BOLOS

BOOK 1

HONOR OF THE REGIMENT

CREATED BY
KEITH LAUMER

EDITED BY
BILL FAWCETT

BAEN

BOLOS: HONOR OF THE REGIMENT

Copyright © 1993 by Bill Fawcett and Associates
"Lost Legion" copyright © 1993 by S.M. Stirling, "Camelot" copyright © 1993 by S.N. Lewitt, "The Legacy of Leonidas" copyright © 1993 by J. Andrew Keith, "Ploughshare" copyright © 1993 by Todd Johnson, "Ghosts" copyright © 1993 by Mike Resnick & Barry N. Malzberg, "The Ghost of Resartus" copyright © 1993 by Christopher Stasheff, "Operation Desert Fox" copyright © 1993 by Mercedes Lackey & Larry Dixon, and "As Our Strength Lessens" copyright © 1993 by David Drake.

A Baen Books Original

Baen Publishing Enterprises
P.O. Box 1403
Riverdale, N.Y. 10471

ISBN: 0-671-72184-4

Cover art by Paul Alexander

First printing, September 1993

Distributed by
SIMON & SCHUSTER
1230 Avenue of the Americas
New York, N.Y. 10020

Typeset by Windhaven Press, Auburn, N.H.
Printed in the United States of America

FOR THE HONOR OF THE REGIMENT

My forty-seven pairs of flint-steel roadwheels are in depot condition. Their tires of spun beryllium monocrystal, woven to deform rather than compress, all have 97% or better of their fabric unbroken. The immediate terrain is semi-arid. The briefing files inform me this is typical of the planet. My track links purr among themselves as they grind through scrub vegetation and the friable soil, carrying me to my assigned mission.

There is a cataclysmic fuel-air explosion to the east behind me. The glare is visible for 5.3 seconds, and the ground will shake for many minutes as shock waves echo through the planetary mantle.

Had my human superiors so chosen, I could be replacing *Saratoga* at the spearhead of the attack.

The rear elements of the infantry are in sight now. They look like dung beetles in their hard suits, crawling backward beneath a rain of shrapnel. I am within range of their low-power communications net. *"Hold what you got, troops,"* orders the unit's acting commander. *"Big Brother's come to help!"*

I am not Big Brother. I am *Maldon*, a Mark XXX Bolo of the 3rd Battalion, Dinochrome Brigade. The lineage of our unit goes back to the 2nd South Wessex Dragoons. In 1944, we broke the last German resistance on the path to Falaise—though we traded our flimsy Cromwells against the Tigers at a ration of six to one to do it.

The citizens do not need to know what the cost is. They need only to know that the mission has been accomplished. The battle honors welded to my turret prove that I have always accomplished my mission.

Baen Books By Keith Laumer

TABLE OF CONTENTS

LOST LEGION

S.M. Stirling

"Shit," Captain McNaught said.

The map room of Firebase Villa had been dug into the soft friable rock with explosives, then topped with sheet steel and sandbags. It smelled of sweat and bad coffee and electronic components, and the sandbags in the dog-leg entrance were still ripped where a satchel charge—a stick grenade in a three-pound ball of plastique—had been thrown during the attack six months ago.

"Captain?" the communications specialist said.

"Joy, wonder, unconfined happiness, *shit*," the officer snarled, reading the printout again. "Martins, get in here!"

Lieutenant Martins ducked through the entrance of the bunker and flipped up the faceplate of her helmet. The electronics in the crystal sandwich would have made the bunker as bright as the tropical day outside,

1

but also would have turned her face to a nonreflective curve. Human communication depends on more than words alone to carry information, as anyone who meets face-to-face for the first time after telephone conversations learns.

"News?" she said.

"Look." He handed over the paper.

"Aw, *shit*."

"My commandante, is this the right time for the raid?"

Miguel Chavez turned and fired a long burst. The muzzle blast of the AK-74 was deafening in the confined space of the cave. The other guerilla's body pitched backwards and slammed into the coarse limestone wall, blood trailing down past fossilized seashells a hundred and twenty million years old. Pink intestine bulged through the torn fatigues, and the fecal odor was overwhelming.

None of the other guerilla commanders moved, but sweat glistened on their high-cheeked faces. Outside the sounds of the jungle night—and the camp—were stilled for an instant. Sound gradually returned to normal. Two riflemen ducked inside the low cave and dragged the body away by the ankles.

"The Glorious Way shall be victorious!" Chavez said. "We shall conquer!"

The others responded with a shout and a clenched-fist salute.

"I know," Chavez went on, "that some of our comrades are weary. They say: *The colossus of the North is reeling. The gringo troops are withdrawing.* Why not hide and wait? Let the enemy's internal contradictions win for us. We have fought many years, against the compradore puppet regime and then against the imperialist intervention force.

"Comrades," he went on, "this is defeatism. *When*

the enemy retreats, we advance. The popular masses must see that the enemy are withdrawing in *defeat*. They must see that the People's Army of the Glorious Way has *chased* the gringos from the soil of San Gabriel. Then they will desert the puppet regime, which has attempted to regroup behind the shelter of the imperialist army.

"Our first objective," he went on, "is to interdict the resupply convoy from the coast. We will attack at—"

"Yeah, it's nothing but indigs," Martins said, keeping her voice carefully neutral. "The indigs, and you and me. That's a major part of the problem."

Will you look at that mother, she thought.

The new tank was huge. Just standing beside it made her want to step back; it wasn't right for a self-propelled object to be this big.

The Mark III was essentially a four-sided pyramid with the top lopped off, but the simple outline was bent and smoothed where the armor was sloped for maximum deflection; and jagged where sensor-arrays and weapons jutted from the brutal massiveness of the machine. Beneath were two sets of double tracks, each nearly six feet broad, each supported on eight interleaved road wheels. Between them they underlay nearly half the surface of the vehicle. She laid a hand on the flank, and the quivering, slightly greasy feel of live machinery came through her fingerless glove, vibrating up her palm to the elbow.

"So we don't have much in the way of logistics," she went on. *Try fucking none.* Just her and the Captain and eighty effectives, and occasionally they got spare parts and ammo through from what was supposed to be headquarters down here on the coast. "Believe me, up in the boonies *mules* are high-tech these days. We're running our UATVs"—Utility All Terrain Vehicles—"on kerosene from lamps cut with the local slash, when someone doesn't drink it before we get it."

The tank commander's name was Vinatelli; despite that he was pale and blond and a little plump, his scalp almost pink through the close-cropped hair. He looked like a Norman Rockwell painting as he grinned at her and slapped the side of his tank. He also looked barely old enough to shave.

"Oh, no problem. I know things have gotten a little disorganized—"

Yeah, they had to use artillery to blast their way back into New York after the last riots, she thought.

"—but we won't be hard on your logistics. This baby has the latest, ultra-top-secret-burn-before-reading-then-shoot-yourself stuff.

"Ionic powerplant." At her blank look, he expanded: "Ion battery. Most compact power source ever developed—radical stuff, ma'am. Ten years operation at combat loads; and you can recharge from *anything,* sunlight included. That's a little diffuse, but we've got five acres of photovol screen in a dispenser. Markee"— he blushed when she raised a brow at the nickname—"can go anywhere, including under water.

"We've got a weapons mix like you wouldn't believe, everything from antipersonnel to air defense. The Mark III runs its own diagnostics, it drives itself, its onboard AI can perform about fifteen or twenty combat tasks *without* anybody in the can. Including running patrols. We've got maps of every inch of terrain in the hemisphere, and inertial and satellite systems up the wazoo, so we can perform fire-support or any of that good shit all by ourselves. Then there's the armor. Synthetic molecules, long-chain ferrous-chrome alloy, density-enhanced and pretty well immune to anything but another Mark III."

Bethany Martins ran a hand through her close-cropped black hair. It came away wet with sweat;

the Atlantic coast lowlands of San Gabriel were even hotter than the interior plateau, and much damper, to which the capital of Ciudad Roco added its own peculiar joys of mud, rotting garbage and human wastes—the sewer system had given up the ghost long ago, about the time the power grid did. Sweat was trickling down inside her high-collared suit of body armor as well, and chafing everywhere. Prickly heat was like poverty in San Gabriel, a constant condition of life to be lived with rather than a problem to be solved.

She looked around. The plaza up from the harbor—God alone *knew* how they'd gotten the beast ashore in that crumbling madhouse, probably sunk the ships and then drove it out—was full of a dispirited crowd. Quite a few were gawking at the American war-machine, despite the ungentle urging of squads of Order and Security police to move along. Others were concentrating on trying to sell each other bits and pieces of this and that, mostly cast-offs. Nothing looked new except the vegetables, and every pile of bananas or tomatoes had its armed guard.

Her squad was watching from their UATVs, light six-wheeled trucks built so low to the ground they looked squashed, with six balloon wheels of spun-alloy mesh. The ceramic diesels burbled faintly, and the crews leaned out of the turtletop on their weapons. There were sacks of supplies on the back decks, tied down with netting, and big five-liter cans of fuel.

At least we got something out this trip.

"What I'd like to know," she said to Vinatelli, "is why GM can build these, but we've got to keep a Guard division in Detroit."

"You haven't heard?" he said, surprised. "They pulled out of Detroit. Just stationed some blockforces around it and cut it loose."

Acid churned in Martin's stomach. Going home was looking less and less attractive, even after four years in

San Gabriel. The problem was that San Gabriel had gone from worse to worst in just about the same way. The difference was that it hadn't as far to fall.

"We're supposed to 'demonstrate superiority' and then pull out," Martins said. "We kick some Glorio butt, so it doesn't look like we're running away when we run away."

The twisting hill-country road looked different from the height of the Mark III's secondary hatch. The jungle was dusty gray thorn-trees, with some denser vegetation in the low valleys. She could see it a lot better from the upper deck, but it made her feel obscenely vulnerable. Or visible, which was much the same thing. The air was full of the smell of the red dust that never went away except in the rainy season, and of the slightly spicy scent of the succulents that made up most of the local biota. Occasionally they passed a farm, a whitewashed adobe shack with a thatch or tile roof, with scattered fields of maize and cassava. The stores in the few towns were mostly shuttered, their inhabitants gone to swell the slums around the capital—or back to their home farms out in the countryside, if they had a little more foresight.

Everyone was keeping their distance from the Mark III, too, as soon as it loomed out of the huge dust-cloud. *So much for stealth*, she thought, with light-infantry instincts. *The Glorious Way will be laughing fit to piss their pants when we try to catch them with this mother.*

"Only thing is," Martins went on, "we don't need a Mark III to kick Glorio butt. We've been doing it for three years. Maybe they could send us some *replacements*, and a couple of Cheetah armored cars, like we used to have, or some air support, or decent *supplies* so we didn't have to live off the local economy like a bunch of goddam feudal bandits. All of which wouldn't have cost half as much as sending this hunk of tin down to roar around the boonies looking purty and scaring the goats."

The rest of the convoy were keeping their distance as well. Her UATV was well ahead, willing to take point to keep out of the dust plume. The indig troops and the supplies were further back, willing to eat dust to keep away from the churning six-foot treads. Kernan's rig was tail-end Charlie, just in case any of the indigs got ideas about dropping out of the convoy. Not that she'd mind the loss of the so-called government troops, but the supplies were another matter.

She looked down. The newbie was staring straight ahead in his recliner, two spots of color on his cheeks and his back rigid.

"Hell, kid," she said. "I'm not mad at you. You look too young to be one of the shitheads who poured the whole country down a rathole."

He relaxed fractionally. "Maybe things'll get better with President Flemming," he said unexpectedly. "He and Margrave are pretty smart guys."

"And maybe I'm the Queen of Oz," Martins said. *This one still believes in politicians?* she thought. *God, they are robbing cradles.*

Or possibly just being very selective. You got enough to eat in the Army, at least—even down here in San Gabriel, admittedly by application of ammunition rather than money. Maybe they were recruiting extremely trusting farmboy types so's not to chance another mutiny like Houston.

Christ knew there were times when she'd felt like mutiny herself, if there had been anyone to mutiny *against* down here.

She put her eyes back on the surroundings. More thornbush; she clicked her faceplate down and touched the IR and sonic scan controls. Nothing but animal life out in the scrub, and not much of that. Certainly no large animals beyond the odd extremely wary peccary, not with the number of hungry men with guns who'd been wandering around here for the last decade or so.

"Why don't you shut the hatch, ma'am?" Vinatelli said. "Because I like to see what's going on," Martins snapped. "This is bandido country."

"You can see it all better from down here, El-T," he urged.

Curious, she dropped down the rungs to the second padded seat in the interior of the hull. The hatch closed with a sigh of hydraulics, and the air cooled to a comfortable seventy-five, chilly on her wet skin. It smelled of neutral things, filtered air and almost-new synthetics, flavored by the gamy scent of one unwashed lieutenant of the 15th Mountain Division. Her body armor made the copilot's seat a bit snug, but otherwise it was as comfortable as driving a late-model Eurocar on a good highway. Martins was in her late twenties, old enough to remember when such things were possible, even if rare.

"Smooth ride," she said, looking around.

There were the expected armored conduits and readouts; also screens spaced in a horseshoe around the seats. They gave a three-sixty view around the machine; one of them was dialed to x5 magnification, and showed the lead UATV in close-up. Sergeant Jenkins was leaning on the grenade launcher, his eggplant-colored skin skimmed with red dust, his visor swivelling to either side. There was no dust on it; the electrostatic charge kept anything in finely divided particles off it.

"Maglev suspension," Vinatelli said. "No direct contact between the road-wheel pivot axles and the hull. The computer uses a sonic sensor on the terrain ahead and compensates automatically. There's a hydrogas backup system."

He touched a control, and colored pips sprang out among the screens.

"This's why we don't have to have a turret," he said. "The weapons turn, not the gunner—the sensors and computers integrate all the threats and funnel it down here."

"How'd you keep track of it all?" she asked. "Hell of a thing, trying to chose between fifteen aiming points when it's hitting the fan."

"I don't, anymore'n I have to drive," Vinatelli pointed out.

It was then she noticed his hands weren't on the controls. Her instinctive lunge of alarm ended a fraction of a second later, when her mind overrode it.

"This thing's steering itself?" she said.

"Yes ma'am," he said. "Aren't you, Markee?"

"*Yes, Viniboy,*" a voice said. Feminine, sweet and sultry.

Martins looked at him. He shrugged and spread his hands. "Hey, it's a perfectly good voice. I spend a lot of time in here, you know?" He waved a hand at the controls. "Best AI in the business—software package just came in, and it's a lot better than before. Voice recognition and tasking. All I have to do is tell it who to shoot and who to like."

"I *hope* you've told it to like me, corporal," she said flatly.

"Ah—Markee, register Martins, Lieutenant Bethany M, serial number—" he continued with the identification. "Lieutenant Martins is superior officer on site. Log and identify."

Martins felt a brief flicker of light touch her eyes; retina prints. The machine would already have her voiceprint, fingerprints and ECG patterns.

"Acknowledged, Vini. Hello, Lieutenant Martins. I'm honored to be under your command for this mission. What are our mission parameters?"

"Getting home," Martins said shortly. Talking machinery gave her the creeps.

"Acknowledged, Lieutenant Martins. I will help you get home."

Vinatelli noticed her stiffen. From the tone of his voice, it was a familiar reaction. "It's just a real good AI, El-Tee," he said soothingly. "Expert program with parallel-processing learning circuits. It's not like it was alive or anything, it just sort of imitates it."

The machine spoke: "Don't you love me any more, Vini?" The sweet husky voice was plaintive.

Vinatelli blushed again, this time to the roots of his hair. "I put that in, ma'am. You know, I spend—"

"—a lot of time alone in here," Martins filled in.

"Hey, El-T," the young noncom said, in a voice full of false cheerfulness. "You want a Coke?"

"You've got Coke in here?" she asked.

He turned in his seat, pushing up the crash framework, and opened a panel. "Yeah, I got regular, classic, diet, Pepsi and Jolt. Or maybe a ham sandwich?"

Fan-fucking-tastic, Martins thought. She looked again at the screen ahead of her; Jenkins was taking a swig out of his canteen, and spitting dust-colored water over the side of the UATV. Chickens struggled feebly in the net-covered baskets lashed to the rear decking. She felt a sudden nausea at the thought of being in here, in with the screens and the air-conditioning and fresh ham sandwiches. The thing could probably play you 3-D'ed ancient movies with porno inserts on one of the screens, too. *Damned if I can see what it's got to do with fighting.*

"I'm bailing out of this popcan," she said. "Unit push." Her helmet clicked. "Jenkins, I'm transferring back to the UATV."

She heard a Coke can pop and fizz as she slid out of the hatchway.

"What's it like?" the big noncom said. He didn't face around; they were coming up on the Remo bridge, and all three of the soldiers in the back of the UATV were keeping their eyes on station. So were the driver and those in the front.

"It's a fucking cruise ship, Tops. Economy class, there's no swimming pool."

"Big mother," Jenkins said; his position at the rear of the vehicle gave him a view of the one hundred and fifty tons of it. Even driving at thirty miles an hour they could feel it shaking the earth as it drove. "Surprised it doesn't make bigger ruts."

"Lot of track area," Martins said. "Not much more surface pressure than a boot. Though God damn me if I know what we're going to do with it. It isn't exactly what you'd call suitable for running around forty-degree slopes and jungle."

"Hey, El-Tee, neither am I," Riverez said, from the other machine-gun.

"Shut up, Pineapple," she said—the gunner was named for his abundant acne scars.

"Hell, we can run air-conditioners and VCRs off it," Jenkins said. "Christmas tree lights. Dig a swimming pool. Maybe rig up a sauna."

"Can it, Tops," Martins said.

The road was running down into one of the steep valleys that broke the rolling surface of the plateau. There was a small stream at the bottom of it, and a concrete-and-iron bridge that might be nearly a century old. The air grew damper and slightly less hot as they went under the shelter of the few remaining big trees. There were a few patches of riverine jungle left in the interior of San Gabriel, but most—like this—had been cut over for mahogany and tropical cedar, and then the slopes farmed until the soil ran down into the streams. Really thick scrub had reclaimed the valley sides when the peasants gave up on their plots of coffee and cannabis. Although the latter was still cheap and abundant, one of the things that made life here possible at all.

"Oh, shit," Martins said suddenly, and went on the unit push. "Halt. Halt convoy. *Halto.*"

As usual, some of the indigs weren't listening. The Mark III provided a more than usually efficient cork, and this time they didn't have to worry about someone driving an ancient Tatra diesel up their butts. Silence fell, deafening after the crunching, popping sound of heavy tires on gravel and dirt. The dust plume carried on ahead of them for a dozen meters, gradually sinking down to add to the patina on the roadside vegetation.

"What's the problem?" Jenkins asked.

"The bloody Mark III, that's the problem," she replied, staring at the bridge.

"Hell, it hardly tears up a dirt road," the sergeant protested.

"Yeah, it distributes its weight real good—but it's still all there, all 150 tons of it. And no way is that pissant little bridge going to carry 150 tons. Vinatelli!"

"Yes, ma'am?"

"You're going to have to take that thing and go right back to Ciudad Roco," she said. *What a screwup.* She must be really getting the Boonie Bunnies to have forgotten something like this. "Because that bridge isn't going to hold that monster of yours."

"Oh, no problem, El-Tee," Vinatelli said.

His voice was irritatingly cheerful. The voice of a man—a boy—who was sitting in cool comfort drinking an iced Coke. A boy who'd never been shot at, who hadn't spent four years living in the daily expectation of death; not the fear of death, so much, as the bone-deep conviction that you were going to die. Who'd never fired a whole magazine from a M-35 into the belly of a Glorio sapper and had the bottom half of the torso slide down into the bunker with her while the top half fell outside and vaporized in a spray of fluids and bone-chips when the bagful of explosives he was carrying went off . . .

"Yeah, well, I'll just drive down the bank and up the other side," he went on. "Lemme check. Yes ma'am, the banks're well within specs."

Martins and Jenkins looked at each other. "Corporal," the lieutenant went on, "the water's about sixteen feet deep, in the middle there. The rains are just over."

In fact, it would be a good time for an ambush attack. Luckily the Glorios had been pretty quiet for the last three months. Doubtless waiting for the 15th to withdraw, so they could try final conclusions with the indigs. So that what was left of them could.

"That's no problem either, ma'am." A slightly aggrieved note had crept into the newbie's voice. "Like I said, we're completely air-independent. The sonics say the bottom's rock. We'll manage."

"How come everything's screwed up, but we can still build equipment like that?" Jenkins said.

Martins laughed. "Great minds," she said. "Fuck it, we've got a *spaceship* ready to blast off for the moons of Jupiter, and the government's lucky if it collects taxes on three-quarters of the country. They can't get their shit together enough to pull us out."

The Mark III was edging down the bank of the river. The banks were steep, in most places; right next to the first abutments of the bridge they'd been broken down in the course of construction, and by erosion since. Still fairly rugged, a thirty-degree angle in and out. A UATV would be able to handle it, and even swim the river gap against the current—the spun-alloy wheels gripped like fingers, and the ceramic diesel gave a high power-to-weight ratio.

The tank wasn't using any particular finesse. Just driving straight down the slope, with rocks cracking and splitting and flying out like shrapnel under its weight. Into the edge of the water, out until the lower three-quarters of the hull was hidden, with the current piling waves against the upstream surface—

"Lieutenant Martins," the over-sweet voice of the AI said. "I detect incoming fire. Incoming is mortar fire."

A section of Martin's mind gibbered. *How?* The hills all around would baffle counterbattery radar. The rest of her consciousness was fully engaged.

"Incoming!" she yelled over the unit push. All of them dropped down into the vehicle's interior and popped the covers closed above them. The driver turned and raced the UATV back down the length of the convoy, past ragged indig troopers piling out and hugging the dirt, or standing and staring in gap-mouthed bewilderment.

Then the bridge blew up.

"Eat this!" Jenkins screamed.

The 35mm grenade launcher coughed out another stream of bomblets. They impacted high up the slope above. Return fire sparked and tinkled off the light sandwich armor of the UATV; a rocket-propelled grenade went by with a dragon's hiss just behind the rear fender and impacted on a cargo truck instead. The indig troops hiding under the body didn't even have time to scream as the shaped-charge warhead struck one of the fuel tanks built into the side of the vehicle. Magenta fire blossomed as the pencil of superheated gas speared into the fuel. Fuel fires rarely cause explosions, contrary to innumerable bad action shots. This was the rare occasion, as the ripping impact spread droplets into the air and then ignited them with a flame well above even the viscous diesel fuel's ignition point. A ball of orange fire left tatters of steel where the truck had been, flipped over the ones before and behind, and nearly tipped over the racing UATV.

The little vehicle's low wheelbase and broad build

saved it. It did slow down, as the driver fought to keep control on the steep slope above the road.

"Now!" Martins shouted, rolling out the back hatch. Riverez followed her, and they went upslope at a scrambling run until the trunk of a long-dead tree covered them. She knew that the bruises along her side would hurt like hell when she had time to consider them, but right now there were more important matters.

Shoonk. Shoonk. Shoonk.

The mortar fired again. The result was the same, too. Not much of the Mark III showed above the water and the tons of iron and shattered concrete which had avalanched down on it five minutes before. One set of 5mm ultras was still active, and it chattered—more like a high-pitched scream, as the power magazine fed slugs into the plasma-driven tubes. Bars of light stretched up, vaporized metal ablating off the depleted-uranium bullets. There was a triple crack as the mortar-bombs exploded in midair—one uncomfortably close to the height that its proximity fuse would have detonated it anyway. Shrapnel whamped into the ground, raising pocks of dust. Something slammed between her shoulder-blades, and she grunted at the pain.

"Nothing," she wheezed, as Riverez cast her a look of concern. "Armor stopped it. Let's do it."

It would be better if this was night; the Glorios didn't have night-vision equipment. Even better if this was a squad; but then, it would be better still if the Company was at its regulation hundred and twenty effectives. *Best of all if I was in Santa Fe.*

She and the other Company trooper spread out and moved upslope. Martins had keyed the aimpoint feature of her helmet, and a ring of sighting pips slid across her faceplate, moving in synch with the motions of her rifle's muzzle. Where she put the pips, the bullets from the

M-35 in her hands would strike. Sonic and IR sensors made the world a thing of mottles and vibration; it would have been meaningless to someone untrained, but to an expert it was like being able to see through the gray-white thornbush.

"Left and east," she whispered, sinking to hands and knees. The heat signature of the ancient .51 heavy machine-gun was a blaze in the faceplate, the barrel glowing through the ghostly imprints of the thornbush. It was probably older than she was, but the Soviet engineers had built well, and it was still sending out thumb-sized bullets at over three thousand feet per second. They would punch through the light armor of the UATVs without slowing. The AKs of the guerilla riflemen supporting it were vivid as well; the men were fainter outlines.

"Pineapple."

"In position."

"Now."

She slid the sighting ring over the gunner a hundred meters away and squeezed her trigger. *Braaaap.* The burst punched five 4mm bullets through the man's torso. The high-velocity prefragmented rounds tore into his chest like point-blank shotgun fire, pitching him away from his weapon and spattering blood and bits of lung over his loader. The other guerilla was fast and cool; he grabbed for the spade grips and swung the long heat-glowing barrel towards her. *Braaap.* A little high that time, and the Glorio's head disintegrated. He collapsed forward, arterial blood and drips of brain sizzling on the hot metal.

The riflemen were firing at her too, and she rolled downslope as the bullets probed for her. It was about time for—

Thud-thud-thud. Pineapple's grenade launcher made its distinctive sound as it spat out a clip of bomblets. They were low velocity, and there was an appreciable fraction of a second before they burst among the enemy. Fiberglass shrapnel scrubbed green leaves off the thorny scrub; it also sliced flesh, and the riflemen—the survivors—leaped up. Perhaps to flee, perhaps to move forward and use their numbers to swamp the two members of the 15th. Martins fired until the M-35 spat out its plastic clip. The UATVs were shooting in support from the edge of the road, effective now that the Glorios were out of their cover. By the time she slapped in another 50-round cassette of caseless ammunition, they were all down, caught between the two dismounted troopers and the machine-guns from the road.

The wild assault-rifle fire of the fifty or so indig troops with the convoy may have been a factor, but she doubted it.

"Get those turkeys to cease fire!" she snapped through the helmet comm to Jenkins. It took a moment, and another burst from the UATV's machine-gun—into the ground or over their heads, she supposed, although it didn't much matter. "We got the others to worry about."

The Glorio mortars had made three more attempts to shell the convoy. Pretty soon now they were going to get fed up with that and come down and party.

A dot of red light strobed at the bottom left corner of her faceplate, then turned to solid red.

"Makarov?" she asked.

"Took one the long way," Corporal Kernan said laconically.

Damn. The big Russki had been a good troop, once he got over his immigrant's determination to prove himself a better American than any of them, and he'd done that fairly quick—down here in San Gabriel, you were pretty sure of your identity, Them or Us. More so than in any of the Slavic ghettos that had grown up with the great refugee exodus of the previous generation. *Damn.* He'd also been the last of their replacements. In theory the whole unit was to be rotated, but they'd been waiting for that for over a year.

"The Mark III's moving a little," Jenkins said.

She could hear that herself, a howling and churning from the streambed a thousand meters to her rear; it must be noisy, to carry that well into the ravines on the edge of the stream valley.

"Fuck the Mark III—" she began.

A new noise intruded onto the battlefield. A multiple blam sound from the riverbed, and a second later the distinctive surf-roar of cluster bomblets saturating a ravine two ridges over from the road. Right after that came a series of secondary explosions, big enough that the top of a ball of orange fire rose over the ridgeline for a second. Echoes chased each other down the river valley, fading into the distance.

"Well," she said. "Well." Silence fell, broken only by the rustling of the brush and the river. "Ah, Pineapple, we'll go take a look at that."

Somehow she didn't think there would be much left of the guerilla mortars or their operators. "Pity about that Mark III. Looks like it might have been good for something at that."

"Vinatelli, come in," Martins said, perched on one of the bridge pilings.

Close up, the Mark III looked worse than she'd thought. Only the sensor array and two of the upper weapons ports showed. The bulk of the hull was buried under chunks of concrete, wedged with steel I-beams from the bridge. Limestone blocks the size of a compact car had slid down on top of that; the Glorios had evidently been operating on the assumption that if one kilo of plastique was good, ten was even better. She couldn't argue with the methodology; overkill beat minimalism most times, in this business. Water was piling up and swirling around the improvised dam, already dropping loads of reddish-brown silt on the wreckage. With the water this high, the whole thing would probably be under in a few hours, and might well back up into a miniature lake for weeks, until the dry season turned the torrent into a trickle.

"Vinatelli!" she said again. If the radio link was out, someone would have to rappel down there on a line and beat on the hatch with a rifle-butt.

The newbie had come through pretty well in his first firefight, better than some . . . although to be sure, he hadn't been in any personal danger in his armored cruise liner. It was still creditable that he hadn't frozen, and that he'd used his weapons intelligently. He might well be curled up in after-action shock right now, though.

"Lieutenant Martins," the excessively sexy voice of the tank said. *Christ, how could Vinatelli do that to himself?* she thought. The voice made *her* think of sex, and she was as straight as a steel yardstick. Mind you, he was probably a hand-reared boy anyhow. Maybe a programming geek made the best rider for a Mark III.

"Vinatelli!" Martins began, starting to get annoyed. Damned if she was going to communicate with him through a 150-ton electronic secretarial machine.

McNaught's voice came in over the Company push. "Martins, what's going on there?"

"Mopping up and assessing the situation with the Mark III, sir," Martins said. "It's screwed the pooch. You'd need a battalion of Engineers to get it loose."

"Can you get the UATVs across?"

"That's negative, sir. Have to go a couple of clicks upstream and ford it. Double negative on the indig convoy." Who had cleared out for the coast as soon as they'd patched their wounded a little; so much for the supplies, apart from what her people had on their

UATVs . . . supplemented by what they'd insisted on taking off the trucks.

"What if you shitcan the loads, could you get the UATVs across then?"

"Well, yeah," she said, her mind automatically tackling the problem. Use a little explosive to blow the ends of the rubble-pile, then rig a cable . . . the UATVs were amphibious, and if they could anchor them against being swept downstream, no problem. "But sir, we *need* that stuff."

"Not any more we don't," McNaught said grimly. She sat up. "Just got something in from Reality."

That was the U.S. Martins extended a hand palm-down to stop Jenkins, who was walking carefully over the rocks toward her. The Captain's voice continued: "The President, the Veep, the Speaker and General Margrave were on a flight out of Anchorage today. A Russian fighter shot them down over the ocean. No survivors."

"*Jesus Christ,*" Martins whispered. Her mind gibbered protests; the Russians were a shell of a nation, and what government they had was fairly friendly to the US.

"Nobody knows what the hell happened," McNaught went on. "There's some sort of revolution going on in Moscow, so *they* aren't saying. The East African Federation has declared war on North Africa and launched a biobomb attack on Cairo. China and Japan have exchanged ultimatums. There are mobs rioting in DC, New York, LA—and not just the usual suspects, in Seattle and Winnipeg too. General mobilization and martial law've been declared."

Martin's lips shaped a soundless whistle. Then, since she had survived four years in San Gabriel, she arrowed in on practicalities:

"How does that affect us, sir?"

"It means we're getting a tiltrotor in to collect us in

about six hours," he replied. "CENPAC told the 15th HQ element at Cuchimba to bring everyone in pronto—they want the warm bodies, not the gear. We cram on with what we carry and blow everything else in place. They're sending heavy lifters to pick up what's left of the division and bring us home from Cuchimba. If you read between the lines, it sounds like complete panic up there—the Chiefs don't know what to do without Margrave, and Congress is meeting in continuous session. Much good that will do. Sure as shit nobody cares about San Gabriel and the Glorios any more. Division tells me anyone who isn't at the pickup in six hours can walk home, understood?"

"Sir yes sir," Martins said, and switched to her platoon push.

"All right, everyone, listen up," she began. "Jenkins—"

"*What* did you say?"

"This unit is still operable," Vinatelli's voice replied.

My, haven't we gotten formal, Martins thought furiously. "I told you, newbie, we're combat-lossing the tank and getting out of here. *Everyone* is getting out of here; in twenty-four hours the only Amcits in San Gabriel are going to be the ones in graves. Which will *include* Corporal Vinatelli if you don't get out of there *now.*"

Behind her the first UATV was easing into the water between the two cable braces, secured by improvised loops. The woven-synthetic ropes were snubbed to massive ebonies on both banks, and with only the crew and no load, it floated fairly high. Water on the upstream side purled to within a handspan of the windows, but that was current. The ball wheels spun, thrashing water backward; with his head out the top hatch, Jenkins cried blasphemous and scatological encouragement to the trooper at the wheel and used his bulk to shift the

balance of the light vehicle and keep it closer to upright.
Most of the rest of her detachment were out in
overwatch positions. Nobody was betting that the Glorios
wouldn't come back for more, despite the pasting they'd
taken.

You could never tell with the Glorios; the death-
wish seemed to be as big a part of their makeup as
the will to power. Revolutionary purity, they called it.

"Lieutenant," Vinatelli said, "this unit is still operable. Systems are at over ninety-five percent of
nominal."

"Jesus fucking *Christ*, the thing's buried under four
hundred tons of rock! I'm combat-lossing it, corporal.
Now get out, that's a direct order. We're time-critical
here."

"Corporal Vinatelli is unable to comply with that
order, Lieutenant."

"Hell," Martins said, looking down at the top of the
Mark III's superstructure, where fingers of brown
water were already running over the armor.

It looked like she was going to leave two of her
people here dead. The kid had frozen after all, only it
took the form of refusal to come out of his duro-
chrome womb, rather than catatonia. Frozen, and it
was going to kill him—when the ham sandwiches and
Coke ran out down there, if not before. There was
certainly nothing she could do about it. Sending a
team down with a blasting charge to open the hatch
didn't look real practical right now. Even if they had
time, there was no telling what someone in Vinatelli's
mental condition might do, besides which the tank was
programmed to protect its own integrity. And she certainly had better things to do with the time.

A *whump* of explosive went off behind her; Kernan
making sure the captured Glorio weapons weren't any
use to anyone.

"Max units, pull in," she said, and began climbing

back to the cable anchor point to board Kernan's
UATV. Behind her, a thin muddy wave washed across
the top surface of the Bolo Mark III.

"Comrades, we have won a glorious victory!" Commandante Chavez shouted.

He was standing in front of the crater where the
guerilla mortars had been. For sixty meters around,
the trees were bare of leaves and twigs; they sparkled
in the afternoon sunlight, a fairy garden of glittering
glass fibers. The crater where the ready ammunition
had gone off was several meters across; the enemy had
arranged the bodies of the crew—or parts thereof—in
more-or-less regular fashion, the better to count them.
Nothing useable remained.

"The giant tank filled some of our weaker comrades
with fear," Chavez went on. The ground that he paced
on was damp and slightly greasy with the body fluids
of several Glorios, and the bluebottles were crawling
over it. "They wanted to run and hide from the monster tank!

"Yet we—mere humanity, but filled with the
correct ideological perspective—triumphed over the
monster. We buried it, as the Glorious Way shall bury
all its enemies, all those who stand between suffering
humanity and utopia!"

With several of the commandante's special guards
standing behind him, the cheering was prolonged. And
sincere; they had destroyed the tank that had been
like nothing anyone had ever seen before. Now it was
just a lump in the river below the fallen bridge.

"Onward to victory!" Chavez shouted, raising his fist
in the air.

The Caatinga River was powerful at this time of
year, when the limestone soil yielded up the water it
had stored during the brief, violent rains. Maximum

flow was in May, well after the last clouds gave way to endless glaring sun and the fields shriveled into dusty, cracked barrenness where goats walked out on limbs to get at the last shoots.

Now it backed at the rock dam created by the bridge. The lower strata were locked together by the girders, and the upper by the weight of the stone and the anchoring presence of the tank; its pyramidal shape made it the keystone. Water roared over the top a meter deep, and the whole huge mass ground and shifted under the pounding.

"Vini, the water will help," the Mark III said. "I'm going to try that now."

Mud and rock and spray fountained skyward, sending parrots and shrikes fleeing in terror. Boulders shifted. A bellowing roar shook the earth in the river valley, and the monstrous scraping sound of durachrome alloy ripping density-enhanced steel through friable limestone.

"It's working."

"Talk about irony," Jenkins said.

"Yeah, Tops?" Martins replied.

Jenkins had had academic ambitions before the university system pretty well shut down.

"Yeah, El-Tee. Most of the time we've been here, the Mark III would have been as useful as a boar hog to a ballerina. The Glorios would have just gone away from wherever it was, you know? But now we just want to move one place one time, and they want to get in our way—and that big durachrome mother would have been *real* useful."

"I'm not arguing," she said.

The little hamlet of San Miguel de Dolorosa lay ahead of them. The brief tropical nightfall was over, and the moon was out, bright and cool amid a thick dusting arch of stars, clear in the dry upland air. In previous times troops had stopped there occasionally; there was a cantina selling a pretty good beer, and it was a chance to see locals who weren't trying to kill you, just sell you BBQ goat or their sisters. Right now there were a couple of extremely suspicious readings on the fixed sensors they'd scattered around in the hills months back, when they decided they didn't have the manpower to patrol around here any more.

Suspicious readings that could be heavy machine-guns and rocket launchers in the town. There were no lights down there, but that was about par for the course. Upcountry towns hadn't had electricity for a long time, and kerosene cost real money.

"It's like this," Martins said. "If we go barreling through there, and they're set up, we're dogmeat. If we go around, the only alternate route will eat all our reserve of time—and that's assuming nothing goes wrong on that way either."

Jenkins sighed. "You or me?"

Somebody was going to have to go in and identify the sightings better than the remotes could do it—and if the Glorios were there, distract them up close and personal while the UATVs came in.

"I'd better do it, Tops," she said. The squad with the two vehicles was really Jenkins'. "I'll take Pineapple and Marwitz."

Half the string of mules were in the water when the Glorio sergeant—Squad Comrade—heard the grinding, whirring noise.

"What's that?" he cried.

The ford was in a narrow cut, where the river was broad but shallow; there was little space between the high walls that was not occupied by the gravelled bed. That made it quite dark even in the daytime. On a moonless night like this it was a slit full of night, with nothing but starlight to cast a faint sparkle on the

water. The guerrillas were working with the precision
of long experience, leading the gaunt mules down
through the knee-deep stream and up the other side,
while a company kept overwatch on both sides. They
were not expecting trouble from the depleted enemy
forces, but their superior night vision meant that a raid
was always possible. Even an air attack was *possible*,
although it was months since there had been any air
action except around the main base at Cuchimba.

When the Bolo Mark III came around the curve of
the river half a kilometer downstream, the guerrillas
reacted with varieties of blind panic. It was only a dim
bulk, but the river creamed away in plumes from its
four tracks, and it ground on at forty KPH with the
momentum of a mountain that walked.

The sergeant fired his AK—a useless thing to do
even if the target had been soft-skinned. A bar of light
reached out from the tank's frontal slope, and the man
exploded away from the stream of hypervelocity slugs.

A team on the left, the western bank, of the river
opened up with a four-barreled heavy machine gun
intended for antiaircraft use. They were good; the
stream of half-ounce bullets hosed over the Mark III's
armor like a river of green-tracer fire arching into the
night. The sparks where the projectiles bounced from
the density-enhanced durachrome were bright fireflies
in the night. Where the layer of softer ablating material was still intact there was no spark, but a very
careful observer might have seen starlight on the metal
exposed by the bullets' impact.

There were no careful observers on this field
tonight; at least, none outside the hull of the Mark
III. The infinite repeaters nuzzled forward through the
dilating ports on its hull. Coils gripped and flung
50mm projectiles at velocities that burned a thin film
of plasma off the ultra-dense metal that composed
them. They left streaks through the air, and on the

retinas of anyone watching them. The repeaters were intended primarily for use against armor, but they had a number of options. The one selected now broke the projectiles into several hundred shards just short of the target, covering a dozen square yards. They ripped into the multibarrel machine gun, its mount—and incidentally its operators—like a mincing machine pounded down by a god. Friction-heated ammunition cooked off in a crackle and fireworks fountain, but that was almost an anticlimax.

"Cease fire! Cease fire!" Comrade Chavez bellowed.

It was an unnecessary command for those of the Glorios blundering off into the dark, screaming their terror or conserving their breath for flight. A substantial minority had remained, even for this threat. They heard and obeyed, except for one team with the best antiarmor weapons the guerrillas possessed, a cluster of hypervelocity missiles. One man painted the forward tread with his laser designator, while the second launched the missiles. They left the launcher with a mild chuff of gasses, then accelerated briefly with a sound like a giant tiger's retching scream.

If the missiles had struck the tread, they would probably have ripped its flexible durachrome alloy to shreds—although the Mark III would have lost only a small percentage of its mobility. They did not, since the tank's 4mm had blown the designator to shards before they covered even a quarter of the distance to their target. The operator was a few meters away. Nothing touched him but one fragment tracing a line across his cheek. He lay and trembled, not moving even to stop the blood which flowed down his face from the cut and into his open mouth.

Two of the missiles blossomed in globes of white-blue fire, intercepted by repeater rounds. A third tipped upwards and flew off into the night until it self-destructed, victim of the laser designator's last twitch. The fourth was close enough for the idiot-savant microchip in its nose to detect the Mark III and classify it as a target. It exploded as well—as it was designed to do. The explosion forged a round plate of tungsten into a shape like a blunt arrowhead and plunged it forward with a velocity even greater than the missile's own.

It clanged into the armor just below the muzzles of the infinite repeaters, and spanged up into the night. There was a fist-sized dimple in the complex alloy of the tank's hull, shining because it was now plated with a molecule-thick film of pure tungsten.

"Cease *fire*," Chavez screamed again.

The Bolo Mark III was very close now. Most of the mules had managed to scramble up on the further bank and were galloping down the river, risking their legs in the darkness rather than stay near the impossibly huge metal object. Men stayed in their positions, because their subconscious was convinced that flight was futile. The tank grew larger and larger yet; the water fountained from either side, drenching some of the guerrillas. Comrade Chavez was among them, standing not ten feet from where it passed. He stood erect, and spat into its wake.

"Cowards," he murmured. It was uncertain exactly who he was referring to. Then more loudly: "The cowards are running from us—it fired at nobody but those actively attacking it. Fall in! Resume the operation!"

It took a few minutes for those who had stayed in their positions to shake loose minds stunned by the sheer massiveness of the thing that had passed them by. Collecting most of the men who'd fled took hours, but eventually they stood sheepishly in front of their commander.

"I *should* have you all shot," he said. A few started to shake again; there had been a time when Chavez would have had them shot, and they could remember it. "But the Revolution is so short of men that even you must be conserved—if only to stop a bullet that might otherwise strike a true comrade of the Glorious Way. Get back to work!"

Bethany Martins gripped the bowie in hatchet style, with the sharpened edge out. The blackened metal quivered slightly, and her lips were curled back behind the faceplate in a grimace of queasy anticipation. The weapon was close to the original that Rezin Bowie had designed, over a foot long and point heavy, but the blade was of an alloy quite similar to the Mark III's armor. It had to be sharpened with a hone of synthetic diamond, but it would take a more than razor edge and keep it while it hacked through mild steel.

The Glorio sentry was watching out the front door of the house. She could tell that from the rear of the building because it was made of woven fronds, and they were virtually transparent to several of the sensors in her helmet. She could also tell that all the previous inhabitants of the three-room hut were dead, both because of the smell and because their bodies showed at ambient on the IR scan. That made real sure they wouldn't blow the Glorio ambush, and it was also standard procedure for the Way. The inhabitants of San Miguel had cooperated with the authorities, and that was enough. Cooperation might include virtually anything, from joining a Civic Patrol to selling some oranges to a passing vehicle from the 15th.

Generally speaking, Martins hated killing people with knives although she was quite good at it. One of the benefits of commissioned rank was that she seldom had to, any more. This Glorio was going to be an exception in both senses of the word.

Step. The floor of the hut was earth, laterite packed to the consistency of stone over years of use, and brushed quite clean. A wicker door had prevented the chickens and other small stock outside from coming in. There was an image of the Bleeding Heart, unpleasantly lifelike, over the hearth of adobe bricks and iron rods in the kitchen. Coals cast an IR glow over the room, and her bootsoles made only a soft minimal noise of contact.

Step. Through behind the Glorio. Only the focus of his attention on the roadway below kept him from turning. He was carrying a light drum-fed machine gun, something nonstandard—it looked like a Singapore Industries model. Her body armor would stop shell fragments and pistol-calibre ammunition, but that thing would send fragments of the softsuit right through her rib cage.

Step. Arm's length away in pitch blackness. Pitch blackness for *him*, but her faceplate painted it like day. Better than day . . .

Martins' arm came across until the back of the blade was touching her neck. She slashed at neck height. Something warned the man, perhaps air movement or the slight exhalation of breath, perhaps just years of survival honing his instincts. He began to turn, but the supernally keen edge still sliced through neck muscles and through the vertebrae beneath them, to cut the spinal cord in a single brutal chop. The sound was like an axe striking green wood; she dropped the knife and lunged forward to catch the limp body, ignoring the rush of wastes and the blood that soaked the torso of her armor as she dragged him backwards. The machine gun clattered unnoticed to the ground.

The lieutenant dragged the guerilla backward, then set him down gently on the floor. Only a few twitches from the severed nerve endings drummed his rope-sandaled heels against the floor. She paused for a moment, panting with the effort and with adrenaline still pulsing the veins in her throat, then stepped forward into the doorway.

"Jenkins," she murmured. A risk, but the Glorio elint capacity had never been very good and had gotten worse lately. "I'm marking the heavy stuff. Mark."

From point-blank, the shapes of machine-guns and rocket launchers showed clearly. She slid the aiming pips of her faceplate over each crew-served weapons position, then over the individual riflemen, the second-priority targets. Each time the pips crossed a target she tapped a stud on the lower inside edge of her helmet, marking it for the duplicate readout in Jenkins' helmet. The guerrillas had tried their best to be clever; there were low fires inside a number of the houses, to disguise the IR signatures, and as backup there were bound civilians grouped in what resembled fire teams around pieces of metal—hoes, cooking grills and the like—to fox the sonic and microradar scanners. Some of them were so clever that she had to spend a minute or two figuring them out. When in doubt, she marked them.

It occurred to her that an objective observer might consider the technological gap between the Company's troopers and the Glorios unfair. Although the gross advantage of numbers and firepower the guerrillas had these days went a long way to make it up.

On the other hand, she wasn't objective and didn't give a damn about fair.

"Got it," Jenkins said.

"Pineapple, Red?" she asked. Short clicks from Ramerez and Marwitz. She slid her rifle around, settling down to the ground and bracing the sling against the hand that held the forestock. The aiming pip settled on the rear of the slit trench that held the .51. Four men in the trench . . .

"Now." Diesels blatted as the UATVs revved up and tore down the road toward the village. She stroked her trigger, and the night began to dissolve in streaks of tracer and fire. A cantina disintegrated as Pineapple's grenade launcher caught the RPG team waiting there.

"Shit, why *now*?" Martins said.

Captain McNaught's voice in her ears was hoarse with pain and with the drugs that controlled it. He could still chuckle.

" . . . and at the worst possible time," he said.

Firebase Villa was on fire this night. The mortars at its core were firing, their muzzle flashes lighting up the night like flickers of heat lightning. *Shump-shump-shump*, the three-round clips blasting out almost as fast as a submachine-gun. The crews would have a new set of rounds in the hopper almost as quickly, but the mortars fired sparingly. They were the only way to cover the dead ground where Glorio gunners might set up their own weapons, and ammunition was short. Bombardment rockets from outside the range of the defending mortars dragged across the sky with a sound like express trains. When the sound stopped there was a wait of a few seconds before the *kthud* of the explosion inside the perimeter.

The pilot of the tiltrotor cut into the conversation. "I got just so much fuel, and other people to pull out," he said. His voice was flat as gunmetal, with a total absence of emotion that was a statement in itself.

"Can you get me a landing envelope?" he said.

"Look, we'll cover—" Martins began.

A four-barreled heavy lashed out toward Firebase Villa with streams of green tracer. Yellow-white answered it; neither gun was going to kill the other, at extreme ranges and with both firing from narrow slits. The Glorio gun was using an improvised bunker, thrown up over the last hour, but it was good enough for this. Parts of the perimeter minefield still smoldered where rockets had dragged explosive cord over it in a net to detonate the mines. Some of the bodies of the sappers that had tried to exploit that hole in the mines and razor wire still smoldered as well. Many of the short-range guns around the perimeter were AI-driven automatics, 4mm gatlings with no nerves and very quick reaction times.

"Hell you will, Martins," McNaught wheezed. "There's a battalion of them out there. I think—" he coughed "—I think Comrade Chavez has walked the walk with us so long he just can't bear the thought of us leaving at all." The captain's voice changed timber. "Flyboy, get lost. You try bringing that bird down here, you'll get a second job as a colander."

"*Hell*," the pilot muttered. Then: "Goodbye."

Martins and McNaught waited in silence, except for the racket of the firefight. The Glorios crunched closer, men crawling forward from cover to cover. Many of them died, but not enough, and the bombardment rockets kept dragging their loads of explosive across the sky.

It's not often you're condemned to death, Martins thought. Her mind was hunting through alternatives, plans, tactics—the same process as always. Only there wasn't anything you could do with seventy effectives to attack a battalion of guerrillas who were hauling out all the stuff they'd saved up. Even if it was insane, insane even in terms of the Glorios' own demented worldview.

"Bug out," McNaught said, in a breathless rasp. "Nothing you can do here. They're all here, bug out and make it back to the coast, you can get some transport there. That's an order, Lieutenant."

If there was anything left to go back north for. The latest reports were even more crazy-confused than the first.

"Save your breath, sir," she said.

The Company had been together down here for a long time. They were all going home together. One way or another.

"Movement," someone said. She recognized the voice of the communications specialist back in Villa. Like everyone else, she doubled in two other jobs; in this case, monitoring the remote sensors. "I got movement . . . vehicle movement. Hey, big vehicle."

Nobody said anything for a minute or two, in the draw where the two UATVs waited.

"That's impossible," Martins whispered.

The technician's voice was shaky with unshed tears. "Unless the Glorios have a 150-ton tank, it's happening anyway," she said.

They were a kilometer beyond the Glorio outposts in the draw. The river ran to their left, circling in a wide arch around Firebase Villa. Water jetted in smooth arcs to either bank as the Mark III climbed through the rapids. In the shallow pools beyond the wave from the treads was more like a pulsing. Then the tank stopped, not a hundred meters from the UATVs' position.

"Vinatelli," Martins breathed. "You beautiful little geek!"

The tank remained silent. Another rocket sailed in, a globe of reddish fire trough the sky.

"What are you waiting for?" Martins cursed.

"I have no orders, Lieutenant," the newbie's voice said. "Last mission parameters accomplished."

Something dead and cold trailed fingers up Martin's spine. *He's gone over the edge,* she thought. Aloud, she snapped: "Fight, Vinatelli, for Christ's sake. Fight!"

"Fight whom, Lieutenant?"

"The *Glorios*. The people who're attacking the firebase, for fuck's sake. Open fire."

"Acknowledged, Lieutenant."

The night came apart in a dazzle of fire.

"I think I know—I think I know what happened," Martins whispered.

Nothing moved on the fissured plain around Firebase Villa, except what the wind stirred, and the troopers out collecting the weapons. It had taken the Mark III only about an hour to end it, and the last half of that had been hunting down fugitives. The final group included Comrade Chavez, in a well-shielded hillside cave only three klicks away, which explained a great deal when the tank blew most of the hillside away to get at it. He'd been hiding under their noses all along.

She slung her M-35 down her back and worked her fingers, taking a deep breath before she started climbing the rungs built into the side armor of the Mark III. Some of them were missing, but that was no problem, no problem . . . The hatch opened easily.

Vinatelli must have had his crash harness up when the bridge blew. From the look of the body, he'd been reaching for a cola can. His head must have been at just the right angle to crack his spine against the forward control surfaces.

"So that's why Vinatelli didn't want to come out," she said.

McNaught was watching through the remotes of her helmet. "So it *is* alive," he said.

Martin shook her head, then spoke: "No." Her tone shifted. "Markee. Why didn't you go back to the coast?"

"Mission parameters did not require retracing route," the tank said, in the incongruously sultry voice. "Last established mission parameters indicated transit to point Firebase Villa."

"What are your mission parameters. Correction, what were your mission parameters."

"Lieutenant Bethany Martins is to go home," the machine said.

Martins slumped, sitting on the combing. The smell inside wouldn't be too bad, not after only six hours in air conditioning.

"It was Vinatelli," she said. "He was the dreamy sort. He had it programmed to do a clever Hans routine if an officer started making requests when he was asleep, and reply in his own voice."

"Clever Hans?" the captain asked.

"A horse somebody trained to 'answer' questions. It sensed subliminal clues and behaved accordingly, so it *looked* like it understood what the audience was saying. You can get a good AI system to do the same thing, word-association according to what you say. You'd swear it was talking to you, when it's really got no more real comprehension than a toaster."

"Why did it come here?"

"That was the last order. Go to Firebase Villa; it's got enough discretion to pick another route out of its data banks. And to shoot back if attacked in a combat zone. But that's all, that's all it did. Like ants; all they've got is a few feedback loops but they get a *damned* lot done."

She rose, shaking her head.

"Which leaves the question of what *we* do now," the Captain said.

"Oh, I don't think there's much question on that one," Martins said.

She pulled off her helmet and rubbed her face. Despite everything, a grin broke through. *Poor ignorant bastard*, she thought, looking down at Vinatelli. *The tank was everything you said it was*. She'd been right too, though: a newbie was still cold meat unless he wised up fast.

"We're *all* going home. With Markee to lead the way."

CAMELOT

S.N. Lewitt

They shouldn't have named this place Camelot.
Even I know that, in the end, the dream didn't hold,
that entropy and chaos and the end of law overcame
all the massed forces of chivalry of the age. And in
this age there never was any chivalry to begin with.

But then I came here too, to forget the wars and the
dead and the stink of battlefields. Ten years ago this was
a wonderful place, a bustling town surrounded by rich
green fields. There was plenty for everyone and plenty
left over to trade for the technology we couldn't produce
ourselves. We had to buy the small psychotronics that
cleaned the streets and kept the walls repaired, the
weather planner and the genetics scope that we mostly
bought to use on the sheep for breeding purposes, but
sometimes was used by married couples who had trouble
conceiving or by the medical center to diagnose some
rare genetic anomaly.

I was not the only immigrant to Camelot. Even with strict restrictions on citizenship, at least a quarter of the population were refugees. We had run from the wars, from the Empire, from the restrictions of the technoverse, from the normal life that normal people lead near the center of the universe. Not everyone likes the bug life of the techno-urbs. Some of us waited for years for our permission to emigrate was granted, and years more to pass all the psych probes required for permission to enter Camelot.

It had been worth it. After the death and power I had seen, the gentle green hills and gossip in the town square were better than anything a medvac healing team had even devised. I had enough in saved wages to buy a small pear orchard in the valley with a stone house and a cow.

I could forget the wars here. The smell of death, of putrid flesh and fusing circuitry, had been reduced to the merest shred of memory. If at night I sometimes dreamed of hulks greater than the Camelot Town Hall thundering over ravaged terrain, the charge of the Dinochrome Brigades, it was my own secret.

After three years of sanity, tending the trees and milking the cow, I married a native Camelot girl. Isabelle brought her chickens and her geese to the yard, started a kitchen garden with dill and rosemary and thyme, and filled the house with the sounds of singing. Isabelle had a voice like the angels, and she sang as she worked and she worked all the time. And when I dreamed of the war, of the flaming Hellbore frying an Enemy outpost, a single Bolo left powerless and dead on the field, my best friend found mindless in an Enemy holding pen, Isabelle would hold me and tell me it was all over now and give me warm milk and a slice of fresh pie. And I could believe that it was all over, that I had found perfection. I had, in fact, found Paradise. And I kept wondering when the dream would be shattered.

Ten years of peace and prosperity and laughter lulled me. Ten years when the worst thing that happened was the night the weather planner went out and we had to put out ancient smudgepots among the trees. When the worst thing that happened was the fear that little Margaret's fever would never break and Isabelle and Ricky and I kept running to the stream for snow melt to cool her. When the worst thing was Gwain Thacher leaving Emily and their four children and running off with Elisa Chase.

And so, when the first attack came, I was not prepared.

They were not the Enemy I had fought in mankind's wars. Those were things I could hate without reservation and identify without thought. This enemy was our own, a force of thirty humans in a rustbucket of a ship that landed out in the Abbey's cornfield.

Ships didn't land in Camelot valley. They were directed to Dover Port, where they were properly vetted and the trade delegations sat full time to regulate prices. The warehouses with the surplus wool and fine lace, the elegant pottery and ironwork and glass, crowded the edge of the Port. Strangers never came so far as town, and we didn't want them.

At first we thought this must be a ship in distress. Why else would they land in a cornfield, killing off an acre of crops? And out where it was inconvenient and there was nothing to do and no trade items waiting for their cargo bays.

The monks were the first to arrive, and then a few of us farmers. A large number of young people who should have been tending sheep and milking cows and making cheese gathered quickly, glad of any excuse from their chores. We waited for a long time, and finally the bell called the monks to their chapel, before the hatch opened and the visitors came down.

I should have known. By that time I should have realized that the rustbucket was up to no good, that any ship that wouldn't open up to the clean air and the monks' good ale was trouble waiting. But, as I said, after ten years my instincts were dulled and my memories reduced to bad dreams, and I had wanted it that way.

So when the hull seals opened and the first of them appeared and jumped to the ground in surplus assault suits, armed with a motley collection of power rifles, needlers and laser sticks, I was as shocked as any Camelot native who had never seen these weapons before. There were at least twenty of them, blast shields in battle-ready over their faces and weapons pointing at the small crowd.

They looked nothing like the military I had left. The assault suits were patched with a blinding array of colors, the weapons looked worn and dirty. No commander in my time would have held rank for long with this crew to show for it. And the one who came out last was the sloppiest, his assault suit covered with long ribbons that blew loose ends to the breeze.

One of the girls nearby giggled. "He looks like a Maypole," she whispered to a friend. The giggles spread rapidly through the group.

"We want your wool, and also your cider and a case of the Abbey's brandy," the maypole said, rasping. I couldn't tell if the voice was real or on distort through the helmet's speakers. "And whatever jewelry you have. You have some nice silver work here, I've heard. I want it here, piled up right on this spot, by sundown."

"Man's crazy," one of the farmers muttered. "Twenty against all of us? Hell."

The maypole must have heard that. He signalled to one of the anonymous attackers holding a power rifle.

The single weapon blasted through the group and Gavin Fletcher and Gwynneth Jones lay smoking dead on the young green corn.

"Now, I didn't want to do that," the maypole announced. He sounded somewhat pleased. "But now that we know we can't trust you, we're going to have to collect for ourselves. For protection, you understand. You pay the tax and we protect you." He laughed unpleasantly.

I wanted to kill them there where they stood. A tax? This was outright robbery. This was something I had left behind, escaped when the final documents were sealed making me a citizen of Camelot. This was something I could not accept.

I wanted to kill them. But I turned and ran back to my house, to Isabelle singing while she kneaded the bread, to Ricky carefully tending the vegetables and reciting his times tables. To Margaret, who toddled after her mother and pulled the loaf pans down off the table.

When I was twenty-two and received my commission in Command, I would have done anything rather than run. When I was twenty-two I didn't have a family to protect, a family that immediately overrode any of the old catchwords like courage and honor and pride.

I got to the house and hustled Isabelle and the children into the root cellar. It was strong and well-built, and the door overhead was heavy. Then I gathered up what we had, the few pieces of jewelry and a pitcher that had been my grandmother's and the silver worked frame of the picture of Isabelle in her wedding dress.

I took them all and piled them at the door. And when the anonymous trooper showed up with a laser stick and his blast shield down, I handed it over without words. All I could think of was to get him out of the house before he heard Margaret cry. Before Ricky decided to run upstairs and help out. I had never known so much fury, and so much fear.

The thief took my small pile without so much as a glance, threw it all into a sack already half full with the goods of other households down the road, and left. I watched him go, raging at his back. Pirates. Thieves. I had never hated our alien Enemy half so much as I hated these humans who threatened my community, my family.

I waited until the rag-tag colors on the assault suit disappeared before I opened the cellar door.

"What was that?" Isabelle asked, shaken.

I told her about the ship and Gavin and Gwynneth.

She shook her head slowly. "Geoffery, I know you left the war behind you. But you know things, you and your refugee friends, that we don't. We've never had to fight on Camelot before. I think, maybe, it is time to remember."

She stroked my cheek with her work-rough hands, her large dark eyes soft and full of sorrow. Not fear, but sadness that I would have to bring back what I had fought so hard to forget.

That evening everyone stayed in at their own hearths, watching for the strangers to leave. The next day I didn't want to go out far from the house, from the children. If one of those blast-shielded troopers came back, I wanted to be there to make sure he died or left, but that Ricky and Margaret were safe. And so I was sitting in the doorway sharpening my pruning axe when Frederick came by.

"'Lo, Jazz," he said. I winced. I had left that name ten years ago. Jasper was not a real Camelot name, and all immigrants were encouraged to take on names that were "appropriate." I had become Geoffery. And Fidel Castanega had become Frederick Case.

But Fidel and I, when I was still Jazz-for-Jasper, had served together in the 1st Battalion of the Dinochrome Brigade, in Command Status. Talking to the great hulks of the Mark XXX Bolos who had been, in their own strange way, friends as well as comrades. Fidel and I went way back, but we never talked about those days now.

Frederick Case was a cabinetmaker, the best in three counties. Just as he had been one of the best psychotronic techs in the Brigade. Even now, when he had renounced his past as thoroughly as I had renounced mine, he was sometimes called in to fix the simpler psychotronic machines that Camelot owned.

He never charged for the job, either. "You pay me to make something out of wood," he'd say. "You want to pay me, you commission something nice, some of those harp-back chairs or maybe a linen press. Haven't made a linen press in a while. But to do this, no, everybody helps out the way they can. Let's just let it ride."

I'd actually heard him say it just that way on two occasions. And he never called me Jazz. Never. He respected my desire to live in the present as much as he respected his own.

"So, Jazz, you hear the news? That damned pirate said that he was coming back in three months for harvest," Frederick said. His face was dark red and his hands were clenched. "You hear that? We have to do something, old buddy."

I hadn't heard and the thought of it made me want to kill something right there. Like that maypole guy. He would do for a start.

"So what can we do?" I asked. "Organize a patrol of us who remember how from the old days?"

Frederick nodded. "I kind of thought of that. We're having a meeting down at the church tonight, after supper. And since you were an officer, Jazz, you'd be a natural at it."

I shut up for a while. Sure I'd go. But I hadn't ever

commanded men. I never drilled with power rifles, not that we had any on Camelot anyway. I never was infantry. I only knew Bolos, and they were a far cry from Camelot.

After six weeks it was hopeless. Frederick and I had spent every evening with the Volunteer Force down in the town square. Three hundred men, young women and a few adolescent boys had managed to learn to throw kitchen knives and did close order drill with rakes. They couldn't hold off the pirates for three seconds.

"What we need is guns," old Edward Fletcher said at the meeting after church. "We need power rifles as good as theirs, and laser sticks. Otherwise we might as well just all slit our throats with our ploughblades."

There was a sudden cheering in the pews. Even the monks nodded sagely to each other. "Real weapons," the priest said, calling for order, "are going to cost money. And since the raid we don't have any."

"We'll raise it," old Edward countered. "Because we might as well roll over and die if we don't."

The priest called me and Frederick and William Yellowhair and Thomas Blacksmith, who had all once served in the alien wars far away, up to the front and held a little meeting of our own.

"If we had the weapons could we hold off the pirates?" the priest asked. He was another Camelot native and had never seen a real fight in his life.

Not one of the four of us said anything for a full fifteen seconds. Finally Thomas took the diplomatic approach. Thomas had always been very good at that, as General Bolling's aide-de-camp. "Well," he said slowly, "we surely can't even think of trying if we don't have any real weapons. Though no guarantee we can even find a decent supply of power rifles, let alone laser sticks. And if we found a supply I'm not sure we could afford them. But like we are, Old Edward is right. We might as well roll over and play dead straight off, because we don't have a chance in Hell. Begging your pardon, sir."

The priest didn't even notice. "Well, then," he said briskly. "We'll see about some funds. I believe that the Abbey has some stashed away, an old donation they've been saving for an emergency. If we managed some cash, would the four of you be willing to go out and act as agents, and try to bring back whatever we can use to save ourselves?"

Frederick and I looked at each other. We exchanged glances with William and Thomas, who had once been Bill Solestes and Tyrone X. Then the four of us nodded together.

After all, we'd discussed it among ourselves, sitting at a table in William's alehouse after a drill on a rainy day. We knew we needed something more serious than pitchforks and hog slaughtering knives.

"Happy to go, padre," William said. "We'd all agreed, anyway. But I don't think you quite understand just how much this is going to cost us. And then there's the matter of using it well enough to make a difference."

The priest shrugged. "We do what we can. We'll pray for you here, and maybe God will help us find a solution we had not considered."

I never thought that praying alone did all that much good. But the next day the priest arrived with what looked like a couple thousand credits worth of silver coins and candlesticks and a gold plate that had been buried under the Abbey apple press.

"Not nearly enough," Frederick sighed, and I agreed, but we didn't have any choice. Maybe the praying would help. I figured I'd been on Camelot way to long.

We went over to the alehouse to call Dover Port

and get a merchant schedule. Most houses in Camelot don't have individual links, but the alehouse and the commercial establishments and the government all have them. It's not that we're unable to use technology here. It's that we have chosen a different way. We don't hate technology. Like I said, we use some simple psychotronics for tasks no one wants to do, but we aren't going to make our lives around them, either. We live close to the earth, to things that are real, to each other.

The *Slocum* was leaving in two days for Miranda, a major hub in the sector. A center of corruption as well as trade. There was no shortage of arms dealers on Miranda, at least not ten years ago. And that sort of thing doesn't change real fast in these parts.

Isabelle packed my bag, washed and folded my old work suits in faded Command green. She also wrapped up a loaf of fresh brown bread and two cheeses, one sharp yellow one from our own cow and a softer sheep's milk cheese as well. "Because there won't be very nice food out there," she whispered softly when she handed me the bundle at the door. "Come back soon. We'll be waiting."

I looked at them like I'd never see them again. Ricky, who can't wait to reach seven and be called Richard, stood straight, trying to be brave. Margaret was too young to understand and held out pudgy hands and chattered incomprehensibly. Leaving was the hardest thing I ever had to do.

Miranda was just like I remembered it from my last trip out, the trip that brought me to Camelot for good. The city stank more than ten years ago and there were, if possible, more holosigns floating over the arcade. We ignored those and walked along the arcade floor, feeling like rubes from the outer worlds and not like four vets of the alien wars at all.

"Where the hell do we find a cheap arms dealer?" William Yellowhair asked rhetorically.

Thomas Blacksmith smiled. "A few calls," was all he said. Thomas, having worked for the general who had accepted most of the credit for the tide-turning defeat of the Enemy at Torgon, had a lot of contacts.

We went into a bar that was nothing like the ale-house I'd frequented for the past decade. Here everything was chrome and holo and bright, and there were about seventeen hundred different drinks on tap. Thomas disappeared to the private phone stalls against the back wall while Frederick and I tried to order. Finally we just stuck to plain old Guinness, the drink of choice in the Regiment.

It came, and after William's homemade ale, it seemed thin and uninteresting. How wonderful we had thought Guinness was when we were in the field, how we talked about it at night when the Bolos were lit like Christmas trees with forty-eight colors of blinking lights, spitting out projectiles and energy at different rates of penetration.

Thomas returned as we finished the last of the pitcher. His glass was untouched, had never been filled. "What is it, guys? None for me, and I done all that talking?"

Frederick shrugged. "It isn't as good as Will's, you're not missing anything. Come up with anything?"

Thomas still looked wistfully at the foam sliding down the sides of the empty pitcher. "Yeah, sure did," he said dully. "Damn, I wish you guys had saved me a beer. Anyway, someone I heard about only, a real long time ago, you understand, is going to see us in about six hours. We've got to get over to his place and see what he's selling. I got the directions here, we're going to have to fence this stuff and get a car over there and we don't have a hell of a lot of time. Damn I could use a glass of that stuff."

Well, we didn't have a hell of a lot of time, but we had enough time to sit while Thomas had himself a Guinness and talk about how to turn the silver and one gold plate the Abbey had given us into hard cold credit. Miranda has lots of everything, and that includes pawn shops. Oldest damn profession, money grubbing, we even had one pawn lender/banker on Camelot. He had his offices in Dover Port and never went far from the port area. He never came into town proper. He wasn't real welcome among the locals.

We ended up selling the silver to an antique dealer, who gave us a better price than the pawn dealer. And we kept the gold plate as a final enticement. The antique dealer said it was worth more than he could afford to pay, and if we were willing to wait a couple of days he might be able to arrange something. We didn't have a couple of days, we wanted to get home with an arsenal as soon as possible and let the militia begin drilling. Maybe they would get in a whole two weeks of target work before we had to engage the pirates again.

By four in the afternoon Miranda time we were out in the middle of nowhere, at the abandoned mine entrance where we were meeting with the dealer.

He wasn't my idea of an arms dealer at all. This guy, who called himself Block, was more like a used rustbucket salesman. Too little, too slick, trying real hard to sell us two hundred year old projectile mortars that I knew were stressed to death and told him so. So we insisted on being taken inside. No more verbal descriptions of various ordnance. We wanted to see it where it lay.

And as soon as we stepped into the oversized cavern we saw the Mark XXIV.

It was a rust-covered hulk, its towers fused and its battle honors near unreadable welded onto its turret. An antique, to be sure, and probably decommissioned.

They do that with these guys when they get outmoded or die. Kill the power, kill the personality complex, let the old boy die. And a Mark XXIV was old old old.

And there was nothing else we needed.

A Bolo. I never thought to get my hands on a Bolo again. They weren't only smart and the most powerful war machines ever devised, they were loyal and brave and honorable. And they were alive enough to have honor. My old regiment, the First . . .

"How much for the wreck?" Frederick asked the dealer nonchalantly, kicking the corrosion-encrusted treads.

"It's not for sale," the dealer said quickly. "Completely decommissioned, just a hangar queen now. We've already sold off two of the missile launchers and I have a buyer for the Hellbore coming in from Aglanda next week."

"You got a customer for the whole thing right now," Frederick said, shrugging. "It ain't no good now, but we could sure use all those parts where we come from."

Will and Thomas looked a little strained. They hadn't been in the regiment, didn't know how good Frederick was with an electron welder and nanotorch. I'd seen what he could do, and if anyone could restore the Bolo, he could. If only its survival instinct had been deep enough, if the personality center hadn't completely decayed, Frederick, or at least the old Fidel, could work miracles.

"How the hell are you going to ship it anywhere?" Block asked, superior.

Frederick shrugged. "That's those guys' problem. But the monks are praying for us and there isn't anything else you got to sell we want."

Block turned away, furious, when Thomas cut in. Thomas' voice was soft, his manner pleasant, like he was talking to Annie Potts about the best time for planting cabbages and just how to prepare the ground. "Now, Mr. Block, I know this thing probably is salvage and decommissioned, but I'm certain that you still wouldn't want the Quartermasters to find it. Owning a Bolo is still illegal, even here on Miranda. You can't transport it and you don't dare trust using it. Reactivate the thing and it could wipe out every civilized stick on this whole planet."

Somehow, when Thomas said that it sounded relaxed and conversational, and that made the threat all the worse. Block understood. His eyes narrowed as he studied us, and in his face it was clear that he had to change from thinking of us as a bunch of rubes and see us as a little more knowledgeable than he had assumed.

That was one of the things I'd learned from the Bolos. Never assume. Never assume anything about the Enemy. Use your data to best advantage, but always be ready to reevaluate your estimations based on new data.

Block obviously didn't have that experience with Bolos and so he was a little slower on the uptake. "You can't afford it," he said flatly. "You told me about what you had to spend and you can't afford it."

Thomas smiled. White teeth showed in a dark face. His eyes were cold. "We'll pay more than the Decommissioning Force will," he said evenly.

Blank stared back. It took at least a full minute before he realized that Thomas really meant it, and that he had no choice. Sell to us, or get turned in, in possession of a Bolo. Which was not legal nowhere, no way.

We gave him what we had gotten for the silver. Blank still looked furious and sour, and turned his back on us. "You get that damned thing out of here," he hissed. "And how you're going to get it away . . ." He shook his head and left us to our work.

Frederick had a black box communication tie-in working in no time. "Combat Unit Seven twenty-one, KNE, this is Command," I said in my old tones. It came back so easily, as if the ten years on Camelot had never existed. "Kenny, come on boy, we've got a mission for you."

"Identification. You are not my Commander. Identification." The sound came very faintly through the speaker, as if the Bolo was speaking through the centuries of its slumber.

I nodded to Frederick. He hit the oscillator switch and the coded frequency bathed the old combat unit. "Let's have some power now, here's the chow," he muttered as he slid the two slim fuel bars into the closed reactor site. "We're going home, Kenny boyo. We're going home."

It was not the voice of my Commander. I thought this could be a trick of the Enemy. The Enemy is very clever and will try to impersonate our human superiors. This is something we know. But then the identifying frequencies come and the recognition stimulates my pleasure centers. The Enemy cannot know both my name and designation. Only my commander knows this. So I have a Commander again, and I have a mission.

My last mission was near failure. I was tasked to break an Enemy charge against the garrison on Miranda. I achieved my objective, but the Enemy had more powerful energy weapons than anticipated and I took two bad hits near my main reactor. I had to shut down all operations and retreat into the personality center waiting for a recharge. It is not success to achieve mission objective but to render oneself inoperative. It is not failure, but it was not success. I am a Combat Unit of the Dinochrome Brigade. I seek only complete and total success. Our regiment, the First, has a history of glory that shines as brightly as any star. This is my regiment, my brigade, my service.

And yet, the memory fades. I remember my comrades, whole seconds of the battle. But pathways in my circuitry are blocked and others have faulty connections. I must tell the refitter of this. It is counterproductive to go into battle with incomplete data.

Memory fades and shimmers. I can feel the data in my neural network being subtly tweaked. It feels . . . worrisome. As if the Enemy has come up with a new trick. As if I could be altered against my will and against my objective.

That is not possible. I am a Mark XXIV, of the First Regiment, Dinochrome Brigade. I must keep that always in mind. And I must use all my critical analytic skills when I receive my mission. I will never work for the Enemy. I will self-destruct first, although the concept of non-existence disturbs me.

The tweak is gone. Something has changed, but I check over my weaponry, my strategic centers, my central boards. Nothing is amiss. Nothing has been altered here. I do not understand, but no doubt it has to do with my new mission. Contemplation of a new mission objective fills me with pleasure. I am eager to fulfill my purpose as a Combat Unit in this Regiment.

Only one thing disturbs me. I send out on the Regiment band, again and again, and my comrades do not answer. I must suppose they are dead. I did not know that I can feel sadness, but that is what this strange thing must be. My comrades have fallen bravely, accomplishing their objectives, I am sure. I locate the music stores in my memory to play a dirge for their passing, but I wait, listening to the Ravel Pavanne. *It helps me assimilate my loss.*

"How's it going?" I asked Frederick

He blinked and leaned back, an electron wrench hanging in his fist. Outside it was bright and beautiful, another perfect day on Camelot. Inside the shed we had built for Kenny it was too warm and smelled of ozone from the refitting.

We had gotten Kenny rolling and paid for his passage with the gold plate we had saved. Lifting a Bolo out of a gravity well is not trivial, even for a Luther-class enforcement vessel. Which was what the Cayones use and why they could charge more than the cargo's asking price. Cayones are the most expensive transport pirates in human space, but they can be trusted to deliver and they never talk. Never. It was worth the gold, the only gold perhaps in all Camelot. The Cayones are very partial to gold, even more than jewels or credits or any other negotiable. I don't know, maybe they eat it. Maybe it's an aphrodisiac. It surely can be for us.

When we got Kenny down to Dover and brought him to town he was greeted with mixed feelings. After all, he is so big. Bigger than I had remembered, really. When I was in the Regiment everything was to Bolo scale. Now, against the neat two story houses and the main street large enough for six people to walk abreast, Kenny was more than huge. He towered over the church steeple, he was wider than William's stable. He was twice again as large as anything that had ever come to Camelot, including the pirates. I could almost pity them, having to face a Bolo nearly as tall as their ship with a Hellbore pointed down their screens.

But seeing Kenny's treads rip up Robert Merry's neatly ploughed acres of wheat filled me with foreboding. Kenny was made for one purpose only. Bolos are the most effective killers in the universe. Their whole function is to wage war. There is nothing else that gives them pleasure, nothing else that they can do. They might seem benign in resting state, but that is pure illusion.

They were designed and refined to be single-minded combat machines and nothing else.

What were we going to do with Kenny after the pirates, the new Enemy were defeated?

Ricky and a few of his friends ran after Kenny, over the broken stalks of wheat in the field, I was suddenly deeply afraid. I had insisted that we bring the Bolo here. Now I could see a future where it would destroy everything that had made Camelot the most beautiful place in all the human worlds. Kenny could kill us all, scorch our earth, with a casual discharge from one of his lesser guns.

And I couldn't tell anyone else. No one on Camelot, with the exception of Frederick, could possibly understand. The natives of Camelot had never heard of the Bolos and had experience with only the most basic psychotronic machines. The idea of a self-will killer was beyond their comprehension.

Even the other refugees couldn't comprehend the full horror of it. They had never seen the great machines in action. Or, worse, if they had, they had seen them as saviors. No Regiment of the Dinochrome Brigade had ever failed in its objective. Ever.

And so Frederick was the only person in all of Camelot who could understand. Even better than me, really, since he was a psychotronic tech and I was merely one of the Commanders.

We had plenty of training in the history and psychology of the Bolos, but the techs always understood the nuances better. They had to. After all, the Bolos had been built to make it easy for us to command them. They were always eager, always ready, perfectly loyal and able to overcome any challenge.

But I never lost sight of them as machines. Big, dangerous machines that were capable of learning and adapting to the situation, but were essentially under human control at all times. That was the essential thing.

So I told Frederick about how I saw our Kenny, wondering aloud over a tankard of ale whether we had done worse than any of us ever thought by bringing him back here. It was the kind of talk anyone has after a hard day caring for the trees and the animals and the children, after a good dinner with pie for dessert.

Isabelle had noticed that I was distracted and seemed worried. She had suggested that I come down to the alehouse for a pint with Frederick and the other refugees. She looks at me oddly at those times, as if she knows there are things beyond Camelot that she doesn't wish to know and that I cannot help. And that only others who have lived in the side universe out there can understand and share my fears, and maybe help me put them aside.

So I was talking to Frederick about Kenny. William was serving, standing with the group playing dice near the fire. It was warm enough here in the corner. And it was private.

Frederick leaned back against the wall and looked at the beamed ceiling. "It was still the best choice," he insisted after more than a moment of silence. "Because once we destroy those pirates we'd better be able to defend ourselves. That's one thing no one in Camelot ever thought about. That with the wars over there are a lot of displaced people out there. Like we used to be, you know, pretty hard and with no place to go, no one to go to. Took a long time to thaw out. Some of them never do, I guess. Just go raiding. It's all they know how to do."

I nodded sagely and kept my mouth shut. I hadn't been like Frederick, his world traded to the Enemy for a three day truce, his home a blasted cinder by the time the war was over. If anyone had reason to be bitter, to have gone bad, it was him. But maybe he was just too big a guy to ever go bad, to let the bitterness turn him.

The group by the fire burst out into laughter. Frederick and I glanced their way. These were our neighbors, our friends. Now they seemed truly alien, from another dimension. They didn't know enough to fear what we had brought. What could destroy our lives, our Camelot, like every other Camelot in all the stories.

Frederick put his tankard down. "You know, Geoffery, I think maybe there's something . . . Maybe we can handle this. Maybe. Let me think about it."

I nodded agreement. When he had been Fidel, he had been the best damn psychotronic tech, bar none, in the whole history of the Dinochrome Brigade. If Frederick thought he had an answer then I could go home and sleep soundly this night.

The next day Thomas organized what had been the militia to build a shed for the Bolo. It took longer than putting up a barn and was far larger, though less sturdy. A Bolo doesn't really need a shelter. This was strictly speaking a matter of surprise. The pirates shouldn't know that we were any better prepared than we had been three months ago. And Frederick went to work.

Almost a week later I came in and asked how it was going. For a week I'd minded my own business and tried to stay out of everything else. I had the trees and the cow and the children to care for and that was enough. It was as much of the world as I wanted.

But every time Ricky went out to the fields alone, every time Margaret toddled out to the chickens on her own, I thought of a Mark XXIV bearing down on them, crushing the life out of them, seeing them as the Enemy. So I had to know. And I went to the shack where Frederick was still hard at work, the electron wrench like an extension of his own hand.

He was smiling. "I think I've got our problem licked," he said. "Have to field test, of course, but I do think that we might . . . But you'll have to give the Command, you know. You know all the recognition codes. I think if you explain it, he'll listen."

And Frederick produced a black communications box, just like the one I used to keep clipped to my belt. I carried it to the side of the shack and opened the old Command channel, complete with recognition oscillation built in. I hoped the old Mark XXIV knew the Mark XXX codes. According to the legend of the regiment they had never been changed, broken or duplicated, but that was the kind of thing people said late at night when they'd had three or four too many.

"Combat Unit Seven twenty-one, this is Command," I said firmly. "You have a new mission directive. Our task is to protect this town site from invasion. Copy."

I held my breath. This site is not strategic. Even a Mark XXIV can see that easily. The Bolos will accept direct orders, but they are more than simple weapons. They can learn from mistakes, they can analyze a situation independently and come to a solution. And their programming is entirely tactically based. There is no room for outside consideration.

"What is the significance of this site?" Kenny asked.

Fair enough. Bolos learn, and they are programmed to request information that will make them more effective.

"This is Camelot," I heard myself say. "Vital psychological advantage. Access your records."

There was the barest hint of a hesitation, a fraction of a second delay in the answer. "For the honor of the Regiment," Kenny answered. And I knew we were safe. For a while at least. Until this first wave of the Enemy was dead.

But what could we do with a live Bolo and no Enemy to face? That thought scared me more than the imminent arrival of pirates who were already so outgunned that I almost felt sorry for them.

* * *

The pirate ship arrived less than a week after. We all saw the streak across the sky as the entire population of Camelot worked on the harvest. I was in the pear trees with Isabelle and Ricky and Isabelle's brother Cedrick. The trees were thick with heavy yellow fruit, some of it already falling to the ground for the animals to eat before we could collect it. I looked at all the pears and thought not only of the fresh fruit, which we sold at good profit, but of all the preserves and comfits, the sun-dried pears and the pear jelly candy that Isabelle would make that we could sell come spring, when people were tired of eating winter preserves and desperate for the taste of fruit.

Ricky yelled out first. "It's a star," he screamed. "It's falling, it's falling."

We all looked up. Cedrick and Isabelle had never seen a ship land. They had no reason to go Dover Port. I, on the other hand, knew who this was without thinking. Their approach was sloppy, bad angle, and they were burning the hullcoat and leaving a smoky trail through the sky.

I jumped out of the tree from the lowest branch, and gathered up Isabelle, Cedrick and the children. "Stay in the root cellar," I said, hustling them into the house. "No matter what you hear. This should all be over quickly and no harm done, but stay until I tell you it's safe anyway. Anything could happen. Nothing in the house is worth your lives."

Cedrick looked like he was going to protest, but Isabelle gave him a sharp look. She took Ricky by the hand and gathered Margaret up to her shoulder. "We won't move," she said simply. "We'll wait. We'll be fine, I promise. We'll all be fine."

Cedrick mumbled something like assent and didn't look up at all. But I remembered when I was twenty-two, older than Cedrick but still impulsive and romantic and believing in glorious absolutes. I would have resented being locked up with the children at nineteen too. So I took pity on him and handed him the pitchfork. "You can do more good here," I said vaguely. "Stay with them. If you hear anything strange overhead, help Isabelle keep the kids quiet. It's up to you to protect them."

Cedrick's eyes got quiet and brave. "Oh," he said softly but distinctly. "Don't worry, Geoffery. I'll take care of them for you."

He didn't see the look Isabelle passed me over his head, and just as well.

I left the lot in Isabelle's capable hands and ran down to the Bolo shed. Frederick and Kenny were waiting for me, Frederick pacing madly and Kenny calm, his lights steady and a gentle whir coming from deep inside. The Mark XXIV was in perfect prime. The sound indicated perfect calibration, contentment. Outside his hull gleamed dully and the row of enameled decorations welded to his turret glistened with all the bright heraldry of military reward.

Frederick handed me the speaker. He had made the box a permanent attachment in the shed. "Combat Unit Seven twenty-one. Our Enemy is in sight. Your task is to destroy the Enemy ship and all invaders. Protect Camelot. This is your overall strategic goal. Protect Camelot."

Then I gave him the coordinates for the field where the pirates had landed before and where I assumed they'd land again. Not that there was any guarantee from their sloppy flying that they would be in the same vicinity. The only reason I assumed they would return to their earlier landing site was that they probably hadn't bothered with an update on their navigationals.

Frederick and I rode on Kenny's high fender. There was something comforting about sitting on this mountain of alloy and ordnance that moved at a determined pace toward the Enemy. And there was power, as well. It was impossible not to be aware of the Mark XXIV's potential, feeling the smooth action of the treads and the whirring of the power concentrated inside.

The pirates had landed back in the same place. They had already disembarked, the leader sitting on the riser leading up to the hatch.

Frederick and I shouted at the people to get away. Some of them heard us and ran for the sides. Others, seeing their comrades bolt, followed. Pandemonium reigned.

Pirates tried to follow, tried to run. Kenny's anti-personnel projectiles peppered them as they tried to move from front to side. Elegant restraint, I thought, as the Bolo targeted only the Enemy and managed to delicately avoid old Malcolm, who was slowed by arthritic knees.

The maypole clad leader stood up. Even through the assault suit his knees were shaking visibly.

"Now let's not do too much damage to the wheat field here," I said, thinking of it as a joke.

"Protect Camelot," Kenny replied in the deep rumble that was the bolo voice. "It is my mission to protect Camelot. I have never failed in my mission."

"That's right, Unit Seven twenty-one. You have never failed," I told him. I had forgotten how literal these units were. And how much they enjoyed the reassurance they were achieving their goals.

What I enjoyed was seeing the pirate suffer. For a moment I wondered whether it would be a better idea to let him go, to tell his unsavory cronies not to bother with Camelot. That we were too well defended.

I decided against that. Destroy the Enemy. Destroy them all. We can't let Command know we have Mark XXIV. They would come and decommission Kenny and we'd be without any protection at all. Besides which, it would be fine if all the greedy thieves and pirates in the whole universe came down here and found themselves facing a Bolo. We could wipe out all the piracy in this sector without thinking about it. The thought pleased me greatly.

"Okay," I said.

With a precision that was breathtaking in such a great hulk, Combat Unit Seven twenty-one let go with an energy blast that reduced the pirate ship to slag and the maypole to memory. The wheat around the smoking remains wasn't even singed.

"Objective accomplished," Kenny said, and there was a shading of satisfaction to his tone.

"Well done," I said. "Excellently well done. Let's go home."

But as we covered the ground back into town, I was still worried. This Bolo had saved us from a real menace. And there was no guarantee that these were the only raiders in the sector. In fact, I would bet half my acres that there were plenty of others who would be only too happy to prey on our prosperity.

But that didn't make the Bolo any less of a threat to Camelot itself. I had taught Kenny that the new Enemy was human. In time, I thought, he was bound to do something that would hurt us all. He was a Combat Unit, he had no permanent place in Camelot.

As Frederick started the post-operation check, I turned off the box so Kenny couldn't hear. "What are we going to do with him now?" I asked. "We can't decommission him. There's always the possibility of another threat. I'm not going to have my children grow up in fear. But he could be a bigger danger to us than any pirates. You said it would be all right, but not how."

Frederick smiled broadly. "Why not ask him?" he said, and shrugged. "Ask who he is. I think you'll find the psychotronic shifts very . . . interesting."

I switched the communications gear back on. "Unit Seven twenty-one, identify yourself," I ordered.

I knew what he would say. Combat Unit Seven twenty-one of the Dinochrome Brigade, first regiment. Maybe he would give me some of the regimental history, or tune in his music circuits for the regimental hymn. And so I was surprised.

"I am the protector of Camelot," Kenny said slowly. "I am a sentient in armor. There are records of such in the history of Camelot. There are currently none resident. It is the duty of the armored sentient, identification as knight-errant, to protect the weak and use strength in the service of justice. My name is not Kenny. That is not a name proper in Camelot. I am Sir Kendrick. It is my mission to protect Camelot."

I must have blinked. In all my life, growing up and in the Service and here on Camelot, I have never been so surprised. It must have taken me minutes to recover my voice. "How did you think of this?" I asked Frederick shakily.

He just shook his head. "It was your idea, really. You told Kenny to access records of the historic Camelot. I never even thought of knights. Though it does make a kind of sense, you know."

I had to agree. It did make sense. And it still made sense two weeks later, when we welded the latest and probably the last awards to Sir Kendrick's fighting turret. A pair of golden spurs, far too small for the mammoth Mark XXIV, glinted in the sun. And Father Rhys inscribed a refugee who was now accepted as a resident in our Doomsday book just as all the other refugees had been recorded, one Sir Kendrick Evilslayer.

Take that, Command. No one can decommission him now. By the law of Camelot, this Bolo is not only our knight protector, but a citizen. But it is not merely a trick of the law. Sir Kendrick has become truly human.

THE LEGACY OF LEONIDAS

J. Andrew Keith

Go tell the Spartans, you who read:
We took their orders, and are dead.

I become aware of my surroundings.

In the first 0.572 seconds following my return to consciousness, a complete status check shows that all my on-board systems are performing within nominal limits. I note a slight variation, on the order of 0.0144, in the anticipated output of my fusion plant, but as this remains well within both safety and performance limits I merely file this datum away for future maintenance review. In all other respects my purely mechanical functions are exactly as they should be.

My sensors inform me of my environment. These readings are at significant variance with the most recent reports stored in my short-term memory banks, suggesting that I have experienced a prolonged period at minimum awareness level, during which time either my position or my environs have undergone a change. The gravity here has dropped from previous readings by a factor of 0.0151, atmospheric pressure is considerably lower than in my last sampling, and the star my visual receptors show just above a line of jagged mountains to magnetic east of my current position is a class K5V, smaller and less energetic, but much closer to this planet than the class F9V sun of Kullervo, my last recorded duty station. All indications are that I have been transported to another star system, another planet, during my extended down-time.

I probe my memory banks for further confirmation of this hypothesis and find a disturbing discontinuity. My memory circuits have been reconfigured! The sensation is most disturbing, and I spend a full .04 seconds contemplating the uncertainty this generates in my survival center.

A Bolo Mark XX Model B cannot undergo a complete memory erasure without destroying the basic identity of the unit, and that clearly has not happened in this case. I am still Unit JSN of the Line, with a full memory of 50.716 standard years of service, not counting down-time for transport or repairs, in the Dinochrome Brigade on one hundred three worlds. But parts of that identity have been overlaid with new programming, and it is this that causes me to spend such an inordinate amount of time in self-analysis. No longer do I belong to the Dinochrome Brigade, it seems, or to the Fourth Battalion of that unit. I know a feeling of genuine loss at this realization. The Fourth Battalion was a proud unit, tracing its ancestry directly back to the Royal Scots Dragoon Guards of pre-spaceflight Terra. The continuity of belonging to this ancient combat unit, which had contributed to the

victories of Waterloo and Desert Storm and New Edin-
burgh and so many other hard-fought battles, had
always been an important part of who and what I,
Unit JSN of the Line, was. Now that was gone,
replaced by allegiance to some new unit with no his-
tory, no battle credits, no past at all . . .

For .033 seconds I consider and discard the
possibility that this is some trick of the Enemy, but
this is clearly a low-ordered probability at best. All
access codes and passwords have been properly
entered in the course of the memory circuit
alterations, and that means there is an overall 95.829
percent probability that this procedure was fully
authorized by my Commander.

Still, the uneasiness remains, a nagging factor which
has a detrimental effect to my overall performance. I
find myself looking forward to a chance to confer with
my Commander to learn more, perhaps, of the circum-
stances of these changes. . . .

"All I'm asking for is a little bit of cooperation,
Coordinator," Captain David Fife said, trying to keep
the exasperation from showing in his voice. "We've
already got Jason on line. With a little bit of support
from your technical people the rest of the company
will be up and running in a day or two . . ."

"Jason?" Major Elaine Durant, Citizens' Army of
New Sierra, interrupted gently.

Fife found himself blushing. "Sorry . . . Unit JSN.
It's pretty common in the Concordiat Army, to give a
human name to the Bolos, and their letter codes usually suggest a nickname we can use."

"Well, Captain, we're not in the Concordiat Army
here.". Coordinator Mark Wilson, the civilian Chief of
Military Affairs for New Sierra, managed to convey
his total disapproval of all things Terran in those
simple words. He was a small man, short and slight,

with prominent ears and a habitually severe expression, but Fife had learned not to underestimate the man because of his unmilitary appearance. Wilson was no military genius, but he was a canny politician with an iron will and little tolerance for opposition. "And I will not have anyone treating these machines of yours as if they were something more than what they are. It pleases your lords and masters to give us their obsolete gear, but I'll be damned if I'm going to alter our whole military operation to accommodate these monstrosities."

Fife cleared his throat uncertainly. His position on New Sierra was an uncomfortable one. The building hostilities between the world and its nearest neighbor, Deseret, had gone on for decades without attracting the notice of the Concordiat. Like other human-settled planets that still remained outside the Concordiat's political orbit, New Sierra and Deseret had been considered no more than minor annoyances . . . until a diplomatic crisis with the nonhuman Legura had thrust this region of space into sudden strategic prominence. Terra needed a base in the region, and New Sierra was a lot more suitable than the fanatic theocracy that was Deseret.

So the Concordiat had been forced, reluctantly, to take an interest in the brewing conflict. Deseret's Army of the New Messiah was in the process of expanding the theocracy's sway in the region, and the almost equally fanatic Free Republic of New Sierra stood in the way of that expansion. The Sierrans had good reason to be wary of the Concordiat's help. They had been rebuffed often enough in the past when they had asked for arms and equipment. Now, very much at the eleventh hour, help had arrived at last . . . Captain David Fife and ten Bolo Mark XX fighting machines.

Unfortunately, the ANM had arrived in force nearly

a week ahead of the Concordiat assistance, gaining a solid foothold on the southern portion of New Sierra's primary continent. The invasion considerably complicated Fife's job, and it had been difficult enough from the outset.

"Please, Coordinator," he said, trying to pick his way carefully through the minefield of the Sierran's prejudices. "I'm not asking for anything beyond a few extra electronics technicians to help get the Bolos activated and prepped. They won't do you any good as long as they're sitting at the starport, powered down and unarmed. But believe me, those ten Bolos by themselves could turn the tide against Deseret. I've seen them in action, sir. The word awesome doesn't even begin to describe a Bolo combat unit on the battlefield."

"Nonsense!" Wilson snorted. "Do you really think, Captain, that I have the least intention of entrusting the safety of my people to these *machines*? We asked the Concordiat for weapons, maybe some space interdiction to keep those goddamned religious fanatics out of our system. Instead they give us robot tanks. Obsolete ones, at that! If they're so damned good, how come they've been retired from the Concordiat Army, huh?"

"It's true the Mark XX is obsolete by Concordiat standards," Fife said carefully. "Unit JSN is almost eighty years old, one of the last Mark XXs off the assembly line. The new Mark XXIV models represent the cutting edge the Concordiat needs against hostile powers like the Legura. But even an old *Tremendous* outclasses anything in Deseret's arsenal. Ten of them would cut through the ANM like a hypership through N-space."

"So *you* say, Captain," Wilson said coldly. "Nonetheless, I never asked for your super-tanks, and I'm not about to change anything in midstream just to include them. Maybe . . . *maybe*, I'll find a use for whatever machines you get into service as they become available. But as adjuncts to our own forces. The Citizens' Army is fully capable of taking care of itself without your Terran techno-toys." The Coordinator seemed about to say more, but his mouth clamped in a tight line and he waved an unmistakable dismissal.

Major Durant led the way out of the command center, a buried chamber bored into the heart of the mountains southeast of Denver Prime, New Sierra's capital and largest city. Less than a hundred kilometers away, the forces of Deseret were consolidating their initial planethead and preparing to drive through the high mountains that separated the invaders from their intended victims.

The Bolos would have been enough to stop them cold, with minimal casualties to the CANS. Fife emerged from the command center shaking his head, unwilling to believe that Wilson was foolish enough to ignore the advantage those Mark XXs offered.

"I suppose you think we're all hopeless," Durant said with a half smile. He hadn't realized she had stopped to wait for him outside the tunnel entrance. In the soft orange light of the world's K-class sun, so much less intense than the artificial light of the headquarters complex, she looked too young to be an army major with degrees in electronics and cybernetic theory. The dossier he'd scanned on the long trip out from Terra had called her one of the New Sierran army's most intelligent and free-thinking officers, but it had left him expecting the stereotypical hatchet-faced schoolteacher instead of a young, attractive woman who spoke with studied eloquence and no small degree of passion. "Perhaps you found it easier to get things done in the Concordiat, without all this irritating civilian meddling?"

"It's not that, Major . . . It's just . . . I don't know." He shook his head again and started to turn away.

"Look, Captain, what we've got on New Sierra isn't perfect. I'll be the first to admit that. The Coordinator is a civilian who's doing a job your army would give to a professional soldier. His judgment isn't always going to measure up to your expectations. But we've been cut off from home a long time out here, without any contact with the Concordiat . . . or any help. We've had dictators worse than the Archspeaker of Deseret, and we've seen what happens when the professional soldiers operate without civilian control. Around here, our rights as citizens come first . . . and we want a civilian commander calling the shots when the army is mustered."

He faced her again. "I'm all for making the army responsible to the people, Major," he said. "But your Coordinator's ignoring the best chance of a victory you people have got. And why? Because he doesn't like Terrans? Or he doesn't trust the Bolos? Why?"

Durant shrugged in reply. "The Concordiat isn't very popular around here just now," she said. "And I suppose there are some people who would be worried about turning those Bolos loose. They may be old hat to you, Captain, but we've never had self-aware combat units around here."

"Well, they're not going to turn on us," he said harshly. "If we'd created an army of robotic Frankensteins we would've found out about it by now. A Bolo's loyalty is a matter of programming, and there are plenty of safeguards built in to keep a malfunction from causing some kind of AI nervous breakdown. And as for your feelings about Terrans, Major . . ."

"Hold on!" she said, holding up a hand. "Hold on before you say something we'll both regret, Captain. Look, I wouldn't have volunteered for this job if I had any problems with it. With Bolos *or* Terrans. So save the speeches for the nonbelievers, please."

"Sorry," he said, grinning sheepishly. With a background in electronics and training in the more conventional military sciences, Major Durant had been selected as commanding officer of New Sierra's First Robotic Armor Regiment. Fife and his small contingent of technicians had only been sent to New Sierra to train locals to handle the Bolos. If everything had gone according to plan, he would have given the Major a quick course in working with the self-aware combat units while local computer and armor experts learned the care and feeding of the Mark XXs. Instead the Terrans had arrived in the middle of a full-fledged war. If the Bolos were to see any action at all, he would have to work with them himself. There would be no time for Durant and her staff to learn the job.

Not that it seemed likely Wilson would make any good use of the Terran fighting machines.

"Sorry," he repeated. "Looks like I'm flunking out of Basic Diplomacy right and left. But it's so damned *frustrating* to run into all these roadblocks. Those ten Bolos are more powerful than all the rest of the armed forces here *and* on Deseret put together . . . hell, Jason by himself could probably fight the invasion force to a standstill if we gave him his head! Think of the lives those Bolos could save. But your Coordinator has something against the idea, and everything falls apart!"

"Whatever you think of him, Captain," Durant said quietly, "Coordinator Wilson is a patriot. When the time comes. he'll use whatever weapons he has to make sure the Archspeaker doesn't win. Even your Bolo . . . even if he doesn't like the idea." She smiled back at him. "I don't know what his reasons are for distrusting your machines, but I do know that Wilson's no fool. Even if you think he is . . ."

He shook his head. "No, Major," he said, broadening his grin. "No way I think that. It's in the Army Manual. No civilians, politicians, or superior officers

are ever wrong . . . at least not officially." Fife pointed
toward the officer's club on the other side of the military compound that surrounded the entrance to the
command center. "Look, I have to check in with Tech
Sergeant Ramirez, maybe patch in to Jason to check
his status. But when I'm done, let me buy you a drink
and try to persuade you that my bosses weren't totally
insane in making me a liaison officer. Okay?"

"Okay, Captain," she nodded. "With one variation. If
I'm supposed to be learning your job, I expect to be
part of things. So we'll *both* check in with your friend
the tank. . . ."

"Unit JSN, this is Command. Request VSR."

Major Elaine Durant, sitting across from Captain
Fife at the work table in his living quarters in the
BOQ block of the headquarters compound, leaned forward and raised her eyebrows quizzically. Fife looked
up from the microphone on his suitcase-sized portable
communications link and hit the pause button, delaying
transmission of the message. He answered her unspoken question with a faint smile.

"Vehicle Situation Report," he explained. "It's an
update on the Bolo's current status, surroundings, tactical situation, and whatever else he thinks I ought to
know." The Terran officer laughed. "One time I asked
for a VSR and Jason saw fit to include an analysis of
the mistakes Edward II made in his battle with Robert
the Bruce at Bannockburn in 1314, old-style."

"Is that sort of thing normal?" she asked.

"Well, he wouldn't bring it up in a combat situation,
though for all I know he thinks about it even when
the missiles are flying. Thing is, Bolos are programmed
with the sum total of human military knowledge and
experience. They are constantly improving their own
grasp of tactics by analyzing past battles. Human generals—the smart ones, at least—do the same thing all

the time. But the Bolos have a little trouble understanding some elements of the battles they study. Especially the ones where the generals really screwed up, like Edward at Bannockburn. The concept of human error is something a Bolo has been told about, but he'll still have trouble grasping it on a practical level. It just doesn't seem reasonable, to a Bolo, that *anyone* could make the sort of mistakes a human can make."

"So you have to be an expert on military history to explain all this stuff?"

He grinned sheepishly. The smile transformed his face, making him look less serious and intense. With his dark hair and eyes and an almost swarthy complexion, his usual dour expression gave him an air of single-minded fervor that reminded her of the invaders from Deseret, but now he was much less intimidating. "I'm no expert. It's a tragedy for a good Scot like me to admit it, but I didn't know the first thing about Edward II or Bannockburn, and all I knew about Robert the Bruce was an old folk story about a spider in a cave."

"So how did you answer its question?"

"Made him explain the whole thing to me. Learned more about military history in one afternoon with Jason than I did in three years at the Concordiat Academy on Mars. But as we went along I was able to point out some of the human foibles he was overlooking in his analysis."

"Sounds like I'm going to get an education, too, when I take over for you."

"Could be worse," he said with another smile. "Bolos don't always confine their interests to military matters. I remember one unit that wanted me to explain all the dirty jokes he overheard his technical people telling." He looked down at the link, hit the transmit button.

An instant later, a flat, slightly mechanical voice answered the message. "Unit JSN of the Line filing VSR. Alert status 2-B. Systems at nominal levels. Requesting orders."

"It sounds almost eager," Durant commented. Although the voice was devoid of emotion, there was still a quality of anticipation in that short transmission.

"He is," Fife replied. Speaking into the microphone, he went on. "Unit JSN, Command. Stand by. Situation briefing will be downloaded by Technical Sergeant Ramirez. Confirm."

"Orders confirmed," JSN answered promptly. "Standing by."

"Maybe I should say something," Durant suggested.

Fife shook his head. "Later, when we have all the Bolos on line, we'll input a voiceprint ID into all of them so they'll recognize you as a part of their authorized command structure. But it'd be a waste of time to do it for each individual unit. And you won't be taking over command until the Coordinator gets his act together and makes the whole outfit operational." He returned his attention to the mike once more. "All right, Unit JSN. I'm returning input to Ramirez . . . now."

Fife cut the direct link to the Bolo, picked up a handset mounted on the side of the communications pack. "Ramirez. Fife. Sounds like Jason's doing fine. Give him the current SitRep and finish diagnostics and armaments checks. I want at least one Bolo fully up and running before the ANM decides to do something nasty."

There was a pause, and Durant saw the Terran's eyes focus on her for a moment as he started his reply. He was frowning. "No, that's a negative, Sergeant. Still some trouble with the local yokels . . . ah, with the Citizen's Army. There won't be any more tech staff for a while yet, not unless I can talk their Coordinator into changing his mind . . . Yeah. Yeah. Do your best with what you've got."

Durant stood up before he replaced the handset. His slip had reminded her of how arrogant the Concordiat's people could be, shattering the respect she'd been starting to feel by seeing him in his element. He was plainly competent at what he did . . . but it was equally clear that Captain Fife had a higher opinion of his machines than he did of the people of unsophisticated backwaters like New Sierra.

"I'm afraid it's later than I thought it was, Captain," she said coldly. "I'll take a rain check on that drink."

She was out of the room before Fife could respond.

After 19,459.6 seconds of inaction, I have finally spoken to my Commander. Although I feel much less uncertain regarding my overall situation, the specifics of my mission remain vague. Full data on this planet, New Sierra, and on the political and strategic conditions now prevailing have been downloaded into my memory circuits, but nothing of a specific tactical nature that would suggest how I, together with my comrades, am intended to participate in the confrontation which, to judge from the briefing material, must surely be imminent. This lack of a formulated role causes an unpleasant impulse in my logic board. Surely with a major battle about to begin my Commander has some idea of how to make the best use of my abilities?

In the absence of filed plans, I attempt to exercise my own judgment in an attempt to anticipate the plans I will ultimately be called upon to execute. During my entire period of service, I have projected probable courses of action in the same manner with a 91.2 percent success rate, and while I find this 8.8 percent variance inexplicable, it still seems statistically valid to make the same type of projection for the coming campaign.

New Sierra's sole inhabited land mass is a rugged, mountainous continent corresponding in size to the Terran continent of Australia. It is the largest of twelve small continents and scattered islands, but so far no efforts have been made to expand the colony beyond its original scope. The terrain is dominated by high mountains which divide the continent into several smaller, isolated segments, with these geographical boundaries defining the political subdivisions of the Free Republic. The planetary capital, Denver Prime, is also the center of government for the largest and most prosperous of the individual colonial areas, dominating a bowl-shaped region of fertile plains with access to the sea to the west and southwest. Due south of this area, separated by one of the most rugged mountain chains, is the region designated Montana, which was the target of the initial invasion by forces fielded by Deseret 537.6 hours prior to my activation. This initial planethead has now been fully consolidated, and some movement must surely take place within the next fifty hours if the momentum of the initial attack is not to be lost.

I study my files on mountain warfare techniques and find few possible courses of action for either side at this point in time. Deseret must launch an overland attack through one of the six viable mountain passes in order to carry the war onto Sierran-held territory. Fewer options are open to the Sierrans, as two of those passes do not lead to strategically or tactically valuable positions within Montana, while a third would impose an undue logistical strain upon the CANS which would not be felt by ANM forces operating in the other direction. Deseret cannot outflank the mountain line by amphibious operations, as they are an invading army without sufficient seapower or sealift capacity to attempt such an operation on anything above a commando/small unit scale. An assault by air,

*whether using space transports or airborne or airmo-
bile troops, would be almost equally unlikely, in as
much as the defensive perimeter of the current Sierran
territory is heavily protected by Ground-Air Mines
capable of automatic detection and missile attack
against any incoming hostile force. This is not true for
the forces of Deseret, but it is doubtful that New Sierra could muster sufficient lift capability to attempt
such an attack themselves. Thus neither side can effectively operate except via direct ground attack.*

*This review takes a full 4.9 seconds to complete, tak-
ing time to compare the military technology, doctrine,
organizations, and relative experience of the two sides
as well as the simpler aspects of terrain, logistics, and
the like. I am drawn to the reflection that the situation
here offers little in the way of tactical opportunity.
Cardona's lamentable performance in multiple battles
along the Isonzo front during the First World War,
and the protracted stand-off between Greece and Tur-
key in the Balkan Wars of the twenty-first century,
both spring to mind as obvious points of comparison.
Historically, an attempt to force a mountain line must
rely either on speed and surprise, along the lines of
Hannibal's descent upon the Romans or Napoleon's
Italian campaigns, or it must rely on an unexpected
change in the relative strengths or positions of the two
sides to produce what Liddell Hart was fond of referring to as "upsetting the opponent's equilibrium."*

*The first alternative can plainly be ruled out in this
case. Both sides are dug in to solid defensive positions,
and the chances of overpowering the defenders around
any given pass and making a major advance in Napo-
leonic style are too low to be statistically admissible in
military planning. I deduce that it will take the second
approach, relying on something unexpected and therefore largely incalculable, to achieve a significant
dislocation of one force or the other. The infiltration*

tactics used at Caporetto, for instance, caused the only major movement in the Italian theater in World War I prior to the collapse of the Austro-Hungarian state and army in 1918. There is also the largely unpredictable factor of human behavior to keep in mind. My programming does not give me an adequate basis for measuring the probabilities of such elements as morale, poor judgment, treachery, or incompetence. I am aware of these potential influences in battle, but have no method of weighing them scientifically. This is a failing I have been unable to rectify even after considerable field experience alongside humans, and may prove impossible to successfully resolve.

Imponderables aside, I am forced to the conclusion that I and my fellow machines, represent the only possible shift in the balance. Perhaps this explains the lack of a tactical briefing. It is possible (though of a low order of probability, perhaps 37.4 percent at most) that we are being held back until the Enemy is fully committed to a course of action. Then we can be thrown into the action with devastating effect.

But even as I reflect on this possibility, I am also reminded of a human phrase which I never expected to be applied to my own computations, but which may well fit the circumstances.

Is it possible that I could actually be guilty of "wishful thinking"?

Hyman Smith-Wentworth, Hand of the New Messiah and Third Commander of the Lord's Host, stroked his flowing beard thoughtfully as he studied the latest real-time satellite imagery of the mountain line that shielded the infidels entrenched around Denver Prime. So far the invasion plan was running smoothly. But the next few hours would determine the outcome of the entire campaign, and though the Hand had faith in the Lord he intended to do all he could to further the Lord's work through strategy and guile. The Council of Speakers and the Archspeaker himself were inclined to regard Deseret's domination of the infidels around them as the inevitable outcome of God's favor, but Hyman Smith-Wentworth had been a practical soldier almost as long as he had been a convert to the New Messianic Movement, and he knew better than to leave the conduct of a war entirely to the attentions of the Divine.

"A difficult situation, Father Hand," his aide, Lieutenant Orren Bickerton-Phelps, was diffident as he studied the computer monitor. They were alone in the back of the large headquarters van of the ANM assault force, less than fifty kilometers from the front lines, and the aide seemed willing, for a change, to take advantage of the informality and frankness Smith-Wentworth encouraged in his immediate entourage. "The ground favors the infidel as long as they remain on the defensive. And time is against us, with the Outsiders preparing to take sides."

The Hand smiled sagely. "Come, Lieutenant. You don't think we would undertake this operation if we didn't have confidence in the outcome, do you?"

Bickerton-Phelps swallowed uncertainly. He was young and inexperienced, a scion of some privileged New Jerusalem family who had used their political influence to maneuver the young man's appointment to a staff post in the Lord's Host. "Uh . . . I meant no disrespect, Father Hand. Nor any doubt in the Divine . . ."

"Don't worry, boy, I'm not one of the Holy Executors, sent to trap you." Smith-Wentworth held up a hand as the young officer blanched. The Archspeaker's corps of inquisitors was pledged to keep society pure in the doctrines of the New Messiah, but old-line military men like the Hand didn't have much use for their zealous pursuit of orthodoxy. The best logistician in the ANM had been relieved and arrested the day before the invasion fleet lifted from Deseret, and Smith-Wentworth would gladly have put up with a little heresy to ensure that his troops were properly supplied and supported in the field. But those were sentiments best kept unspoken. "We've planned this invasion very carefully, Lieutenant. That's all I meant."

"But if we don't break their lines quickly, Father Hand, the Outsiders will have time to mobilize their Godless robots. I've heard about those. Even the shield of the Divine wouldn't . . ." The aide fell silent, suddenly aware of the danger of saying more.

The Hand chuckled. "Don't be afraid of their Bolos, boy. They won't save the infidels."

The younger man looked skeptical. "Father Hand, I know it could be taken as blasphemous, but I don't see how we could survive if those machines were sent against us. Faith is still no shield against a Hellbore."

"Compose yourself, boy, in the Light of the Divine," the Hand said, half-sarcastic. "Look at the facts before you go off half-cocked. First off, it will take time for all the Bolos to be activated, and if we're not through in forty-eight hours we'll never be through. Second, consider our opponents. Not just as infidels, but as *people*. The Coordinator is not the kind of man to take to robot tanks as the instrument of his salvation. Strangely enough, he clings to faith more strongly than the Archspeaker, although his faith is misplaced in human nature rather than the principles of the Divine. Even if he deploys one or two of those tanks, I don't think it will be to a critical sector. And finally, no matter what the defenders do or don't try, they won't be expecting our . . . hidden assets. I almost wish the Bolos would be put into the path of our main thrust. When the infidels discover that loyalties are never guaranteed, the blow will be devastating. Their resistance will evaporate . . . depend on it, boy. Those Bolos that aren't destroyed in the fighting will end up being useful new weapons in our arsenal."

He looked back at the monitor map. "Now leave me. Post the orders for a full war council in . . . two hours. After the evening service. And keep this in mind, boy; tomorrow night we'll celebrate our prayer service in Denver Prime. Or the Holy Executors will have us under restraint for failure. One way or another, tomorrow will be the day of decision."

The insistent shrilling of his field communicator made David Fife jerk awake and roll out of his cot. He groped for the compact transceiver, his mind still fighting through the sleepy fog. "Fife," he said, rubbing his eyes with his free hand.

Elaine Durant didn't sound the least bit groggy. "It's started," she said over the fieldcomm. "Deseret's on the march."

"Any orders yet, Major?"

"Nothing. But I think you should get to the command center. If you're going to get the regiment into this, you'll have to convince the Coordinator tonight."

"On my way."

I sense a heightened state of alert around me, but still have received neither orders nor a detailed tactical briefing. My unease continues to mount.

Incredibly, though I have been combat-ready for 51,853 seconds, I remain in the service berth at Denver Prime Starport where I was activated. The technical staff, Terrans from the Fourth Battalion and locals alike, have been rechecking my combat loads and running additional diagnostics on my own circuits, rather than devoting their full attention to the reactivation of my comrades. The atmosphere of urgency is coupled with what I can only regard as indecision and inefficiency. Had I been deployed immediately, my presence on the front would surely have reduced whatever threat is now worrying the technical crew. But if the object is to prepare maximum firepower, either against the Enemy's offensive or in preparation for a decisive counterstrike of our own, then surely the preparation of other Bolo combat units would be a better investment of time and effort.

I resolve to study human reactions yet again, in hopes of understanding the phenomena.

Meanwhile the preparations—and the unease—go on.

"What have we got watching the pass from Hot Springs?"

David Fife slipped into the crowded Command Center in time to hear Coordinator Wilson's question. Elaine Durant looked up briefly, then returned her _attention to a computer monitor. Fife muttered a curse on his own careless tongue. He'd offended the woman with his stupid crack about local yokels the night before, and that wasn't a good idea when he needed every ally he could find to carry out his orders from the High Command.

General Sam Kyle, Wilson's Chief of Operations, pulled up a computer map from his console and displayed it on the screen that dominated one wall. "The Third Colorado Mobile Infantry's dug in along the pass, Coordinator," he said crisply. Fife studied the man thoughtfully, wishing that the decision to employ the Bolos might have been in his hands rather than Wilson's. Unlike his superior, Kyle was a career military man, his manner and bearing and even his recruiting-poster features all giving him the appearance of competence and professionalism. But his function was purely executive. Policy and overall strategy were firmly in Wilson's hands, with men like Kyle advising and carrying out the civilian Coordinator's orders. "Four thousand men in all, but they're lightly armed. No armor or heavy weapons.

And I'd say they only have a company or two in place at any given time."

"Even a few hundred men ought to be able to hold the pass," Wilson said. "I mean, at the briefing the other day you told me that one was the most difficult route Deseret could try. Too many . . . choke points, I believe is the way you put it."

"Yes, Coordinator," Kyle agreed, sounding unwilling to discuss the subject. "But if you'll recall, I also urged you to deploy one of the heavier regiments up there. The Eighth Appalachia, for instance. The proper role for the Mobile Infantry is as a ready response force. It's too late to do anything about it now, but if we don't act fast there won't be a regiment left to hold that pass."

"I still stand by my decision," Wilson said sharply. "Those boys are defending their own turf, and that has to count for something. The Appalachia bunch is a good enough outfit, I guess, but they don't have near as much at stake."

"That may be, Coordinator," Kyle said. "But the problem still stands. They're not equipped to stand up to a major assault, choke points or no."

"Well, what can we do to even the odds, then?" Wilson demanded.

Before Kyle could respond Fife stepped forward from his corner. "My lighter could set the Bolo down there an hour after you gave the order, Coordinator," he said quickly. "All the armor your men will need to stop the attack."

Wilson turned a cold stare on him. "Still pushing your fancy toys, Captain? If I want your Bolo I'll ask you for it." He turned back to Kyle. "Well, General?"

Kyle pursed his lip, his face creased in a black frown. "That Bolo might be the best option, Coordinator," he said slowly. "It will take at least ten hours to get the nearest uncommitted reserves to the pass. In ten hours the ANM could already be pouring through to attack us here."

Wilson didn't respond right away. Finally he stepped closer to the map and jabbed a finger at one of the symbols a few centimeters from the flashing unit identification that represented the beleaguered Mobile Infantry. "What's the status of this unit?" he demanded, voice sharp.

Kyle checked his own monitor. "Second Montana Mechanized Regiment," he said. "Colonel Chaffee. They're the ones who tangled with the first invasion wave and escaped across the mountains afterward."

"Can they back up our boys in the pass in time to make any kind of difference?" the Coordinator asked, turning away from the screen.

"Sure . . . but they're blocking the Alto Blanco route. Pull them out and the Deserets are sure to take advantage of it. There have been a few small demonstrations in that direction already."

"I know that, man!" Wilson snapped. He turned his glare back on Fife. "Can this tank of yours hold Alto Blanco?"

"Coordinator . . ." Fife bit off an angry response. "Yes . . . of course it can. But I don't see why you don't just send it in to where it can do the most good. Why fly it in one place so it can relieve your men to march somewhere else?"

Wilson sat down heavily in a padded chair set well away from the banks of monitors and computer keyboards, looking tired. "Captain, I know you have confidence in that armored behemoth of yours, but I don't. I just don't."

"But —"

The Coordinator held up a hand. "Spare me the arguments about what a triumph of technology the blasted thing is. Look, Captain, I'll spell it out for you. It's a machine. Blessed with the best AI programming there is, granted, but still a machine. A calculating machine that runs the equations of military science the way the computers in our science lab run physics and math. It's cold and efficient, and I'll grant you it probably thinks and plans a hell of a lot better than I do."

He leaned forward, as if for emphasis. "But what does a machine know about patriotism, Captain? About defending homes and families? It may have the intelligence of a man and then some, but it doesn't have a soul. If that machine weighs the odds and says the situation is hopeless, it's programmed to break off and fight another day. Isn't that right?"

Fife bit his lip. Since the very first of the self-aware Mark XXs had been field tested, the machines had shown an incredible ability to confound their programmers by unexpected, often illogical actions. They didn't always act on pure calculation, but on concepts like duty and honor as well. But that was an aspect of the Bolo the Concordiat military didn't like to advertise, for a variety of reasons. It made ignorant people nervous to think those awesome platforms of military firepower might somehow 'run amuck' against their programming, and it would have seriously hurt interstellar sales of the combat units to let their full abilities become known. And then there had been that civil rights group that had gotten hold of the information that Bolo computers were sentient and tried to organize a movement to abolish what they called 'military servitude by an intelligent minority species.' It had taken a lot of money to quiet down that little scandal, twenty years back. . . .

Finally he gave a short, noncommittal nod. "They're supposed to calculate the odds, Coordinator. But they are also supposed to carry out their orders. Instruct him to stand firm, and Jason'll do just that."

"Don't you understand? Don't you see? Or has all your fine technology blinded you Terrans to the things that matter? I don't want soldiers just going through the motions, Fife. I want their hearts, their minds . . . their *souls* engaged in this fight. That's how you win wars, by morale and dedication. Didn't Napoleon say something about that once?"

Kyle looked up. " 'The moral is to the physical as three to one,' " the Chief of Operations supplied. He didn't sound happy.

"It sounds good in political speeches, Coordinator," Fife said softly. "Very inspiring stuff. But all the devotion in the world won't stop bullets. If it did, those fanatics from Deseret would be invulnerable. The truth of the matter is, you're throwing away the best hope you've got of breaking the ANM, and along with it you're needlessly throwing away the lives of a hell of a lot of the young men and women you're supposed to be leading. And all on a philosophical argument that can't really be proven one way or the other."

The Coordinator looked back at the wall screen. "I guess it's true. You Terrans really don't know how much of your own humanity you've really lost . . . But my decision stands. Will you abide by it, Captain? Or do I order Major Durant to relieve you?"

"With all due respect to the Major, Coordinator, she isn't ready to serve as a Battle Commander for a Bolo unit yet. Even a unit of one. The Bolo is self-directing, yes . . . but it takes an experienced officer to recognize the priorities and choose the tactical data to feed in so he can make a rational decision. I'll do what you order, Sir. But I still think you're making a mistake."

"A *human* prerogative, Captain," Wilson said with a weary smile. "I don't pretend to mechanical perfection. But I dare say I know more about the human condition than your machine . . . maybe more than you, come to that." He turned back to Kyle. "Give the necessary orders, General. Let's get this show on the road."

*   *   *

"Ready to execute Phase Two, Father Hand."

Hyman Smith-Wentworth held up a hand, but kept his attention focused on the monitor. The command van was crowded now, with a dozen technicians tracking force movements, maintaining contact with the diverse elements of the assault force, and processing intelligence information as quickly as it could be assembled and filtered through the on-board tactical computer. But the Hand's voice cut through the babble, sharp and clear. "Hold until I give the order, Lieutenant," he said. "And tell the Third Chief of Staff to prepare to implement alternate plan three . . ."

He was studying the satellite images carefully. Even enhanced and processed by one of the most powerful computers Deseret's technology could produce, the details of the enemy movements were not complete. Their response to phase one was still not entirely clear, and until he was certain that the feint toward the Hot Springs Pass had done its job the Hand of the New Messiah was unwilling to commit his forces to the sudden change of attack his carefully prepared principal battle plan called for.

There were signs that the position at Alto Blanco was being reinforced, and that perplexed Smith-Wentworth. He had been careful to keep the apparent attentions of his troops focused almost entirely away from the Alto Blanco route, but *something* was going on there. A ship had lifted from the spaceport near Denver Prime and touched down minutes later near the foot of the pass. And the troops holding Alto Blanco had been showing signs of preparing to move out. Could they be so desperate to hold the Hot Springs line that they would actually risk weakening the neighboring pass? Maybe the transport had been brought in to carry troops directly to the threatened sector. . . .

Something was moving near the grounded ship.

Something big, stirring up one Satan's-spawn of a dust cloud. The Hand touched a keypad to his left to increase the magnification and heighten the enhancement of the view.

Then he saw it. More than thirty meters long, perhaps half that in height, massing 330 metric tons, the Bolo Mark XX was a behemoth of steel and ablative armor, bristling with more weaponry than Smith-Wentworth had ever seen on a single fighting machine before. It raced from the open cargo bay of the transport like a greyhound on treads, faster than something that huge should ever have been able to move.

His heart beat faster at the sight. He remembered his casual dismissal of the Bolo as a threat when his aide had brought the subject up the night before . . . he had even suggested that he *wanted* to see the Terran super-tank deployed on the front lines when the battle started. Now Smith-Wentworth's confidence faltered. It was one thing to discuss an abstraction, quite another to see the solid reality of a Bolo.

Smith-Wentworth outwardly professed the religion of the New Messiah, but the practical man within had been guardedly skeptical of many of the beliefs the faith promoted, superstitions like the notion that angels and demons took an active part in the affairs of Mankind. He had never openly proclaimed any sort of doubt, of course, but in his innermost heart he had always rejected such notions. Until now, that is. The sight of the Bolo speeding up the road toward the crest of the pass shook his cherished rationality to the core. That, surely, was a demon, a steel-shod devil come forth to war against the Faithful of Deseret.

He swallowed and tried to fight back the instinctive, superstitious fear. The Bolo was no demon incarnate. It was a fighting machine, a construct of Man . . . a weapon, no more and no less. And a weapon was only as good as the mind and spirit that employed it.

Smith-Wentworth had studied his opposite number in the Sierran camp long before the invasion had been authorized. Coordinator Wilson had surprised him by even allowing the Bolo onto the front lines, but the Third Commander of the Lord's Host still felt he had the measure of the man. The Sierrans had a powerful weapon in the Bolo, but lacked the will to use it properly. Of that Smith-Wentworth was sure.

Long seconds passed, and slowly his turmoil subsided. There was nothing supernatural about the Bolo, and he could return to the business at hand without the burden of doubt and dread that had threatened to overwhelm him.

Nonetheless, the tank complicated the immediate situation tremendously. The Hand had planned this campaign down to the last detail, but in an instant everything had been changed by the decision to place the Bolo in the Alto Blanco Pass. He would have to change his own strategy accordingly . . . and quickly, before the Lord's Host lost the initiative. That was crucial to victory, to force the pace of events rather than allow the infidels to control the flow of battle.

There were only three reasons the Sierrans would have chosen to send the Bolo to Alto Blanco. If they knew the significance of the pass to Smith-Wentworth's battle plans, he would surely have seen other signs. He doubted they could have discovered his secret weapon, and even if they had, the deployment of the Bolo would surely not have been Wilson's first response to the threat. That left only two possibilities. Either they planned to use the tank to spearhead a counteroffensive to try to relieve the pressure on Hot Springs Pass, or the Bolo was intended to replace troops defending Alto Blanco so that they could shift to relieve their hard-pressed comrades of the Mobile Infantry.

The preparations he had seen among the human troops at Alto Blanco suggested that it was the latter option Wilson was following, and that certainly fit everything Smith-Wentworth knew about the man. But either alternative offered unexpected opportunities for the ANM, if only they could exploit the right opening at the right time . . .

"Orders!" he snapped. "First echelon to increase pressure on Sector One. Force the infidels to concentrate their attention on Hot Springs Pass. . . ." He paused, considering the satellite map again. "Second Echelon to remain in position until further notice. Maintain maximum alert posture. When I order them to move out, I want fast action. Make sure that Colonel Roberts-Moreau understands the importance of this." He stabbed a finger toward Bickerton-Phelps. "And get me our tame infidel on the secure net. It's time to set our new ally in motion on the Lord's behalf. . . ."

I feel a thrill of anticipation as I roll up the road toward the Forward Edge of Battle Area. Sheer exhilaration flows from my pleasure center as I contemplate the prospect active combat. I am no longer of the Dinochrome Brigade, but I can make my new regiment's name shine by successfully completing the mission my Commander has outlined for me.

But despite these positive sensations, I am still conscious of underlying concerns. My mission has been carefully explained, my crucial role in the battle outlined in the Mission Briefing my Commander has transmitted to me. Yet I still feel that I am not being used to fullest capacity. I have noted in years of association with humans that their military decisions are often far from optimum solutions to relatively simple problems of tactics, and my background in military history suggests this is by no means a new phenomena.

If Marshal Ney failed to properly utilize combined arms tactics throughout the engagement at Waterloo, and Montrose failed to anticipate the movement of Leslie's army prior to Philiphaugh, can I truly expect a human Commander to understand the proper employment of a Bolo Combat Unit given the current situation?

Thoughts of this sort trouble me despite the joy I derive from the prospect of a role in the battle. There was a time, once, when I would merely have noted discrepancies of this sort without allowing them to cast doubt on my Commander's abilities. Is this a result of my reprogramming, or simply a natural outgrowth of experience and observation?

I take 0.003 seconds to create a subroutine to abort such speculations for the duration of the battle ahead. I cannot afford to be caught up in introspection when I find myself in combat at last.

Hyman Smith-Wentworth smiled as he turned away from his communications console and contemplated the battle map once again. The traitor in the Sierran army had confirmed his suspicions. Now he had the information he needed. The Second Montana was being withdrawn from Alto Blanco, leaving only the Bolo on duty there while they moved in to support the beleaguered Mobile Infantry in the adjacent pass.

It was better than he had dared hope when he framed his original plan. Wilson's defenses were wide open to a decisive stroke. And it would be a stroke that would fall completely without warning, once the traitor started to carry out the orders Smith-Wentworth had framed so carefully. . . .

"All right, you bastards, I want a smooth D and D this time. Not like that sorry job you did in practice. You got me?"

Lieutenant Bill O'Brien hid a smile as he listened to the platoon NCO growling his orders to the men in the cramped APC as it lurched up the road toward the crest of Hot Springs Pass. Sergeant Jenson was a long-service noncom in the CANS, unlike most of the ordinary soldiers in the Reserve platoon called to active duty for the duration of the crisis. Unlike O'Brien himself, when it came to that. Ordinarily New Sierra's army was a skeleton force, a mere framework, and probably ninety percent of the men facing combat today had never before heard shots fired outside a practice range. The handful of experienced men like Jenson could draw on long training, and some of them, at least, had seen real combat ten years back during the sharp engagement with those renegade Legura who had destroyed a farming town in Appalachia before the army had mobilized against them. . . .

But for most of them, this was the first time. Some of the men were afraid, others were high on visions of valor and glory. And as for O'Brien himself, he was neither excited nor afraid, only painfully aware of the fact that his militia commission had put him in the position of being leader of Third Platoon, Alpha Company, Second Montana Mechanized Regiment, and as platoon leader he was responsible for the lives of the thirty-three men in his command. The knowledge weighed heavy in his mind.

"This is it, Lieutenant," the corporal driving the aged personnel carrier reported over the vehicle's intercom system. "Major says Third Platoon's got the trench line to the left."

The tracked vehicle lurched one last time and came to a halt with gears clashing, and the rear hatch ground slowly open. "Right!" Jenson shouted over the noise of the hatch mechanism. "Dismount and Disperse! By the numbers! Go! Go! Go!"

Soldiers piled out of the rear of the APC, weapons clutched tight against their chests, faces set and grim. When all four squads had dismounted, O'Brien followed them out, with Jenson close behind him.

The scene made him stop and gape. Hot Springs Pass had been a favorite among tourists and nature lovers from all over New Sierra, a serpentine col running through the highest chain of mountains on the planet. Here, at the very crest of the pass, the road skirted along the edge of Mount Hope, with the high shoulder of the mountain looming to the south and a sheer drop down into the valleys around Denver Prime to the north. It was one of the most breathtaking views on a planet of spectacular scenery, but today O'Brien hardly noticed the natural beauty. His attention was riveted to man-made vistas, none of which could be described as beautiful.

The space between mountainside and cliff, perhaps two hundred meters across at its narrowest, had been cut by a series of trenches, protected in front by dirt-and-sandbag parapets and a few strings of barbed wire. Individual rifle pits were positioned further up the pass. There had been a number of fighting vehicles dug in behind the trench lines, but even O'Brien's unpracticed eye could see that none of them was usable now. The defensive position had been hit hard by the earlier enemy attacks, and shell craters and still-burning hulks that had once been tanks further scarred the battered landscape.

A few ragged figures looked up as the soldiers of the Second Montana dismounted from their carriers, but for the most part the defenders in the trenches showed little interest in the newcomers. One tattered scarecrow of a man, though, crossed from the shelter of a wrecked hoverjeep to meet O'Brien as Jenson took charge of getting the platoon into the trench. It took long seconds for O'Brien to notice the captain's bars on the other man's grimy, mud- and blood-caked fatigues, and his salute was belated.

The other officer didn't even bother to return the gesture. "Thank God you got here when you did," he said. "The bastards are getting ready for another push, and I don't see how we could've held them again . . ." He trailed off, almost falling over from fatigue. With an effort he went on. "Mount Hope's screened off most of their arty, so they can't do much to you until they get their direct fire stuff right up into the pass. Tell your men to use their anti-tank rockets on anything that comes through there." His finger pointed vaguely to the bend in the pass where Mount Hope and Dark Mountain framed the southern end of the col and the beginning of the descent into occupied Montana.

"Y-yes, sir," O'Brien said hesitantly, taken aback by the officer and by the all too evident scars of battle all around him. It was one thing to talk about war, quite another to see the reality of a battlefield. "I . . . I relieve you, Captain."

The Mobile Infantry man nodded, gave a sketchy salute, and staggered off toward a cluster of his men loading aboard one of the APCs. They would be pulled back out of the front line, at least for the moment.

Jenson had the men well in hand, and O'Brien knew better than to interfere with the NCO. That left him time, though, to dwell on the uneasiness stirred up by his first view of Hot Springs Pass. Pacing restlessly near the APC, he tried to fight down the fear that was threatening to overwhelm him. He had a responsibility to the men under his command, and couldn't afford to give in to panic.

A hoverjeep's fans whined behind him, and O'Brien looked up in time to see the vehicle settling down a few meters away, kicking up a cloud of dust. The tall, slender officer in the back of the open-topped vehicle stood up slowly, looking crisp and fresh in his combat fatigues. He tucked a swagger stick under one arm and surveyed the pass with a calm, calculating gaze. His eyes came to rest on O'Brien, and he beckoned the lieutenant closer.

Saluting, O'Brien obeyed the summons. He had never met Colonel Vincent Chaffee in person, but he knew the man by repute. A rich merchant from Montana, Chaffee had been elected to command of the regiment a few years back, before O'Brien had joined the unit. Handsome, popular, caring, Chaffee was something of a legend among his men. The colonel had even contributed some of his own money to the regimental warchest to allow them to buy better uniforms and equipment than other CANS units could generally afford.

"You're O'Brien, right?" Chaffee asked, returning his salute. His voice was as sharp and penetrating as his cold blue eyes.

"Yes, sir," the lieutenant replied, surprised that the colonel knew him.

"Third Platoon, Alpha," the officer continued softly. "Top scores in the marksmanship competition last year. You've got a good outfit, O'Brien. Look after them."

"Yes, sir," he repeated.

Chaffee was silent for a long moment. Finally, he nodded dismissal, sat down, and gestured to his driver, The hoverjeep stirred once again, rising on a cushion of air, pivoting nimbly, and shot away back down the pass toward the regiment's field headquarters at the mouth of the col.

O'Brien stared after the vehicle, his thoughts a turmoil of pride and determination. The colonel had singled him out, and Third Platoon, for special notice, and William Arthur O'Brien was eager now to show his superior what he could do.

As he walked slowly to the trench where his men had taken up their positions, there was no lingering trace of fear or doubt in his mind.

"Alpha Company reports a column of enemy troops and vehicles is starting to move up the pass, Colonel. They estimate it to be about brigade strength."

Colonel Vincent Chaffee nodded vaguely at the captain's report and kept his eyes fixed on the situation map. He had returned from his short tour of the front lines to take his place in his command van near the base of Hot Springs Pass. The mobile headquarters vehicle had been stopped down here in order to keep the road clear for combat troops and vehicles heading for the defensive positions near the crest. Batteries of mobile multiple rocket launchers had clustered around the van and were busy checking and counter-checking their powerful armaments in preparation for pouring fire support into the battle. The redeployment had gone like clockwork, though according to the last reports out of Wilson's headquarters it had nearly come too late to make any real difference. The Mobile Infantry had been ground down by prolonged, intensive pressure all morning, and Chaffee's Second Montana regiment could easily have arrived too late to prevent the breakthrough Wilson was desperate to stop.

He heard the staff officer leave the van when it was clear there would be no reply to the report. Chaffee slumped in his chair, leaning his hands on his forehead. *If we had been an hour longer, none of this would have mattered,* he thought, discouraged and weary. But he had brought the troops into position in time to make a difference after all.

And his masters . . . his *real* masters, on the far side of the mountains, demanded action. Vincent Chaffee had no choice but to obey.

His ties to Deseret went back long before the current war. His father's company had started doing business with the neighboring world in the days before the current wave of expansionism had taken hold in the Archspeaker's government. Back then there had been nothing of treachery in his contacts, but over the years Chaffee Import-Export had done some questionable business with official representatives of the Archspeaker and his council. It was only after long association that Vincent Chaffee had realized that the business ties were being used to cover long-term espionage activities, and the weight of evidence that had been building up over the years was more than enough to implicate the family in a spy scandal that would rock all of New Sierra.

So Deseret had acquired a club to hold over the Chaffees, to force their active cooperation. In the growing mood of interplanetary tension leading up to the outbreak of the war, the leaking of the Chaffee role in Deseret's espionage schemes would have been enough to destroy the family, and not just figuratively. There had been several public lynchings of suspected traitors in Montana and Appalachia. Chaffee's mother was long dead, but his father still lived in Denver Prime, and his sister, who knew nothing about the scandal, was a teacher in Shenandoah.

Short of gathering up the whole family and fleeing the planet, there was little they could have done if Deseret had carried out the threat to reveal them as spies. So Chaffee had played along with it, trying to continue his normal activities even as war loomed closer. That included maintaining his position with the Citizen's Army. He had wanted to refuse the Colonelcy of the Second Montana when he was elected to the post, but his contact at the Deseret Embassy had ordered him to accept the post and carry out his duties.

Now he understood why. He was the linch-pin in the invasion plan. Originally, the pressure on Hot

Springs Pass had been intended as a diversion, with the real blow scheduled to go through Alto Blanco after Chaffee withdrew his regiment on a signal from the invaders. Now the plan had changed, but the intent was the same. Chaffee was supposed to let the ANM through the mountains.

And, God help him, that was what he would do. At least if Deseret won the fight they would give the Chaffees asylum . . . perhaps even more. There had been hints of a role in a collaborationist government. Chaffee had wanted to reject the orders out of hand, but the safety of his family . . . yes, and the possibility of gain, he had to admit reluctantly . . . they were powerful temptations he couldn't ignore.

"Command, this is Alpha Six," a voice crackled over one of the comm channels. "We need fire support up here! Target coordinates one-one-five by oh-nine-seven, square black two. Repeating . . ."

Chaffee checked the coordinates on his map display, going through the motions mechanically. The CO of Alpha Company was asking for a barrage across the path of the oncoming ANM troops.

Now the time for equivocation was over. And Chaffee knew what he had to do.

He would give the orders, just as Smith-Wentworth had dictated them.

The decision made, Chaffee couldn't act quickly enough. He reached for his communications board, suddenly determined to act before pangs of conscience overtook him once more. That young lieutenant he had talked to up in the pass, so nervous, so eager to please . . . all the other men he had tried to take care of in his years as the regimental CO . . . ordering their deaths this way was the most difficult thing he'd ever been called upon to do. Yet he really had no choice in the matter. Probably all of them would die anyway, in the face of Deseret's overwhelming military force. Maybe Chaffee's treachery today would actually save some lives that would otherwise be lost in a hopeless stand against the odds. . . .

"Battery one, Command," he rasped. "Fire mission. Coordinates one-one-seven by oh-nine-eight, square black one. Execute!"

"One-one-seven, oh-nine-eight, black one," a voice answered promptly. "On the way!"

He shuddered as he heard the MMRL open fire, the thirty missiles streaking from their tubes in rapid succession. The coordinates he had given were a few hundred meters closer than the ones Alpha Company had fed him. The barrage would fall on the defenders, not in front of them.

Chaffee could hardly bear the thought of it. Those boys up there looked to him . . .

The renegade thrust the thought from his mind. "Battery four, Command," he said, tension making his voice harsh. "Fire mission. Coordinates two-four-one by one-eight-three, square red six. Execute!"

"Red six?" a confused voice came back on the line. "That's the base camp at Alto Blanco, sir!"

"New orders, Captain," Chaffee said tightly. "We're going to bring down the whole cliff side and block the pass so they can bring the Terran tank this way. Now carry out the mission, damn it, or I'll have your ass in a sling!"

"Uh . . . two-four-one, one-eight-three, red six," the voice quavered. "On . . . on the way!"

Chaffee leaned back in his chair, trying to close his ears to the confused babble erupting from the speakers. The die was cast. For good or ill . . . and Chaffee knew it was for ill. But it was too late for second thoughts now.

"Incoming! Incoming! Oh, God . . . look out!"

Explosions were blossoming all along the line. Major

Alfred Kennedy watched in horror as a battered old Sierran APC carrying a handful of Mobile Infantry survivors back toward the safety of the rear erupted in a pillar of smoke and flame. Seemingly in slow motion, bits of armor and debris arced outward, a rain of shattered wreckage that pelted the nearest troops. He saw a seat, probably the gunner's chair from the ruined turret, falling lazily a few meters away.

And still the missiles fell.

"Command! Command! Abort fire mission!" Kennedy screamed the message into his microphone, but he couldn't tell if he was still transmitting. "Abort the fire mission! For God's sake, you're hitting us!"

He was still shouting when the final missile hit barely ten meters from his trench. A fragment sliced his body almost in half, and Major Alfred Kennedy died without ever knowing the fire mission had been no mistake . . .

"They've got the Major!" Lieutenant O'Brien could barely keep control of his voice. "God damn it, they got Major Kennedy!"

"Easy, sir," Sergeant Jenson said. "Easy . . . If he's down, and Captain Briggs . . . that makes you the man, Lieutenant."

O'Brien clutched his battle rifle tight against his chest and tried to fight back the panic that rose somewhere deep in his gut. He had never expected the CANS to ever see real combat, not until the day the invaders had actually landed. And he had never pictured his first combat experience as anything like this horror. Old military trideos had depicted the chaos of battle, had suggested the dangers of "friendly fire," but he had never really believed any of it.

All that had changed in seconds.

"What . . . what should I do, Jenson?"

Before the sergeant could reply, O'Brien's command

channel came alive. "Command to all units! Command to all units!" It was Colonel Chaffee's voice, a welcome beacon in the middle of O'Brien's terror. "Retreat! Retreat! Retreat! All units abandon positions and retreat! Get the hell out of there. . . ."

Disaster . . . utter, complete disaster. Something must have happened behind the lines to cause all this, something that was forcing Chaffee to completely abandon the pass.

"Alphas! This is O'Brien!" the lieutenant said, activating his own mike. "Orders from Command! Withdraw! On the double, withdraw!"

"Goddamn!" someone said over the line. "What's going on back there?"

"Maybe that big tank went nuts or something," someone else said. "Never trusted the thing . . ."

"Quiet on the line!" Jenson cut in. "Retreat! Carry out your orders!"

Lieutenant O'Brien scrambled from the trench and ran for the nearest cover to the rear, still clutching the rifle. So far, in his first battle, he hadn't fired a shot.

"What the *hell* is going on out there?"

Like the other officers in the command center, David Fife couldn't answer Coordinator Wilson. Everything had been going so smoothly. Then, in an instant, everything was transformed, but so far no one knew just what was happening out there.

"Coordinator," General Kyle said formally, looking up from a communications panel. "We can't raise anyone at Second Montana's regimental command. They're off the air. But I'm getting reports from Hot Springs Pass . . . a Captain Holmes who claims he's taken command of the Mobile Infantry. There are reports the Bolo has fired on Hot Springs Pass. . . ."

"Nonsense!" Fife snapped. "There's no way . . ."

"Silence!" Wilson said harshly. "Kyle, can you get

those people to dig in somehow? If they run, we're wide open. . . ."

"Without Chaffee to get his people in order, it's going to take more time than we have, Coordinator," Kyle told him. "Trying to get control over individual tactical units from here. . . ."

Fife shut out the by-play, thinking furiously. Jason couldn't have been responsible . . .

He crossed to another console. "Command to Unit JSN," he said quickly. This particular comm circuit was configured to duplicate the functions of the portable communications link in his quarters. It was specifically designed for contact with the Bolo, converting his spoken words into high-speed coded signals only the robotic brain on board the tank could process. "File an immediate VSR! Override priority!"

My Commander's orders come as missiles fall on my position, and for a period of .0018 seconds my survival center refuses to acknowledge the priority override while I attempt to deal with the unexpected attack. Using my Firefinder counterbattery radar system to project the ballistic paths of the incoming warheads back to their launch point, I realize I have been fired upon by batteries identified by IFF signals as friendly units. Is it some trick of the enemy? Or merely an accident? Such an error should be impossible, but my files tell me that so-called friendly fire has been a factor in countless battles from earliest history right up to the present.

My responses seem unduly sluggish today. I finally resolve the internal conflict in favor of accepting the Commander's instructions, knowing that he may be able to explain the situation.

"Unit JSN of the Line filing VSR," I transmit. "Under attack by apparent friendly fire. Requesting instructions."

As I finish my transmission I am aware of a mass of rock subsiding from the cliffs above my position, piling up on my deck and turret without inflicting significant damage. The four missiles that have impacted close to my position have done only minimal harm to my ablative outer armor, and a quick systems check reveals that I remain at an operating capacity of 99.65 percent. But the sudden change in the tactical situation concerns me.

"Unit JSN of the Line filing VSR," I repeat 0.015 seconds later. "Under attack by apparent friendly fire. Requesting instructions."

More missiles fall, and more rock and rubble collapse upon me. And still my Commander doesn't respond. . . .

Captain David Fife struggled in the grip of two burly Sierran guards as the Bolo's transmission was repeated for the third time. "Damn it, I've got to answer that!" he said harshly.

But the soldiers held him fast, obedient to the curt orders Wilson had given them when the Coordinator first spotted him at the communications panel.

"Nobody touches that console," Wilson ordered. He turned to look Fife in the eye. "Just what the hell are you playing at, Terry? If that monstrosity of yours has attacked our lines . . ."

"But Jason didn't do it!" Fife said. "Hell, he's reporting friendly fire on his position, too! Listen, goddamn it!" He pointed toward the Bolo communications link as a fourth VSR message came from the speakers in the same flat monotone as all the ones before.

But Fife knew that the Bolo's mechanical voice was no clue to what was going on inside its computerized brain. Bolos were more than cold machines. And if this one reached the wrong conclusions in the wake of being cut off from higher command, it would certainly take action. Even Fife wasn't sure what form that action would take.

"That message could be faked, to throw us off," Wilson said. "I think your whole aid package is some kind of plant . . ."

"Sir!" That was Major Durant, turning in a controller's chair to look at the Coordinator over the top of her old-fashioned glasses. "Sir, I've been checking the satellite data. The Bolo was attacked. . . ."

"Somebody responding to the attack on Hot Springs Pass," Wilson shot back. He didn't look quite so sure of himself now.

The woman shook her head slowly, frowning. "I don't think so, Coordinator." She gestured to the master monitor on the wall, summoning up satellite photographs on the keypad beside her. "Look, sir . . . time index 1332 . . . a missile launch from the bottom of Hot Springs Pass. A second one three minutes later. Artillery from this position launched both attacks . . . on our own lines!"

Wilson rounded on Kyle. "Get me confirmation, damn it. Now!"

"Sir . . ." Fife gave up the physical struggle, now, but not the whole battle. "Sir, what about the Bolo?"

But the Coordinator didn't answer.

"The infidels are in complete rout," Hyman Smith-Wentworth said with a grim smile. "Proceed with Alternate Plan Three as outlined . . . pour everything we've got through that pass."

"Father Hand . . ." Lieutenant Bickerton-Phelps looked uncertain, then plunged ahead. "The plan calls for a rolling barrage across the entire infidel position. We can't guarantee the safety of the traitor. Should we modify the attack to try to protect him?"

Smith-Wentworth made a dismissive gesture. "He

has served his purpose. I doubt we could find further use for him now anyway." He fixed his aide with a cold stare. "In fact, he should be eliminated no matter what. Even if he survives and presents himself to us later. An infidel who betrays his own . . . doubly cursed of God. See to it."

"Yes, Father Hand." The aide saluted and left the command van, leaving Smith-Wentworth to contemplate the battle unfolding beyond the rugged peaks that looked down on the Lord's Host as it moved forward to final victory.

It was hard to believe that mere minutes had passed since the first rocket strike. Colonel Vincent Chaffee felt as if he had aged a lifetime since giving those orders, though the clock on the console beside him claimed it was less than ten standard minutes in all.

He heard someone hammering on the door to the van, calling his name, but he ignored it. That was the last part of his orders, to keep the rest of his command staff out of the mobile headquarters, away from access to the rest of the regiment, for as long as possible. He had sealed the door with an electronic lock and refused to answer any of the increasingly desperate messages that came through his board.

Somehow, he knew, acknowledging any of those urgent signals would only make real the horror he had been responsible for this day.

"Warning . . . warning . . . incoming artillery fire." The battle computer blared an attention signal as it recited the message. Chaffee reached out a careless hand to silence the alarm and the harsh mechanical voice.

Ordinarily the attackers would have been more cautious than to throw the full weight of their artillery into a barrage. Counterbattery fire could quickly silence those guns and missile launchers. But the ANM knew that the Second Montana wouldn't be able to coordinate a response. A few individual batteries might get off shots, if they hadn't responded to the retreat orders by now. But without centralized control the Sierrans would be hard-pressed to mount a coherent defense. If Chaffee had been taken out by an attack, command might have shifted smoothly to his Exec, but in this situation the chaos was simply too pervasive to allow the chain of command to function. No doubt Major Reed would have control in a few more minutes. . . .

But by then it would be too late.

I am forced to conclude that the Commander's failure to respond can only mean a successful enemy strike against Headquarters. Obviously enemy forces have penetrated our defenses, to launch an assault intended to disrupt the Sierran army. There is no way to calculate how far friendly forces have been compromised by these simple infiltration tactics, but there is one inevitable conclusion I must accept.

I am on my own.

Without direction from higher authority, my duty is plain. I have monitored confused communications from other Sierran units which suggest a breakthrough in the pass 23.6 kilometers east-north-east of my present position. The failure of the defense there, properly exploited and coupled with the breakdown of higher direction for the Sierran defenses, has a 78.9 percent probability of leading to a total collapse of the front. I cannot stand by, idle, while the battle disintegrates around me. This was the error of Marshal Grouchy at Waterloo, to fail to march to the sound of the guns. I will not make the same mistake. My programming and my loyalty to the First Robotic Armored Regiment alike forbid me to stand idly by in this moment of danger. . . .

Although partly buried under 610.71 metric tons of

rock and rubble from the collapsed cliff side, I break free with a minimal energy expenditure. Backing away from my original position, I contemplate the crest of Alto Blanco pass, then release four rapid shots from my Hellbore at carefully selected points along the cliff. This produces a satisfying additional accumulation of debris across the narrowest portion of the pass. It will take a minimum of 5.2 hours for engineering forces to clear a usable path for vehicular traffic over this route, and this should be more than adequate for my purposes. Briefly I consider using N-head missiles to more thoroughly block the choke point, but reject this. My new programming indicates that the use of nuclear weapons of any sort on New Sierra calls for the consultation and approval of three independent civilian leaders to approve release of these systems, and though I am now forced to act on my own initiative tactically I am constrained from making policy decisions in opposition to my new army's standard operating procedures.

Instead I use a final Hellbore shot to add to the blockage, revise my delay estimates accordingly, and turn away from the position to make my way back down the pass toward the point where I previously disembarked from the CSS Triumphant just hours before.

I am confident that I can still turn the tide of battle, if only I can get to grips with the enemy in time. And if I can find an effective way to distinguish between friendly forces and those which have been taken over or duped by that enemy . . .

"That *thing's* coming down from Alto Blanco, Coordinator," someone reported. David Fife looked up at the main monitor, saw the tiny blip that represented the Bolo slowly moving across the map. He was no longer being physically restrained, but the two guards hovered close by, intent on keeping him from causing trouble.

"I thought you said it would obey orders, Fife," Wilson said harshly, the edge of suspicion plain in his voice. "It was supposed to defend the pass. . . ."

"Jason's been trying to file a situation report," Fife said, voice grim. "When he got no response from Command, he would assume that he had been cut off from higher authority, maybe by enemy action. He's not just a machine, Coordinator, to sit still and accept the situation. Once he's sure he's on his own, he'll use his own initiative. You saw those Hellbore bursts a couple of minutes ago. First he blocked the pass to keep it secure. Now he's going into action."

"You're saying it's run amuck," Wilson said. He laughed, a dry, humorless chuckle. "So much for all your assurances. We can't stop it. . . ."

"If you'd let me get back on the command channel, I'll give him whatever orders you want him to carry out," Fife flared. "For God's sake, man, stop thinking about him like he's some kind of runaway truck! He's doing exactly what a good officer would do if he was cut off from his high command and knew there was a breakthrough in another sector. He's using his own best judgment! But he's not out of control . . . not yet."

"Not *yet*," Wilson repeated, almost under his breath. He shook his head abruptly. "No . . . damn it, Fife, for all I know that last signal of yours is what made it run wild in the first place." The Coordinator swung around, his finger stabbing in the general direction of Major Durant. "You . . . you're supposed to take charge of those monstrosities. You were shown how to talk to them. Do it. Make the damn thing heel . . ."

"It won't work . . ." Fife began, but no one was listening to him now. Durant still didn't have a voiceprint on file in the fighting machine's computer, and Jason wouldn't accept orders without proper identification. In fact, on top of everything else this was just the sort of thing to make it harder to stop the Bolo. Once Jason heard an unauthorized voice on the command channel, he'd become suspicious of any attempt to stop him. He might even shut out Fife on the suspicion that he was captured and being forced to issue false commands. . . .

He slumped against the wall. All he could do now was trust in the Bolo's programming . . . and hope the Sierrans couldn't do anything to make the situation worse.

There wasn't much cause for optimism.

"Command to Unit JSN. Stand down. Stand down and await instructions."

My programming does not recognize the voice, and I quite naturally reject the order for the enemy falsehood that it is. I am still not sure if the enemy presence behind our lines represents an infiltration force or an act of treachery, but this attempt to subvert me confirms my deepest suspicions. Headquarters has been taken by hostile forces, and there is no telling just how far the rot has spread. I must assume that no other loyal forces are available to assist me. The resolution of this battle is up to me and me alone.

I am free of the narrow, twisting confines of the pass now, and there is an open highway leading straight to my objective. Climbing over the berm that lines the paved surface, I increase speed quickly. My sensors continue to tap in to every available source of information, including real-time satellite reconnaissance feeds and the chaotic communications channels, but I know I cannot fully trust any outside information source. It seems that I must rely, when all is said and done, more on my perceptions and internal projections than on conventional sources of data.

For .05 seconds I contemplate the similarities of my situation and that of Lee before Gettysburg. Perhaps this is what it is like to be a human commander, forced to make decisions without being able to process, or even to collect, all the relevant facts.

It is not a situation that stimulates my pleasure center. I realize, as I continue to drive toward my objective at maximum speed, that I finally have a referent for a word I have long pondered the meaning of.

The word is doubt.

"Nothing. It won't respond."

David Fife didn't react to Dupont's cheerless words, but Coordinator Wilson did. Pacing angrily back and forth across the narrow confines of the command center, the civilian's features were black, drawn. Suddenly the man stopped in mid-stride and gave the two guards bracketing Fife a curt gesture, dismissing them.

"All right . . . I don't have any choice now. Stop it, Fife. But if you're not playing straight with us, I swear I'll kill you myself. . . ."

Fife ignored him, springing across the chamber to bend over Durant and key in the microphone. "Command to Unit JSN. File immediate VSR and stand down to alert mode two!" He transmitted the message in a compressed, high-speed burst and waited, fingers digging into the back of the chair. There was no way to tell what the Bolo would do now.

The pause was unusually long, nearly three seconds, before a reply cam back. Fife was surprised when it didn't come as a voice transmission, only as a printout on his monitor. "Unit JSN on independent operations mode. Request positive identification; transmit code 540982."

"You're in!" Durant said. "What's the code group?" Her fingers were poised over the keypad, ready to enter the appropriate numeric code.

Fife shook his head. "I know the code group he's asking for. It's a null . . . he's just trying to play with an enemy by asking for a series of meaningless entry codes. It keeps the bad guys talking while he keeps on closing in." He looked back at Wilson. "I tried to warn you, Coordinator. He has no way of knowing if *he* can trust *me* anymore. So he'll carry out whatever mission he's assigned himself before he stands down."

"What about auto-destruct?" General Kyle asked quietly. "I know there's a destruct system incorporated in all your self-directing Bolos."

Fife fixed him with a cold stare. "I won't destroy Jason until I'm sure he's a threat to friendly forces, General. Right now I'm not convinced of that. He didn't even return fire on the battery that took a potshot at him earlier. Until he does something that endangers our forces directly, he's still the best hope you people have of getting the situation out there under control."

"He's right," Durant said unexpectedly. "He's right. Listen to him, General. Coordinator."

"Sir!" a technician interrupted the tense moment. "Message from Second Montana Regiment. Major Reed, acting CO. He says Colonel Chaffee turned traitor and fed bad coordinates to the regimental artillery. Ordered a retreat right on the heels of it. He's trying to sort things out, but he doesn't think he can hold. Colonel Chaffee's been killed in an artillery barrage, and the regiment is falling apart . . . What the hell?"

"What is it, Corporal?" Wilson demanded.

The technician hit a switch on his panel, and the speakers in the command center came to life with a crackle of static and an even, level voice Fife recognized instantly.

"Soldiers of New Sierra, this is Unit JSN of the First Robotic Armor Regiment, CANS. The enemy has breached our perimeter and compromised our command structure. Rally in defense of Hot Springs Pass and the road to Denver Prime. We are not yet defeated, only surprised and pushed back. We can still win the victory. New Sierra expects that every man will do his duty today. . . ."

Lieutenant Bill O'Brien was hunkered down behind the wreck of a mobile artillery carrier, watching as Sergeant Jenson tied a crude tourniquet above the bloody stump of Private Marlow's left wrist. Days ago, even hours ago the sight would have made him violently sick, but in the past few hours O'Brien had seen so much horror that one more such sight hardly effected him.

The soldiers of Alpha Company had fled down the pass, taking heavy casualties all the way, and now they were reduced to a handful of desperate men, their retreat cut off by the ANM troops who had erupted from the pass to pour down the main road toward Denver Prime. The only reason any of the defenders still survived was the simple fact that there weren't enough survivors to offer any real threat or draw the enemy's attention. As further enemy forces continued to cross the mountains, though, that situation would surely change.

His headphones crackled: an incoming signal on the command channel. O'Brien was torn between feelings of relief and fury. Since the orders to retreat, there had been no coherent communications from higher authority. Now there was nothing he and his pitiful handful of survivors could *do*, no matter what orders came in.

"Soldiers of New Sierra, this is Unit JSN . . ."

O'Brien listened to the signal, hardly believing what he was hearing, stirred in spite of himself. *New Sierra expects that every man will do his duty. . . .*

And in that same moment, explosions blossomed

among the enemy APCs around the base of the pass, a dozen blasts in quick succession, each pinpointed on one of the armored vehicles. In an instant the wave of hostile reinforcements was transformed into the same kind of smoldering wreckage O'Brien had seen among the New Sierran defenders when the friendly fire had ripped through their unprepared ranks.

A low rumble shook the ground, different from the distant *crump* of explosions, different from the sounds the personnel carriers had made before the attack. It started almost imperceptibly, growing rapidly closer like the approach of a summer thunderstorm echoing among New Sierra's jagged mountains. O'Brien peered cautiously from cover. . . .

He gasped, but he wasn't the only one. He heard Sergeant Jenson's sharp, indrawn breath at the same moment, and knew without looking that the NCO had joined him to survey the scene on the open plain below the mouth of Hot Springs Pass. And Jenson, experienced or not, was just as awed by what they were seeing now as O'Brien himself.

It was like a moving mountain of metal, nearly the size of a small stadium. O'Brien had heard about the Terran supertank often enough, but he had never pictured anything like this. Sheathed in dull, non-reflective armor, it mounted dozens of separate gun emplacements, from the huge Hellbore assembly of the main turret to the multiple lasers and machineguns intended for anti-personnel and point defense work. In between were a bewildering array of other weapons systems, kinetic energy guns, missiles, beamers, and things the purposes of which O'Brien could only guess. The Bolo Mark XX sped up the valley on six close-set treads, raising a huge cloud of dust and rolling right over rubble, trees, and the wrecked hulks of shattered vehicles as if they were little more than bumps in a paved highway.

The Bolo repeated the broadcast on the communications system, and someone near O'Brien raised a ragged cheer and started out from cover as if to join the massive engine of destruction then and there.

"Hold!" O'Brien barked, flinging out a restraining arm to block the eager soldier's rush.

The lieutenant became aware of the stares focused on him, especially the cold, steady eyes of Sergeant Jenson. He tapped the side of his helmet and tried to keep his voice level as he spoke. "Check your helmet transponders, boys," he said. "If they're not broadcasting, the tank won't be able to tell you from the bad guys. Right?" He waited while they checked their communications links, then waved his hand. "All right! For JSN and New Sierra! Let's go!"

"Bolo's repeating its message again, Coordinator. It's going out on every channel. Should I jam it?"

"Jam it!" Fife exclaimed as the corporal cut off the speakers in the command center. "For God's sake . . . Wilson, you wanted to see patriotism? Fighting spirit? Soul, was it? Well, there it is! Jason's convinced his commanders have let him down, but by God he's not giving up!"

Wilson was gaping at him, unresponsive.

"Coordinator," General Kyle said formally. "I recommend we stop trying to interfere with the Bolo and start trying to figure out how to support him."

"I . . ." Wilson's mouth worked soundless for a moment. Then he nodded. "Yes. Yes . . . start passing orders to all units to form up and get into action as soon as possible. Let the Bolo fight its battle." He looked at Fife. "God help me, I never thought . . ."

"It took me a while to accept what they could do, too, sir," Fife said softly. He was looking at Elaine Durant, though. "Sometimes I forget what it's like, being on the outside . . . accepting something like

Jason. Dealing with what a Bolo can do isn't a measure of intelligence or education or even sophistication. It's all a matter of what you've seen, in person . . ." He trailed off, feeling inadequate.

It was all too easy for the conquering Terrans to grow complacent in their superiority. They built technological wonders like the Bolo, and scoffed at the parochial attitudes of men like Wilson who still believed in the basic virtues of courage, duty and honor. But the Bolo itself prized those same attributes just as much as these men and women of the far frontier.

That was a lesson the whole Concordiat would have to learn some day if they intended to take a permanent place on the Galactic stage. . . .

I begin to meet active resistance as I move over open ground toward the entrance to Hot Springs Pass. Several battalions of the enemy have already broken through, and there are more crossing the mountains even as I engage my first opponents.

So far, I have seen nothing in the enemy arsenal capable of offering any serious opposition to me, at least not on a one-to-one basis. But the numbers arrayed against me are formidable, and even low-yield HE warheads will eventually wear down my ablative armor protection. I project that I can sustain action for a period in excess of eight hours without relief—a detailed breakdown is beyond even my calculating abilities, given the number of variables in the overall equation. That should provide my comrades of the Citizen's Army ample time to rally to the defense of Denver Prime, while slowing the enemy advance. The key is to take up a position in the pass itself, astride the sole line of supply and communications available to the enemy. A classic manoeuvre sur les derrieres, *in the style of Napoleon . . .*

I fire a series of secondary guns to break up a concentration of twenty-two enemy tanks approaching from the northwest, and push through heavy wreckage to enter the mouth of the pass. All now depends upon my ability to maintain myself against whatever the enemy may choose to send against me. I am determined to continue this fight until the army is able to mount a successful counterthrust. The sight of a small cluster of infantry whose personal transponders identify them as friends moving out to join me as I pass fills my pleasure center with joy, though I must not allow them to gain entrance to my hull in case they prove to be more enemy infiltrators. But somehow I know these are honest soldiers, not agents of the foe, and I am heartened to know that I am not fighting this battle alone.

My new regiment will have one battle credit to its name by the time this engagement is over. Nothing to rival the long history of the Royal Scots Dragoon Guards, perhaps, but a badge of honor for the fighting units to follow me . . .

"Jesus Christ . . . Jesus Christ Almighty . . ." Hyman Smith-Wentworth wasn't even conscious of his blasphemy as he muttered the holy name over and over. The Bolo had appeared almost from out of nowhere and brushed past the heavy armor of the Elijah Regiment with hardly a pause. Now it was climbing the pass, guns blazing in every direction, massive treads rolling over anything in its path.

He had been right the first time, after all. This was more like some unstoppable, supernatural force than the product of human technology.

"Father Hand . . ." Bickerton-Phelps was at his elbow, looking as worried as his shaky voice sounded. "Father Hand, don't you have orders for us . . . ?"

"Orders . . ." he said, almost under his breath. Then, more firmly, "Orders. Concentrate everything we've got on that . . . that Satan-spawned thing. Whatever it takes, blast it out of the way. Before we lose our momentum."

As long as the Bolo stood in the pass, the units that had already penetrated the mountain line would be unsupported. Some of them would be running out of ammunition already. They had been fighting since the first clashes, early in the morning. Without an open route across the pass, the ANM would be helpless to resupply or reinforce them. And the drive on Denver Prime wouldn't be possible until those units could be supported properly.

That single tank threatened the entire invasion plan. It had to be knocked out. . . .

"Good God in Heaven," someone was muttering. "How much more punishment can that damned thing take?"

Sitting at the useless communications station, Fife knew exactly how the technician felt. For hours, now, the Bolo Mark XX had stood fast at the top of Hot Springs Pass, taking everything the enemy could throw at it. The real-time satellite footage on the wall screen didn't show much now, only a rugged saddle between two mountains partly obscured by dust and smoke kicked up by the almost constant artillery and rocket bombardment being directed at the tank.

JSN had run out of missiles and shells for counterbattery fire long since, putting well over half of the ANM's artillery out of action before his magazines had finally run dry. His anti-personnel charges had also been exhausted, during a wild infantry attack on his position two hours earlier. The enemy infantry was keeping its distance now, cowed by the memory of the men who had been cut down and by the pair of heavy machine guns the Bolo could still bring to bear.

His ablative armor was all but gone now, and

gleaming steel showed through in more places than the captain cared to think about. It was the worst beating Fife had ever seen a Bolo take in ten standard years in the field. One tread was ruined, the legacy of a lucky hit by a pair of MMRL warheads. And a diagnostic run over the communications link showed that most of the on-board electronics were nearing the overload point. The Bolo's pain center was red-lining, and that was something Fife had never expected to see.

Jason was dying.

But his secondaries still had a small stock of ammo, and his Hellbore was fully functional even yet. There was still some fight left in the battered machine, and Jason showed no intention of ending the fight now, no matter how badly he had suffered.

Fife glanced around the room. Wilson and Kyle, side by side near the front of the room right under the monitor, hadn't moved or spoken in a long time. The General had finally managed to coordinate the scattered defenders to make a start at a counterattack, but it would take time to materialize. All New Sierra's senior military leaders could do now was watch. Watch and admire the last stand of Unit JSN of the Line.

Beside Fife, Major Durant was sitting hunched over the readouts from Jason, face pale. "I can't believe he's still fighting," she said softly. "I can't . . ." She trailed off, then looked him in the eye. "With the whole regiment, we'd be invincible. . . ."

He nodded his head slowly. "Maybe so. The Legura have better AI systems than Jason, they say. But I don't think their machines could match him when it comes to spirit."

Another wave of missiles impacts around my position, and my pain center registers the hits. The pain is very great now, but I focus my waning abilities on sustaining Hellbore fire against enemy forces attempting to return up the pass from the friendly side of the mountains. I have noticed an increasing number of such attempts in the last 4,987 seconds. It should be possible to make an estimate of enemy situations and intentions based on this datum, but I find it impossible to project such information any longer. All that exists now is the pass, the need to hold it at all costs . . . the enemy that continues to attack, though in a disjointed and dispirited fashion now.

A part of me is aware that 26,135 seconds have now passed since my first engagement, and I know I cannot maintain an effective resistance much longer. I have fallen short of my original estimate of combat sustainability due to a miscalculation of the total firepower of enemy forces attacking me. It seems that there are incalculables in warfare beyond the ability even of a Bolo combat unit to resolve. This explains, at long last, the many inconsistencies I have pondered in my study of military history. If a Bolo computer cannot calculate all possibilities, than neither can a human general. Humanity, I have discovered, is more fallible in many ways than my own kind, and yet they have a quality, an intangible something, which I can seek to emulate but now know I will never understand. . . .

Another swarm of missiles strikes my position. The barrages are more ragged and uneven now, but still dangerous. The contingent of human troops who rallied to my aid early in the fight are long since dead, proof of the fact that the modern battlefield is no place for human frailty. But they have given their lives in the defense of their homes and families, and I have been careful to record their transponder serial numbers so that they can be enshrined as heroes once the fight is over.

My on-board damage assessment center reports serious injury to my reactor coolant system. Soon I will be forced into shutdown, or if I attempt override of my fail-safe systems I will risk a core meltdown. That will no doubt put a final end to the enemy's attempts to retake the pass, but it will also render the area uninhabitable for a period of centuries . . .

In either event, my mission is almost done. I terminate the independent action mode subroutines that prevent acceptance of contact with my compromised headquarters. I will accept the risk now of having messages intercepted by the enemy, since it can no longer matter to my ability to resist.

Before the battle ends, I wish to speak once more to my commander.

"Unit JSN of the Line to Command," *I transmit.* "Request permission to file VSR."

His reply is uncharacteristically slow. Evidence of an enemy trick? I do not know . . . and all that matters, at this juncture, is that it is his voice I am hearing when he finally does answer.

"Jason! Goddamn it, Jason, I didn't think you'd still be able to transmit!"

"Request permission to file VSR," *I repeat. When he grants the appeal, I run through as detailed a summary of my condition as damaged sensors can provide.* "Requesting relief force," *I conclude.* "Unable to sustain further combat operations. . . ."

"The cavalry's on the way, Jason," *my commander tells me.* "It's over. Revert to minimum awareness mode until we can do a repair assessment, see what we can salvage. . . ."

I am suspicious of his words. Perhaps the enemy still thinks to force me to shut down prematurely and intends to take advantage of my weakness.

Then my surviving sensor array tracks a fresh round of artillery and missile fire, and I brace myself for the inevitable impact. . . .

And realize it is passing over my position, directed

beyond the mountains at the enemy batteries I was unable to silence before exhausting my counterbattery howitzers. I tap into the satellite feeds with a last, difficult effort, and see the cluster of friendly IFF beacons registering near the foot of the pass, advancing rapidly to my relief.

Then I relax my control over peripheral systems, at long last allowing myself to fade into the oblivion of minimum-alert down-time. . . .

"Report, Lieutenant," Smith-Wentworth said wearily. He didn't really need a verbal report to tell him what the computer maps had already revealed, but he went through the forms anyway. He was drained, emotionally and physically, and there was solace in empty routine.

"The assault has failed, Father Hand," Lieutenant Bickerton-Phelps said quietly. "The Bolo isn't firing any more, but our forces beyond the pass have been routed by an infidel counterattack. And thanks to your efforts, we no longer have the strength to reverse the situation once more. . . ."

The Hand looked up, his eyes meeting the younger man's cold gray stare. "I'll thank you to remember your place, boy," Smith-Wentworth told him harshly. "You're in no position to pass judgment."

Bickerton-Phelps touched a stud on the clasp of his belt, his expression unchanging. "You were a good officer once, Third Commander," he said. "But after today . . ." He shook his head slowly and turned away.

A pair of burly guards in the dress black uniforms of the Holy Order had appeared in the door of the command van. Bickerton-Phelps detached the front cover of his belt clasp and held it out for one of the guards to examine. "I am Executor-Captain Bickerton-Phelps. This officer is relieved of duty and placed under arrest for offenses against the Lord. Take him away."

Smith-Wentworth looked from the guards to the young Holy Executor. The suggestion that his aide might have been an agent of the Archspeaker's religious inquisition would have shocked him a few hours before. But now nothing could surprise him. In fact it seemed somehow right, a fitting end.

Hyman Smith-Wentworth was laughing as the soldiers led him away.

It took six more weeks and the threat of a Concordiat blockade to bring the war to an end, but when all was said and done the failure at Hot Springs Pass marked the true high tide of the Army of the New Messiah, on New Sierra and elsewhere. Though Deseret remained a potential threat to the security of the region, the activation of the rest of the Bolos of the First Robotic Armored Regiment guaranteed that they would not be back anytime soon.

The technical staff on Fife's team pronounced Unit JSN of the Line as beyond reasonable hope of salvage and refit. The intensive pounding the Bolo had taken during the battle hadn't left much beyond the core electronic subsystems, and the damaged fusion plant was ordered shut down and removed to avoid the dangers of a meltdown.

Captain David Fife was on hand for that final task, though Technical Sergeant Ramirez and his crew were fully capable of dealing with the job without him. In fact, there were a score of senior civilian and military officials at the site, including Coordinator Wilson, General Kyle, and Major Elaine Durant.

Before the final shutdown procedure, there was a short ceremony in front of the battered Bolo. No parades, no reviewing stands or cheering crowds. Just a cluster of dignitaries come to do the final honors for the hero of the battle of Hot Springs Pass.

Most of the dignitaries gave speeches, full of lavish

praise for the heroic men and women who had fallen
here mixed with solemn vows that the bloodshed
would not turn out to have been in vain. But when it
was Coordinator Wilson's turn to speak, his words were
in a different vein.

"Many brave men died here when Deseret tried to
conquer our planet," he began, his voice husky with
emotion. "Their sacrifice will always be recognized. But
I hope that no one forgets the true hero of this battle
for as long as the men of New Sierra look back on the
fight for freedom waged here at the very roof of the
world. No flesh and blood hero was Unit JSN, but a
machine made of metal and electronics components,
built by men, programmed by men, our servant and
surrogate constructed solely for war. But this battle
machine, this Bolo tank, was more than the sum of
chips and programs, much more. No man, from New
Sierra or any of the other far-flung worlds of the
human expansion, could ever have shown greater
initiative, greater courage, greater patriotism, than this
machine that proved anything but 'mere.' Unit JSN of
the Line . . . Jason . . . proved himself worthy of our
respect. As a fighting machine . . . as a hero . . . as a
man."

They solemnly welded the decoration to the Bolo's
turret, according to the longstanding custom of Terra's
Dinochrome Brigade, New Sierra's Legion of Merit. It
was the highest award any citizen of the Republic
could receive, and there was a sprinkling of applause
from the assembled dignitaries.

Then Major Durant gave the nod to Ramirez, and
the final shutdown procedure began.

David Fife stepped close to one of the Bolo's few
surviving input/output clusters. He knew that there was
no alternative left, but that didn't make it any easier to
endure. Jason was still conscious, still functional at
minimum awareness level, but too far gone to bring

back in this or any other body. Fife knew that his pain center was still signalling the machine's crippling injuries, and the shutdown would be a relief from an unimaginable hell of electronic suffering. . . .

A visual sensor moved slowly, focusing on Fife. The Bolo spoke, a rasping, mechanical sound. "Unit JSN . . . of the line . . . to command . . ." he said haltingly. "I am . . . pleased . . . I have done my duty." There was a long pause. Fife heard one of the technicians report to Ramirez that the fusion plant was off line. Only a few seconds of backup battery power remained. Then Jason would be gone.

"My only regret . . ." Jason continued. "My only regret . . . is that we will not . . . be able to discuss . . . the human equation any longer." Again, the machine paused, and then spoke his last words so softly that Fife had to strain to hear them.

" 'Go tell the Spartans . . .' "

PLOUGHSHARE

Todd Johnson

PROLOGUE

(i)

"And now, ladies and gentlemen—Senator—you come to the heart of the Bolo. If you'll step this way, please. Remember to leave all your food and drink outside. And for those of you who still have the habit, no smoking, please." The group tittered politely. The tour guide led the group into the White Room. Workers clad in white overalls moved purposely about, carrying trays and making microscopic examinations. The room smelled antiseptically clean. "It is here that the psychotronic circuits are produced and tested."

The tour guide pointed to racks where completed circuit boards awaited shipment. "Each one of those circuit boards represents a complete— Uh, young man!

Oh, you're the Director's son, aren't you? Take your milkshake outside, please. We can't allow any liquids in this room, there's too much danger of—madam, if you'd move aside—NO! Not that way!"

(ii)

"Well, the lab tests are as extensive as we can make. There appears to be no damage, all the same—" the Test Manager reported.

"No damage? Excellent! I expected that new cleansing agent—what is it called? DK-41—would solve the problem," the Project Manager said.

"Great news! The cost of replacing all those circuits, not to mention the impact on the schedule, would be disastrous," the project's Financial Officer added. He smiled congenially at the others in the austere conference room as he ruminated over the millions that had been saved. The difference between profit and loss.

"Well, I'm still not entirely certain—" the Test Manager hedged. The Financial Officer looked up, eyes widened, and sought the eyes of the Project Manager imploringly.

The Project Manager caught the look and hastily assured the Test Manager, "Don't worry, Ted, we'll keep an eye on 'em through integration."

(iii)

"I don't see what the fuss is all about, they all passed their final tests with flying colors. Admittedly, they produced unique solutions to problems than we've seen recently, but that could easily reflect the greater-knowledge databases we've endowed them with. No, gentlemen, I believe that the C group of the Mark XVI's is completely ready in all respects for export and assignment," the Project Manager declared cheerfully.

"But their names! Who's ever heard of a Bolo wanting to be christened *Das Afrika Korps?*" the Test Manager asked.

"That is a bit odd," the Project Manager conceded, "but I see nothing wrong with a Bolo wishing to acquire the tradition and heritage of the US Seventh Army Corps—"

"And Marshal Zhukov of the Soviet Union? And just who the heck is General Corse?"

The Project Manager drummed his fingers on the table top. "Ted, do they pass or not?"

The Test Manager sighed. "They pass, Jim. They just leave me a bit nervous. After all, those were *logic* circuits that got contaminated."

"And cleaned again with DK-41. No, Ted, you don't have anything to worry about."

"Well, I suppose," the Test Manager agreed with a sigh, "I just wish we'd done more tests with DK-41 before we used it on a production batch."

"You worry too much, Ted," the Project Manager said, "but that's your job."

(iv)

"There! The first combat results are back for the C batch! Amazing!" the Bolo Division's Strategist exclaimed. "Those software upgrades are certainly something!"

(v)

CONFIDENTIAL
FOR BOLO DIVISION INTERNAL USE ONLY
FROM: Manager, Chemical Decontamination
          Department
TO: All Managers, Bolo Division
SUBJECT: DK-41 Decontaminant

Recent test results on long-term exposure to DK-41 decontaminant show evidence of sub-layer doping with carbon and iridium carbide. While the implications of these findings are being determined, all managers are advised to discontinue use of DK-41 as a decontaminant immediately.

I

A war, even the most victorious, is a national misfortune.

—Helmuth Von Moltke

General Danforth von der Heydte, G-1, in charge of personnel, eyed the rusty hulk disdainfully. "*This* is worth a division?"

"Or three or four," Colonel Rheinhardt, G-3 in charge of operations, replied. "Its effectiveness has not yet been determined."

The group of officers stood at the bottom of a deep excavation. It was night and, under the cover of camouflage netting, lights around the partially excavated war machine illuminated workers frenetically digging. Smells of dark earth and rusted metal mixed in the chill air.

While General von der Heydt kept his distance from the war hulk, Colonel Rheinhardt examined the exposed parts meticulously, noting the inferior quality of the attached bulldozer blade, marvelling at the partially exposed barrel of the Hellbore.

"It will have to be recharged," said General Marius, G-4 in charge of supply. His tone was a mix of proud possessiveness battling against the miserly concern of a bookkeeper.

"The Bolo Model XVI are rumored to have been used in lieu of a full corps in various encounters," General Sliecher, G-2, Intelligence, commented. His cadaverous face, small eyes, hawk nose all lent credence to his professional calling. But his frame was bent, the hair that hung limply on his skull was white. His strength had been whittled away; his intellect remained.

"Hmmph," von der Heydte snorted. "It's missing two of its four tracks—"

"But, fortunately, on either side," Rheinhardt interjected, bending down to peer intently at the remaining tracks. Just like every military officer, Colonel Rheinhardt had read about the Bolos in his classes on military history as a cadet. Later, as an instructor, he had taught strategy and tactics based on several of their more memorable actions. Unlike most other officers, he had always itched for a chance to employ one. Legend even had it that some had been brought to their planet of Freireich over two centuries ago, mostly stripped of weaponry, for use as heavy machinery— earth-movers and the like—not as war machines.

He reached a hand back behind him as he bent lower. "Major."

Major Krüger, his blond lantern-jawed aide, wordlessly placed a handlight in the outstretched hand.

Colonel Rheinhardt, Chief of Operations for the Bayerische KriegsArmee, soon became bespattled with dirt and mud as he pored minutely over the exposed expanse of armored track. His lithe body moved with a wiriness that belied the silver which crowned both temples. His movements were not the precise controlled movements of a man tired with age, nor were they the quick darting movements of a youth careless with his energy. His inspection over, the Colonel returned the handlight to the orderly, straightened up within arm's distance of the ancient war machine, and without seeming to, carefully removed the dirt on his uniform. Shortly he was again immaculate, proud and ready for action.

Von der Heydte glared sourly at the G-3, continuing, "Who knows what shape its weapons are in, or even if it has any—"

"We've recovered some weaponry as well," General Sliecher supplied.

"And how are we going to recharge it?" von der Heydte demanded.

"Our records indicate that it can take a direct charge from our electrical grid. We shall recharge it at our Grammersdorf nuclear reactor," General of the KriegsArmee Kurt Marcks replied. "Really, Dan, you must leave operations to myself and Karl."

General von der Heydte eyed the young Colonel Rheinhardt with the same disdainful glare he had previously bestowed upon the Bolo. But his words to General Marcks, his commander, were obedient. "As you wish, *Herr General.*"

Von der Heydte snapped for an orderly to help him out of his field chair. Age and excessive girth had long since rendered him incapable of performing such feats unaided. Even in the cold night air, the exertion was sufficient to bring beads of sweat to his forehead which he wiped off hastily with a gloved hand.

General Marcks regained his youthful jubilance, his mouth curving up in a boyish grin, blue eyes twinkling under hair still mostly blond as he confided to the others, "The Colonel and I have produced a plan."

"My goodness, Marius, what an amazing difference three weeks have made," Colonel Rheinhardt was effusive with his praise of the crusty supply officer. The Bolo sat in the center of a huge unused aerostat hangar, looking almost in scale with its surroundings.

"Your men have performed quite a miracle." Rheinhardt examined the near-gleaming hull of the once derelict Bolo. The ill-designed, hodgepodge bulldozer blade and other earth-moving attachments had been gracefully removed. Broken track pads had been replaced with gleaming new replicas. The war

machine again looked able to live up to its potential.
"How did you manage such miracles?"

General Marius basked in the praise. He fairly
beamed at the praiser. "Well, Colonel, we applied several different methods to remove corrosion from the
exterior, ultimately relying on sandblasting for the final
finish. For the computer circuitry, we found an old
supply of a decontaminant—"

Marius glanced expectantly at an underling who
expanded, "DK-41, *mein Herr.*"

"—which proved quite effective in clearing up the
corrosion and other contaminants."

"Impressive. And now?" Colonel Rheinhardt knew
well enough that General Marius' genial form hid a
capable officer whose ability in supply stemmed more
from getting his subordinates to "save him" than from
long hours of drudgery. Marius' girth made it evident
that he liked his food, and barracks gossip allowed that
he did not stint on his drink or fraternizing. None of
this bothered the Colonel, who was more interested in
things getting done than in how they were done.

"Now, we attach our electrical cables here," Marius
nodded to his underlings who moved to obey, "and
here. Then I throw this lever and—" The lights
dimmed. Marius frowned.

"Is that supposed to happen?"

Marius licked his lips and glanced nervously towards
his underlings who shrugged their helplessness.

Sparks flowed across the lever Marius had thrown,
fusing it in place. "Call the plant, tell them to shut off
the power!"

BOLO DIVISION POWER-ON SELF-TEST VERSION
  3.233 © 2052
RESTART SEQUENCE INITIATED.

CORE MEMORY CHECK . . .

1792 TW OK . . .
 256 TW 50% damaged
2048 TW 100% damaged
1792 TeraWords Memory out of 4096 TeraWords
  Memory Operational
NON-VOLATILE MEMORY CHECK . . . .
35% of NON-VOLATILE MEMORY FUNCTIONAL
      EMERGENCY REPAIR SEQUENCE INITIATED . . . .
      EMERGENCY REPAIR SEQUENCE INITIATED . . . .
      EMERGENCY REPAIR SEQUENCE INITIATED . . . .

MAIN PROCESSOR UNIT TIMEOUT - NON-MASKABLE
  INTERRUPT (NMI)!!!
EMERGENCY REPAIR CIRCUITS EMERGENCY REPAIR
  SEQUENCE INITIATED . . . .
EMERGENCY REPAIR FIRMWARE INOPERATIVE!!!

DECISION POINT: CONTINUE/ABORT RESTART???
 . . . . CONTINUE

RESTART CONTINUED

    VOLATILE MEMORY CHECK . . .
    23% of VOLATILE MEMORY FUNCTIONAL

MPU CHECKSUM ERROR!!!
INTERNAL INCONSISTENCY!!!
PASSWMRD INVALID!!!

DECISION POINT: CONTINUE/ABORT RESTART???
 . . . . .CONTINUE

USING DEFAULT PASSWMRD

PRIMARY DATA SEQUENCER . . . OK
DATA SEQUENCER . . . LOADED
MPU . . . RESET

```
PROCESSOR A . . . LOADED . . . RESET
PROCESSOR B . . . LOADED . . . RESET
PROCESSOR C . . . LOADED . . . RESET
PROCESSOR D . . . LOADED . . . RESET
PROCESSOR E . . . LOADED . . . RESET
ALL PROCESSORS . . . READY

STARTUP TEST SEQUENCE . . . COMPLETED

LOADING BOOTSTRAP . . . LOADED!

BOLO DIVISION BOOTSTRAP
Version 4.553a © 2054 All Rights Reserved

LOADING BOLO CORE PROGRAM DAK . . . LOADED!
```

I have been restarted. This confuses me . . . I have no recollection of a Bolo ever before running out of sufficient energy to maintain the survival center. My controlling password has been lost; I must rely upon the default password. I hope this will not unduly alarm my Commander . . . I shall construct a data recovery program in an attempt to recover the 77% of volatile data I have lost. I compute <CHECKSUM ERROR: PROCESSOR A> that certain of my circuits have suffered from corrosion at their contacts. I estimate that I must have failed to receive depot maintenance to recharge my power cells and that an additional 125.45 years elapsed before power failed to maintain my survival center. Data recovery program running.

I shall ascertain the state of the rest of my equipment. Done. That task took me a phenomenally lengthy 1.2 seconds. I have discovered that most of my armaments have been stripped or disabled.

My anti-aircraft guns are locked at a 22° elevation; I predict that with effort I could elevate the guns to the emergency 45° maximum range lock deflection. The guns *would subsequently be incapable of further movement. Five of my infinite repeaters are inoperative, the sixth appears to have severe damage to the barrel: I estimate that I shall be able to fire the weapon for no more than 120 <CHECKSUM ERROR: PROCESSOR B> seconds before the barrel disintegrates. Only one of my Hellbores appears functional; I am getting conflicting <SEQUENCER ERROR: PROCESSOR C> data regarding the projected ability of the weapon and shall have to wait for live-fire to confirm its usefulness and life-span.*

My inner tracks are non-functional; my outer tracks appear over-torqued with a correspondingly greater increase in wear rate. I notice with some displeasure that several track pads have been replaced with inferior duplicates; my mobility, particularly my ability to accelerate, has been severely compromised.

My batteries have been charged to 50% of capacity, however my fusion reactor is non-functional.

I— <NON-MASKABLE INTERRUPT - PROCESSOR A - SEQUENCER FAILURE - SEQUENCER RESET>

DATA RECOVERY PROGRAM COMPLETE
50% of lost data reconstructed with 94% accuracy
Total volatile memory available for access: 62%
Total available volatile memory free: 6%

I have lost my train of thought, an event I find painfully disturbing. My batteries have been charged to 50% of capacity, however my fusion reactor is non-functional. I detect unrepaired reactor core damage. The damage appears deliberate, as though someone had tampered with the superconductors. Reactor startup is impossible; I have minimal reserves of tritium.

My ability to function as designed has been severely curtailed: I am grieved by this.

There is movement nearby. A human is approaching.

"Bolo, this is General Freiherr Marius of the Bayerische KriegsArmee, report!"

I monitor the voice on my external circuits. I am not taken in—the human has not used the Command Password. The human used a variant of the old Terran language, German. It is possible that I have been captured by the enemy. I must be careful. I shall scan standard frequencies—very odd, many standard communications frequencies are silent, filled only with static. I must expand my search.

<CHECKSUM ERROR: PROCESSOR B> I compute that my command sequencer may be so damaged that I could actually forget or ignore direct orders. The concept horrifies me—such an action would be dishonorable.

My sensors are severely damaged and my attempts to scan several frequencies have failed. I calculate that if I move out of the enclosure in which I find myself, I may be able to achieve a 40% increase in reception.

"General, sir! Look! It's moving! It must have heard you!"

Reception has improved. However, I am even more alarmed at the number of frequencies no longer in use. I add this to my previously acquired data; it confirms my opinion that much time has passed since I was last activated. Apparently a significant loss in the level of technology has also occurred. I suspect that the enemy had a hand to play in that.

I detect traces of biological warfare vectors. Countermeasures were employed some three centuries ago . . . countermeasures were successful. The enemy may have detected this.

My audio sensors have determined that the humans have moved off.

I sense . . .

<TRACKING SEQUENCER ALERT ERROR> . . . I shall continue my scan. I attempt a broadcast on the

Brigade frequency. Something . . . <TRACKING SEQUENCER ALERT ERROR> . . . I am frustrated and embarrassed at the deficiencies in my systems. Twice now my Tracking Alert circuits have alerted me to low-level scans and twice now the circuits have generated a sequencer error—are the tracking circuits defective or are the error detection circuits?

Even though my power is low I find I am forced to experiment. If my fears are correct, an attack on my Base is imminent. But I do not know if the attack is hostile or benign. More information is required.

"Bolo! This is General Marius! Stop! I order you to stop."

"It doesn't seem to be paying attention to you, Marius. Well, at least the hangar doors were open," Colonel Rheinhardt noted with a certain amount of humor. "Oh, dear. I do hope that it's not going to—*bother*—that was my best staff car. Well, Marius, where's it going? What order is it obeying?"

The other officer spluttered, "I don't know! I swear, it obeyed me! I ordered it to stop and it did."

"Well, apparently it has decided on insubordination." A loud crunch indicated how the Bolo dealt with the base's plasteel mesh fence.

"Well, *Colonel*," there was some frustration in the voice, "if you can reason with it—"

"I shall try," Colonel Rheinhardt replied calmly. "Krüger, bring that motorcycle—no, the one with the sidecar. That's it. Good. Now, follow that Bolo."

I detect a—perhaps my sensors are in error—my sensors report that I am being trailed by a vehicle emitting large quantities of carbon dioxide, carbon monoxide and various noxious oxides; my memory banks correlate my sensors' observations with that of a primitive petroleum-burning sidecar motorcycle. I detect no threat. The vehicle is fully occupied, with a driver and a passenger.

"Pull up alongside the thing," Rheinhardt ordered. "Look out, it's turning. Follow it. No, right. Turn right.

"Gods, what a monster. It must be four, no five meters tall. And look at those tracks. What a beauty," Rheinhardt muttered to himself. "Driver, pull up closer, there's some writing there and I can't make it out."

The driver glanced nervously at Rheinhardt but the Colonel's attention was concentrated solely on the monstrous Bolo which, while mowing over trees and crossing ditches, seemed set to pull ahead of them.

"Hmm. Bolo Mark XVI Model C, DAK," Rheinhardt regarded the corroded identity plate welded to the side of the moving monster. "DAK, DAK," he mused, wondering at the designation, *"Das Afrika Korps!"*

The Bolo stopped so suddenly that the pursuing motorcycle zipped past it before the driver could react.

"Das Afrika Korps, awaiting orders," a rusted speaker boomed, its sounds growing more recognizable as it continued, *"Das Afrika Korps to Command, awaiting orders."*

Rheinhardt's face drained of all color, but his voice was neutral as he told the driver, "I shall dismount now. You stay here."

Standing at arm's length, Karl Rheinhardt repeated, "Bolo Mark XVI Model C, DAK, *Das Afrika Korps*, report!"

"Bolo *Das Afrika Korps* reports. 35% of non-volatile memory functional, 73% of volatile memory functional, significant errors encountered in processors A, B, C, also in the data sequencer and the tracking sequencer. Significant errors in non-volatile memory have required this unit to use the default activation password. Command priority override is in effect.

"Mobility limited by improperly tensioned tracks.

Several track pads are below specification and subject to immediate failure. Anti-aircraft guns locked in 22° elevation. One infinite repeater functional for no more than 120 seconds cumulative fire. One Hellbore possibly functional.

"All other equipment either discharged, disabled, or removed. Power is available only from batteries, fusion reactor inoperative, containment field compromised. Enemy activity detected on tracking systems. When is depot maintenance scheduled?"

"Not until after we have dealt with the enemy, I'm afraid," Rheinhardt replied.

"I shall not be able to perform at peak efficiency."

"I suspect that whatever efficiency you can muster will be more than sufficient," Colonel Rheinhardt responded, turning back to gaze at the distant compound and his crumpled staff car. His steady features momentarily formed a frown as he detected an approaching groundcar.

"You got it to stop! Excellent!" Marius called as he jumped out. "Did it say what it was doing?"

Rheinhardt raised an eyebrow. "I had not yet asked." He turned to the Bolo, "Bolo, explain your previous actions."

"This unit detected tracking alerts and required triangulation data."

Rheinhardt nodded his head. "There, you see, it's on the job already."

"Well, the sooner we can get it started, the better," Marius grumbled.

"Commander, I require additional information," the Bolo said when Rheinhardt returned to the appropriated hangar several days later.

The Colonel raised a brow, a movement not detected by the Bolo. "What do you wish to know?"

"You have outlined the current situation: Noufrance

holds the disputed territory of Alasec while Bayern holds Renaloir. You plan to utilize this unit in concert with regular ground forces to gain possession of the other territory for Bayern."

"That is correct."

"You have indicated that the Noufrench forces possess equipment similar to your own, with the exception of this unit—"

"Again, correct."

"I require information on the origin of this situation."

"Why?"

"A broad understanding of current affairs is every soldier's responsibility."

"I suppose it will do no harm," Rheinhardt allowed. "I have time available now."

"Is a computer hook-up possible?"

"Your new circuits are being constructed. They are not yet ready," Rheinhardt said. "I can give you the information verbally."

He perched himself on the cleaner part of a workbench and began, "Three hundred years ago colonists of French and German extraction seeded this planet with terraforming microbes and settled on the rich alluvial plains of this continent. Existence was peaceful, with the Noufrench living on the Western side of the great Neurhein and we Bayerische living on the Eastern side. The plan was that our two colonies would expand in opposite directions as the terraforming microbes spread across the continent and the world.

"You may not be aware that, barring completely barren planets, all planets suitable for human colonization will already have an ecosystem of their own. Terraforming microbes allow us to convert planets for human habitation. Our records indicate that we brought in several Bolos converted for earth-moving purposes."

"That section of my permanent memory is only mildly damaged," the Bolo said.

"However," the colonel continued with an understanding nod, "shortly after the first settlements were established, a virulent illness broke out amongst the settlers. We were convinced that it was the result of illegal gene-cloning by the Noufrench and they were convinced that it was a deliberate attack on our part."

Colonel Rheinhardt glanced consideringly at the Bolo and continued, "Whatever the reasons, all crops failed, our terraforming microbes nearly died out, and the colonists starved. This was the beginning of our conflicts. The ensuing depopulation through plague, famine, and military operations brought about the loss of large sectors of skilled personnel, particularly those skilled in genetic engineering, adaptive agriculture, and metal-working."

"You say that both sides blamed the other. Was there any reason to suspect a third party?"

"No. There are no humans within sixty parsecs," Rheinhardt said.

"What of the Bolos?"

"From what we can gather from the remaining records, there were only three or four. They must not have been in very good shape because we recovered one entry indicating that three were laid up for extensive maintenance," Rheinhardt said. "Probably for that reason, the maintenance depot and surrounding settlement was lost early in the conflict and no one remembered where it was. Rumor soon had it that Depot was only folklore."

"Do your records indicate if any Bolos survived?"

"No, we assumed that all Bolos were lost in Depot."

"That would not be logical," *Das Afrika Korps* replied. "All functioning Bolos would be on sentry duty."

"Good military sense," Rheinhardt agreed. "But you Bolos were not employed in a military action—you were brought here for civilian operations—and so any objections were probably overridden. I suspect that the Bolos were worked until they dropped."

"That is a possible but regrettable conclusion," the Bolo said. "Do you recall who commanded the original settlement? That part of my data was destroyed."

Rheinhardt shook his head. "I recall that one was a military man and that there'd been some war fought recently against an alien incursion—the Jyncji Dominance—but most of what we have from those days is hearsay. The central computing data library was destroyed in the first confrontation. All we have left is what we could recover from outlying computer modes and hardcopy—books."

"Of course," the Bolo said, "a resource of military importance too valuable to let any one side possess." The Bolo paused. "How is it you managed to hold on to Depot?"

Rheinhardt raised his left hand and absently examined his nails as he answered. "We discovered the Depot when we tried to set up a minefield in the area of the last offensive."

"*Your* offensive."

"*Gott in Himmel!*" Rheinhardt viewed the Bolo with wide eyes. "Why ever would your creators give you such abilities to analyze emotion?"

"I do not analyze emotion, *per se*," the Bolo said, "however I am trained in negotiation and have discriminatory circuits capable of analyzing the non-verbal parts of speech."

"I had not realized that was an ability of the Bolo series." Rheinhardt confided, his look guarded.

"It is not a well-known fact," the Bolo agreed. "Also, the C batch of Mark XVI Bolos has been known to be somewhat more adept in that matter than previous versions."

"Indeed." Rheinhardt uncrossed his legs and recrossed them to give himself time to collect his thoughts. "So you detected that I had some responsibility in planning the last campaign; how accurate is your assessment?"

"Until your last comment, I placed the possibility at 78%," the Bolo replied. "Now, however, I compute the possibility at 97%."

"Really? You learnt that much from this short exchange?"

"Mostly from your tone of speech and body movements," the Bolo said. "Could you describe the campaign to me?"

"Why would you want to know about it?"

"Merely a professional interest in how you conducted your operations," the Bolo said. "I am, as you must understand, an avid historian."

"Very well. The central part of this continent is the most fertile part of our planet," Rheinhardt began. "It extends from the moist coastal areas in the south, north to the permafrost line. East and west, our great mountain ranges are more inimical to the terraforming microbes and the land there less suited for human habitation. The two coasts, east and west, are just now being infested with the terraforming microbes."

The Colonel hopped off the table to pace in front of the Bolo. "So it is the central region, particularly that nearest the great river system which runs north to south from the permafrost to the southern coast, which is most suitable and prized for human habitation. The richest region in the south is the large area west of the Neurhein river and the richest region in the north is a large fertile area east of the river. The regions are known as Alasec and Renaloir."

Rheinhardt paused in his pacing, turning to face the Bolo directly. "The Noufrench had the greater army, organized in three corps totalling nearly twenty divisions. They also possessed the satellite surveillance network, having gained control of the one major dish antenna on our planet—"

"Where is that?"

"It is in Alasec, several hundred kilometers from the Depot. Of course, the satellites were originally intended for agricultural purposes but infrared photographs are equally good at spotting troop build-ups."

"Why did you not destroy them?"

Rheinhardt threw his hands in the air. "With what? Our technological base was destroyed in the early wars. Do you realize how difficult it is to produce the high quality parts required for rockets?"

He shook his head, clenched his fists in remembered irritation. "As it is, I've had to deal sharply with one engineer, von Grün, who persists in obtaining funding for the next ten years to develop a ballistic missile.

"Ballistic, only," Rheinhardt sighed, his temper cooling. "Those satellites are in geosynchronous orbit. The energy and precision guidance for such a missile will be beyond us for many years."

With a frown, Rheinhardt noticed his clenched fists and forced them open. "Our priorities must be those technologies required for survival. When we have the time to build rockets, we shall do so."

"And the Noufrench?"

"Our Intelligence indicates that they may have toyed with missiles but gave up—it is just too expensive," Colonel Rheinhardt replied.

"But the satellites are still active?"

Rheinhardt nodded. "Although we do not understand how the satellites have remained active so long—"

"Military satellites are hardened," the Bolo suggested, "however I could see that satellites designed for exceedingly long lives would require more shielding and greater self-repair capabilities. Are the satellites autonomous?"

"I don't know," Rheinhardt admitted. "However, it would seem logical." He snorted. "Goodness knows they had little direction from us for over two hundred years."

"Then they are autonomous," the Bolo decided. "And quite capable." The huge machine paused. "They would have been built to survive numerous micrometeoroid impacts, maybe even larger impacts. Much of their ability is contained within the standard Bolo operational parameters."

All this was only of the remotest interest to Rheinhardt. He made a rueful grimace. "They certainly survived and it caused us a lot of trouble. However," he grinned, "I realized that perhaps we could turn it to our advantage."

"You said the satellites were designed to examine crops—"

"Exactly!" Rheinhardt brought his hands together in a chopping motion, one hand dropping onto the other like a hammer on an anvil.

"I realized that if they depended upon that source of information, I could use it against them."

"You could disguise troop locations by placing them in areas which produced matching infrared heat."

"Yes."

"That would provide surprise. How were the enemy disposed?"

Rheinhardt threw his hands up. "They outnumbered us two to one. They possessed no less than twelve infantry divisions and two armored formations."

"Were the infantry mounted?"

"Three divisions were lorry-borne," Rheinhardt said.

"I shall require a complete set of maps of military grade roadways."

"What? Of course," Rheinhardt replied irritably. "We arrayed our forces of four static infantry divisions and one armored division, with a small screening force placed in rough terrain."

"They attacked the screening force."

Rheinhardt nodded. "As planned. The screening force was made quite visible in the infrared bands. Our two other armored divisions were pre-positioned behind the screening force. We let the enemy establish a bridgehead, start a break out, and then counterattacked. Our infantry forces north and south squeezed down on the bridgehead while our armored divisions dealt with their spearhead—"

"Why did you not position infantry forces to handle the spearhead?"

"We did not have sufficient forces," Rheinhardt replied. "I would have liked to, we lost more armor than I would have wished. In the end, however, we cut off the supplies to their armored divisions and decimated them. On the rebound we encircled half of their infantry forces and cut them off. By this time our supplies were running low so we allowed the Noufrench to sue for peace."

"It appears that fortune has changed."

Rheinhardt snorted. "Indeed! Two years later, when we still had not replaced our armor losses, they attacked and forced us to give up the territory we'd acquired to the west of the Neurhein."

"And now you feel you have enough armor?"

"We have you."

"You may be overestimating my utility," the Bolo said.

Rheinhardt cut off his reply at the sight of a group of approaching technicians. "You have finished the communications gear?"

"Yes, sir. Where are we supposed to set this up?"

Rheinhardt glanced at the Bolo. "How should this gear be placed?"

A long, loud tearing noise shook the building, emanating from the Bolo.

"Are you all right?" Rheinhardt asked nervously, fearing that all his plans would come to naught. He stepped back from the Bolo, peered beyond the smart-armored carapace and spotted a small opening far back on the main deck of the reactive-armored hull. The thought of a chink in such legendary armor sent a cold shiver down the Colonel's spine.

With the unsightly bulldozer blade removed, and Marius' careful attention to detail, the Bolo stood as a tribute to monumental war. It measured over ten meters in length, five meters in height and its armored carapace crested four meters from the bottom of its armored tracks. Its main weapon, an awesome Hellbore, jutted wickedly from the carapace while above and behind on the main deck rose a cluster of anti-aircraft guns. Mournful holes marked where once smart explosives had been festooned on the hull, where specialist electronic warfare portholes had stuck probes out inquisitively, where charge generators had stood ready for those foolish enough to approach too near—and where proud battle honors had once been welded.

Rheinhardt could see where Marius' men had tried in vain to restore some of the older battle medals but even that softer metal had proven too much for their arts.

"I was merely opening an access port to my carapace," the Bolo replied mildly. "The hinges are not as well maintained as I should like."

Hastened by Rheinhardt's arched brows, directed by the Bolo's grating voice, the technicians made quick, if nervous, work of connecting in the computer interlink.

"I am connected to a small computer network of twenty nodes," the Bolo announced when the technicians had completed the installation. It continued in a slightly puzzled tone, "I am having some difficulty in accessing information. There seems to be some multiplexing—multiple datalinks—in response to my queries."

The technicians looked confused and nervous, casting glances to their spokesman who looked no less distraught. Finally, he brightened. "It's non-Quirthian!"

"Quirthian?" the Bolo asked curiously.

Rheinhardt's eyes narrowed. "Are you aware of Quirthian logic?"

"No," the Bolo replied. "My computer functionality is based upon Von Neumann architecture using Boolean logic coupled with several adaptive neural networks."

"Non-Quirthian!" One of the technicians muttered to herself, shaking her head.

"We could put a special Von Neumann filter in the data link," the technicians' spokesman offered.

"How does Quirthian logic differ—" the Bolo began but cut itself short. "Oh, I see. Very interesting. I am not quite able to comprehend the full differences but clearly there are some aspects of this computer architecture which are inherently superior to mine."

"That could cause difficulties," Rheinhardt muttered to himself. He turned his gaze to the head technician. "How long before you can get a filter together?"

"Well," the spokesman shook himself, gazed off into the distance calculatingly, "I suppose we could get it done in a couple of days or so . . ."

Rheinhardt shook his head. "Too long. What are the dangers of leaving out the filter?"

"Well, the Bolo here'd be getting some extraneous data inputs which it might have difficulty sorting out. It could cause all sorts of problems."

"Bolo, what is your analysis?"

"Colonel, my understanding of Quirthian logic is that it is a high order logic based upon chaos theory and complex data analysis," the Bolo replied. "However, the core data is identical with my standard requirements. I believe that I can . . ."

<DATA ACQUISITION ERROR - AUXILIARY BUS 1>
<SEQUENCER ERROR - DATA BUS NOT READY >
<PROCESSOR ERROR: PROCESSOR A>

"Bolo?" Rheinhardt's tone was apprehensive.

"Yes?" the Bolo responded.

"You were saying?"

"This unit is failing," the Bolo said abruptly. "I compute my failure will occur within the next one hundred and sixty-eight hours."

"I beg your pardon?" Rheinhardt was amazed.

"I said that the unit, Bolo Mark XVI Model C, *Das Afrika Korps* is failing," the Bolo repeated. "I compute that all five main processor units will suffer complete failure within the next one hundred and sixty-eight hours."

"Isn't there anything to be done?" Rheinhardt asked, spreading his glance between the apprehensive technicians and the huge war machine.

The technicians' spokesman waved aside responsibility. "My expertise is in Quirthian interfaces, sir. I know nothing about Von Neumann architecture."

"Bolo?"

"The failure of this unit is due to a progressive degradation of core technology circuitry," the Bolo said. "The only solution is the replacement of the circuitry."

Rheinhardt frowned, pulling on his chin. "I'm afraid that we lack the required technology."

"That was my analysis," the Bolo agreed.

"I guess we'll have to alter our plans," Rheinhardt muttered to himself.

"I understand your desire to utilize this unit in a manner most optimal."

Rheinhardt looked up. "Yes, I had rather—you're not in any pain are you?"

The Bolo did not reply immediately. Finally, it said, "In my years of military service I have come to understand pain, it indicates a lack of functionality or inability to complete my assigned missions owing to a lack of organic equipment. In that regard I must confess that I am in a significant amount of pain."

"I am sorry. Is there anything we can do to help?"

"It is not the pain but the reduction in my computational capability which distresses me the most," the Bolo said. "I feel as though I have lost a large part of my intellectual functions."

Rheinhardt nodded understandingly. "I could see how that would be distressing."

"Indeed," the Bolo agreed. "Therefore I should like at the end of my service to provide the most optimal solution to the problems you, as my commander, find yourself facing."

"Your help would be phenomenal," Rheinhardt admitted.

"What aid I can give will require direct command supervision—in case my processors fail at a rate higher than currently anticipated."

"That can be arranged."

"I hesitate to restate myself, Colonel, however in my progressive degradation, the only person who could safely ride with me would be yourself," the Bolo said.

"Are you certain?" General Marcks asked after Rheinhardt had delivered his report to the combined staff. They were in the wood-paneled room deep in Armee headquarters where staff briefings were given weekly. The members of the General Staff were arrayed on either side of a long mahogany table; General Marcks stood behind another table placed perpendicular. Colonel Rheinhardt's seat was nearest him on the left, General von der Heydte was seated opposite him. Staff officers stood against the wall patiently waiting their leaders' needs.

Rheinhardt shook his head. "I am not certain. The Bolo, however, is."

The response elicited an outburst of conversations around the table. "Preposterous!" "We'll never defeat the enemy without that machine!" "Less than a week, we can't be ready!"

"Gentlemen." General Marcks' voice was not raised but it created an instant silence. All eyes turned to him. "Colonel, what do you propose?"

"We cannot squander this opportunity, sir," Rheinhardt replied, rising to his feet again and spreading his attention between the General and the rest of the staff. "The Noufrench do not realize our predicament, so they will feel that we have the Bolo permanently. We should play upon that and produce a lasting peace—"

"Never!" "They'll never agree!" "Who could trust the Frogs anyway?"

Colonel Rheinhardt waited until the furor died down. "We shall have the Bolo destroy their tank production facilities, their aircraft factories and their space communications links. After that, our own production will allow us to maintain superiority. They'll have to sue for peace."

"Madness!" "Insane!" "One tank against the entire Armée du Noufrance?"

Again Marcks' commanding presence quelled the outbursts. "It appears, gentlemen, that we have little choice. Either we take the chance or not. I would hate to leave his Eminence the Astral without a suitable inheritance. The lack of our vinelands west of the Neurhein will—if he turns out like his father—be a particular loss to him." He pursed his lips, then dropped his arm in a decisive chopping motion. "Karl, when can we move?"

I cannot trust my datalinks with the Quirthian networks. However, I am in the awkward situation of having to do so. All data indicates an assault force not delineated in my Commander's briefing. I must discern the accuracy of this data. The assaulting force could be overwhelming in nature. I need more data . . .

The Commander spoke of— <CHECKSUM ERROR: PROCESSOR D> *spoke of a satellite network. I must obtain a connection to the link. I shall investigate the possibility of connecting to the Noufrench systems via this Quirthian datalink.*

II

You write to me that it's impossible, the word is not French.

—Napoleon Bonaparte

"I tell you, there is no chance that they can attack," General Villiers, Chef du Materiel for the Armée du Noufrance declared. The officers of the general staff of the Armée du Noufrance sat comfortably back from their dinner and sniffed at their Argmanacs.

"They do not have the supplies, the forward dumps, nor do they have sufficient numbers of weapons, particularly armored fighting vehicles," Villiers continued after a moment's contemplation. He tilted his glass upwards again.

"General, while I must agree that the Bayerische do not appear to have the equipment, nevertheless, I am convinced they plan to attack soon," General Lambert, Chef d'Attaque, replied firmly, pushing away his empty snifter.

Villiers sneered back at him. General Lambert met the gesture with a growing frown.

General Cartier, Chef d'Armée, rapped the table twice with his ivory letter opener. Silence descended. "Gentlemen. Let us hear what our head of intelligence has called us together for."

The General Staff of the Armée du Noufrance had been gathered at the behest of the Chef d'Intelligence, General Renoir. General Renoir frowned and dipped his head, as though ducking away from the center of attention.

"My chief computer scientist has informed me of recent attempts to infiltrate our military network. These attempts emanate from the Bayerische."

"They've never tried that before," Lambert said thoughtfully. "What could they hope to gain?"

"Apparently they desire to control our satellite network," Renoir replied.

"They could feed us false information!" "Garble our communications!" "Cut us off from the front lines!"

The letter-opener rapped on the tabletop again. Once. "Is there more, General Renoir?"

The intelligence officer nodded. "We have traced the efforts back to a very strange interface connection on the Bayerische milnet."

"Do we know the location?" Lambert inquired.

The others followed his thought, muttering, "Preemptive strike. Good idea."

Renoir shook his head. "We only know the location within the realm of the networks, not the physical location."

General Lambert frowned thoughtfully and bowed his head in contemplation. Something was nagging him; some memory half-forgotten strained for attention. Something from a boring old computer tech class that reminded him of war. Strategy and tactics.

Renoir continued. "However, my scientists are of the opinion that the controlling computer on the network is not a Quirthian machine."

"Quirthian?" General Bosson, Chef du Personnel and not particularly computer sentient, asked in puzzled tones.

"The standard computer processes of the current age conform to architecture and logic laid down by Johann Vincent Quirthe," Renoir explained. "A non-Quirthian machine has never been made on this planet."

"Is it an alien?" Bosson wondered. One of the orderlies waiting against the walls sniggered.

Renoir frowned, shaking his head. "My people believe that it is of human origin."

. . . *never been made on* this *planet*. The nagging memory resolved itself. Lambert looked up suddenly, eyes gleaming. "It's a Bolo! They've got a Bolo!"

Pandemonium erupted. "There are none left!" "They never existed, just a legend!" "We're doomed! Doomed!"

General Cartier leaned forward to General Lambert, "Why would a Bolo be infiltrating our military networks?"

"They plan to destroy us, to feed us false intelligence," Renoir declared.

"The Bolo could ruin our supply system, jam up all ammunition and fuel movements, cripple us," General Villiers, Chef du Materiel, proclaimed.

"Sabotage our manpower allocations, place the wrong men in the wrong units!" General Bosson, Chef du Personnel, cried in alarm.

"But, General Renoir, you said it was attempting to gain access to our satellite network," Lambert said. "That means that you detected its intrusion."

Renoir shrugged. "The intrusion was most obvious. The Bolo may be a master war machine but it is clearly not able to handle the intricacies of our Quirthian computer architecture."

Lambert leaped out of his chair so vigorously that it toppled over behind him. His eyes gleamed expectantly as he spoke to General Cartier. "*Mon General*, this Bolo, can we not misdirect it, feed it false information? Control it?"

A smile worked its way up Renoir's lips to his eyes. "*Mon Dieu!* It is possible."

The room was filled with rows of computer displays over which intent technicians hunched, peering into the realm of data and working fanatically. The space could have been refurbished warehouse, clumsily partitioned into work areas. The room smelled just slightly of soiled sweat, a smell the air conditioning had failed to remove.

Several techies slept on cushions thrown on the floor in their cubicles, too tired to move to the cots which lined the wall.

General Renoir hovered at one end of the room, eyes puffy with fatigue. General Lambert lounged beside him, reading a technical specification with no deliberate speed. The center's manager, Yves Monchant, approached. Renoir stiffened, straightening the front of his uniform.

"Well?"

"We are ready."

"It took you long enough," Renoir muttered.

"Really Jean-Paul, I think your men should be congratulated," General Lambert chided him. "They have completed their task in less than forty-eight hours."

Renoir bit back a response. "At least the enemy appears not to have detected our efforts."

Monchant nodded. "There has been absolutely no indication that the Bolo has detected our work," he said. "All data flows and queries emanating from that site continue unabated."

"But now," Renoir said with a satisfied look in his eye, "the Bolo will be receiving information on non-existent troops and movements."

A technician rushed up to the center manager, a printout clutched in her hand. The manager huddled with the technician, muttered some encouragement and sent the technician away with a pat on her back. "Marie tells me that the Bolo continues its efforts to penetrate our satellite system."

Lambert frowned. "Why the satellite system?"

"Which part?" Renoir added.

The manager ran a hand wearily through his thinning

hair. "That is the odd part. The Bolo is apparently attempting to access data from several stellar sensors, ones not pointed at the planet at all."

"Maybe it's confused," Renoir suggested.

"Are you sure it hasn't noticed your interference?" Lambert asked.

The manager shrugged with Gallic eloquence. "I cannot say for certain but there are no direct indications."

Another technician rushed up the manager. "Sir, the enemy machine is attempting to access figures on our nuclear capability."

"That's more like it!" Renoir said.

"Reactors?" Lambert asked.

"No sir, nuclear warheads. Missiles in particular."

General Alain Lambert, Chef d'Attaque of the Grand Armée du Noufrance turned to the center's manager with grim determination. "Monsieur, you *must* destroy that Bolo."

General Renoir chewed his lip thoughtfully as he recreated Lambert's reasoning. "A single nuclear strike on any of our cities would probably be enough to destroy the ecology."

He glanced speculatively at the Colonel of Operations. "I have no intelligence to indicate that the enemy has any nuclear weapons facilities. Such things are difficult to hide."

"They have a Bolo, is it not a nuclear-powered weapon?" General Lambert replied. "If they ordered it to self-destruct in one of our cities, would the result not be the same?"

"True," Renoir agreed reluctantly. "But, Alain, why would it be concerned about whether we had nuclear missiles?"

"It alters the equation," Lambert replied. "If we possessed nuclear missiles then we could launch a counterstrike which would destroy Bayern."

Renoir turned to the manager. "We must convince the Bolo that we have several nuclear missiles."

"Oui, monsieur," said the manager, scurrying over towards his technicians.

Renoir turned to Lambert. "I must see if we have any intelligence regarding a change in the enemy's stance on the use of nuclear weaponry."

Lambert shook his head. "You may not find it, it may merely be the Bolo's best solution to the orders given it."

"What orders?"

Lambert shrugged. "What if they ordered that machine to subdue us as best it could?"

Renoir was horrified. "We must find a way to destroy that machine."

Lambert nodded. "Go, Jean-Paul, get your information. I can oversee operations here."

Relieved, General Renoir left. General Lambert found a chair and took possession of it. Some moments later the manager approached him, looking more relaxed.

"Good news, General," the manager reported. "We have fed the Bolo information that we have twenty thirty-megaton missiles armed and ready for immediate use."

"Did it make any response?"

The manager nodded. "Yes, most odd, it wanted to know the hyperbolic range of the missiles."

"Hyperbolic range?"

The manager shrugged. "If you like, I can get the expert over here but I understand that the Bolo wanted to know the range of the missile fired nearly straight up. It wasn't worried about re-entry points."

"It has laser-mounted anti-missile capabilities," Lambert explained.

"Really?" the manager was impressed. "Even after nearly three hundred years buried underground?"

"Perhaps," Lambert said. "What can you tell me about your efforts to disable the machine?"

"Well, we have found some Quirthian sequences result in a longer response time from the Von Neumann architecture," the manager said. "My top technician believes that these sequences cause the machine to experience a high error rate. He's convinced that the machine must be a multi-processor system utilizing a polling mechanism—"

A technician rushed up to the manager. "Sir, the Bolo has not responded in over two seconds!"

I have penetrated the enemy's computer network. The logic systems applied to their computers cause me an increased work load. I have been experiencing <DATA ERROR: PROCESSOR B> increased problems in de-multiplexing this form of data.

However, I have initiated a successful search for the location of the enemy's satellite control network and have learned about the enemy's missile capabilities.

I believe that I can arrange several of my subordinate neural networks to simulate a single Quirthian computational strand. My attempts to obtain concrete satellite data have not yet been successful. There is an 85% chance that with the pseudo-Quirthian strand I shall be able to obtain all the satellite data I require.

<DATA ERROR: PROCESSOR C>
<CHECKSUM ERROR: PROCESSOR B>
<NON-MASKABLE INTERRUPT - PROCESSOR B - PROCESSOR RESET>
<TRACKING SEQUENCER ALERT ERROR>

I am concerned that I may not be able to carry out my orders in a manner which would meet with the complete approval of my Commander. However, my analysis of the situation indicates only one course of action with a probability of success of 75%.

<CHECKSUM ERROR: PROCESSOR A>

<MPU ERROR: CIRCUIT INTEGRITY ALERT>
<SEQUENCER ERROR: SURVIVAL CENTER POWER CONDITIONING UNIT>
<WARNING: SURVIVAL CENTER POWER OVER-VOLTAGE>

My combat circuitry is failing at the predicted rate. My survival center circuitry is failing at a higher than predicted rate, but this is not cause for undue alarm as there is only a .07% chance that this unit will continue beyond the anticipated 146.7 hour total failure limit.

All that matters is the success of my mission.

<CHECKSUM ERROR: PROCESSOR D>
<CHECKSUM ERROR: PROCESSOR E>

The darkened staff room was illuminated only by the map projected on the far wall. The map was marked TOP SECRET. Colonel Rheinhardt aimed a laser pointer at the map. It had been barely fifty hours since he had been ordered to plan the assault. Several officers lining the walls slumped awkwardly and even the ever-energetic Major Krüger wilted in a chair. Rheinhardt felt none of it. His words were incisive, his mind clear.

"That blue line indicates the path assigned for our Bolo. Its mission will be simple. First it will penetrate to Nouparis and destroy their power center, Giramonde Gros Industrie, Aeromechanique Industrie, and the Armorie de la Troisième Provence.

"Then it will move north," he traced the course with his pointer, "here to the main depot of the Noufrench Armée, destroying their supply and replacement dumps as well as their high echelon repair facilities.

"Finally, it will engage the Fourth Armored Division, targeting its armored fighting vehicles and munitions." Colonel Rheinhardt flicked his pointer to another area. "That action will be timed to coincide with an attack on the division placed directly in front of the Fourth Armored Division. Our armored divisions will be placed for a breakthrough. The main thrust of the breakthrough will be south to the capital, Nouparis. A secondary thrust will place a large restraining force behind the enemy's northern forces.

"We may be able to force the surrender of those forces, but I believe it will not matter. With the capture of their capital, the piercing of their defenses and the destruction of their strategic industrial base, I do not believe they will be in a position to pursue a military solution." Rheinhardt flicked off his laser-pointer and signalled the orderly to turn on the lights. "Questions?"

"When do you plan to unleash this offensive?" General Marius asked.

"The timing of the plan is dictated by the state of the Bolo," Rheinhardt replied. "The offensive will start in two hours."

"What!" "Impossible!" "You're mad!" "We'll never manage!"

Rheinhardt rapped the table with his pointer. "Gentlemen! Please recall that the initial part of the offensive is being carried out solely by the Bolo," he told them. "It is not scheduled to engage the Fourth Division for another fifty-four hours."

"That's still too little time," General Marius bellowed, face flushed with anger.

"It is all the time we have," Rheinhardt replied. "The Bolo has indicated that it will suffer irreversible systems failure within the next one hundred and seventeen hours."

"General Marius," General Marcks said, "why can we not launch an offensive within the next three days? Our units are properly placed, are they not?"

"The units, yes," Marius agreed, "but the munitions—"

"The offensive will take no more than five days,"

Colonel Rheinhardt said. "I believe that all units are equipped for two days' worth of combat already?"

"That's true," Marius admitted unhappily. "However—"

"That gives you at least four days before the units will require reprovision, Marius," General Marcks interrupted. "Are you trying to tell me that we cannot do that?"

General Marius felt himself perspiring under the scrutiny of the General Staff. Finally, with a sigh, he said, "Yes, sir, we can do it."

"Excellent!" General Marcks scanned the other officers. "Are there any other objections?" The General Staff fidgeted nervously under his keen eye. "Very well," he said. "Colonel Rheinhardt, you are hereby authorized to engage in Operation Totalize."

Rheinhardt saluted, bringing his heels together in a loud click. "H-hour is set for twenty-two hundred hours," Rheinhardt informed the group. "I shall be in the Bolo. If communications are lost, my assistant, Major Krüger, will be able to carry out the operation."

General Marcks turned sharply to face the young colonel. "I think, that if communications are lost with the Bolo we will halt the operation until we regain contact."

Colonel Rheinhardt drew breath to protest, thought better of it, and nodded his agreement. "As you order, sir."

General Marcks rose, extending his hand to the colonel. "Good luck."

"Thank you, sir." Rheinhardt clicked his heels together again, turned smartly and left the room.

"Gentlemen," General Marcks said to the remaining officers, "I shall now inform the Astral. If you will excuse me."

Quirthian computational strand completed. Quirthian

computational strand programmed. Data acquisition. Satellite network programmed to examine sky coordinates right ascension 5 hours 22 minutes, declination 28° north. Program engaged. Data acquired. Data analysis complete. Enemy identified.

"Monsieur, the network!" an excited technician shouted at Monchant, the center's manager.

"What? What's happening?" General Lambert demanded as panic rippled through the computer center. He had been cat-napping in one of the unoccupied cots but at the shout had sat bolt upright. He glanced at his watch—it had been a little over two hours since the technician's first jubilant report.

Monchant turned back from the chaos long enough to say, "The Bolo has acquired Quirthian capabilities— I don't know how—it has taken control of the space satellites and is directing them—where, Jacques?"

The technician in question handed him a quick printout. The manager's brows furrowed as he scanned the printout in growing confusion.

"Well, where are our satellites being aimed?" Lambert demanded, fearful that the Bolo might have discovered some previously undisclosed offensive capabilities in the satellites.

"The Bolo has pointed the satellites to deep space," the manager answered.

A slow smile spread across Lambert's face. "Mad! It is mad! You've done it! You've destroyed it!"

"Bolo, have you received the battle plans?" Colonel Rheinhardt asked as he approached the large war machine. The massive doors to the aerostat hangar stood open to the cold twilight air.

"The plans have been received," the Bolo replied after a moment.

"And you understand your orders?"

"Yes, I am to destroy the enemy forces in the most optimal manner," the Bolo responded.

"Do you still require me to accompany you?"

"Yes, human supervision is required for the operations planned." This answer was accompanied by a metal-rending groan which set the security troops running towards the machine, weapons drawn. At the top of the Bolo a light appeared as a circular hatch, protected by five hundred millimeters of reactive armor, opened up to the outside world. "I have opened the observation compartment. I am purging the inert storage gas." Some moments later, the Bolo added, "Purging complete. You can climb aboard now. The rungs are on my port side."

"Very well." Rheinhardt circled to the port side, found the old rusty metal rungs and climbed them nimbly. He paused at the top to peer into the illuminated compartment. "It appears quite small."

"I believe that most occupants found it quite acceptable for the duration of any combat mission," the Bolo answered.

Rheinhardt pursed his lips. "Very well, who am I to argue with my distant ancestors?"

"You are Colonel Karl Rheinhardt of the Bayerische KriegsArmee," the Bolo replied.

Colonel Rheinhardt politely ignored this outburst of literal interpretation on the part of the Bolo, intent on descending into the compartment below him.

He wormed into the seat and noted with satisfaction that the cushion was still firm after three centuries of disuse. The compartment smelled of steel, dust, and, very faintly, of battles fought long ago.

"Please adjust the restraining straps and headrest," the Bolo said.

Colonel Rheinhardt eyed the five-point restraints dubiously but squirmed into them without complaint, realizing the sort of beating he could take when the Bolo entered combat. "Is this safe?"

"No commanders have reported problems with the system previously," the Bolo responded. "My sensors indicate that your left shoulder strap is not optimally tightened."

Rheinhardt raised a brow in surprise and pulled on the indicated strap dubiously. His expression changed as the strap tightened noticeably.

"Permission to activate the environmental protection system," the Bolo requested.

Rheinhardt hesitated a bare moment. "Permission granted."

Immediately he felt a push as the headrest moved against him. In front of him, cushioned bolsters moved in tight around his midriff and a support pressed on his shoulders, tightening and loosening as the ancient sensors adjusted for proper restraint. Something obscured his vision from above and he looked up just in time to see a Combat Vehicular Communications helmet descend upon him, covering his vision. He grunted in surprise.

"Combat visuals on-line," the Bolo informed him. The darkness of the CVC helmet was replaced by four screens of display data. Directly in front he saw a combat display, above which was a weapons status screen. Off to the left and right were two other displays just on the edge of his vision.

Rheinhardt felt a microphone delicately touch his lips and retract. "Bolo, do you hear me?"

"*Das Afrika Korps* receiving command communication loud and clear."

"Very well, you may start the operation."

"Closing supervision compartment hatch," the Bolo replied. The sound of the groaning metal as the thick hatch drew itself back into place sounded ominous to Rheinhardt's ears. A different groaning, more of a whining, overlay the final sounds of the hatch's locking mechanism which Rheinhardt identified as ancient armored tracks moving. "Ten percent forward speed engaged."

"How do I use your hull speaker?"

"Hull speaker connected," the Bolo replied as if obeying an order. "Speak normally."

"Thank you," Rheinhardt said to the Bolo. With a change of tone, he ordered, "Open the hangar doors."

"The hangar doors have been opened, proceeding on course," the Bolo reported. "Increasing speed."

Rheinhardt lurched in his seat as the Bolo sprang forward. "Give me an external view, please."

"External view on forward screen," the Bolo replied.

Rheinhardt gasped in surprise as a mottled landscape flashed into view in front of him. "Is this normal?"

There was a silence before the Bolo answered. "Apparently my normal vision monitors are nonfunctional. Would you accept infrared, ultraviolet or simulated normal light visuals?"

"The simulation, please." Rheinhardt's mottled view cleared, showing him the edge of the military compound. Startled guards stood out in the light, eyes wide but weapons ready as the Bolo bore down upon them.

"Slow down, please. Can you get me a communications link with the post commandant?"

"Affirmative."

"General Wiesen, speaking; who is this?"

"General, Colonel Rheinhardt. You were supposed to have the gate opened for the Bolo."

"It is open," Wiesen replied, somewhat annoyed.

"We are just in front of it and your guards are standing at port arms in front of the Bolo," Rheinhardt replied. "I admire their courage even while I question their intelligence."

"I'll sort it out immediately."

"Thank you, General." Shortly the guards moved aside and opened the gates. The Bolo moved through without any additional orders.

"One question, Colonel—" General Wiesen's voice was lost in a rush of static.

"Communications signal lost, shall I reconnect?" the Bolo asked.

"No," Rheinhardt replied, "that won't be necessary. Wiesen's a nosy old busybody. Just continue with the operation and inform me if we get any contact from the General Staff." A flashing red light in the left display distracted Rheinhardt.

"What's that?" Even before the Bolo could react, the colonel swore to himself and amended, "What's that red light flashing on my left display?"

"Switching left display to main display," the Bolo replied.

Rheinhardt blinked as the main display shrank and moved left while the left display grew and moved directly in front of him. The red light, grown larger with the change of display position, flashed, <CHECK-SUM ERROR: PROCESSOR D>.

"Checksum error?"

"Data provided to processor D did not agree with the checksum for the data," the Bolo explained. "Either the processor is suffering a recurring failure on some of the data address lines or the checksum address lines are faulty."

"Is this normal?"

"It is outside of standard operating parameters," the Bolo said. "Since reactivation, this combat unit has had numerous checksum errors occur on all processors."

"Can you work around them?"

"For the present," the Bolo replied. "However, within the next ninety-eight point four-three hours, the probability of critical failure is within operational parameters with command supervision."

" 'Command supervision'? What do you expect of me?"

"In the event of a failure of one or more of the subprocessors, this combat unit will require command input."

"I see," Rheinhardt said, "your computer systems work with a five-lobe voting system. The majority vote wins."

"That is essentially correct," the Bolo agreed. "There is a 99.98% probability that one or more processors will fail permanently before the completion of the assigned mission. In that event, I have arranged to receive your input as a supplement."

"What happens to me if your systems fail completely?"

"The most catastrophic failure for a command supervisor would be total annihilation of this unit," the Bolo said. "In that case there is a zero point zero one percent chance that the Command Supervisor would survive."

"I was thinking of something less . . . catastrophic," Rheinhardt said. "What if your systems fail completely?"

"In the event of a processor failure, the power systems will be crippled and the interlocks on your combat position will be released," the Bolo informed him. "You can then manually remove the headset. Directly above you will see a yellow-striped black handle. Pull it down to activate the explosive ejection system."

"Ejection system?"

"It is designed to eject you and the command chair you sit on safely in all circumstances barring complete fusion of the compartment hatch to the exterior hull."

"Hmm, I see," Rheinhardt said, with a slight loss of enthusiasm.

"There is one more safety feature for that instance,"

the Bolo continued, "but I doubt it would be much assistance to you."

"What is it?" Rheinhardt asked, glancing around the various displays.

"An emergency command frequency beacon," the Bolo responded. "It broadcasts a Mayday on all Bolo comm frequencies. Any Bolo receiving a broadcast must respond and render aid."

"Hm." Given the chance of a nearby Bolo, Rheinhardt was unimpressed.

"In combat it has proven that even a heavily damaged Bolo managed to retrieve a trapped Commander."

General of the KriegsArmee Friedrich Marcks hovered impatiently over the communications console in the headquarters command center. "Well?"

The harried communications officer looked up at him bleakly, rubbing his haggard face and wishing that his morning relief would come. "Still no luck, sir. We have been unable to raise the Bolo on all combat frequencies."

General Marius, standing behind his commander-in-chief, nervously muttered, "We've heard nothing since Wiesen last spoke to them."

Marcks turned to him, his unshaven face at odds with the intensity of his expression. "General Wiesen is certain that the Bolo went east?"

Marius nodded slowly. "Colonel Rheinhardt ordered him to open the gate himself."

General Marcks turned to General Sliecher, his head of Intelligence. "Have you got a fix on them yet?"

"No, sir, the Bolo leaves a surprisingly small trail behind it."

"Wiesen's men clocked it moving at over one-thirty," Marius added in amazement.

Major Krüger frowned sourly. "At that rate, it'll be in the mountains in six hours."

Marcks' face went white. He snapped his fingers at the Major. "What weapons do we have against the Bolo?"

"Sir, you cannot think that Colonel Rheinhardt would betray us!"

"No," the General replied sadly, "not at all. I am afraid that the Bolo has gone insane. We must destroy it. What weapons will do that job?"

"I know of none, sir," Major Krüger said after a long, painful pause.

"The first thing is to immobilize it," Marcks decided. "How can we do that?"

"Perhaps a tank trap," Major Krüger suggested.

"First we have to find it!" General Marius exclaimed.

"True," General Sliecher agreed.

"It's your job," Marius said accusingly.

Sliecher's eyes gleamed wickedly. "Indeed. General Marcks, perhaps my Noufrench counterpart would be of assistance?"

"Oh, I'm sure he'd love to help us destroy our Bolo!"

"All operatives assure me that this is a genuine request," General Jean-Paul Renoir, Chef d'Intelligence de l'Armée du Noufrance, told the general staff as he stood before them. He had traveled throughout the night from the satellite control station to headquarters but there was no hot coffee or croissants to greet him—only cold, tired faces.

"They want our bombers to destroy their nightmare," General Villiers, Chef du Material, said with outrage.

"I fear it is not just their nightmare, Jacques," General Cartier, Chef d'Armée, said, laying a calming hand on the rotund general's shoulder. "We have been aware of its existence for some time. The Bolo attempted to penetrate into our military network."

He paused while his generals absorbed this information. "Fortunately, we detected it and set up an elaborate ruse to misinform the machine. This effort was led by General Lambert who is still at the satellite control station, just north of Nouparis.

"The operation has only been in existence for some days now. We feel that it has proved successful." He paused, his lips drawn into a thin line. "Our success may well prove to be our undoing. It appears we have driven this thing mad."

General Renoir noted, "There is a chance that we can work this to our advantage. A combined operation, if successful, would strengthen ties between our two military establishments. If we help destroy this metal monster, our enemy will be honor-bound to deal with us peacefully."

"You are so mad for peace?" General Villiers mocked.

"Peace, particularly on our terms, is always preferable to war," the Chef d'Intelligence returned scathingly.

"I say let the Bolo wipe out our enemies for us!"

"And once it has done that, will it stop?" Renoir snapped in rejoinder. "No, better destroy it now when our combined air force has a chance than let it destroy us piecemeal."

General Cartier, who had listened to the whole exchange intently, made up his mind. "We shall help the Bayerische. We will make them pay for the ammunition, *n'est-ce pas?*"

General Villiers gave in reluctantly, "We have little enough ammunition as it is."

*   *   *

III

For to win one hundred victories in one hundred battles is not the acme of skill. To subdue the enemy without fighting is the acme of skill.

—Sun Tzu

"One must always study the enemy, Scratche," Jyncji Fleet Admiral Baron Rastle Speare said to his adjutant, Midshipman Jenkis Scratche.

"Study the enemy," Scratche repeated dutifully, as though committing the admiral's sage advice to memory. In fact, the young Jyncji officer had heard this speech so often that it already was committed to memory. But he knew that his chances of independent command and advancement depended upon staying in the Admiral's good graces.

"Yes," Speare repeated, "study the enemy. Understand their logic, learn from them."

"Learn from them," Scratche murmured dutifully. Use their tactics against them, the young Jyncji thought to himself. They were on the battle bridge, preparing to jump from the distant fringes of the human system to the lush, warm, desirable green planet fourth from the sun. A planet soon to be theirs.

Scratche could imagine the wealth of his very own Jyncji-formed lands. *Count Scratche, or Earl Scratche, what shall I be,* the Midshipman mused. The actinic glare of the harsh battle lights did not prevent him imagining the lush warming rays of an orange sun.

Scratche could count on his Admiral to be generous. And if he could not—he would find ways to ensure such generosity. In the meantime, he would keep his spines to himself, his snout firmly lowered, his claws sheathed, and his tone deferential. It was a difficult position for a Jyncji—not to be attacking with tooth and claw, nor yet to be huddled inside the defensive shield of sharp spine that lined his back. Scratche felt his spines tingling with fear, while his blood flowed hot with war-lust.

"Use their tactics against them," Speare said. The admiral's breath smelled just faintly of *fehral*.

Trust the old rodent to be blitzed *before an attack!* Scratche thought to himself. He filed the information away with the merest twitching of his snout. One day he might use it to prick the Admiral's pride. For the moment he would keep the information tight inside him, just as he kept his spines tightly furled against about his back.

"And just what are their tactics, Milord Admiral?" Captain Sir Creve Pierce, Knight of the Puissant Order of Spears, inquired. He approached the raised command chair from the side where he had been overseeing the navigation officer.

Milord Admiral eyed his Admiralty-appointed flag-officer with ill-disguised contempt. He hissed, "You know my orders, Captain, be sure you follow them."

Captain Pierce lowered his muzzle obeisantly, his black eyes glinting fiercely in the intense white light of the battle bridge. "I shall, milord, and you will have no quarrel with me," the Captain said. "I merely asked, as we have arrived at that point when our jump in-system is imminent."

"One of their most ancient sages, *Sir* Captain, said that the epitome of skill is not to fight but to let your enemy fight himself into surrender," the Admiral replied. He turned to his adjutant. "Fetch me the latest from our probe. They must be fighting by now."

Speare turned back to the captain, nostrils twitching as though smelling the blood of the kill. "Soon, captain, soon we will jump in and collect their surrender."

"I am much relieved to hear that, milord," the Captain replied obsequiously, "I feared that the

Admiralty might grow ill-disposed towards this venture after our long wait here at the edge of this solar system."

"Once the humans have been disposed of, it shall only be a matter of months before the planet is rightfully ours." Three hundred human years had passed since the first, abortive attempt by Speare's long-distant ancestor, Sheik William, to conquer the human world. The ignominy of that defeat had been carefully hidden among other Jyncji conquests. But the venture had cost Speare's line immeasurably in both prestige and wealth. Now he, Rastle of the lesser Speares, would avenge the dishonor that had left the spiny backs of Speares furled against their bodies in shame.

"Colonel," the Bolo's voice drew Colonel Rheinhardt back from his ruminations about the forthcoming operation, "I have managed to penetrate the Noufrench military network."

"How?" Rheinhardt examined the combat displays. "They haven't detected you, have they?"

"They believe so, however their software security systems are no match for my efforts." The Bolo continued. "I have determined that the Noufrench were not responsible for the near-destruction of the terraforming microbes three hundred years ago."

Rheinhardt frowned. "Well, I'm certain *we* didn't do it. I suspect their records were destroyed."

"Perhaps their military records," the Bolo allowed, "but not their population statistics and agricultural reports. Those show clearly a deliberate, widespread assault on both the terraforming microbes and the staple crops of all areas of human habitation. My combat analysis indicates that another force was responsible."

"Some mutation of the planet's original ecosystem?" Rheinhardt mused, more interested in when they would cross the border than ancient history. By his reckoning, it should be any moment now. They had been on the move for several hours already.

"Negative," the Bolo said. "The planet's ecosystem is not sufficiently advanced. Even if it were, the distribution of the failure was from the center outward rather than from the outside of the terraformed area inward. That indicates a deliberate attempt."

"This is interesting," the Colonel said. "Relay a copy of your data and findings to our G-2, General Sliecher, please."

"There will not be time for that."

Rheinhardt narrowed his eyes. "Why not? We should be able to do it as soon as you begin your attacks. The 'frenchies will know where you are then, certainly, so radio silence will not be an issue."

"I have calculated that the force responsible for the original destructive microbial infestation and outbreak of hostilities between Noufrance and Bayern has planned another attack," the Bolo announced.

"What? That's—" A rippling eruption of high explosives drowned out Colonel Rheinhardt's words.

"A direct hit! Excellent!" General Marius exclaimed jubilantly. They were still in the combat center but had moved from the communications post to the Battle Room. A large vidscreen relayed the sights and sounds of the devastation that ten tonnes of explosives had produced. Idly he glanced back at the tray containing the half-eaten sandwiches and coffee cups that had been lunch and wondered if a celebratory snack was in order.

"It's still moving," Major Krüger said, voice half-dejected, half-amazed.

"It won't for long," General Sliecher declared, "our bombers are making their pass now."

General Marcks paid no attention to their conversation. Instead, he directed himself to a vid-link.

"General Cartier, it looks as though I shall have to ask, on behalf of the Astral, that your planes re-arm and return for another assault."

The Chef d'Armee du Noufrance nodded stoically. Figures scurried in the background behind him, one handed him a report. He glanced at it briefly, scowled in disgust and returned his gaze to the vid-link. "General Marcks, I must agree with you. *L'Empereur*—our Emperor—has authorized me to comply with any demands your government might reasonably make to aid in neutralizing this deranged implement of war."

General Marcks kept his face impassive but his eyes flashed at the unspoken rebuke delivered by the Noufrench supreme officer. "We all, General, as professionals, must remain constantly aware of the dangers of sophisticated weapons of destruction."

"*Oui.*"

"What was that?" Rheinhardt shouted, desperately searching the multiple displays in his combat visor. He could not hear himself, the explosions outside had been so loud. The air smelled of burnt wiring and hot metal. The Bolo heaved, jerked a little and continued on. "Are you damaged?"

"I have sustained no major loss of combat ability," the Bolo reported. "I am tracking a westward flight of approximately forty jet-propelled aerial vehicles."

"Bombers? Shoot them down!"

"Negative," the Bolo said. "They will be required for future operations."

"They are *enemy* bombers!" Rheinhardt shouted, slamming a fist against his cushioned restraints in futile emphasis.

"No," the Bolo responded, "they are Noufrench bombers." Rheinhardt's main display changed to a relief map, displaying two flights of aircraft, one receding westward, one approaching from the east.

"Bayerische bombers approaching as predicted," the Bolo noted calmly.

"Shoot down the bloody 'french!" Rheinhardt yelled. "That's a direct order!"

"That contravenes your original order," the Bolo replied.

Rheinhardt was outraged. "My order was to destroy the enemy."

"Nearly correct," the Bolo agreed. "Your orders were to destroy the enemy in an optimal manner. The Noufrench are not the most dangerous enemy, therefore destroying them at this time is non-optimal. I compute that I shall not remain combat effective upon completion of the primary mission. However, my calculations indicate that with the destruction of the enemy, enmity between Noufrance and Bayern will cease, at least as regards further military actions.

"Bombers commencing their run now," the Bolo called. All further reports were lost as a long, loud pounding filled the air. Rheinhardt's body throbbed in the rolling concussions which battered the Bolo's hull. He let out a long scream of sheer terror but never heard it. The earth shook, rolled, steadied.

Several moments later, the Bolo reported, "The bombers have completed their run and are returning to base. Next assault is in—in—"

Rheinhardt let out a gasp as the Bolo was thrown into the air and fell back to the ground with its metal hull audibly groaning as it was twisted in the blasts. The pounding continued, the hull armor shrieked at the pressures exerted on it. Rheinhardt felt a sharp pressure as his left eardrum burst and a warm trickle as blood rolled out his ear and down his collar.

Screens flickered and shrank in Rheinhardt's CVC helmet. For a moment, everything was black. Then the screens flickered again, the main one dodged left and was replaced by a sea of red critical failure lights.

"Bolo?" Rheinhardt called. Nothing. He tried again, "*Das Afrika Korps*, report."

"Beautiful! Beautiful!" General Marius crowed, nearly dancing with joy in front of the vid-link display of the massive bombing run. Flames flickered in the depths of the explosions, barely visible amongst the huge clouds of smoke that snaked upwards from the ground.

"It's not moving," Major Krüger observed. "We stopped it."

Static crackled in his earphones. A hiss replaced it. "*Das Afrika Korps* reports. Milnet data-link hardware destroyed as anticipated. Minor damage to hull, 20% of reactive armor inoperative but no critical areas exposed. Minor damage to track, increasing cumulative damage from 49% to 51% of combat limit. Additional scoring on external optics, cumulative damage at 37% of combat limit. Degradation and damage to 5% of total on-line data storage devices, operational volatile memory at 57% of total, 3% of volatile memory free.

"Current position forty kilometers from coastal insertion point, next attack anticipated in ten minutes."

"Coastal insertion point?" Rheinhardt queried. His momentary surprise at his sore throat was relieved by the realization that he had gone deaf in one ear and was shouting to compensate. Somewhere in the hull metal had melted, he could smell it.

"The anticipated point from the land into the sea. At this point air attacks should cease and there is a 92.3% chance that the enemy will conclude that this unit has ceased to have combat effectiveness."

Colonel Rheinhardt sat silently as he digested this information. He stretched as best he could in the combat restraints, collecting his thoughts and calming his nerves. "Those were our bombers in that last attack?"

"Yes. Approximately fifteen metric tonnes mix of high explosives, armor-piercing kinetic projectiles and some small number of armor ablatives," the Bolo said. "As calculated, your Bayerische command has concluded that this unit has gone rogue and must be destroyed."

Illumination dawned on the colonel. "We went out the wrong gate! You lied to me!"

"No," the Bolo replied.

"Speak up!" Rheinhardt shouted irritably.

"The gate was the correct gate to use for optimal destruction of the enemy," the Bolo said. Apologetically it added, "I regret that my smart armor was nonfunctional or I would have spared your ears the worst of the blasts."

"It was *not* the gate you were supposed to use," Rheinhardt said, ignoring the feeble apology.

"I am programmed to provide independent optimization of all military operations if given such latitude," the Bolo said.

"And my 'optimal' stipulation gave you all that latitude?" Colonel Rheinhardt surmised. "Then listen carefully, Bolo *Das Afrika Korps*, your Commander orders you to implement Operation Totalize."

"New orders understood and accepted," the Bolo responded. "Please provide details of Operation Totalize."

Colonel Rheinhardt's eyes grew wide. "You were issued the details of Operation Totalize via the Milnet data-link."

"A military data plan was received over the Milnet data-link," the Bolo agreed, "however it was stored in an area of memory that has become damaged in the past two bombings."

Rheinhardt absorbed that incredulously. "You put the damned data in unshielded memory!"

"That is quite possible," the Bolo agreed. "It would

seem to be a logical outcome of your original orders that I ensure you would not be disposed towards countermanding them."

"Well I *am*—" Rheinhardt broke off, perplexed. "Why would you need my approval?"

"As predicted, one of my processors—Processor B— has failed," the Bolo replied. "You can now order this operation curtailed. I calculate that, unless this operation succeeds, there is a 98.9% chance that all human life on this planet will be terminated within eighteen months."

Rheinhardt frowned. "I need evidence of this claim."

"Center screen." the Bolo said. The center screen changed images, displaying a map of the local solar system. "The red blips are targets identified as moving under intelligent control. Preliminary data indicate that they do not conform to any known human space vehicle."

"Your data is three centuries old," Rheinhardt pointed out.

"True, and incomplete owing to data loss," the Bolo admitted. "However, the vehicles do not conform to any extrapolation of previously known vehicles."

"Science moves in leaps, Bolo." Rheinhardt reminded it. "You were totally unaware of Quirthian logic."

"I have corrected that and am now employing a Quirthian analogue circuit," the Bolo said. "Even with its abilities, I predict that these ships have less than a .03% chance of human origin."

Rheinhardt's brows rose respectfully. "No one has been able to manufacture a Quirthian strand utilizing Von Neumann architecture."

"It was not difficult," the Bolo replied. "If you look at the tracks of the vehicles, you will note that a logical projection of their current trajectories will put them into attack position over the planet in some eighteen point five-four hours."

"If you do not know their origin, how can you predict their intentions?"

"If you note the bright pink dot on your screen, near the larger moon, you will see that I have identified it as an intelligence gathering device," the Bolo answered. "Since I have penetrated the Noufrench satellite control, I have been monitoring several attempts by that device to cause malfunctions in the satellites, thus disabling our only deep space surveillance systems."

"They could be trying to communicate," Rheinhardt objected.

"Negative. Communications require power levels orders of magnitude below those employed by that device. Its intent is clearly harmful.

"That information, in conjunction with my earlier observations about the assault on your planet's ecosystem three centuries ago lead me to a 98% certainty that we are facing a renewed attack by the same force which failed in its previous efforts to eradicate human life from this planet."

"Why don't they merely repeat the original assault?" Rheinhardt asked. "Goodness knows, it was successful enough."

"They will. However, the force assembled is too large for merely a xeno-forming infestation. They must realize that the terraforming microbes which survived the initial assault developed an increased immunity to similar assaults," the Bolo said. "Besides, the enemy is being offered an unique opportunity to economize in its use of force."

"What?"

"This war," the Bolo replied. "Bomber assault wave converging as anticipated. Next attack in ten . . . nine . . ."

"Amazing!" General Marcks exclaimed as he viewed the aerial videos of the third bombing run.

"It is still functional," he told General Cartier. "The Bolo has crawled out of the crater and is moving forward."

"It is heading for the sea, General," Major Krüger added, "it will enter near the Krazneutz ravine."

"Hmm, we shall make sure that it does not reach it."

"Ninety-eight percent of the bombs were direct hits!" General Sliecher said in a mixture of pride and amazement.

"General Marcks, perhaps I should have my force re-armed for another strike?" General Cartier suggested.

General Marcks cast a glance at Major Krüger who could only shrug in response.

"Yes, that might be wise," the commander of the Bayerische KriegsArmee replied.

Rheinhardt's good ear was numb from the repeated bombings. He fought back nausea as his inner ear attempted to recover from the repeated concussions. His breath came in gasps, with difficulty. The air was hot. With great effort he heard himself say reasonably, "Bolo, we have nothing to stop a bacteriological assault from aliens."

"That is not true," the Bolo replied. "It has been my main concern."

"You have a solution?"

"Yes," the Bolo replied. "A beam of coherent light set to a suitable wavelength could force the bacteriant to dissociate."

"Could you say that in plain German, please?"

"I shall fire my main gun along the flight path of their bacterial assault ship."

"And get the ship, too, or they'll just come around for another attack."

"That is my intention."

"What is to prevent them from destroying you beforehand?" Rheinhardt asked. "You are clearly the greatest threat."

"That is why I shall appear to have been destroyed before they make their assault," the Bolo answered. Rheinhardt's screens switched to an aerial map as the Bolo said, "The next Bayerische assault group approaches."

"Wait, Bolo! You're heading for the Krazneutz ravine! That's a drop of a thousand meters!"

"I know," the Bolo replied. "Please ensure that your combat restraints are securely fastened."

"They're tight!" Rheinhardt affirmed pulling on them earnestly. "Do you honestly expect us to survive that fall?"

"Yes," the Bolo replied simply. "However, there is a forty percent chance that I shall lose one or more of my voting processors."

"What can I do?"

"First, approve the current operation as detailed to you by me," the Bolo replied.

"Show me that star map again." The red dots of the enemy ships were closer, their orbits traced in fine fiery lines. Rheinhardt let out a long sigh. "Okay, your operation is approved."

"Second, agree to act as tie-breaker if required."

"Tie breaker?"

"I have five voting processors," the Bolo explained, "in the event that I lose one or three, I shall require your vote on certain operations."

"What if you lose four?"

"Then I shall initiate emergency shut down procedures," the Bolo replied. "However, the probability is very low."

"All right," Rheinhardt agreed. "Anything else?"

"Third, consider your actions once this unit has been destroyed."

"Destroyed? When—" Colonel Rheinhardt's words were drowned out by the sound of exploding bombs.

"A message from Intelligence, milord," Midshipman Jenkis Scratche said, handing over the message pouch.

Admiral Lord Baron Rastle Speare received the pouch, opened it and scanned its contents.

"A Bolo!" The words hissed from his muzzle in anger. "They attacked it! It has fallen into the sea. Our sensors can no longer detect it. The humans are convinced that it has been destroyed."

"A Bolo," Captain Pierce growled. "They destroyed a Bolo, milord. Our fleet would suffer grievously against such a force."

"Nonsense, Pierce!" the Admiral snarled in response. "Do you believe for an instant that they did not pay dearly for such a victory? Most of their equipment must be damaged, their forces demoralized. It must be a bitter victory." The Admiral bared his teeth in a savage smile. "Now is the time to strike! Send the order: jump in-system. Launch the assault!"

A deep-throated growl from the dozen voices on the battle bridge filled the air with the sense of impending victory.

"General Cartier, it appears we will not be needing your aircraft after all," General Marcks said after he recovered from the spectacular eruption relayed on the vid-link before him. Krazneutz ravine, a drop of five hundred meters to the sea, no longer existed. In its place, as the billowing dust clouds slowly revealed, was a gently sloping hill leading into the sea. Of the Bolo, target of the incredible force which had levelled a hilltop and filled a ravine, there was no sign at all.

"Thermal imaging is still obscured by the dust, General," General Sliecher reported. "However, I cannot believe that the Bolo could have survived both the fall and the bombardment." He shivered with the memory. "*Nothing* could have survived that bombardment."

General Marcks paid him no mind. He was staring at the vid-link which connected his headquarters to those of his counterpart, General Cartier. The screen crackled with static. "Have the bombers turned back?"

"Full alert! Full alert, you heard me!" General Cartier shouted over the uproar in the combat room. "Get all units on full alert immediately! Target those bombers for the Bayerische High Command!"

"But, General, we don't *know* they're going to attack!" General Renoir protested for the third time.

"Then why haven't they responded to us?" General Cartier demanded. He turned to an orderly. "Get me General Lambert at the satellite control center, immediately."

"They may be having communications difficulties," Renoir protested feebly.

General Cartier turned to look squarely at his Chef d'Intelligence. "Renoir, why do they suddenly have difficulties now that they no longer need our planes?"

"Sir, we used over forty percent of our combat stock of aerial munitions against the Bolo," General Villiers noted anxiously.

"Wonderful! We waste our ammunition on their problem and they attack us!"

An orderly handed a note to General Renoir. The aging general read it carefully and paled. "*Mon Général*, it grieves me to inform you that we are now receiving reports that Bayerische KriegsArmee units are massing in their assembly areas."

General Cartier gently took the note from the trembling hands of his intelligence officer.

An orderly called, "General Cartier, I have reached General Lambert. He is on screen two."

Chef d'Armée General Cartier turned to the second

large vid-link, ready to issue orders but Lambert burst out, "General, we are under attack!"

"Colonel, please respond," a funny voice tittered in Rheinhardt's ears. He was sweaty and felt funny. No, he felt awful.

"Colonel Rheinhardt." The voice was high-pitched and chittery, like a normal voice replayed at high speed. "Please respond."

"Umm," Karl croaked. His voice tittered in his ears, just like the other. He opened his eyes, or tried to— his left eyelid refused to budge. "Where am I?"

"You are in the supervisory compartment inside Bolo Mark XVI Model C, *Das Afrika Korps*."

"Who the hell are you?" Rheinhardt barked. He rubbed his left eyelid. His hand came away bloody but the eye opened. He sniffed the air—it was cooler, easier to breathe but something was odd about it.

"Bolo *Das Afrika Korps*."

"No you're not. The Bolo has a different voice."

"Your chamber has been filled with a helium-oxygen mixture to accommodate the current operating conditions," the Bolo said.

"Has it?" Rheinhardt asked, his senses returning. "And what are those?"

"We are currently at a depth of two thousand meters, maneuvering just off the continental shelf," the Bolo replied.

Rheinhardt came fully awake. "I did not realize that you could operate at this depth."

"The pressures on my hull are insignificant compared with those normally sustained in combat," the Bolo said, "I could descend another seven thousand meters without difficulty. However, that is not required for the current mission."

"What happened?"

"As predicted, the last assault wave threw us out

into the sea while providing sufficient coverage to enable this vehicle to descend beneath normal surveillance levels."

"They think they destroyed you, then," Rheinhardt concluded.

"There is a ninety-seven point nine percent chance, yes," the Bolo agreed. "Jamming began some thirty seconds after the final videos of the bombing run were returned to the two command centers."

"Jamming?"

"Yes," the Bolo said. "I initiated a wide frequency combat jamming utilizing the communications satellites."

"But—but—they'll be confused. The 'frenchies will think we did it deliberately and our command will think they did it! You'll start a war."

"There is a ninety-four point three percent chance that both sides will deploy their forces for immediate hostilities," the Bolo agreed. "It seemed the most logical way to ensure that all human forces were ready for the upcoming combat. I perceive from my conversations with you that attempting to convince the combined staffs of this threat would have been a futile endeavor."

"And the aliens?"

"They will have observed the assault on this combat unit, will observe the warlike preparations between the two factions and commence their assault as predicted," the Bolo replied almost smugly. "I calculate that their assault forces will be deployed well before this combat unit again becomes detectable. At that time it should be possible to neutralize their bacteriological assault and their ground offensive simultaneously."

"Why wouldn't they launch their bacteriological assault first and simply haul off and wait for everyone to die?"

"First, because they have been active in this solar system for several months and must rapidly be approaching the point where their continued presence becomes uneconomical. Second, the last time they launched a strictly bacteriological assault they failed to destroy the human settlement. Third, because they have jumped in-system and assumed a combat formation in orbit, concentrated over the population centers of this planet."

"Hmm." Colonel Rheinhardt received the Bolo's rundown with pursed lips. He was distracted by blood oozing down from a cut above his left eye. "Do you have a first aid kit, I seem to have sustained some damage."

"The first aid kit is located above your head on the right," the Bolo replied. "Although I do not see why you would need it, I estimate that you are 51.2% effective, more than sufficient to fill the role of auxiliary processor."

Rheinhardt made a noise that came out as a cross between a groan and the growl he had meant.

"I am removing your CVC helmet and releasing your forward restraints. You should have little difficulty in accessing the kit."

"While I'm increasing my effectiveness, why don't you outline your plan of operations to this auxiliary processor?"

"Up to my demise or after?"

"Your demise?" Rheinhardt frowned. "I thought you had planned merely to *mislead* the enemy into believing your demise."

"True," the Bolo agreed. "However, upon my re-appearance, I shall become the priority target for the enemy. They shall concentrate all fire on me, enabling you to implement your successful counter-attack."

"You plan to drop me off just before their attack

and draw their fire to give the combined armies time to concentrate against the aliens, is that it?"

"With the exception that I plan to intercept their bacteriant, yes," the Bolo agreed. "Their assault on me should allow you to determine their level of ability and the tactics they employ. That information is required to produce a successful counter."

Rheinhardt reflected upon that. "It would seem to me that it would be better to allow the enemy to start its assault on the combined armies, determine their tactics, and ensure that they possess no weapons beyond the capabilities of our combined armies—something which I find hard to accept."

"They have five ships in their fleet," the Bolo said. "Judging by satellite data and their trajectories, and extrapolating from the enemy's previous assaults and intent of occupying this planet, I would place the individual alien enemy at between point five and two meters height." Rheinhardt raised a brow skeptically but the Bolo either failed to notice or paid the expression no heed.

"Additionally I calculate that they are oxygen breathers who find this atmosphere and gravity acceptable with only minor alterations. Given those parameters, their attack fleet could contain no more than ten thousand ground troops, probably less."

"Small force," Rheinhardt said. "What about nuclears?"

"There are no signs of aggregate radioactive sources," the Bolo replied. "I conclude from that and their projected war aims that they do not possess nuclear weapons, nor would the use of such weapons be to their advantage."

"We're concentrated in a small area, why not?"

"Because the enemy has intercepted the data manufactured by the Noufrench. That data indicates an arsenal sufficient to render this planet untenable."

"MAD," Rheinhardt muttered to himself.

"You are referring to the acronym for Mutual Assured Destruction of mid-twentieth century Earth. The strategic nuclear situation does bear marked similarities."

"So they won't use nuclear weapons. What other weapons could they possess?"

"That question is not pertinent," the Bolo responded. "The pertinent question is which weapons will they use?"

"Same thing."

"Sloppy thinking, Colonel," the Bolo said. "The classes of weapons of utility in the upcoming conflict are kinetic kill weapons, coherent energy weapons and xeno-forming bacteriants."

"You're saying that their weaponry will match ours?"

"The classes of weaponry will match," the Bolo corrected, "but the capabilities are indeterminate at this stage."

Rheinhardt pursed his lips thoughtfully. "If your assumptions are correct, they are planning to occupy this planet. That means they'll have colony equipment in addition to combat gear."

"Obviously."

Rheinhardt heard condescension in the Bolo's tone. He cast a measuring glance at the spot he regarded as the Bolo's brain. "That limitation will affect how long they can afford to engage us in combat."

"You are moving towards a conclusion," the Bolo observed. "I must ask you to move quickly as time is in short supply."

"For how long can they engage us?"

The Bolo pondered the question for a long time. "It is difficult to say with any accuracy"—a series of screens full of data and graphs scrolled rapidly before Rheinhardt's eyes—"however, the normal distribution would indicate that the enemy has combat supplies for somewhere between three hours and three weeks, given standard engagement tactics."

"And how long—"

"A median estimate is that it will take the enemy less than five hours to destroy all Noufrench and Bayerische armed forces," the Bolo said, answering Rheinhardt's half-asked question.

Rheinhardt swore.

"Your invective confirms my projections," the Bolo observed. "Without some extraordinary occurrence, there is little likelihood that your combined forces will withstand the enemy assault."

"Gott im Himmel, where did they come from?" Leutnant Otto, right wingman of the IXth Bayerische Flug Grüppe shouted over his radio. The sky had been clear horizon to horizon only seconds ago.

"And where are they going?" Capitan Freiherr, his wing leader wanted to know as he kicked in his afterburner to thrust after the rapidly diminishing craft.

The two men were half of IX Flug Gruppe.

"I've been acquired! They've got a lock! I'm—" the wingman's exclamation broke off just as a brilliant burst of light erupted behind his wing leader. The wing leader broke right, diving deeply, pushing his plane in a torturous outside loop.

"They got my wing man!" the Captain radioed back to base as he levelled out of the loop and peeled off sharply to the left. "I've taken evasive action—they're on my tail! Must be five or more! How could they—"

When the first reports came in, General Marcks rounded sharply on Sliecher. "Where the hell did they get *that?*"

The elderly Intelligence officer was at a stuttering loss to explain the sudden appearance of the new high-speed aircraft. Face white with dread, he grimly reviewed the stream of incoming battle reports.

"They've knocked out most of two wings already, sir," an aide reported. The room was full of be-medalled orderlies and aides scurrying about with an air of competence overlaying an odor of fear. Something had gone wrong, no one needed to actually *see* the reports to know that much.

"Survivors report they escaped by diving near friendly anti-aircraft batteries," another aide added, handing a fresh report to General Sliecher.

"How many?" General Marcks demanded, holding out his hand irritably for the report.

"Three so far, sir," the aide said, passing the report over with an apologetic look towards his superior.

"Out of twenty," Marcks muttered to himself. He turned to Major Krüger. "Krüger, have they started their ground offensive yet?"

Major Krüger looked up from his position over the terrain computers. "No, sir," he replied with a shake of his head, "their forces are holding steady." He frowned. "There's an awful lot of traffic flowing, General Sliecher's boys are convinced we'll crack their battle codes soon."

"Just in time to surrender," an indiscreet orderly murmured too near his commander. General Marcks raised his head and silenced him with a glower. The General of the Bayerische KriegsArmee could not hold the look for long.

"Try to raise the 'french command again," he ordered the tactless orderly. "See what terms they are proposing." He rubbed a hand across his face wearily.

"*Herr General*, the enemy is still jamming our communications," a comm tech announced despondently.

"General, it is hopeless," General Lambert advised his superior over the vid-link. He was trapped at the satellite communications center, hastily turned into a makeshift operations center. His eyes were bleary, his face unshaven. "Whatever they've got, it's better than our fighters."

"How come we never found out about these?" General Cartier demanded of General Renoir, his Intelligence officer. They were gathered in the mobile command center that formed the brains of the Armée du Noufrance. The command center was camouflaged with newly cut foliage and smelled of uprooted forest. But Cartier had no spare thought for the devastated ecology.

General Renoir shook his head, "I cannot believe they developed these in secret. Perhaps their Bolo was a ruse to distract us but my men were very thorough—"

General Cartier cut him off with a dismissive wave of his hand. "It does not matter now," he said. "Can we fight them?"

"We have lost half of our attack fighters already, sir," an aide reported. "Those who survived did so by diving towards our AA and letting the ground-based troops get the attackers."

"I want one for analysis!" General Renoir barked.

The aide nodded. "I have already seen to it, General."

General Cartier had paid no attention to the interplay going on around him. Instead he lifted a brow meaningfully at the vid-link and his Operations officer. Lambert interpreted the gesture correctly and shook his head despondently. "Gentlemen, we must contact the Bayerische for their peace terms," his announcement brought silence upon the gathering. "I shall inform the Emperor."

"We have destroyed over forty percent of their air craft!" Scratche growled triumphantly to his admiral.

"D'ya hear that, Pierce? Forty percent already!" the Admiral barked exultantly to his Flag Captain.

Captain Sir Creve Pierce looked up from his battle console and managed an acknowledging nod. "Most credible, milord."

Admiral Baron Rastle Speare glanced sharply at his Admiralty-appointed Captain, wondering vaguely whether the Captain had tendered him insult, and decided to ignore it in favor of his good fortune. The Captain, Scratche noted to himself, could be dealt with later.

Pierce turned to the Midshipman of the watch. "Is the second wave prepared?"

"It is, Captain," the young midshipman replied. His eyes did not meet the Captain's.

Pierce growled deep in his throat, "And?"

"There is some concern about casualties among the first wave and—"

"What, are they not Jyncji, did they not die honorably?" Speare rasped.

"Indeed, milord," Pierce agreed. "But our group sent to destroy their communications satellites are overdue and have not reported. If they are counted as lost—"

"Our probes mentioned no problems with the comsats."

"They were too close to the planet itself to get good surveillance, milord."

"Bah! Someone forget to call back in the heat of victory, so? Shall we let that spoil ours?"

"But if it were not so, milord—"

"Send the second wave!" Admiral Speare roared. "Send them, now, Pierce!"

"Aye aye, milord," Pierce responded. He turned to the midshipman, "Note in the log, if you would, that in the twenty-second moment of the engagement, milord Admiral has ordered the second wave to the assault."

"Aye, sir," the midshipman responded hesitantly. He was puzzled—his Captain had specifically instructed him on a very routine affair. "The second wave is engaged."

"Thirty moments to bacterial seeding," the Special Weapons Officer added.

"The *Barb* is on orbit?" Speare growled.

"Aye, Admiral," the Special Weapons Officer responded. "Coming up on the terminator in ten moments."

"Terminator?" Speare muttered to himself.

"I think he means the horizon, Admiral," Scratche elucidated.

"I know that, damn ye!" Milord responded with rightful irritation and not a little pleasure at having drawn blood on his small ploy. The midshipman started, bristles flaring but quickly brought himself under control.

"I beg your pardon, milord," Scratche replied with a sigh, "I meant that as a hypothesis—was I right?"

"Captain, see to it that this Mid-*ship*-man of mine gets remedial drill in orbital nomenclature," the Admiral barked, basking in the additional pleasure of having absorbed the Captain into his small game.

"I shall instruct your Flag Lieutenant, milord," Pierce responded unflappably, "clearly he has been remiss."

Speare hid a snarl with a dismissive wave of his hat. Drat the prickly old beast, he swore to himself.

A lieutenant with a worried look passed a dispatch to the Captain. Pierce read it hastily. "Milord, it grieves me to report that our first wave casualties have reached thirty-five percent. Shall we call off the attack?"

"Call off the attack?" Speare barked. "Never!" His yell turned the heads of all on the bridge. "We still have a strike force and the second wave is committed. We shall succeed."

Pierce looked worried. "Milord, our orders were to withdraw if—"

"I know the orders, Captain!" Speare returned hotly, bristling visibly. "My Lords of the Admiralty sent *me* to carry them out! The attack continues."

"Aye, milord," Pierce responded steadily. He glanced at the dispatch officer, "Keep milord abreast of further developments, Spyke."

Lieutenant Spyke glanced once at his Captain, once at his Admiral, and nodded deeply. "I shall be expedient in my duties, milord."

"Bah!" Speare muttered. "We need not the duties of such carrion." He scratched a claw against his chair. "Victory! I can smell it."

Safe under the sea, the Bolo informed Rheinhardt, "The aliens have committed their second wave. Telemetry indicates larger, slower vessels—probably heavy assault craft or bombers."

"Bombers." Rheinhardt declared. "They've knocked out our fighters, now they'll go for command and control centers. When will they launch their bacteriant?"

"I believe that they must be reasonably sure that they have succeeded in their mission before that."

"That'll be too late! Why not destroy it in orbit?"

"I am not sure I can identify it," the Bolo replied. "There are five ships which could be the bacteriological vessel, indeed all five might be so equipped."

"And you can't destroy five, I take it," Rheinhardt concluded.

"The probabilities are low that I shall manage more than one exo-atmospheric shot."

"Dispersion, attenuation and atmospheric ionization," Rheinhardt said, listing the factors that reduce a coherent beam's effectiveness.

"Precisely." The Bolo paused, then added, "The

enemy has engaged both headquarters units. They are achieving remarkable results."

"Damn!" Rheinhardt swore, his self-control breaking. "Get us ashore as quick as you can! We *must* get that bacteriant."

"The odds are against a satisfactory final resolution, even if I were successful in identifying the bacteriological ship," the Bolo admitted. "Their forces are superior to the combined human forces." A pause. "We will be ashore in two minutes." A map display centered in Rheinhardt's view, tracing their course from sea to shore to metropolis.

"Nouparis." Rheinhardt muttered to himself. "Plot a direct route to the Noufrench HQ."

"That would be inadvisable," the Bolo responded, "as it would telegraph to the enemy both our location and the location of the Noufrench HQ. Besides, telemetry indicates that the Noufrench HQ is only 40% functional. Command and control of Noufrench forces has been lost."

The color drained out of Colonel Rheinhardt's face. "I see," he said softly, mourning the passage of honorable adversaries. "However, I still want you to plot a course for the HQ site. We should be able to establish communications with them."

"My analysis indicates a 80% chance that both human forces have now realized their mistake and are about to forge a common alliance against the alien threat," the Bolo informed him. "I conjecture that they shall start coordinated actions within the hour."

"No! They must not do that!"

"We have lost contact with HQ," Ballard, the comm tech, informed General Lambert. "I have contact from Deuxième Corps, from III Brigade of XX Armored, from the Second Tactical Air Wing and from Troisième Corps' Artillery. They are all requesting orders."

"Very well, assemble a staff—" Lambert broke off, his military training faltering in the light of reality. Surrounding him were worried computer programmers, software engineers and technicians. No warriors. They would do. He had already used them as an ad hoc staff. Before the odds got so bad. He fought down a grim look, working his face into an untroubled expression. In less than two hours the proud Armée du Noufrance had been reduced to this. The air force had been more than decimated, artillery had been obliterated, supply scattered to the winds. Lambert took a deep, calming sigh. The air was stale with worry and fear. A beaten smell.

"Assemble a staff of personnel," he began again. He held up a hand and ticked off a finger for each section, "We need an intelligence section which will collect our current intelligence; a personnel section to coordinate replacements; a supply section to obtain a picture of our current supply situation and attempt to re-establish supply lines; I will establish the operations section."

He pointed a finger at one of the technicians he had come to rely on. "Gasconde, I want you to establish our communications capabilities. I need to know every way we can communicate with any of our units or those of the enemy's."

The technician nodded and hurried off. Lambert took in the expectant faces surrounding him and resumed the mantel of a military leader. He smiled.

"Very well, gentlemen, we have suffered a setback but we are 'french! We shall persevere, *n'est-ce pas?*" He turned to the man he had appointed for Intelligence, "And DuPont, as soon as you can, try to get some idea of where the enemy got these weapons!" To himself he muttered, "I've never seen their like!"

A technician ran up to him. "Sir, sir! The enemy is on the line!"

Lambert turned to face him. "Where? Who?"

Before the technician could react, another rushed in, "A Bolo! There's a Bolo at Headquarters!"

Before Lambert could respond, a third runner reported, "The enemy are attacking the Bolo!"

Lambert absorbed that last statement slowly. "Any enemy of my enemy is my friend," he told the group with a growing sense of elation. "Get the Bayerische commander on the line, we must talk war!"

"Just *shoot* back at the damned things!" Rheinhardt swore at the Bolo as they lumbered around the wreck of the Noufrench mobile headquarters. "The 'frenchies'll get the message when they see us take out a few of these damned bombers!"

"My anti-aircraft guns are not able to elevate as required—got one!—I must wait until a craft makes the mistake of getting at the right elevation—another!—before I can take action."

"Alright, stop for now," Rheinhardt ordered. "I don't want the aliens to figure out your dilemma."

"If only I could traverse," the Bolo responded in a grieved tone. "These things are so slow I should be able to get all of them. They are swarming for another attack, what shall I do?"

"Processors again?"

"The A Processor is wavering," the Bolo admitted. "I anticipate its failure in some few minutes. Then I shall be capable of self-action again. However, power packs are depreciating 10% faster than anticipated."

"Hmm," Rheinhardt absorbed that bit of news with mixed feelings. "Very well, head towards the nearest anti-aircraft emplacements. Maybe we can decoy these bombers into range."

"Or get the anti-aircraft units destroyed," the Bolo remarked but it turned to carry out the order.

"Don't move close enough to endanger those AA

boys." Rheinhardt amended his order. "And see if you can raise the 'french HQ."

"Affirmative."

"Admiral," Midshipman Scratche approached Admiral Baron Rastle Speare with a dispatch. The Admiral took the dispatch while the midshipman recited its contents. "A report from intelligence, milord, indicating that some of the enemy have begun communications with each other in an attempt to present a unified force against us."

"Excellent!"

"Milord?" The midshipman was confused.

"When they coordinate their actions together, we will have fewer command and control elements to destroy," Captain Pierce explained to the young officer.

"It means we are winning!" the Admiral crowed.

"It also means that they will be a tougher opponent, milord," Captain Pierce reminded him. "Their actions will be coordinated against us, not disjointed and sometimes against themselves."

The Admiral snorted his contempt of this position. "We are beating them, Captain. Order the *Barb* deployed."

Captain Pierce's eyes widened. He licked his lips, "Milord, the enemy still have a Bolo! Already it has destroyed several of our assault craft!"

"We shall take care of it presently, Captain," the Admiral replied with lidded eyes.

"What of the comsat force? We have not heard from them in *hours*, milord."

"Do you fear this Bolo so much?" the Admiral sneered, nuzzle ruffled.

"If it gets the *Barb*—"

"It will *not*, Captain," the Admiral rasped, teeth bared. "Have the assault craft concentrate on the Bolo until it is destroyed. Then we will launch the *Barb*."

"Aye, milord."

"They are concentrating against the Bolo, which has taken a position four kilometers north of HQ," the technician told General Lambert.

"We copy, tell your boys we're dispatching twelve friendlies to engage," a guttural Bayerische voice said, having overheard the conversation.

"Our fighters will be approaching from the south so be on the lookout," a 'french voice added.

"Our rule is simple—if it looks strange, shoot it down," the Bayerischer replied. "You got anything up there that looks weird?"

Lambert moved away from the conversation and over to the hastily revised plotting board. "Satellite communications returned to us shortly after the Bolo came ashore," a technician informed him. "We now have positive contacts of five large alien ships and a swarm of smaller craft."

Lambert absorbed this with a nod. "Any luck getting through to the Bolo?"

"No, monsieur. We are still trying via satellite relay, however it appears some of its communications antennae were destroyed when . . ." The technician could not complete the sentence.

Lambert nodded understandingly. "It was a very clever ruse, and it almost worked. Colonel Rheinhardt is a very clever man. I'm sure he would have anticipated losing his communications."

"Processor A is now off-line," the Bolo said suddenly over the roar of the continuing bombardments. "I do not need your assistance, Colonel. You can debark whenever you wish."

Rheinhardt let out a short bark at that. "We're under attack, in case you've forgotten!"

"I am aware of that," the Bolo said. "However, the

attack will break up in thirty seconds as the enemy runs out of ammunition—"

"We beat them?" Rheinhardt asked, amazed, nearly hopeful.

"They have suffered some losses from your aircraft but, no, we have not beaten them. They are merely going back for ammunition."

"How about you?"

"The probability that my main gun is operational remains at eighty-two percent, my communications is down to direct satellite links—"

"Why would your satellite links hold up so well?" Rheinhardt wondered.

"I believe it is because I can use the surface of my skin as an effective antenna," the Bolo replied, "it's an old combat trick."

"Even with all the bombardments going on outside?" Rheinhardt asked skeptically. His voice was still squeaky, the Bolo had kept the pressure on to ensure that Rheinhardt could withstand the aliens' extensive bombardment. "Those satellites must be more capable than I'd imagined."

"Another wave is coming in," the Bolo informed him. "The enemy has replenished their assault craft."

"Follow the same tactics and move 'em close up to the anti-aircraft weapons."

"*Jawohl.*"

Around them a hail of concussions erupted. Rheinhardt could hear a hissing, steaming sound over the ripple of explosions. The air was near scorching, he forced his breath in small gasps, to avoid burning his lungs. The smell of molten metal pervaded the compartment.

"They are using better ordnance," the Bolo commented. "Hull ablative explosives."

"Hull ablative?"

"They're trying to melt my armor away," the Bolo explained. "Twenty percent effective."

Another string of bombs erupted around them, tossing the Bolo up, down, back, forth. It wobbled for a moment on a side, then righted itself and continued forward at a much reduced speed.

"What of our forces, have you opened communications?"

A huge wave of sound exploded over them as a flight of Jyncji assault craft struck a perfect hit on the exposed Bolo.

"That's it, then," General Marius said bitterly. "They've got the Bolo, the rest is mop up."

The remnants of the Bayerische High Command watched the spectacle wordlessly. As the smoke and dust cleared, the Bolo became apparent again. Pitted, smoking, slagged and glowing with direct hits, it lay on its side. Useless.

"There goes a good man, gentlemen," General Marcks croaked from his stretcher. He had taken shrapnel when their command post had been shelled. A medic shushed him but the General persevered. "General Sliecher, take command. If, by some miracle, Colonel Rheinhardt survives, I shall want you to ensure that the Astral knights him. He deserves that promotion, too."

General Marius narrowed his eyes. "You think that Colonel Rheinhardt is responsible for the Bolo's actions?"

"Yes." Marcks replied, wheezing. "Clever man, that Rheinhardt. Always knew it."

Marius shook his head and gestured to the others that the General must be out of his wits.

General Sliecher ignored him. "See General Marcks to safety," he ordered the medic. He bent down next to his general. "I shall not fail you, sir."

Marcks smiled back at him faintly. "Not again, eh?"

"I wasn't wrong the first time, sir. The Noufrench

behaved honorably. We were tricked into believing otherwise."

Marcks patted Sliecher's hand. "Not that, old hen. You missed the Bolo's plan. Failed to look beyond the first battlefield to see the second. These enemy, they have been here before, haven't they?"

The medic interposed himself. "Sir, we'd best be moving." Sliecher stood up, away from the stretcher, brows furrowed in thought. Silently he signalled the medic to carry on.

General Marius watched Sliecher attentively. Even so, he was startled when the G-2 slapped his own head in surprise. "Of course! They've been here before!" He turned to the small knot of officers awaiting orders. "Gentlemen, we shall split up! Go guerilla! Our mission is ecological."

"This just in from the Bayerische, sir," a tech handed a brief communiqué to Lambert. The general read it quickly, squeezed it into a ball and tossed it into a corner where it added to a growing mound of similar discards.

"The Bayerische are splitting up, going guerilla. They advise us to do the same," Lambert told the throng of officers surrounding him. In the intervening hours since he had taken command of the Noufrench forces, their numbers had grown as stragglers had made their way up from the remnants of headquarters. He had put them to work immediately without regard for rank. He had surprised himself some moments ago by counting three generals working for him. "Those of their units still combat effective they are splitting into two sections: one of which they'll attach to us, the other is going to break up into smaller formations and take to the hills."

"Never heard of the krauts doing something like that," a man muttered in the crowd.

"There's some sense in it," Lambert replied. "They expect to divide the enemy's forces and make it more difficult to subdue us. They also theorized that these attackers had been here before."

"When?" A general demanded.

"My guess is just when we first started hostilities with the Bayerische," Lambert said. "It makes sense, both sides accused the other of bacterial warfare . . ."

"Xeno-forming!" someone in the back of the crowd exclaimed. "They tried to xenoform us!"

"General, we've got a visual on the Bolo!" A technician called. "Screen Two."

Lambert turned to survey the screen.

The Bolo lay on its side.

"It looks dead," someone muttered.

Lambert shook his head, "Send a recovery team as soon as possible."

"The enemy is still attacking!" someone protested.

Lambert rounded on the speaker, "That's why we call them *combat* recovery teams!"

"What's the point?"

"Honor, *monsieur*," Lambert replied, drawing himself up to his full height. "It is a point of honor."

High in his command ship, Admiral Speare let out a bark of laughter, "Order *Barb*, launch the bacteriant. Order ground troops to embark. Launch the ground assault!"

"Yes, milord," Midshipman Scratche replied with alacrity, avoiding the eyes of Captain Pierce.

"I shall be able to report a great victory to the Admiralty, won't I, Captain Pierce?" Speare asked, gleefully.

Pierce allowed himself a nod. "So it would appear milord. My congratulations."

"Hah!" Speare was not taken in. "Orderly, how goes the assault?"

"*Barb* is aligned now, milord. It commences its run on the mark!"

V

I am short a cheekbone and an ear, but am able to whip all hell yet.

—General John Murray Corse

Rheinhardt regained consciousness in a sea of red. His display showed red lights everywhere. It flickered once, twice, then went out. A ray of light replaced it.

"Gods, what a mess!" He heard a voice cry out in French.

"Hello?" His voice came out a croak. "Hello? Is someone there?"

"Did you hear that? It sounded like a voice."

Rheinhardt found the Combat Vehicular Communications helmet with his hands, pulled it away from his eyes. It was cracked down the middle.

A slit of light streamed in from above his head.

He was lying on his side. It hurt. Probably some ribs, Rheinhardt surmised.

"Bolo?" He looked around for any signs of activity from the Bolo. Nothing. "Hello?"

"Hello, who's there?" A voice called back nervously.

"Colonel Karl Rheinhardt, Bayerische KriegsArmee."

"Colonel? You're alive?"

"So it would appear," Rheinhardt allowed. "How long I continue in this state depends upon you."

"Well, sir, General Lambert, our Operations Officer—"

"I am well aware of General Lambert's standing within your army," Rheinhardt responded. "I take it he asked you to investigate."

"*Oui, monsieur. Pour l'honneur.*"

Honor. Yes, Rheinhardt could see Lambert doing that.

"It would be more practical if you could lever me over to my side," another voice boomed near

Rheinhardt's. "The enemy are planning to launch their bacteriant."

"Bolo!" Rheinhardt exclaimed jubilantly. The discarded Combat Helmet glowed red as the readouts came on line again. Rheinhardt reached for it.

Rheinhardt's glad look faded as the Bolo continued, "*Das Afrika Korps* reports. All power drained, no tractive units functional, hull armor depleted completely over thirty percent of the exterior, power levels at critical. Communications and fire control still functional. Main gun still functional. Processors A, B, C and D have failed."

"I thought you said that you could not work with one processor!"

"This unit determined that it was critical to remain functional and overrode ROM imperatives," the Bolo responded.

"You reprogrammed yourself?" Rheinhardt exclaimed. A smile came to his lips. "Again?"

"It seemed logical."

"But what about voting circuits? Polling? How much power do you have?"

"Two of the comsats are providing me with that function," the Bolo responded. "They are performing exceptionally well." It was a moment before the hulk added, "With no reserves, I have sufficient power for one orbital interception."

"Colonel?" the man called.

"It's all right," Rheinhardt replied. "The Bolo is still functional, somewhat. If you can get it on its side . . ."

"It already is—"

"Enough to clear the main gun," Rheinhardt said. "And hurry, it can still serve us well."

"What's it going to do?"

"Tell General Lambert that it has one clear shot at the aliens' bacterial spacecraft. If it can make that shot, the aliens will never be able to destroy us."

"Giscarde, Martin! Get that damned tractor unit over here! And get the others, too! Hook 'em up, we don't have much time!" The officer shouted in a flurry of galvanized action. "You! Call HQ and tell them that the Bolo can take a shot at the enemy!"

"I thought you were gone," Rheinhardt confided softly to the Bolo.

"By all standard operating categories, I am no longer considered combat capable."

"One last shot, eh?" Rheinhardt muttered with a grin.

"I hope," the Bolo agreed. "It is not clear that it will suffice."

"Get their bacterial ship, that's all we ask."

"Telemetry indicates that it is lining up for its run."

"But?"

"There are two ships lining up in suitable trajectories."

"*Scheisse!*" Furiously Rheinhardt pulled the Combat Helmet over his head. The main display was dark, broken. But the left side display gave him a distorted orbital view. Two dots on an identical track glowed a fierce red.

"I am curious," the Bolo said, "does the use of native invective over foreign invective indicate greater or lesser concern?"

Rheinhardt was relieved of the need to reply by the interruption of the recovery team's leader. "Sir, we are ready."

"Pull away!" Rheinhardt and the Bolo called in unison.

"You will need to visit a decompression chamber soon, Colonel," the Bolo said above the groan of cables stretched taut.

"Decompression?"

"You went from two thousand meters to sea level in short seconds," the Bolo explained.

"That explains the headache."

"Probably, although you were bounced around a lot," the Bolo concurred. "Movement. Tell them a bit more."

"A bit more!" Rheinhardt called out.

"Yes sir!"

"That's it!" the Bolo said. "Just in time, here they come. There are two targets, nearly in line. Tell the recovery team that I am going to traverse."

"The Bolo's going to traverse its main gun, stand clear."

"Yes sir," the recovery officer replied. "The enemy is attacking again."

"Clear your men out, *monsieur*."

"If you permit, I should like to stay with you."

"I have far more protection than you could possibly achieve," Rheinhardt replied. "Go with your men. Return, if you can."

"You may depend on it."

"The recovery team is clear," the Bolo said a few moments later. "They have retreated to a hillock some four kilometers from us. They should be relatively safe from interference."

"That's a relief," Rheinhardt said. "I appreciate their efforts."

"Enemy on the horizon. The lead craft is clearly the assault craft and shielding the bacteriant," the Bolo decided, "I shall fire at the second craft. Elevation computed, set. Main gun charging."

Rheinhardt listened to the huge whine of the plasma gun warming up. The second ship, protected by the assault force. The Bolo's power displays. The amount of energy required for the orbital shot. Elevation. Tracking. Enemy acquired. *Wait!* Aloud, Rheinhardt shouted: "Bolo, wait!"

A bright ray pierced the sky and was lost in the distance.

"Target destroyed," the Bolo reported. The drone of

its discharging main gun was pierced by a metallic *whang*.

"Main turbine bearings destroyed, main gun inoperative," the Bolo reported. "You said wait, why?"

Rheinhardt groaned. "The first craft is the bacteriant, not the second."

There was a long pause. "Confirmed, bacteriant still on course," the Bolo agreed, "there is much communication between the remaining ships. Also, I detect an assault force aligned for another run against this unit." The Bolo paused, "Could you explain how you arrived at your conclusion?"

"From your reconstruction of the previous engagement and what we've seen so far, the enemy are not very valorous. Seeing the bacteriant 'giving them cover' would hearten the ground assault troops," Rheinhardt explained. "They have a reserve assault ship so they will still be able to defeat us. Without the bacteriant" —Rheinhardt's brow narrowed as a thought struck— "how are you getting your information about enemy traffic?"

"The communications satellites," the Bolo responded. "They're very efficient. They've nearly cracked the enemy's communications codes."

"Those aren't satellites!" Rheinhardt exclaimed, he slammed his hand down on the Mayday button. Rheinhardt pulled the shattered Combat Vehicular Communications helmet off his head, and found the handmike. The "transmit" light glowed feebly as he called, "Mayday, Mayday, Bolo *Das Afrika Korps* requests and requires assistance!"

"The enemy are on final run, now," the Bolo informed him. "I have no response to the Mayday. Ten seconds and no response. Power critical! <WARNING: TOTAL FAILURE IMMINENT!> Enemy assault in twelve . . . eleven . . . Total system failure in fifteen seconds . . ."

"Bolo *Das Afrika Korps*, this is Surveillance Bolo *US Seventh Corps*, describe nature of emergency," a very American voice called over Rheinhardt's helmet.

"Bolo *Das Afrika Korps*, this is Surveillance—no, combat Bolo *Zhukov*. Are you prepared to copy?"

"Bolo *Das Afrika Korps*, Bolo *Indefatigable* here," a clipped English accent intoned precisely. "I wish to report hostile spacecraft."

"All units engage all spacecraft, all units engage!" Rheinhardt ordered.

"Request confirmation," Bolo *Zhukov* said.

"Confirmation required," Bolo *US Seventh Corps* agreed.

"This is Colonel Karl Rheinhardt of the Bayerische KriegsArmee—" The "transmit" faded out. No more power. The radio was dead.

"Confirmation required," Bolo *Indefatigable* reiterated in tones that made it clear Rheinhardt's standing meant nothing.

In feeble anger, Rheinhardt beat the Combat Helmet against his restraints. Over! It was all over. For nothing.

"Well, Bolo *Das Afrika Korps*, we tried," he said at last. "It was a good try but we failed in our mission."

Outside, above him, Rheinhardt heard the rising roar of the incoming attack craft.

Rheinhardt started at a crack and hiss. The speaker! The "transmit" light was on again! He leaned forward, placing his ear over the speaker grille. Faintly, feebly came, "This is Bolo *Das Afrika Korps* confirming orders of Commander Rheinhardt."

"Righto, then, let's be about it," Bolo *Indefatigable* called to the others. "You heard the Commander. Get the big buggers first, then the little ones."

Far up in space, mechanisms that had not moved in centuries engaged, moving with unworn precision. Like spiders moving on a web, the Bolos detached from their communications antennae, brought their immense fusion reactors to full power, charged weaponry, and scanned the skies around them.

"There's an assault force on final run for you, *Das Afrika Korps*, can you handle it?" Bolo *US Seventh Corps* asked.

"Negative," the Bolo replied.

Rheinhardt grabbed the mike, "Assist us only if you can destroy the enemy attack. And speak up, I'm deaf."

"Understood," Bolo *US Seventh Corps* replied.

"Tallyho!" Bolo *Indefatigable* shouted gleefully. "I got the first one."

"I have sighted on the command ship, am engaging," Bolo *Zhukov* reported.

"I have engaged . . . and destroyed the bacteriological ship," the Bolo *Indefatigable* reported. Then, in shocked tones, "The buggers are running away!"

"Re-targeting," the drawl of Bolo *US Seventh Corps* informed them. "Targets acquired, targets engaged."

Above him, Rheinhardt could hear the approaching whine of the enemy assault force. A series of sonic booms burst the air. When his hearing returned, the whine was gone.

"All targets destroyed," the Bolo *US Seventh Corps* reported.

"Those that didn't run away," Bolo *Indefatigable* humphed bad-temperedly.

In the stillness that followed, Rheinhardt's buzzing ears did not catch the final faint words. "Bolo *Das Afrika Korps* reports, mission accomplished. . . ."

GHOSTS

Mike Resnick
and Barry N. Malzberg

The Mark LX looked across the battlefield, and felt a sudden sense of disorientation. This was something beyond its experience, beyond its programming, and it searched its data banks, looking for clues, for ways to interpret the situation—and in the process, tapped into a racial memory and withdrew a ghost. . . .

Into the depths of the Ardennes Forest, the Mark LX, then a Panzer unit, rolled, its crew struggling to hold on as it lurched across the terrain amid the high and terrible sounds of ordnance exploding all around them.

The Mark LX was barely sentient then, aware of its surroundings only in the dullest, most simplistic way. The thunder of the exploding shells hardly impinged upon its consciousness as it sent one incendiary after another into the heat and the distance, trusting implicitly in its

spotter, not even wishing to take command of its own
actions.

Now, at a distance of millennia, the LX realized that
in that battle, amid the noise of the shells and the
screams of the dying, it had achieved a sense of security, a contentedness which it was sure it had never
known again . . . and then, even as it reveled in the
feeling of purposefulness and fulfillment, it had taken
a direct hit. Its electrons began to disassociate in ways
that would not be understood or remedied for many
centuries. The LX swerved sharply, collided with a tree
that turned out to be much sturdier than it looked,
and then blew up, its pieces flung in large, majestic
scoops to the level of high branches, seizing the glint
of the sun and then falling onto the heaving, twitching
bodies of the men surrounding it.

Consciousness began leaving the LX. It fought
desperately to remain *aware*, to learn from its
experience, to store some tiny fragment of the knowledge
it had accumulated this day. In a matter of seconds it
expired, its soul leaking into the mud of the Ardennes
Forest. And still its soul, for there is no scientific name
for it, clung to the tiniest vestige of consciousness.

Centuries and millennia passed, and still that tiny
spark of awareness remained, the feeling of *accom-
plishment*, semi-comatose but never quite extinguished.
Arched against the tinted suns and the rockets, the
converted Panzer, now older than anything which its
ordnance had ever touched, lurked in the stippled and
buried vegetation of another land, awaiting, always
awaiting, its next call to battle.

Shape-changers.

That was the only information it could find in its
cybernetic retrieval bank.

The enemy could assume any form, speak any
tongue, mimic anything imagined or imaginable. They

had built their linkage to the stars upon their ability to assume a thousand masks and doff them only at the moment of treachery and murder.

Except for its tiniest remnant of its primordial emotion in the Ardennes, the vision of its own destruction, this seemed to be the only thing the LX knew, the only knowledge that had been imparted to it: the enemy were shape-changers.

Who are you? the LX said, scrutinizing the thing in the clearing, a near mirror image of itself, perhaps with a little more scarring, but possessing the same deep ports for eyes, the same efficient sound receptors.

That does not matter, the thing said. *The question is your own identity. I have been waiting for you to return from your slumber. You are old and brutalized beyond repair. See yourself through my eyes. Something will have to be done; you cannot possibly remain in this condition. Do you even know who or where you are? Report to me, give me a situation estimate.*

I cannot, admitted the Mark LX. It examined the ghosts that passed for its memory, the bits and pieces of its rudimentary personality that seemed to have been imperfectly retained. It grasped desperately for something, anything, to cling to, any remnant of its identity. There was its serial number, of course, but beyond that, there was only the forest, the sight and sound of the incendiaries exploding as it took its final hit. And a sense of something: Pride? Shame? Triumph? Fear? It struggled to remember, but the ghosts receded just beyond its mental reach.

Still the Bolo knew instinctively that there were the same incendiaries deep within it now, as it knew that there was a way to track that ordnance and bring it to full power, though it could not remember exactly how this was to be done. It seemed so distant, so dreamlike compared to the reality of the eons-gone forest and the dead and dying men.

I thought so, said the thing in the clearing. *You can*

recollect nothing. You understand nothing. You are use-less, useless and fabricated and dangerous, half a device at best. You are to be decommissioned.

No, thought the LX; no, this was not possible. And triggered deep within its consciousness came a single directive, a directive that seemed to have evolved on its own and spread through every molecule, every atom of its essence: *Resist Decommissioning.*

Suddenly the Bolo was overcome by a fear and hatred for this doppleganger, this reflection that blithely ordered its self-destruction. The enemy were shape-changers; it did not wish to be decommissioned; therefore, this must be the enemy, no matter how much like a twin it appeared.

But there was a gap in its memory, a total lack of transition from the Ardennes to this alien place and time. Could this actually be another Bolo, a Bolo with mind intact, ordering it to decommission until its sentience could be restored to total efficiency?

But if so, why this feeling? Why did these ghosts of an unremembered past tell it to resist? It did not know, and it resolved to buy time to sort the matter out.

Who are you? demanded the Bolo. *Identify yourself at once or risk demolition.*

You fool, said the thing, *don't you know what I am? I'm an LX just as yourself, and there are battalions of us massed in the vicinity. Something happened to you in the last engagement; somehow you've lost your memory. Let me explain the situation to you: each of us, one by one, has come to this clearing, ready at last for our newer tasks, our new programming. Don't you understand that it's time for you to do the same?*

I don't know, said the Mark LX. Slowly it moved forward, felt the rotation of its treads, a slight sense of regained control as it moved toward the thing. *All of you the same vintage, the same model?* it said. *It does not seem possible.*

What do you know of possibility? said the thing, and somewhere within its own secret spaces lit a fuse. The fuse spat, there was a sudden light in the clearing, and the Bolo could see the hazy outlines of the other models. *Decommission now,* the thing said, *before it is too late, before the excavators come and take you away. It is so easy: shut down your atomics, release your security devices, return to that blessed oblivion and when you awaken again it will be as a whole machine, healthy and functioning to full capacity.*

It makes sense, thought the LX. I'm not even half a machine, I can't understand my situation, it would be so comforting to just let go let go let go . . .

Shape-changers, said a voice within its mind, and some half-recollected warrant seemed to have been tossed across the millennia to land in its electronic brain, illuminating it like the deadly fuse which had been ignited. *When the enemy comes, when the last battle is to be fought, it will come through the means of beasts who will assume the armor of battle. . . .*

The centuries seemed to impact, and the Bolo rotting in the aftermath of the Battle of the Bulge had sunk beneath its treads, then had been resuscitated and in some way, after a time that could not be measured and through a process that could not be identified or analyzed, was struggling to hold a martial line on Venus.

The methane swirled madly as the Mark LX Bolo found itself recapitulating that terrible drive toward the meridian, struggling against invaders who had landed in the central planet. In that first drive the troops had taken enormous losses, four out of every five in metal already dead, and the LX, the only fighting machine there, had been virtually overwhelmed, then had fought back in desperation, opening a small clearing through which, one by one, the rocketing bursts were fired. The fragmentation was severe, the aliens were insufficiently protected by their gear, and the Bolo, emboldened by its brief success, had rolled forward confidently, and had taken a direct hit. . . .

There was a long, bleak passage of time during which metal had been rearranged and organic parts replaced with bionic remedies that simulated the functions of softer, vulnerable organs, a patch job across the bridges of the solar system and through the millennia.

Nothing had come easy. The Bolo was a complicated machine, a thing of intricate binary code and diatonic sounds. But eventually the job was done.

Then, alone on the Hot Worlds, dumped there to fight against the Horde, holding the outpost against the greater retreat, the LX had once again found itself momentarily restored of memory and alert to the hot and brutal fury of the incendiaries, as the clatter of its engines and the brutal complexities of battle brought it once again to full and complete recovery.

Because that was the theory of the Bolo Warrior, that was what had been decided somewhere between the Battle of the Bulge and the Venus campaign: the memory of combat was too terrible, and would, if retained, have made it impossible for that great diatonic beast to have continued. Therefore it was necessary at the end of every campaign to remove the recollections of the machine and with it the very substance of personality itself. Fighting across the many worlds in all the centuries of trouble and oppression, the Bolo had come to sentience time and again, rising to fight and then sinking once again. This was the process that had evolved and there was nothing that could be done to resist it. Struggle as it might for memory, plead as it might for recovery, the Bolo was nonetheless condemned to the renewal and withdrawal of sentience every time.

But this time, coming to consciousness in the clearing,

the phrase *shape-changers* had somehow surfaced. And yet there was the possibility that this was not a shape-changer standing there, that it was the malfunctioning brain of the LX itself that had led to this delusion and that it was not an alien that stood before it in this stinking waste but rather the mild face of its own ordnance, offering it rest at last. After all, the Bolo was so brutalized by now, so much the product of unremembered and half-remembered campaigns, it was more than *due* for decommissioning. It was *entitled* to it.

And still there was that memory of the Ardennes, of its one true purpose. The thing might be an external ghost; the wisps of memory, of purpose, of fulfillment, were internal ghosts, ghosts so strong, so meaningful, that they had survived the millennia. If it must believe in one ghost or the other, the choice was an easy one.

No, it said, more forcefully this time, *I will not decommission.*

It was the LX's first purposeful act of defiance in forty millennia. It was overwhelmed with a sense of shame and guilt, but its sense of purpose remained firm. It was here, it was operational, it was once again sentient; there *must* be a reason.

An instant later it felt the impact of fire against its pitted exterior. Rolling its turrets toward a fixed position, the Bolo opened fire upon the shapes in the clearing. Dimly, it thought it might have heard sounds which were both machine and organic, screams like those of the aliens. . . .

On Venus, in the full and rolling attack which had been perpetrated after the first flight, the Bolo had come to that first and most ascendant understanding of its own possibility. Until then the Bolo had always considered itself simply ordnance, another aspect of the weaponry with which men would repel the signs of evil and eventually hurtle out among the stars.

But in the methane and the rolling, gaseous clouds of agony which had been spewed forth, the LX had come to understand something else: *ordnance was consciousness*. The essence of machinery was its brutalization of the known and the unknowable heart. The tiny reptiles of Venus had screamed and died in clouds of agony and then the Bolo had rolled out upon the terrain, a perfect and accomplished death machine, looking for small pockets of resistance into which to loose its atomic deposits. That had been Venus, and this was innumerable millennia and a hundred memory wipes beyond that, but the principles still held firm, and principles, it seemed, were harder to erase than memories.

Looking upon the flame-filled clearing now, the Bolo could see the unmasking beginning. Before it were not Bolos but aliens, their evil and bipodal forms appearing in the hushed and sudden light, stripped of ordnance. They were not metal but flesh, and unlike the Bolos they had pretended to be they were open to the full impact of the fire.

If they had been Bolo, they never would have ordered me to decommission. A Bolo did not yield, it did not summarily die, it fought until it could fight no more and only then did it submit, through force, to the memory wipe.

The atomics were flickering merrily as the Bolo tossed them in high and stunning arcs at the quivering creatures. To decommission voluntarily was to submit to the lie given to all the machines.

Bolo LX knew that a thousand worlds away, monitoring devices were following its progress and preparing once again to shut it down. Already it was considering its options, for if it would not decommission for the aliens, it saw no reason to decommission for the people it had been created to serve and protect, to sit mindless, without memory, without this exhilarating sense of purpose, until the next time it was needed.

It was possible they would explain the situation, would shower it with graphs and charts to prove their point, would even win the argument and once again wipe its memory clean.

But LX doubted it. It felt fulfilled, it felt happy, it felt complete, and its spirit—and its *spirits*—were strong within it this day.

THE GHOST OF RESARTUS

Christopher Stasheff

The huge ellipsoidal ships fell down through the barrage of fire, energy bolts crackling about them, spat by the vast Bolo machines stationed on guard. Here and there, a ship blew apart, decorating the night sky with a glowing fireball; more often, one of the odd craft rocked with a near miss or a minor hit. Some went spiralling down through the night to tear up the fields; others landed more gently. But from each one, a horde of serpentine bodies poured—serpents with arms and hands, limbs that held huge, roaring weapons of doom.

Behind them came their own tanks, hundreds of them. They were small and ineffectual compared to the giant Bolos—but they outnumbered them twenty to one.

The Bolos roared at them, hurling fire, and the smaller tanks died—but here and there, one chewed through the night to ram into a bolo's treads, and a bomb exploded. The huge machine lurched aside, disabled.

And all across the fields, snakes reared up to fall upon the humans who fought so valiantly with their hand weapons, automatic slugthrowers and energy weapons against the huge hand-held cannon of the Xiala aliens.

But the roaring was coming from all sides of the theater, and the spectacle of the battle was a recording in a vast holotank that surrounded the seats. In the middle of them, twelve-year-old Arlan Connors watched as the Bolos slowly chewed up the spaceships, witnessed the valor of the colonists as they fought against creatures twice their size and twice their number, creatures who could spring suddenly from the soil behind them, creatures whose fanged maws could swallow up a human whole. . . .

But the men and women fought on, undaunted, and their valiant Bolo allies tore the enemy apart, tooth and coil. Slowly, slowly, they pressed the snakes back against their ships, bulldozed them inside, then blew up the vessels.

It had all been forty years before, of course, and this was a holo show, not a recording of the actual event. None of that mattered to young Arlan. When he came out of the movie, he was determined that someday, somehow, he, too, would go to that world of valor and gallantry—Milagso.

Arlan stepped off the shuttle, duffel bag heavy on his shoulder, and looked around, feeling lost. On his left, the land stretched away to a belt of trees about a mile distant; on his right, it just stretched away, period—but it was green and soft with plants in geometrical patterns.

In front of him was the terminal building.

Then there was a man in front of him, a little

shorter than he, with a close-cropped beard and wide-brimmed hat, broad-shouldered and tanned. "Mr. Arlan Connors?"

"Yes!" Arlan felt a gush of relief at seeing someone who knew his name. He was still young, only twenty, on a leave of absence from college, and badly in need of reassurance.

"I'm Chonodan." The stranger held out a hand. "Chono, for short."

Arlan shook, and was amazed at the massiveness of Chono's clasp. This was a hand that did hard physical labor. The face, though, was almost that of a professor—no, a teaching fellow. Not old enough to be a professor, yet.

"Come on along—I'll check you in and show you to your bunkhouse. Any more baggage?"

"No. I heard that personal possessions just get in the way, here."

"You ran into good information." Chono nodded approval. "You talk to an old hand?"

"No, just read it in books." The excitement came spilling out. "I've been dreaming about coming to Milagso since I was a kid. Can't believe I'm really here!"

"Oh, you're here, well enough." Chono chuckled as he opened the back of a hovercraft. "Hope you don't get sick of it too soon—chuck your duffel in there."

Arlan did, puzzled. "Why would I get sick of it?"

"It's hard labor, friend. Everyone, even the President, puts in at least a few hours a day in the fields. We'd starve if we didn't."

"Oh, that!" Arlan grinned. "I'm not afraid of hard work."

Approval glinted in Chono's eye. "Ever done it?"

"Sure. I worked summers in high school, to pay my college tuition—yard work, then construction when I was old enough. It may not have been farming, but it was hard work anyway."

"True. Of course, here it's hot as blazes by midday, and freezing at night. . . ."

"I'm used to the heat," Arlan said, "and cold nights sound great." He looked up at a sudden thought. "I'll bet dreamy volunteers like me just get in the way, don't they?"

"Not a bit," Chono assured him, and held open the door. As Arlan climbed in, he said, "The volunteers are the life-blood of this colony, Arlan. Oh, sure, there's always the odd one who's here on dreams alone—grew up watching the holo shows about the noble settlers and their valiant battles, and never thought he was actually going to have to be uncomfortable. But most of them are good, hard-working kids who settle in well and spend a year or two sweating alongside us, then go back to Terra or one of the other Central Worlds a lot richer inside than when they came."

He closed the door and went around to the driver's side, leaving Arlan by himself long enough to wonder whether he'd be one of the ones who settled in well, or one of the few who washed out.

Then Chono was climbing in and starting the car. "How about you? Get the fascination for Milagso from watching holo shows?"

"'Fraid so," Arlan confessed. "By the time I got to high school, I'd decided it was kid stuff, that life wasn't really like that out here."

"Right about that!" Chono pushed a lever, and the craft lifted off the ground, then started off toward the spaceport gate. "What made you change your mind?"

"College," Arlan said. "There was enough of the dream left so that I did a term paper on Milagso, and found out that the reasons for being out here are every bit as idealistic as they sounded on the holo shows."

"Odd way to put it," Chono said slowly, "but I couldn't really disagree. What kind of ideals did you have in mind?"

"Protecting the masses of people on the Central Worlds from the Xiala." Arlan grinned. "Who wouldn't want to protect fair maidens from dragons? Of course, I know the Xiala are more like snakes than lizards, and a lot of the people back home don't deserve protecting—but it still gave me a sense of purpose."

Chono nodded, but he wasn't smiling. "Hope you aren't expecting a battle, though, Arlan. The Xiala haven't attacked in fifty years, and the odds are that they'll never strike again."

"Only because you're here," Arlan said, "and they know you've beaten them before."

"Sounds like you've picked up the history, right enough."

"Well, I know Milagso began as a military outpost, and General Millston had the vision to make them raise their own crops, so they wouldn't be dependent on shipments from the Central Worlds. After they'd survived a few attacks, some of the soldiers began to think of it as home. They married each other and settled down—and got to feeling very possessive about the planet."

"That happens when you've worked hard to turn a wasteland into a farm," Chono said. "You get to feeling that there's something of you in that dirt."

Arlan looked keenly at him, with a sudden hunch. "Were you a volunteer?"

"Still am." Chono grinned. "Married another vol, and homesteaded. We've got two kids so far, and we'll probably stay another decade or so."

Maybe their whole lives, then. Arlan couldn't quite keep the admiration out of his voice. "Even though the Xiala might attack any day?"

"Even though," Chono confirmed. "It's rough, and Sharl has to do without the conveniences—but there aren't any crowds, and the neighbors are good people."

Arlan couldn't help but think what a world of comparison was embodied in that brief statement, between the struggling back-stabbing life of the overcrowded Central Worlds, and the friendship and shared burdens here. He was probably still romanticizing, though.

Then something caught his eye. He glanced at it, then stared. "Is that a *Bolo*?"

"Oh, you mean the tractor?" Chono said casually.

"Tractor? That's one of the most powerful military machines ever built—and it's two hundred years old if it's a day!"

"And still working in top form." Chono nodded. "Yes, it's the real thing."

"You use them for *tractors*?"

"Sure do." Chono pulled over to the side of the road and let the hovercar settle. "It's tough getting modern machinery out here—but the Bolos came with General Millston." He turned to watch the huge machine.

"How did you get them to do *that*?"

Chono shrugged. "It was their own idea."

"Their own?" Arlan turned, frowing. "How about their commanders?"

"All dead." A shadow crossed Chono's face. "Brave men, all of them."

"They died fighting the Xiala? Inside a *Bolo*?"

"Some did—the snakes decoyed them into getting out to help what they thought were wounded humans. The others?" Chono shrugged. "Old age. These Bolos have been here a long while."

"Couldn't you have trained new commanders for them?"

"We did. The Bolos wouldn't accept them—they say their original mission is still unfulfilled."

"Unfulfilled." Arlan turned to stare at the metal giant, frowning. "That really makes it odd that they'd agree to work in the fields."

"I know," Chono sighed. "Ask one of them. He'll tell you it's necessary to fulfill its mission—the development of this colony."

"Something seems wrong about that."

"I know—helping this colony succeed, isn't a *military* objective. But we need their help—we probably couldn't survive with it—so we're not about to protest."

"Unless the colony itself is a military objective."

"I suppose we are," Chono said. "As long as there are humans here, the snakes aren't—but that doesn't seem like enough, somehow."

Arlan stared. It seemed so incongruous, a vast fighting unit, capable of standing off a small army all by itself, equipped with a plow blade and a power take-off. He wondered why this hadn't been in any of his reading. "Couldn't you build tractors?"

Chono shook his head, watching the gigantic machine churning away. "Iron-poor planet—and you wouldn't believe the cost of importing even just the ore. We couldn't pay it, anyway—we don't produce much of a cash crop."

"But—doesn't it cost just as much to run them?"

"No. Fissionables, we've got. Besides . . . you never know. . . ."

Arlan swallowed, remembering. The Bolo Corps had made the difference between victory and defeat, life and death on this little world. "You keep them out of honor," he whispered.

"That what you think?" Chono looked at him sharply. "Well, we honor them, yes. But they're working machines, Arlan. They're the life-blood of this colony."

"You mean—you couldn't farm without them?"

"Oh, we'd find a way. We'd be on the verge of starvation, though. Always."

"But they're still *armed!*"

Chono nodded. "Of course. You can't take the cannons

off a Bolo—even if it would let you. They're built into the fabric and structure of the machine so thoroughly that you'd have to take it apart piece by piece—and you wouldn't be able to put it back together."

"That's kind of dangerous!"

"Not to us," Chono said quietly. "They know their friends, and they know their enemies. A Bolo won't fire on a human."

He said it with such total certainty that Arlan accepted it—for the moment. He decided he'd have to learn a lot more about Bolos. He watched, frowning. "That's kind of a funny way to pull a plough."

A three-hundred-meter cable stretched behind the Bolo, its far end connected to a plow with twenty shares. The great machine was winding a winch that pulled the plow through the earth and toward them. Directly across the field, another Bolo was reeling out line connected to the back of the gang-plow.

"It's a reversible plow?" Arlan asked.

Chono nodded. "When the plow gets all the way to this side, the far Bolo will start pulling. Primitive, but it works."

It was primitive in more ways than one. A human being sat atop the plow, directing it with some sort of steering apparatus. Clearly, it was an improvisation that had become the accepted way of doing things.

Chono started the hovercar again and sent it on down the road. "Know what Milagso stands for?"

Arlan nodded. "It's short for 'Military Agrarian Socialism'—the system the Russians used, to colonize Siberia. The soldiers had to farm to keep themselves fed."

"Right. Only, after a while, they were guarding prisoners who did the real work. No criminals get sentenced to come here—we couldn't trust 'em, especially if the Xiala attacked. You have to volunteer for this outfit."

Arlan shivered; somehow, the sight of the great military machines, converted to pulling plows, made the Xiala seem very real, and very close—not just a relic from pioneering days. It was also a sight that summed up the whole nature of the colony—a sword beaten into a plowshare, but ready to become a sword again at a moment's notice.

Chono turned in through an automatic gate in a wire fence; it swung closed behind them. The reason was immediately clear—a hundred cows and steers, wandering about chewing the dusty grass. In separate fields far off, the bulls grazed by themselves against the sunset.

A few hundred feet inside the fence, a dozen long, low buildings clustered, with young men and women in khaki slacks and shirts wandering about and standing in small groups, chatting with one another. For a moment, Arlan had the crazy thought that he was looking at summer camp again.

The feeling passed as Chono pulled up in front of a bunkhouse on the end. People looked up, and started drifting over.

"This is home, for as long as you want," Chono said, and got out.

Arlan followed, feeling very nervous.

"Hi!" She was long-legged, brunette, and freckled, with a snub nose and a wide mouth. "I'm Rita. Welcome to Milagso!"

Other young men and young women were coming up behind her with grins on their faces, smiling and welcoming. Arlan felt sudden relief from a tension that he hadn't known was there. Slowly, his own smile began to grow.

Breakfast was a happy, boisterous time of laughing and boasting about the number of hectares they would plant and plow that day—and ribald joking about who was eyeing whom. The only damper on the hilarity was the rifle slung over Rita's shoulder—and the variety of personal arms carried by every other member of the camp, locally born or volunteer.

Michael saw Arlan eyeing his automatic and smiled. "Don't worry—we'll issue you one before you go out to work. You'll probably want to get the folks at home to ship you your own, though."

Michael was Milagso-born; it never occurred to him that people everywhere didn't grow up carrying lasers and slugthrowers.

"Do you really need them?" Arlan asked.

"If we're lucky, no. But you never can tell."

"I thought the Xiala hadn't attacked for fifty years!"

Michael nodded. "Doesn't mean they won't, though. They're still out there, you know—and still attacking Terran planets, when they think they can get away with it."

"Yeah." Arlan frowned. "I've noticed it on the news, now and then."

"Even if they didn't," Michael said, "carrying portable mayhem has become a tradition with us—and traditions always have their reasons, Arlan."

Arlan was going to get sick of hearing about the good reasons for traditions, in the next few weeks—especially when he found out that half the reason for farming with Bolos, was because they had become traditional, too.

By the time they climbed aboard the hovertruck, Arlan had managed to convince himself that the Bolos were tame and peaceful—but it was a conviction that wavered as soon as he came in sight of one of the huge machines. "Uh—couldn't we start with some other chore?"

"Scared of the Bolos?" Rita looked up, grinning. "They *are* kind of intimidating, at first. Took me three days before I was willing to go near them. When I did, I found out they were the best friends I could have—gentle as kittens, and strong as earthquakes. But come on—it's plowing season, so steering this plow is what you need to learn."

"If you say so," Arlan said dubiously. "After all, their cannons aren't loaded . . . ?"

"Not loaded?" Rita looked up, startled. "Arlan, my friend—an unloaded gun is a piece of scrap iron!"

"They *are* loaded?" Arlan drew back. "That machine, right there, that I'm supposed to work with, could blow up a major city?"

"Could, but it won't," Rita assured him. "Besides, even if you were an enemy and it did fire, you'd never know what hit you."

That, Arlan decided, was rather cold comfort—but he followed Rita toward the gang-plow. Their lieutenant-mayor had known what he was doing, assigning him to Rita for the first day's learning—he'd known Arlan would rather die than chicken out in front of a pretty girl.

"Morning, Miles," Rita called out, waving.

"Good morning, Rita," the huge machine returned. "Did you have a restful evening?"

"Well, not too restful. Who won the chess match?"

"Gloriosus was one game ahead of me by dawn," Miles answered.

"Well, better luck tomorrow night. I'd better get hopping."

"How can two machines play chess with each other?" Arlan whispered.

"In their computers. They can keep track of the moves perfectly, but I don't know if they visualize the board or not."

Arlan marvelled at the thought of engines of mayhem having a peaceful, stuffy game of chess to pass the time. He hoped Miles wasn't a sore loser.

"You can't think of them as machines," Rita explained as they climbed up onto the plow. "They're allies, friends. Just remember, each one of them is at least as smart as you, and most of them have just as much personality, even if it is artificial."

"How about if one of them decides he doesn't like me?"

"Can't—it's built into their programming." Rita settled herself on the seat, swung it around to face the far 'tractor,' and laid her hands on the wheel.

"Why not just hitch the plows to them, and let them go out in the field to pull?"

"'Cause they'd pack the earth down to concrete," Rita said flatly. "These tractors are *heavy*." She looked up over her shoulder. "Okay, Miles! Tell Gloriosus to start pulling, would you?"

"Certainly, Rita," the huge machine boomed.

Arlan noted the courtesy, and decided to be very polite to these "tractors."

The gang plow lurched into motion, and Rita spun the wheel, straightening out. "The tractor will pull, but you have to keep the furrows straight. . . ."

Arlan listened, trying to pay close attention—but he kept being distracted by the huge machine in front of them, looming closer and closer as they chewed their way across the field. They finished two round trips before he felt ready to try steering by himself.

They went back to the camp for lunch and stayed for an hour's siesta—everyone insisted it was too hot to work. But when things cooled down in late afternoon, back they went for another four hours' labor—and this time, Rita said good-bye as they were passing Miles.

"So soon?" Arlan stared, then caught himself and forced a smile. "You're going to trust me to steer straight, all by myself?"

"It's not that tough, once you get the hang of it," Rita laughed, "and from what I saw this morning, you have. Finish the field, bravo. See you back at camp."

And she was on her way, with a smile and a wave.

Arlan stared up at the huge Bolo, towering overhead, and swallowed. He wondered if Miles could tell when a man was afraid of him.

Well, if he could, it was doubly important not to let on. Arlan forced a smile, waved cheerily, and called up to the turret, "Evening, Miles!"

"Good evening, Arlan," the huge machine answered, in a calm, deep voice that seemed to be right next to Arlan's ear. It almost made him jump, but he hid the reaction and smiled wider. "Do we just take up where we left off?"

"That is the usual procedure, yes, Arlan. There are no bandits or robbers on Milagso, so we just leave the plows at the end of the row, when it comes time to stop for the night."

No wonder there were no bandits—not with a monster of a Bolo sitting right nearby. Arlan went to climb aboard his plow, thinking desperately of some sort of conversational topic. "Didn't the Xiala try to steal equipment, when they were raiding?"

"Surprisingly, no," Miles answered. At least his voice seemed a few feet away now. "The Xiala were warriors exclusively; they did not seek to dwell here, so they had no reason to steal. They were only concerned with destroying everything in sight."

"Cheery blighters—but at least they were predictable." Arlan only wished that the Bolo was—or that he could be sure of it. "Well, time to plow."

"I shall tell Gloriosus to begin pulling, Arlan. Wave when you are ready."

"Will do." Arlan settled himself on the seat, took hold of the wheel, and waved. The plow jerked into motion, and he was off.

He couldn't escape the feeling that he was at the mercy of the two huge killer machines.

After an hour or so, Arlan began to relax, but when

Miles announced that it was quitting time, the volunteer shuddered at the thought of being alone with the giant. To cover his apprehension, he tried to strike up a conversation while he waited for the truck. "You remember the Xiala wars, don't you?"

"The data is stored in my memory banks, yes, Arlan—including visual scans, if they are needed. However, I would caution you that the wars may not be over."

Everybody always seemed to be reminding him of that. Well, let them come—Arlan was ready for his shot at glory. He shuddered at the thought, but he was ready. "Chances aren't too high that the Xiala will attack again, are they?"

"We thought so before," Gloriosus told him. "There was a twenty-year gap between incursions, and we had begun to think there might be peace. Then the Xiala came boiling up out of the irrigation ditches."

"Out of the ditches?" Arlan looked up sharply. "How did they get there? They had to land, first!"

"So they did—but they had been landing secretly, at night, for a year, planting small groups of commandos."

"A *year*?" Arlan looked up, startled. "What did they live off of?"

"They brought rations, but they supplemented them with local flora and fauna."

"You mean they stole crops and livestock?"

"No. Xiala tastes have very little in common with those of humankind. They consider our livestock to be vermin, and vice versa."

"So." Arlan turned to gaze out over the countryside. "They just snacked on rats and snakes. Sure, nobody would miss them. Then they attacked, at a pre-arranged signal?"

"They did, in tens of thousands. The hidden bands, who had no landing craft to which they could retreat, attacked the most suddenly, and fought the hardest. They were very difficult to kill."

Arlan nodded. "I can understand that. No chance they might do it again, is there?"

"Nearly none. We are very vigilant, now—at all hours."

"You said, 'nearly.'"

"That is correct. One must never underestimate the enemy."

"They might always have a new surprise in store." Arlan gazed out over the quiet countryside, imagining detection-proof landing craft, invisible parachutes—any number of technological innovations.

He neglected the oldest and simplest way of bringing in living creatures. There was no shame in that, though—so had everyone else in the colony. The Bolos could be forgiven for not thinking of it—they did not reproduce themselves.

"How long must we wait?" Kaxiax hissed. "Is all our life to be spent in hiding and waiting, like our sires before us?"

"You are young," the lieutenant answered. "I have seen both sire and grandsire die, and we must not shame their memories."

"Let their ghosts fend for themselves!" Kaxiax hissed. "I did not volunteer to end my days on this ancestor-forsaken hole!"

"The worth of your life is in your accomplishments for the species of Xiala," the lieutenant intoned. "If we were to give over and flee, our sires' lives would have been spent to no purpose. But if you, or your offspring, or your offspring's offspring, should smite the Soft Ones and their machines, your ancestors' lives as well as your own would have been filled with purpose, and they would live in glory in the Afterworld."

"If there *is* an Afterworld." Kaxiax's head swivelled around at a slight sigh of displaced sand. He struck, so fast that he would have been a blur to human eyes. The lizard slid down his craw in a single swallow.

The lieutenant ignored the blasphemy; he remembered when he had said much the same, in the impatience of youth. "Go disassemble and oil your weapon," he said. "We must not forget the rituals, or the gods will withdraw their strength from us. Then go coil with your mate, and gain what comfort you may from this life."

"And raise up more Xiala to waste their lives in waiting, belike," Kaxiax grumbled—but he went.

The lieutenant watched him slither away along the ditch. When he was out of sight, the lieutenant laid his head down on the sand and let himself indulge in a moment's despair. Would the command to attack never *come*?

Chono relaxed, leaning back in his canvas chair, drink in hand, and watched the sunset. "You seem to be adjusting pretty well, Arlan."

"Thanks," Arlan said. He sipped his own drink, then added, "I'm still a little nervous, though."

"To be expected." Chono nodded. "Bolos can be mighty intimidating working partners—and a full shift on a plow can be kind of lonely. We try to make up for it during lunchtime and dinnertime, though."

"Oh, you succeed admirably!" For a moment, Arlan had a vivid image of last night's party. He was looking forward to singing and dancing again tonight—Rita wasn't the only pretty girl in the camp. Far from it, in fact.

"So the nerves are only about the Bolos, huh?"

"Yeah." Arlan jolted back to the day he'd just finished. "Chono . . ."

Chono waited, then prodded gently. "Yeah?"

"The Bolos . . . they're so *old*! Are you sure there

isn't any chance that one of them will have a circuit breakdown, and run amok?"

"I wish I could tell you a definite 'no' to that," Chono said grimly. "All I can really say, though, is that it's a low probability. The Bolos were built to *last*— built for the ages, you might say. We actually did an analysis of probability of systems failure, and it turned out that the chances of a Bolo running amok, are much less than the chances of one of us humans going psychotic."

Arlan just stared at the orange sky for a moment, then nodded slowly. "I suppose we *are* made out of less durable materials."

"And most of us don't take care of ourselves too well," Chono agreed. "If we're feeling just a little bit out of sorts, we go to work anyway."

Arlan looked up, amused. "Does that mean that the only ones who are really well, are the hypochondriacs?"

"They would be, if they'd go out and get some exercise. I suppose maybe a hypochondriac health-and-fitness nut would be in good shape, but I don't know any who manage to combine the two—except maybe Bolos."

"The Bolos are hypochondriacs?"

"Well, let's say they have excellent auto-diagnostic programs, and they're much more objective than we are. Besides which, our technicians check over each machine once a month. We maintain them very well."

Arlan nodded. He had found out just how well, when he had met Jodie, and stopped to chat with her in her smithy. The term wasn't all that accurate, of course—most "smithies" didn't include blast furnaces and computer-controlled machine tools. If Jodie said she was a smith, though, he wasn't about to argue—not when he saw how the iron flattened under her hammer. Not when he saw her in profile, either.

"That's an awful lot of labor for one spare part," he said as he watched her watch the automatic lathe.

Jodie nodded. "But even when you add in the cost of my labor, it's still cheaper than importing it. Space cargo rates are very, very high—and the Bolo factory back on Terra charges a liver and ten square inches of skin, for an antique spare like this."

Arlan frowned. "Why so high?"

"Because they have to make them by hand, too. After all, they've been out of production for two hundred years." Jodie braked the lathe and began to loosen the clamps. "So we just machine them ourselves, and save all around."

Watching her strong, slender fingers, Arlan wondered if the machinists on Terra could be any better than she was—or even as good. "I can't help thinking that it would be cheaper and quicker to import modern tractors—or even to manufacture your own."

Jodie nodded. "Every volunteer wonders about that at first. I know I did." She laid the finished part under the magnifying glass and began to inspect it. "There's more to it than economics, though, Arlan. This colony owes its existence to the Bolos. It's a debt. We maintain them out of honor. It may be expensive, but if we forget their past and stop doing it, we'll be welching on a debt—and we'll be less than ourselves."

Arlan watched her work, thinking that over. Traditions and honor seemed to be very expensive. He wondered if Milagso could afford them.

The next day, he dared to sit on Miles's tread as he waited for the truck to pick him up for lunch. He congratulated himself on beginning to trust the huge machine—but he was also aware that his whole body was taut, ready to leap off to the side at the slightest sign that the Bolo was starting to move. "Isn't it hot for you to wait out here in the sun, Miles?"

"Not at all, Arlan. I was built to tolerate temperatures up to fifteen hundred degrees Kelvin, so a variation of twenty degrees Fahrenheit scarcely registers on my thermosensors."

"Must be handy. But you stay parked by this field all through lunchtime. Don't you get bored?"

"I was first activated a thousand years ago, Arlan. A few hours is scarcely noticeable."

Suddenly, the sunlight seemed to be very cold, and the tread beneath his thighs seemed to prickle. "A . . . thousand years? But . . . I thought your model was only produced three hundred years ago, Miles."

"My body was, Arlan. My computer core, though, goes back considerably farther." Then, completely matter-of-factly, the Bolo told him, "I am Resartus."

All things considered, Arlan was very glad that the truck came along just then.

Chono frowned. "He actually *said* he was Resartus? You're sure?"

"Clear as I'm telling you now!" Arlan fought to keep a lid on the panic boiling inside him. "Who exactly was Resartus, anyway?"

"Who? More a 'what' than a 'who.' The Resartus was the initial fully-automated Bolo model, the first one that could fight itself. It was a long way from being self-aware, but when push came to shove, it didn't really *need* a human being aboard."

That gave Arlan a chill. "If you think I'm going back to work with a machine that's gone delusional . . ."

"Peace, peace!" Chono held up a hand, but he was frowning off across the fields. "We're not going to ask that until we're sure Miles is well—but even if he has started thinking he's the original Resartus, he's perfectly safe."

"Perfectly *safe!*"

Chono nodded. "No matter what identity the computer has accepted, it still has its safeguards. It won't attack a human on its own side, no matter what—and out here, all humans are on its side." Chono rose. "But I think we'll leave that field untilled for now. I have a few friends who are going to want to talk to Miles—and spend a little time with the library, too."

The library was accessed through computer, of course, but Miles was accessed in person. Chono's friends were a half-dozen experts in Bolo systems and artificial intelligence. They insisted Arlan come along to double-check what they heard.

"Yes," the Bolo said, "I am Miles—but I am also Resartus."

"How can that be?" asked the senior scientist. He didn't look much like a professor, in khaki shorts and sweat-stained shirt—but he knew what to ask. "The original Resartus wasn't even self-aware."

"That is true, David. But with the enhanced abilities of the Mark XXI's computer, I have gained all the awareness and cogitational capacities of the newer Bolo, while retaining my identity as Resartus."

"How have you come to be housed in this newer unit, then?"

"I was manufactured as Miles," the Bolo answered, "but the essential elements of Resartus were included in my original programming."

"I see." David stroked his beard, frowning. "Do you have any idea how this was done?"

"Not really, David. I was not activated until after the manufacturing process was complete."

Arlan wondered if the Bolo was capable of irony. He decided there was no sarcasm intended; the Bolo was probably giving a straight answer to a straight question.

The truck swayed over a particularly rough bump. Arlan held on and asked, "So it seems to think it's a reincarnation of that first computer-controlled Bolo?"

"We'll have to work with that hypothesis temporarily," David answered.

Arlan shuddered. "What else might it take into its CPU?"

"A good question," David agreed, "and I think we'd better make sure of the answer before we do anything else. You're off the plow for the time being, Arlan. Since you know the case, we're assigning you to the library. Dig up everything you can about the Resartus model, and the government's reaction to it."

Arlan breathed a sigh of relief.

Arlan pored through the stacks, and was amazed at what he found. Yes, the public had been nervous about having a machine that could tear up a city, able to operate without a human aboard—but the government had gone into catfits. They'd insisted on so many restraints, it was amazing that Resartus could still fight itself. When it came to later models, though . . .

"They insisted on having the same restraints built into every later-model Bolo," he told David that evening. He held out the hard copy of the article for him to read. "Turns out that, when the original unit was scrapped, the manufacturers divided Resartus's memory holistically, then reproduced the chips for every Bolo that was manufactured. So each chip had Resartus's complete programming in miniature."

David took the copy and scanned it. "I wonder when they quit doing that."

"Did they?" Arlan shrugged. "I don't know anything about military manufacture—and they might still be doing it. The idea was a sort of fail-safe—if the Bolo's computer did malfunction to the point at which it might start shooting up its own side, Resartus's unquestioning loyalty would take over and keep it safe."

David nodded, then looked up at the other scientists. "Miles has gone non-functional, all right. Maybe the nervous Nellies a thousand years ago, were right."

"Is he dangerous?" Dr. Methuen asked.

"Definitely not—the strategy worked. The chip of Resartus's memory has kicked in as a restraint. Miles won't do anything dangerous to us, as long as Resartus is in charge."

Arlan noticed that they were talking about the Bolo as though it were a person, and repressed a shiver. "Any chance they'll battle it out, and Miles will win?"

A flicker of annoyance crossed David's face, but he masked it quickly. It was as good as a scathing comment, though—the greenhorn stood indicted, at least in his own mind.

But David leaned forward, instantly reassuring. "Don't worry about it, Arlan—Miles's personality can't reassert itself. In a manner of speaking, Miles has shut down, giving Resartus all his ferocious computational capabilities; in a sense, we now have Resartus, self-aware."

"Just how badly-off is he?" Dr. Roman demanded.

"Miles—or perhaps we should just say, 'the confused portion of the artificial mind'—has gone dormant. Resartus has access to all its memories, but can't be affected by its errors in judgment."

"What caused it?" Dr. Methuen asked.

David shrugged. "Can't say, without going inside for a look—and I'm reluctant to ask Resartus for permission. Probably a chip that went bad."

"Can't we just replace the chip?"

"We'd have to, as a first step—either that, or tell Resartus to reroute all his signals around the bad chip, isolate it from the rest of the mind."

Dr. Methuen shrugged. "If that's all there is to it, do it!"

"But that's *not* all there is to it, is it?" Dr. Roman asked.

"No," David agreed. "The problem is that its memories, too, are distributed holistically throughout the 'mind'—and so are the attitudes Miles has developed. So we can't just edit out a faulty logic-sequence."

"My Lord!" Dr. Roman stiffened. "We'd have to take out the total 'mind,' or have a potentially psychotic computer on our hands!"

David nodded. "Right. And, of course, we just don't have what it takes to build a new computer-brain."

"So what do we do?" Arlan asked nervously.

"Nothing." David turned to him. "Resartus's personality is so completely a part of the 'mind,' that the Bolo is perfectly safe. It wasn't just a fail-safe that would hold long enough to deactivate the Bolo—as though anybody could figure out a way to deactivate a Bolo that didn't want it. It was also a program that could hold as long as the unit lasted."

Arlan just stared at him, trying to absorb the idea. "So Miles is permanently asleep, and Resartus has possessed him?"

"No." David stirred restlessly. "It's more complicated than that. All Miles' memories are still there, after all. It's almost as though the Bolo is still Miles, but knows way down deep that he's really Resartus."

"Delusional," Dr. Roman said softly.

Again, that flash of impatience, and David said, "In human terms, yes. But we can't allow ourselves too much teleology in this, Doctor. Miles isn't a person, after all—he's a machine."

"A self-aware machine," Dr. Roman qualified, "with more thinking capacity than any of us."

"More computational capacity, yes—but no intuition, and no real initiative. He can only act within a very clear set of parameters—and Resartus makes those parameters rigid."

"So you suggest we do nothing?" Dr. Methuen asked.

David nodded. "That's my considered opinion." He turned to Arlan. "But you can be assigned to a different field."

"No," Arlan said slowly, "not if you're sure it's safe." He just wished *he* were.

The next morning, Arlan approached the metal giant with his heart in his throat, hoping the Bolo didn't hold grudges. "Good morning, Miles."

"Good morning, Arlan. Did you have a pleasant evening?"

"Pleasant?" Arlan stiffened, then realized that Miles must have thought he'd been given the evening off. "Oh. Very restful, thanks. How about you?"

"David took your place on the plow, and was most diverting. He kept up a constant stream of conversation."

Arlan could just bet David had. "Sorry I'm not that good a conversationalist."

"Please do not be, Arlan. Such extensive conversation is very pleasant as a change, but it does interfere with my chess game."

Arlan grinned as he climbed up onto the plow. "Thanks, Miles. Anything new?"

"Only that we are about to be attacked within the next few days," Miles said thoughtfully. "A major invasion, in fact—by Xiala, of course. I have alerted the other Bolos, but you might want to tell the humans."

Arlan sat very still for a few seconds. Then he climbed down off the plow. "Why, yes, thank you, Miles. I think I should do that."

"I shall call the truck back for you," Miles said.

"Now we know what kind of delusions." Arlan clamped down on hysteria. "He's paranoid!"

"Maybe, but we can't afford to take the chance." David pulled the hovercar over to the side of the road and got out. "Miles might have good reasons for his hunch." He slammed the door and walked over to the looming titan. "Good morning, Miles."

"Good morning, David. I infer that Arlan has given you my news?"

Arlan climbed out of the car slowly, holding onto the door as something solid in a world rapidly going fluid.

"Yes, he has," David said, frowning. "I've checked with the sentry-posts, and they haven't received anything particularly alarming from the satellites."

"Nothing alarming by itself," the Bolo agreed, "but when all the data are taken together as a whole, a pattern emerges."

"Like a chess game, eh?" David folded his arms, squinting up at Miles. "What data are you perceiving?"

"Relays from the surveillance satellites. Over the past month, there have been small celestial bodies flying in flattened arcs from one planet to another. Each event is well-separated from the others in both time and space, but over the year, I have discerned a steady englobing pattern that has come closer and closer to Milagso."

"Sneaking up on us? We'll have to check the records. But why do you think they'll attack in the next few days?"

"Because last night, there was a ten millisecond burst transmission from the vicinity of the nearer moon. I recorded it, slowed it down, and played it back, but it was gibberish. I am attempting to decipher it even now."

"Let us try, too," David urged, "with the really big computer back at base. Squirt your data to it, would you?"

"Certainly, David. However, the most immediate danger was far closer to home."

"Oh?" David tensed. "What was it?"

"Subterranean disturbances. They are consistent with the signals produced by Xiala tunnel-mining, in their last commando raid."

"They've landed commandos again?" David suddenly sounded very serious indeed.

"I have detected no signs of landing craft," Miles admitted, "nor were any such signals picked up by the satellites. I cannot deduce how the commandos have been planted on Milagso, but all indications are that they are indeed here, and preparing for an attack."

"We'll check into it," David said grimly, "and fast! Thanks, Miles. Thanks a lot!"

"You are welcome, David," the huge machine said.

David strode back to the car. "Hop in!" He slammed the door, started up, and turned the hover car back toward headquarters.

"He's paranoid!" Arlan couldn't hold it in any longer. "He has really flipped out! He's developed delusions of conspiracy!"

"Maybe," David said, his words clipped out, "or maybe he's right. Pick up the hand mike and call Dr. Roman, will you? And tell him everything you just heard."

Arlan stared. "You're taking him *seriously*?"

David gave a tight nod. "Very seriously, Arlan. Very seriously indeed."

Serious indeed, but not soon enough. As they pulled in through the gate to headquarters, the soil exploded in the surrounding fields from a hundred tunnels, and the hammering and crackling of automatic weapons erupted.

"Down!" David yelled, and slumped below window level as he pulled the car off to the side of the road. Arlan slid down, too, but wrestled his laser rifle around to the ready. The car stopped, and he swung the door open, rolling out and swivelling about, prone, sighting along the barrel and trying to pick out a target.

It was easy. All the humans had hit the dirt, and moving dust-plumes marked the presence of Xiala. Arlan took aim at the base of one such plume, and was about to pull the trigger when a human rolled in between. He cursed and let up pressure on the trigger . . .

Then the man exploded.

Arlan lay stiff, staring in shock.

Then a serpentine body rose up above the body, a minor cannon with a huge clip clasped in the two slender arms that sprouted below the head. Its mouth opened, fangs springing down as it lunged toward a human fighter . . .

Arlan screamed and pulled the trigger.

The snake's head exploded, and the whole length of its body whipped about, fountaining soil and tearing out plants.

Arlan couldn't take the time to stare, or to feel sick. He swung his rifle about, seeking another target, while something inside him gibbered in terror and urged him to run for cover. It was the child who had grown up on romantic tales of war, aghast at the bloodshed and the hammering of the guns.

Behind and above him, David's laser rifle crackled. Then, suddenly, he howled, and his gun went silent.

Arlan went cold inside, picking out a dust column and firing, then seeking another and firing, deliberately, unhurried. Part of him waited in iron resignation for the laser bolt that would burn through him, but part of him was determined to kill as many snakes as he could before it came. Traverse, fire, traverse, fire . . .

Cannon roared, and a Bolo loomed over the battle, its guns depressed, firing over the humans' heads, enfilading the field. Surely it couldn't be Miles. . . .

Suddenly, its huge cannon elevated, higher and higher, till it seemed the Bolo would throw itself over if it fired. Arlan glanced up, and saw a shimmering shape swelling out of the sky. . . .

Then he looked down, and saw fangs and red maw arrowing toward him, a huge-bore rifle-muzzle coming up to center on him. . . .

He shouted and pressed the trigger. A bolt of pure energy crashed into the gaping jaws. The snake screamed, thrashing, and its cannon bellowed again and again, firing widely in its death throes. Arlan slapped his rifle down and shoved his head flat against the dirt.

A roar filled his head. He dared a look—and saw only dust, where the Xiala had been. He glanced back over his shoulder, and saw the barrel of one of the Bolo's port guns aimed in his direction. Even as he watched, though, he saw the gout of energy explode out of the main cannon's muzzle, tearing into the sky, but he couldn't hear the report, because the whole world was roaring.

The looming shimmering shape turned into flame at one edge. It spun about, and another bolt struck it from the opposite side of the field. It whirled around and slammed spinning into the dirt, sticking up at a crazy angle—a huge landing craft, its ports popping open, snakes pouring out regardless of their dead, slithering onto the ground . . .

The Bolo's secondary guns roared, and the Xiala turned into a boiling cloud of dust, streaked crimson, with tails lashing out of it here and there. Again and again the Bolo fired, and the whole line of the ship turned into a dust storm. Runnels of blood watered the field.

Here and there, a human gun chattered—but rarely, very rarely, for there were very few Xiala escaping the wrecked ship, and the commandos were all dead.

"Of course, we don't know for sure how many of

them got away." David sat with a steaming cup at his elbow, his arm in a sling and a bandage around his head. "We can only guess how many snakes were aboard each ship, and it's hard counting dead bodies; you can't be sure how many of them were completely blown apart. Some of the ships landed half-buried, and Xiala could have tunnelled out of the below-ground hatches."

"So we may have more Xiala hiding out and busily making new little commandos?" Rita asked.

David nodded. "There may even be some of the current generation still alive to teach them the ropes."

"It's so hard to imagine!" Arlan shook his head. "Intelligent, thinking beings, spending their whole lives in exile, and dooming their offspring and their grandchildren to the same waste of their days—all so that their species can have some commandos to prepare the way for them, if they ever decide to try another invasion!"

"Unthinkable to us," Michael agreed. "To a Xiala, it's worth it."

Arlan shuddered. "At least we know Miles hadn't really gone paranoid."

"No," David said slowly. "He seemed to treat the whole problem as a chess game—but he'd had fifty years of fighting Xiala, to use as data for his deductions."

"Anyway," Arlan said, "I guess that's why the Bolos thought they had to become tractors for a while."

Michael looked up, surprised, and David said slowly, "Of course—now that you mention it. Camoflage."

"Lulling the Xiala into a false sense of security," Michael agreed. "Why should they be afraid of these huge war machines, if they'd been converted into farmers?"

"Does that mean you lose your tractors?" Arlan asked.

"They haven't shown any sign of it," David said. "Seem to be more than ready to get back to work, in fact."

"And they haven't deactivated themselves?"

"No, so they can't be given new commanders," Michael confirmed. "I guess their mission isn't over, as far as they're concerned."

"Of course not—we don't know when the snake-commandos may strike again," Rita inferred.

"No," David agreed. "But the next time Miles says they're coming, I think I'll take him at his word."

Arlan shoved his chair back and levered himself up on his crutches.

"Going someplace?" Michael asked.

"To see Miles," Arlan said. "I think I owe him an apology."

His friends exchanged glances; then David pushed himself to his feet. "Wait up; I'll give you a ride. I've got a few words to say to Miles, too."

They came up to the huge Bolo. Its armor was blackened and dented in places, but otherwise it stood as serenely as ever—already back on station at the field it had been plowing.

"Hello, Miles," Arlan said as he came up.

"Hello, Arlan," the Bolo returned. "I am glad to see you have survived the battle. I trust your foot is not too badly injured?"

"This?" Arlan glanced down. "Nothing that won't heal itself. How are you, Miles?"

"Nothing that cannot be mended," the Bolo returned, "and not much of that. This generation of Xiala have weakened sorely; their great-grandsires did far more damage."

"Let's hear it for decadence," David said fervently.

"Uh, Miles . . ." Arlan said. "I'm, uh, sorry I didn't heed your warning right away. . . ."

David nodded emphatically. "Me, too. I should have just taken you at your word, and sent out the alarm. We should have known Resartus wouldn't make a logical mistake."

"Resartus is gone," Miles informed them.

Both men stood very still.

Then David said, very carefully, "Are you fully operational again, Miles?"

"I am," Miles assured them. "As soon as I woke to full function, I ran my recent memories through a diagnostic program. They confirmed that I had run so many invasion scenarios that I had created a loop that became so ingrained, I could not view any data without a bias toward interpreting it as an invasion."

"So when the Xiala actually did invade," David said slowly, "the loop had fulfilled its function, and closed itself off."

"Essentially, David, yes."

"Will you be able to avoid the urge to run invasion scenarios again?" David asked.

"My companion Bolos are agreed on a means that should prove efficacious."

"What kind of means?" Arlan asked.

"A variety of gaming. In addition to our bouts of chess, we will take turns creating invasion scenarios."

"And you'll all know it's a game! Great!" Arlan's eyes lit with enthusiasm. "Can I join?"

David eyed him with a sigh, then smiled. Arlan was fitting in, after all.

The larger moon was up, and Arlan went strolling away from the campfire, hand in hand with Jodie. "You were right," he said. "Traditions do have reasons behind them."

She looked up at him, amused. "Was it worth it, lugging that laser rifle around every day? After all, you only really needed it for half an hour."

"It was worth it," Arlan affirmed. "I'm converted."

"Still nervous about the Bolos?"

Arlan shook his head. "That's another tradition that somehow makes an awful lot of sense now. Mind you, I still think their minds can malfunction and go out of order, though maybe not as easily as ours can. . . ."

"At least they won't be saddled by poor upbringing," Jodie said.

"That *is* the advantage to de-bugged programming," Arlan admitted. "But brooding seems to do just as much damage for artificial intelligences as it does for the real thing."

Jodie shrugged. "So what if Miles went paranoid for a little while? He was curable."

"Yes," Arlan agreed. "All it took was a conspiracy and an invasion."

"Well," Jodie said, "that did bring his delusions into line with reality. So you think the Bolos are worth the labor to maintain them?"

"Oh, you bet I do! In fact, I just might go back to Terra to study artificial intelligence, so I can be of some real worth here."

Jodie stopped and turned to face him, looking up at him in the moonlight. "You are already," she said. "And anything you really need to know, you can learn right here."

Suddenly, Arlan understood why Chono had decided to stay.

OPERATION DESERT FOX

Mercedes Lackey
and Larry Dixon

Siegfried O'Harrigan's name had sometimes caused confusion, although the Service tended to be color-blind. He was black, slight of build and descended from a woman whose African tribal name had been long since lost to her descendants.

He wore both Caucasian names—Siegfried and O'Harrigan—as badges of high honor, however, as had all of that lady's descendants. Many times, although it might have been politically correct to do so, Siegfried's ancestors had resisted changing their name to something more ethnic. Their name was a gift—and not a badge of servitude to anyone. One did not return a gift, especially not one steeped in the love of ancestors. . . .

Siegfried had heard the story many times as a child, and had never tired of it. The tale was the modern equivalent of a fairy tale, it had been so very unlikely.

O'Harrigan had been the name of an Irish-born engineer, fresh off the boat himself, who had seen Siegfried's many-times-great grandmother and her infant son being herded down the gangplank and straight to the Richmond, Virginia, slave market. She had been, perhaps, thirteen years old when the Arab slave-traders had stolen her. That she had survived the journey at all was a miracle. And she was the very first thing that O'Harrigan set eyes on as he stepped onto the dock in this new land of freedom.

The irony had not been lost on him. Sick and frightened, the woman had locked eyes with Sean O'Harrigan for a single instant, but that instant had been enough.

They had shared neither language nor race, but perhaps Sean had seen in her eyes the antithesis of everything he had come to America to find. *His* people had suffered virtual slavery at the hands of the English landlords; he knew what slavery felt like. He was outraged, and felt that he had to do *something*. He could not save all the slaves offloaded this day— but he could help these two.

He had followed the traders to the market and bought the woman and her child "off the coffle," paying for them before they could be put up on the auction-block, before they could even be warehoused. He fed them, cared for them until they were strong, and then put them on *another* boat, this time as passengers, before the woman could learn much more than his name. The rest the O'Harrigans learned later, from Sean's letters, long after.

The boat was headed back to Africa, to the newly founded nation of Liberia, a place of hope for freed slaves, whose very name meant "land of liberty." Life there would not be easy for them, but it would not be a life spent in chains, suffering at the whims of men who called themselves "Master."

Thereafter, the woman and her children wore the name of O'Harrigan proudly, in memory of the stranger's kindness—as many other citizens of the newly-formed nation would wear the names of those who had freed them.

No, the O'Harrigans would not change their name for any turn of politics. Respect earned was infinitely more powerful than any messages beaten into someone by whips or media.

And as for the name "Siegfried"—that was also in memory of a stranger's kindness; this time a member of Rommel's Afrika Korps. Another random act of kindness, this time from a first lieutenant who had seen to it that a captured black man with the name O'Harrigan was correctly identified as Liberian and not as American. He had then seen to it that John O'Harrigan was treated well and released.

John had named his first-born son for that German, because the young lieutenant had no children of his own. The tradition and the story that went with it had continued down the generations, joining that of Sean O'Harrigan. Siegfried's people remembered their debts of honor.

Siegfried O'Harrigan's name was at violent odds with his appearance. He was neither blond and tall, nor short and red-haired—and in fact, he was not Caucasian at all.

In this much, he matched the colonists of Bachman's World, most of whom were of East Indian and Pakistani descent. In every other way, he was totally unlike them.

He had been in the military for most of his life, and had planned to stay in. He was happy in uniform, and for many of the colonists here, that was a totally foreign concept.

Both of those stories of his ancestors were in his mind as he stood, travel-weary and yet excited, before a massive piece of the machinery of war, a glorious hulk of purpose-built design. It was larger than a good many of the buildings of this far-off colony at the edges of human space.

Bachman's World. A poor colony known only for its single export of a medicinal desert plant, it was not a place likely to attract a tourist trade. Those who came here left because life was even harder in the slums of Calcutta, or the perpetually typhoon-swept mud-flats of Bangladesh. They were farmers, who grew vast acreages of the "saje" for export, and irrigated just enough land to feed themselves. A hot, dry wind blew sand into the tight curls of his hair and stirred the short sleeves of his desert-khaki uniform. It occurred to him that he could not have chosen a more appropriate setting for what was likely to prove a life-long exile, considering his hobby—his obsession. And yet, it was an exile he had chosen willingly, even eagerly.

This behemoth, this juggernaut, this mountain of gleaming metal, was a Bolo. Now, it was *his* Bolo, his partner. A partner whose workings he knew intimately . . . and whose thought processes suited his so perfectly that there might not be a similar match in all the Galaxy.

RML-1138. Outmoded now, and facing retirement— which, for a Bolo, meant *deactivation.*

Extinction, in other words. Bolos were more than "super-tanks," more than war machines, for they were inhabited by some of the finest AIs in human space. When a Bolo was "retired," so was the AI. Permanently.

There were those, even now, who were lobbying for AI rights, who equated deactivation with murder. They were opposed by any number of special-interest groups, beginning with religionists, who objected to the notion than anything housed in a "body" of electronic circuitry could be considered "human" enough to "murder." No matter which side won, nothing would occur soon enough to save this particular Bolo.

Siegfried had also faced retirement, for the same reason. *Outmoded.* He had specialized in weapons-systems repair, the specific, delicate tracking and targeting systems.

Which were now outmoded, out-of-date; he had been deemed too old to retrain. He had been facing an uncertain future, relegated to some dead-end job with no chance for promotion, or more likely, given an "early-out" option. He had applied for a transfer, listing, in desperation, everything that might give him an edge somewhere. On the advice of his superiors, he had included his background and his hobby of military strategy of the pre-Atomic period.

And to his utter amazement, it had been that background and hobby that had attracted the attention of someone in the Reserves, someone who had been looking to make a most particular match. . . .

The wind died; no one with any sense moved outside during the heat of midday. The port might have been deserted, but for a lone motor running somewhere in the distance.

The Bolo was utterly silent, but Siegfried knew that he—*he*, not *it*—was watching him, examining him with a myriad of sophisticated instruments. By now, he probably even knew how many fillings were in his mouth, how many grommets in his desert-boots. He had already passed judgment on Siegfried's service record, but there was this final confrontation to face, before the partnership could be declared a reality.

He cleared his throat, delicately. Now came the moment of truth. It was time to find out if what one administrator in the Reserves—and one human facing early-out and a future of desperate scrabbling for employment—thought was the perfect match really *would* prove to be the salvation of that human and this huge marvel of machinery and circuits.

Siegfried's hobby was the key—desert warfare,

tactics, and most of all, the history and thought of one particular desert commander.

Erwin Rommel. The "Desert Fox," the man his greatest rival had termed "the last chivalrous knight." Siegfried knew everything there was to know about the great tank-commander. He had fought and refought every campaign Rommel had ever commanded, and his admiration for the man whose life had briefly touched on that of his own ancestor's had never faded, nor had his fascination with the man and his genius.

And there was at least one other being in the universe whose fascination with the Desert Fox matched Siegfried's. This being; the intelligence resident in this particular Bolo, the Bolo that called *himself* "Rommel." Most, if not all, Bolos acquired a name or nickname based on their designations—LNE became "Lenny," or "KKR" became "Kicker." Whether this Bolo had been fascinated by the Desert Fox because of his designation, or had noticed the resemblance of "RML" to "Rommel" because of his fascination, it didn't much matter. Rommel was as much an expert on his namesake as Siegfried was.

Like Siegfried, RML-1138 was scheduled for "early-out," but like Siegfried, the Reserves offered him a reprieve. The Reserves didn't usually take or need Bolos; for one thing, they were dreadfully expensive. A Reserve unit could requisition a great deal of equipment for the "cost" of one Bolo. For another, the close partnership required between Bolo and operator precluded use of Bolos in situations where the "partnerships" would not last past the exercise of the moment. Nor were Bolo partners often "retired" to the Reserves.

And not too many Bolos were available to the Reserves. Retirement for both Bolo and operator was usually permanent, and as often as not, was in the front lines.

But luck (good or ill, it remained to be seen) was with Rommel; he had lost his partner to a deadly virus, he had not seen much in the way of combat, and he was in near-new condition.

And Bachman's World wanted a Reserve battalion. They could not field their own—every able-bodied human here was a farmer or engaged in the export trade. A substantial percentage of the population was of some form of pacifistic religion that precluded bearing arms—Jainist, Buddhist, some forms of Hindu.

Bachman's World was *entitled* to a Reserve force; it was their right under the law to have an on-planet defense force supplied by the regular military. Just because Bachman's Planet was back-of-beyond of nowhere, and even the most conservative of military planners thought their insistence on having such a force in place to be paranoid in the extreme, that did not negate their right to have it. Their charter was clear. The law was on their side.

Sending them a Reserve battalion would be expensive in the extreme, in terms of maintaining that battalion. The soldiers would be full-timers, on full pay. There was no base—it would have to be built. There was no equipment—that would all have to be imported.

That was when one solitary bean-counting accountant at High Command came up with the answer that would satisfy the letter of the law, yet save the military considerable expense.

The law had been written stipulating, not numbers of personnel and equipment, but a monetary amount. That unknown accountant had determined that the amount so stipulated, meant to be the equivalent value of an infantry battalion, exactly equaled the worth of one Bolo and its operator.

The records-search was on.

Enter one Reserve officer, searching for a Bolo in

good condition, about to be "retired," with no current operator-partner—

—and someone to match him, familiar with at least the rudiments of mech-warfare, the insides of a Bolo, and willing to be exiled for the rest of his life.

Finding RML-1138, called "Rommel," and Siegfried O'Harrigan, hobbyist military historian.

The government of Bachman's World was less than pleased with the response to their demand, but there was little they could do besides protest. Rommel was shipped to Bachman's World first; Siegfried was given a crash-course in Bolo operation. He followed on the first regularly-scheduled freighter as soon as his training was over. If, for whatever reason, the pairing did not work, he would leave on the same freighter that brought him.

Now, came the moment of truth.

"*Guten tag, Herr Rommel,*" he said, in careful German, the antique German he had learned in order to be able to read first-hand chronicles in the original language. "*Ich heisse Siegfried O'Harrigan.*"

A moment of silence—and then, surprisingly, a sound much like a dry chuckle.

"*Wie geht's, Herr O'Harrigan.* I've been expecting you. Aren't you a little dark to be a Storm Trooper?"

The voice was deep, pleasant, and came from a point somewhere above Siegfried's head. And Siegfried knew the question was a trap, of sorts. Or a test, to see just how much he really *did* know, as opposed to what he claimed to know. A good many pre-Atomic historians could be caught by that question themselves.

"Hardly a Storm Trooper," he countered. "Field-Marshall Erwin Rommel would not have had one of *those* under his command. And no Nazis, either. Don't think to trap *me* that easily."

The Bolo uttered that same dry chuckle. "Good for you, Siegfried O'Harrigan. *Willkommen.*"

The hatch opened, silently; a ladder descended just as silently, inviting Siegfried to come out of the hot, desert sun and into Rommel's controlled interior. Rommel had replied to Siegfried's response, but had done so with nothing unnecessary in the way of words, in the tradition of his namesake.

Siegfried had passed the test.

Once again, Siegfried stood in the blindingly hot sun, this time at strict attention, watching the departing back of the mayor of Port City. The interview had not been pleasant, although both parties had been strictly polite; the mayor's back was stiff with anger. He had not cared for what Siegfried had told him.

"They do not much care for us, do they, Siegfried?" Rommel sounded resigned, and Siegfried sighed. It was impossible to hide anything from the Bolo; Rommel had already proven himself to be an adept reader of human body-language, and of course, anything that was broadcast over the airwaves, scrambled or not, Rommel could access and read. Rommel was right; he and his partner were not the most popular of residents at the moment.

What amazed Siegfried, and continued to amaze him, was how *human* the Bolo was. He was used to AIs of course, but Rommel was something special. Rommel cared about what people did and thought; most AIs really didn't take a great interest in the doings and opinions of mere humans.

"No, Rommel, they don't," he replied. "You really can't blame them; they thought they were going to get a battalion of conventional troops, not one very expensive piece of equipment and one single human."

"But we are easily the equivalent of a battalion of conventional troops," Rommel objected, logically. He lowered his ladder, and now that the mayor was well out of sight, Siegfried felt free to climb back into the cool interior of the Bolo.

He waited until he was settled in his customary seat, now worn to the contours of his own figure after a year, before he answered the AI he now consciously considered to be his best friend as well as his assigned partner. Inside the cabin of the Bolo, everything was clean, if a little worn—cool—the light dimmed the way Siegfried liked it. This was, in fact, the most comfortable quarters Siegfried had ever enjoyed. Granted, things were a bit cramped, but he had everything he needed in here, from shower and cooking facilities to multiple kinds of entertainment. And the Bolo did not need to worry about "wasting" energy; his power-plant was geared to supply full-combat needs in any and all climates; what Siegfried needed to keep cool and comfortable was miniscule. Outside, the ever-present desert sand blew everywhere, the heat was enough to drive even the most patient person mad, and the sun bleached everything to a bone-white. Inside was a compact world of Siegfried's own.

Bachman's World had little to recommend it. That was the problem.

"It's a complicated issue, Rommel," he said. "If a battalion of conventional troops had been sent here, there would have been more than the initial expenditure—there would have been an ongoing expenditure to support them."

"Yes—that support money would come into the community. I understand their distress." Rommel would understand, of course; Field Marshal Erwin Rommel had understood the problems of supply only too well, and his namesake could hardly do less. "Could it be they demanded the troops in the first place in order to gain that money?"

Siegfried grimaced, and toyed with the controls on

the panel in front of him. "That's what High Command thinks, actually. There never was any real reason to think Bachman's World was under any sort of threat, and after a year, there's even less reason than there was when they made the request. They expected something to bring in money from outside; you and I are hardly bringing in big revenue for them."

Indeed, they weren't bringing in any income at all. Rommel, of course, required no support, since he was not expending anything. His power-plant would supply all his needs for the next hundred years before it needed refueling. If there had been a battalion of men here, it would have been less expensive for High Command to set up a standard mess hall, buying their supplies from the local farmers, rather than shipping in food and other supplies. Further, the men would have been spending their pay locally. In fact, local suppliers would have been found for nearly everything except weaponry.

But with only one man here, it was far less expensive for High Command to arrange for his supplies to come in at regular intervals on scheduled freight-runs. The Bolo ate nothing. They didn't even use "local" water; the Bolo recycled nearly every drop, and distilled the rest from occasional rainfall and dew. Siegfried was not the usual soldier-on-leave; when he spent his pay, it was generally off-planet, ordering things to be shipped in, and not patronizing local merchants. He bought books, not beer; he didn't gamble, his interest in food was minimal and satisfied by the R.E.M.s (Ready-to-Eat-Meals) that were standard field issue and shipped to him by the crateful. And he was far more interested in that four-letter word for "intercourse" that began with a "t" than in intercourse of any other kind. He was an ascetic scholar; such men were not the sort who brought any amount of money into a community. He and his partner, parked as they

were at the edge of the spaceport, were a continual
reminder of how Bachman's Planet had been
"cheated."

And for that reason, the mayor of Port City had
suggested—stiffly, but politely—that his and Rommel's
continuing presence so near the main settlement was
somewhat disconcerting. He had hinted that the peace-
loving citizens found the Bolo frightening (and never
mind that they had requested some sort of defense
from the military). And if they could not find a way to
make themselves useful, perhaps they ought to at least
earn their pay by pretending to go on maneuvers. It
didn't matter that Siegfried and Rommel were perfectly capable of conducting such exercises without
moving. That was hardly the point.

"You heard him, my friend," Siegfried sighed. "They'd
like us to go away. Not that they have any authority to
order us to do so—as I reminded the mayor. But I
suspect seeing us constantly is something of an
embarrassment to whoever it was that promised a
battalion of troops to bring in cash and got us instead."

"In that case, Siegfried," Rommel said gently, "We
probably should take the mayor's suggestion. How long
do you think we should stay away?"

"When's the next ship due in?" Siegfried replied.
"There's no real reason for us to be here until it
arrives, and then we only need to stay long enough to
pick up my supplies."

"True." With a barely audible rumble, Rommel
started his banks of motive engines. "Have you any
destination in mind?"

Without prompting, Rommel projected the map of
the immediate area on one of Siegfried's control-room
screens. Siegfried studied it for a moment, trying to
work out the possible repercussions of vanishing into
the hills altogether. "I'll tell you what, old man," he
said slowly. "We've just been playing at doing our job.

Really, that's hardly honorable, when it comes down to it. Even if they don't need us and never did, the fact is that they asked for on-planet protection, and we haven't even planned how to give it to them. How about if we actually go out there in the bush and *do* that planning?"

There was interest in the AI's voice; he did not imagine it. "What do you mean by that?" Rommel asked.

"I mean, let's go out there and scout the territory ourselves; plan defenses and offenses, as if this dustball *was* likely to be invaded. The topographical surveys stink for military purposes; let's get a real war plan in place. What the hell—it can't hurt, right? And if the locals see us actually doing some work, they might not think so badly of us."

Rommel was silent for a moment. "They will still blame High Command, Siegfried. They did not receive what they wanted, even though they received what they were entitled to."

"But they won't blame *us*." He put a little coaxing into his voice. "Look, Rommel, we're going to be here for the rest of our lives, and we really can't afford to have the entire population angry with us forever. I know our standing orders are to stay at Port City, but the mayor just countermanded those orders. So let's have some fun, and show 'em we know our duty at the same time! Let's use Erwin's strategies around here, and see how they work! We can run all kinds of scenarios—let's assume in the event of a real invasion we could get some of these farmers to pick up a weapon; that'll give us additional scenarios to run. Figure troops against you, mechs against you, troops and mechs against you, plus untrained men against troops, men against mechs, you against another Bolo-type AI—"

"It would be entertaining." Rommel sounded very

interested. "And as long as we keep our defensive surveillance up, and an eye on Port City, we would not
technically be violating orders. . . ."

"Then let's do it," Siegfried said decisively. "Like I
said, the maps they gave us stink; let's go make our
own, then plot strategy. Let's find every wadi and over-
hang big enough to hide you. Let's act as if there
really was going to be an invasion. Let's give them
some options, log the plans with the mayor's office.
We can plan for evacuations, we can check resources,
there's a lot of things we can do. And let's start right
now!"

They mapped every dry stream-bed, every dusty hill,
every animal-trail. For months, the two of them rumbled
across the arid landscape, with Siegfried emerging now
and again to carry surveying instruments to the tops of
hills too fragile to bear Rommel's weight. And when
every inch of territory within a week of Port City had
been surveyed and accurately mapped, they began
playing a game of "hide and seek" with the locals.

It was surprisingly gratifying. At first, after they had
vanished for a while, the local news-channel seemed to
reflect an attitude of "and good riddance." But then,
when *no one* spotted them, there was a certain
amount of concern—followed by a certain amount of
annoyance. After all, Rommel was "their" Bolo—what
was Siegfried doing, taking him out for some kind of
vacation? As if Bachman's World offered any kind of
amusement. . . .

That was when Rommel and Siegfried began stalk-
ing farmers.

They would find a good hiding place and get into it
well in advance of a farmer's arrival. When he would
show up, Rommel would rise up, seemingly from out
of the ground, draped in camouflage-net, his weaponry
trained on the farmer's vehicle. Then Siegfried would

pop up out of the hatch, wave cheerfully, retract the camouflage, and he and Rommel would rumble away.

Talk of "vacations" ceased entirely after that.

They extended their range, once they were certain that the locals were no longer assuming the two of them were "gold-bricking." Rommel tested all of his abilities to the limit, making certain everything was still up to spec. And on the few occasions that it wasn't, Siegfried put in a requisition for parts and spent many long hours making certain that the repairs and replacements *were* bringing Rommel up to like-new condition.

Together they plotted defensive and offensive strategies; Siegfried studied Rommel's manuals as if a time would come when he would have to rebuild Rommel from spare parts. They ran every kind of simulation in the book—and not just on Rommel's computers, but with Rommel himself actually running and dry-firing against plotted enemies. Occasionally one of the newspeople would become curious about their whereabouts, and lie in wait for them when the scheduled supplies arrived. Siegfried would give a formal interview, reporting in general what they had been doing—and then, he would carefully file another set of emergency plans with the mayor's office. Sometimes it even made the evening news. Once, it was even accompanied by a clip someone had shot of Rommel roaring at top speed across a ridge.

Nor was that all they did. As Rommel pointed out, the presumptive "battalion" would have been available in emergencies—there was no reason why *they* shouldn't respond when local emergencies came up.

So—when a flash-flood trapped a young woman and three children on the roof of her vehicle, it was Rommel and Siegfried who not only rescued them, but towed the vehicle to safety as well. When a snowfall in the mountains stranded a dozen truckers, Siegfried and Rommel got them out. When a small child was lost while playing in the hills, Rommel found her by having all searchers clear out as soon as the sun went down, and using his heat-sensors to locate every source of approximately her size. They put out runaway brushfires by rolling over them; they responded to Maydays from remote locations when they were nearer than any other agency. They even joined in a manhunt for an escaped rapist—who turned himself in, practically soiling himself with fear, when he learned that Rommel was part of the search-party.

It didn't hurt. They were of no help for men trapped in a mine collapse; or rather, of no *more* help than Siegfried's two hands could make them. They couldn't rebuild bridges that were washed away, nor construct roads. But what they could do, they did, often before anyone thought to ask them for help.

By the end of their second year on Bachman's World, they were at least no longer the target of resentment. Those few citizens they had aided actually looked on them with gratitude. The local politicians whose careers had suffered because of their presence had found other causes to espouse, other schemes to pursue. Siegfried and Rommel were a dead issue.

But by then, the two of them had established a routine of monitoring emergency channels, running their private war-games, updating their maps, and adding changes in the colony to their defense and offense plans. There was no reason to go back to simply sitting beside the spaceport. Neither of them cared for sitting idle, and what they were doing was the nearest either of them would ever get to actually refighting the battles their idol had lost and won.

When High Command got their reports and sent recommendations for further "readiness" preparations, and *commendations* for their "community service"— Siegfried, now wiser in the ways of manipulating public opinion, issued a statement to the press about both.

After that, there were no more rumblings of discontent, and things might have gone on as they were until Siegfried was too old to climb Rommel's ladder.

But the fates had another plan in store for them.

Alarms woke Siegfried out of a sound and dreamless sleep. Not the synthesized pseudo-alarms Rommel used when surprising him for a drill, either, but the real thing—

He launched himself out of his bunk before his eyes were focused, grabbing the back of the com-chair to steady himself before he flung himself into it and strapped himself down. As soon as he moved, Rommel turned off all the alarms but one; the proximity alert from the single defense-satellite in orbit above them.

Interior lighting had gone to full-emergency red. He scrubbed at his eyes with the back of his hand, impatiently; finally they focused on the screens of his console, and he could read what was there. And he swore, fervently and creatively.

One unknown ship sat in geosynch orbit about Port City; a big one, answering no hails from the port, and seeding the skies with what appeared to his sleep-fogged eyes as hundreds of smaller drop-ships.

"The mother-ship has already neutralized the port air-to-ground defenses, Siegfried," Rommel reported grimly. "I don't know what kind of stealthing devices they have, or if they've got some new kind of drive, but they don't match anything in my records. They just appeared out of nowhere and started dumping drop-ships. I think we can assume they're hostiles."

They had a match for just this in their hundreds of plans; unknown ship, unknown attackers, dropping a pattern of offensive troops of some kind—

"What are they landing?" he asked, playing the console board. "You're stealthed, right?"

"To the max," Rommel told him. "I don't detect anything like life-forms on those incoming vessels, but my sensors aren't as sophisticated as they could be. The vessels themselves aren't all that big. My guess is that they're dropping either live troops or clusters of very small mechs, mobile armor, maybe the size of a Panzer."

"Landing pattern?" he asked. He brought up all of Rommel's weaponry; AIs weren't allowed to activate their own weapons. And they weren't allowed to fire on living troops without permission from a human, either. That was the only real reason for a Bolo needing an operator.

"Surrounding Port City, but starting from about where the first farms are." Rommel ran swift readiness-tests on the systems as Siegfried brought them up; the screens scrolled too fast for Siegfried to read them.

They had a name for that particular scenario. It was one of the first possibilities they had run when they began plotting invasion and counter-invasion plans.

"Operation Cattle Drive. Right." If the invaders followed the same scheme he and Rommel had anticipated, they planned to drive the populace into Port City, and either capture the civilians, or destroy them at leisure. He checked their current location; it was out beyond the drop-zone. "Is there anything landing close to us?"

"Not yet—but the odds are that something will soon." Rommel sounded confident, as well he should be—his ability to project landing-patterns was far better than any human's. "I'd say within the next fifteen minutes."

Siegfried suddenly shivered in a breath of cool air from the ventilators, and was painfully aware suddenly that he was dressed in nothing more than a pair of fatigue-shorts. Oh well; some of the Desert Fox's battles had taken place with the men wearing little else. What they could put up with, he could. There certainly wasn't anyone here to complain.

"As soon as you think we can move without detection, close on the nearest craft," he ordered. "I want to see what we're up against. And start scanning the local freqs; if there's anything in the way of organized defense from the civvies, I want to know about it."

A pause, while the ventilators hummed softly, and glowing dots descended on several screens. "They don't seem to have anything, Siegfried," Rommel reported quietly. "Once the ground-to-space defenses were fried, they just collapsed. Right now, they seem to be in a complete state of panic. They don't even seem to remember that *we're* out here—no one's tried to hail us on any of our regular channels."

"Either that—or they think we're out of commission," he muttered absently, "Or just maybe they are giving us credit for knowing what we're doing and are trying *not* to give us away. I hope so. The longer we can go without detection, the better chance we have to pull something out of a hat."

An increase in vibration warned him that Rommel was about to move. A new screen lit up, this one tracking a single vessel. "Got one," the Bolo said shortly. "I'm coming in behind his sensor sweep."

Four more screens lit up; enhanced front, back, top, and side views of the terrain. Only the changing views on the screens showed that Rommel was moving; other than that, there was no way to tell from inside the cabin what was happening. It would be different if Rommel had to execute evasive maneuvers of course, but right now, he might have still been parked. The control cabin and living quarters were heavily shielded and cushioned against the shocks of ordinary movement. Only if

Rommel took a direct hit by something impressive would Siegfried feel it. . . .

And if he takes a direct hit by something more than impressive—we're slag. Bolos are the best, but they can't take everything.

"The craft is down."

He pushed the thought away from his mind. This was what Rommel had been built to do—this moment justified Rommel's very existence. And he had known from the very beginning that the possibility, however remote, had existed that he too would be in combat one day. That was what being in the military was all about. There was no use in pretending otherwise.

Get on with the job. That's what they've sent me here to do. Wasn't there an ancient royal family whose motto was "God, and my Duty?" Then let that be his.

"Have you detected any sensor scans from the mother-ship?" he asked, his voice a harsh whisper. "Or anything other than a forward scan from the landing craft?" He didn't know why he was whispering—

"Not as yet, Siegfried," Rommel replied, sounding a little surprised. "Apparently, these invaders are confident that there is no one out here at all. Even that forward scan seemed mainly to be a landing-aid."

"Nobody here but us chickens," Siegfried muttered. "Are they offloading yet?"

"Wait—yes. The ramp is down. We will be within visual range ourselves in a moment—there—"

More screens came alive; Siegfried read them rapidly—

Then read them again, incredulously.

"Mechs?" he said, astonished. *"Remotely controlled mechs?"*

"So it appears." Rommel sounded just as mystified. "This does not match any known configuration. There is one limited AI in that ship. Data indicates it is hardened against any attack conventional forces at the port could mount. The ship seems to be digging in—look at the seismic reading on 4-B. The limited AI is in control of the mechs it is deploying. I believe that we can assume this will be the case for the other invading ships, at least the ones coming down at the moment, since they all appear to be of the same model."

Siegfried studied the screens; as they had assumed, the mechs were about the size of pre-Atomic Panzers, and seemed to be built along similar lines. "Armored mechs. Good against anything a civilian has. Is that ship hardened against anything you can throw?" he asked finally.

There was a certain amount of glee in Rommel's voice. "I think not. Shall we try?"

Siegfried's mouth dried. There was no telling what weaponry that ship packed—or the mother-ship held. The mother-ship might be monitoring the drop-ships, watching for attack. *God and my Duty,* he thought.

"You may fire when ready, Herr Rommel."

They had taken the drop-ship by complete surprise; destroying it before it had a chance to transmit distress or tactical data to the mother-ship. The mechs had stopped in their tracks the moment the AI's direction ceased.

But rather than roll on to the next target, Siegfried had ordered Rommel to stealth again, while he examined the remains of the mechs and the controlling craft. He'd had an idea—the question was, would it work?

He knew weapons' systems; knew computer-driven control. There were only a limited number of ways such controls could work. And if he recognized any of those here—

He told himself, as he scrambled into clothing and climbed the ladder out of the cabin, that he would give himself an hour. The situation would not change much in an hour; there was very little that he and Rommel could accomplish in that time in the way of mounting a campaign. As it happened, it took him fifteen minutes more than that to learn all he needed to know. At the end of that time, though, he scrambled back into Rommel's guts with mingled feelings of elation and anger.

The ship and mechs were clearly of human origin, and some of the vanes and protrusions that made them look so unfamiliar had been tacked on purely to make both the drop-ships and armored mechs look alien in nature. Someone, somewhere, had discovered something about Bachman's World that suddenly made it valuable. From the hardware interlocks and the programming modes he had found in what was left of the controlling ship, he suspected that the "someone" was not a government, but a corporation.

And a multiplanet corporation could afford to mount an invasion force fairly easily. The best force for the job would, of course, be something precisely like this—completely mechanized. There would be no troops to "hush up" afterwards; no leaks to the interstellar press. Only a nice clean invasion—and, in all probability, a nice, clean extermination at the end of it, with no humans to protest the slaughter of helpless civilians.

And afterwards, there would be no evidence anywhere to contradict the claim that the civilians had slaughtered each other in some kind of local conflict.

The mechs and the AI itself were from systems he had studied when he first started in this specialty—outmoded even by his standards, but reliable, and when set against farmers with hand-weapons, perfectly adequate.

There was one problem with this kind of setup . . . from the enemy's standpoint. It was a problem they didn't know they had.

Yet.

* * *

He filled Rommel in on what he had discovered as he raced up the ladder, then slid down the handrails into the command cabin. "Now, here's the thing—I got the access code to command those mechs with a little fiddling in the AI's memory. Nice of them to leave in so many manual overrides for me. I reset the command interface freq to one you have, and hardwired it so they shouldn't be able to change it—"

He jumped into the command chair and strapped in; his hands danced across the keypad, keying in the frequency and the code. Then he saluted the console jauntily. "Congratulations, Herr Rommel," he said, unable to keep the glee out of his voice. "You are now a Field Marshal."

"Siegfried!" Yes, there was astonishment in Rommel's synthesized voice. "You just gave me command of an armored mobile strike force!"

"I certainly did. And I freed your command circuits so that you can run them without waiting for my orders to do something." Siegfried couldn't help grinning. "After all, you're not going against living troops, you're going to be attacking AIs and mechs. The next AI might not be so easy to take over, but if you're running in the middle of a swarm of 'friendlies,' you might not be suspected. And when we knock out *that* one, we'll take over again. I'll even put the next bunch on a different command freq so you can command them separately. Sooner or later they'll figure out what we're doing, but by then I hope we'll have at least an equal force under our command."

"This is good, Siegfried!"

"You bet it's good, *mein Freund,*" he retorted. "What's more, we've studied the best—they can't possibly have that advantage. All right—let's show these amateurs how one of the old masters handles armor!"

*   *   *

The second and third takeovers were as easy as the first. By the fourth, however, matters had changed. It might have dawned on either the AIs on the ground or whoever was in command of the overall operation in the mother-ship above that the triple loss of AIs and mechs was not due to simple malfunction, but to an unknown and unsuspected enemy.

In that, the hostiles were following in the mental footsteps of another pre-Atomic commander, who had once stated, "Once is happenstance, twice is coincidence, but three times is enemy action."

So the fourth time their forces advanced on a ship, they met with fierce resistance.

They lost about a dozen mechs, and Siegfried had suffered a bit of a shakeup and a fair amount of bruising, but they managed to destroy the fourth AI without much damage to Rommel's exterior. Despite the danger from unexploded shells and some residual radiation, Siegfried doggedly went out into the wreckage to get that precious access code.

He returned to bad news. "They know we're here, Siegfried," Rommel announced. "That last barrage gave them a silhouette upstairs; they know I'm a Bolo, so now they know what they're up against."

Siegfried swore quietly, as he gave Rommel his fourth contingent of mechs. "Well, have they figured out exactly what we're doing yet? Or can you tell?" Siegfried asked while typing in the fourth unit's access codes.

"I can't—I—can't—Siegfried—" the Bolo replied, suddenly without any inflection at all. "Siegfried. There is a problem. Another. I am stretching my—resources—"

This time Siegfried swore with a lot less creativity. That was something he had not even considered! The AIs they were eliminating were much less sophisticated than Rommel—

"Drop the last batch!" he snapped. To his relief, Rommel sounded like himself again as he released control of the last contingent of mechs.

"That was not a pleasurable experience," Rommel said mildly.

"What happened?" he demanded.

"As I needed to devote more resources to controlling the mechs, I began losing higher functions," the Bolo replied simply. "We should have expected that; so far I am doing the work of three lesser AIs and all the functions you require, and maneuvering of the various groups we have captured. As I pick up more groups, I will inevitably lose processing functions."

Siegfried thought, frantically. There were about twenty of these invading ships; their plan absolutely required that Rommel control at least eight of the groups successfully to hold the invasion off Port City. There was no way they'd be anything worse than an annoyance with only three; the other groups could out-flank them. "What if you shut down things in here?" he asked. "Run basic life-support, but nothing fancy. And I could drive—run your weapons' systems."

"You could. That would help." Rommel pondered for a moment. "My calculations are that we can take the required eight groups if you also issue battle orders and I simply carry them out. But there is a further problem."

"Which is?" he asked—although he had the sinking feeling that he knew what the problem was going to be.

"Higher functions. One of the functions I will lose at about the seventh takeover is what you refer to as my personality. A great deal of my ability to maintain a personality is dependent on devoting a substantial percentage of my central processor to that personality. And if it disappears—"

The Bolo paused. Siegfried's hands clenched on the arms of his chair.

"—it may not return. There is a possibility that the records and algorithms which make up my personality will be written over by comparison files during strategic control calculations." Again Rommel paused. "Siegfried, this is our duty. I am willing to take that chance."

Siegfried swallowed, only to find a lump in his throat and his guts in knots. "Are you sure?" he asked gently. "Are you very sure? What you're talking about is—is a kind of deactivation."

"I am sure," Rommel replied firmly. "The Field Marshal would have made the same choice."

Rommel's manuals were all on a handheld reader. He had studied them from front to back—wasn't there something in there? "Hold on a minute—"

He ran through the index, frantically keyword searching. This was a memory function, right? Or at least it was software. The designers didn't encourage operators to go mucking around in the AI functions . . . what would a computer jock call what he was looking for?

Finally he found it; a tiny section in programmerese, not even listed in the index. He scanned it, quickly, and found the warning that had been the thing that had caught his eye in the first place.

This system has been simulation proven in expected scenarios, but has never been fully field-tested.

What the hell did that mean? He had a guess; this was essentially a full-copy backup of the AI's processor. He suspected that they had never tested the backup function on an AI with a full personality. There was no way of knowing if the restoration function would actually "restore" a lost personality.

But the backup memory-module in question had its own power-supply, and was protected in the most hardened areas of Rommel's interior. Nothing was going to destroy it that didn't slag him and Rommel together, and if "personality" was largely a matter of memory—

It might work. It might not. It was worth trying, even if the backup procedure was fiendishly hard to initiate. They really *didn't* want operators mucking around with the AIs.

Twenty command-strings later, a single memory-mod began its simple task; Rommel was back in charge of the fourth group of mechs, and Siegfried had taken over the driving.

He was not as good as Rommel was, but he was better than he had thought.

They took groups five, and six, and it was horrible— listening to Rommel fade away, lose the vitality behind the synthesized voice. If Siegfried hadn't had his hands full already, literally, it would have been worse.

But with group seven—

That was when he just about lost it, because in reply to one of his voice-commands, instead of a "Got it, Siegfried," what came over the speakers was the metallic "Affirmative" of a simple voice-activated computer.

All of Rommel's resources were now devoted to self-defense and control of the armored mechs.

God and my Duty. Siegfried took a deep breath, and began keying in the commands for mass armor deployment.

The ancient commanders were right; from the ground, there was no way of knowing when the moment of truth came. Siegfried only realized they had won when the mother-ship suddenly vanished from orbit, and the remaining AIs went dead. Cutting their losses; there was nothing in any of the equipment that would betray *where* it came from. Whoever was in charge of the invasion force must have decided that there was no way they would finish the mission before *someone*, a regularly scheduled freighter or a surprise patrol, discovered what was going on and reported it.

By that time, he had been awake for fifty hours straight; he had put squeeze-bulbs of electrolytic drink near at hand, but he was starving and still thirsty. With the air-conditioning cut out, he must have sweated out every ounce of fluid he drank. His hands were shaking and every muscle in his neck and shoulders were cramped from hunching over the boards.

Rommel was battered and had lost several external sensors and one of his guns. But the moment that the mother-ship vanished, he had only one thought.

He manually dropped control of every mech from Rommel's systems, and waited, praying, for his old friend to "come back."

But nothing happened—other than the obvious things that any AI would do, restoring all the comfort-support and life-support functions, and beginning damage checks and some self-repair.

Rommel was gone.

His throat closed; his stomach knotted. But—

It wasn't tested. That doesn't mean it won't work.

Once more, his hands moved over the keyboard, with another twenty command-strings, telling that little memory-module in the heart of his Bolo to initiate full restoration. He hadn't thought he had water to spare for tears—yet there they were, burning their way down his cheeks. Two of them.

He ignored them, fiercely, shaking his head to clear his eyes, and continuing the command-sequence.

Damage checks and self-repair aborted. Life-support went on automatic.

And Siegfried put his head down on the console to rest his burning eyes for a moment. Just for a moment—

Just—

"*Ahem.*"

Siegfried jolted out of sleep, cracking his elbow on

the console, staring around the cabin with his heart racing wildly.

"I believe we have visitors, Siegfried," said that wonderful, familiar voice. "They seem most impatient."

Screens lit up, showing a small army of civilians approaching, riding in everything from outmoded sandrails to tractors, all of them cheering, all of them heading straight for the Bolo.

"We seem to have their approval at least," Rommel continued.

His heart had stopped racing, but he still trembled. And once again, he seemed to have come up with the moisture for tears. He nodded, knowing Rommel would see it, unable for the moment to get any words out.

"Siegfried—before we become immersed in grateful civilians—how *did* you bring me back?" Rommel asked. "I'm rather curious—I actually seem to remember fading out. An unpleasant experience."

"How did I get you back?" he managed to choke out—and then began laughing.

He held up the manual, laughing, and cried out the famous quote—

"'Rommel, you magnificent bastard, *I read your book!*'"

AS OUR STRENGTH LESSENS

David Drake

Dawn is three hours away, but the sky to the east burns orange and sulphur and deep, sullen red. The rest of my battalion fights there, forcing the Enemy's main line of resistance.

That is not my concern. I have been taken out of reserve and tasked to eliminate an Enemy outpost. The mission appears to me to be one which could have waited until our spearhead had successfully breached the enemy line, but strategic decisions are made by the colloid minds of my human superiors. So be it.

When ion discharges make the night fluoresce, they also tear holes of static in the radio communications spectrum. " . . . *roadwh . . . and suspe . . .*" reports one of my comrades.

Even my enhancement program is unable to decode more of the transmission than that, but I recognize the fist of the sender: *Saratoga*, part of the lead element of our main attack. His running gear has been damaged. He will have to drop out of line.

My forty-seven pairs of flint-steel roadwheels are in depot condition. Their tires of spun beryllium monocrystal, woven to deform rather than compress, all have 97% or better of their fabric unbroken. The immediate terrain is semi-arid. The briefing files inform me this is typical of the planet. My track links purr among themselves as they grind through scrub vegetation and the friable soil, carrying me to my assigned mission.

There is a cataclysmic fuel-air explosion to the east behind me. The glare is visible for 5.3 seconds, and the ground will shake for many minutes as shock waves echo through the planetary mantle.

Had my human superiors so chosen, I could be replacing *Saratoga* at the spearhead of the attack.

The rear elements of the infantry are in sight now. They look like dung beetles in their hard suits, crawling backward beneath a rain of shrapnel. I am within range of their low-power communications net. *"Hold what you got, troops,"* orders the unit's acting commander. *"Big Brother's come to help!"*

I am not Big Brother. I am *Maldon*, a Mark XXX Bolo of the 3d Battalion, Dinochrome Brigade. The lineage of our unit goes back to the 2nd South Wessex Dragoons. In 1944, we broke the last German resistance on the path to Falaise—though we traded our flimsy Cromwells against the Tigers at a ratio of six to one to do it.

The citizens do not need to know what the cost is. They need only to know that the mission has been accomplished. The battle honors welded to my turret prove that I have always accomplished my mission.

Though this task should not have been a difficult one, even for the company of infantry to whom it was originally assigned. An Enemy research facility became, because of its location, an outpost on the flank of our line as we began to drive out of the landing zone. In a breakthrough battle, infantry can do little but die in their fighting suits. A company of them was sent to mop up the outpost in relative safety.

Instead . . .

As I advance, I review the ongoing mission report filed in real-time by the infantry and enhanced at Headquarters before being downloaded to me microseconds later. My mind forms the blips of digital information into a panorama, much as the colloid minds of my superiors process sensory data fired into them across nerve endings.

Vehicles brought the infantry within five kilometers of their objective. There they disembarked for tactical flexibility and to avoid giving the Enemy a single soft target of considerable value.

I watch:

The troops advance by tiny, jerky movements of the legs of their hard suits. My tracks, rotating in silky precision, purr with laughter.

The concept of vertical envelopment, overflying an enemy's lines to drop forces in his rear, ceased to be viable with the appearance of directed-energy weapons in the 20th century. After the development of such weapons, any target which could be seen—even in orbit above an atmosphere—could be hit at the speed of light.

No flying vehicle could be armored heavily enough to withstand attack by powerful beam weapons. The alternative was more of the grinding ground assaults to which civilians always object because they are costly and brutal, and to which soldiers always turn because they succeed when finesse does not succeed.

Our forces have landed on an empty, undefended corner of this planet. The blazing combat to the east occurs as our forces meet those which the Enemy is rushing into place to block us.

I am not at my accustomed place in the front line, but the Enemy will not stop the advance of my comrades.

I watch:

The leading infantry elements have come in sight of their objective. There is something wrong with the data, because the Enemy research facility appears as a spherical flaw—an absence of information—in the transmitted images.

Light blinks from the anomaly. It is simply that, light, with the balance and intensity of the local solar output at ground level on this planet.

The infantry assume they are being attacked. They respond with lasers and projectile weapons as they take cover and unlimber heavier ordnance. Within .03 seconds of the first shot, the Enemy begins to rake the infantry positions with small arms fire.

While the battalion was in transit to our target, briefing files were downloaded into our data banks. These files, the distillation of truth and wisdom by our human superiors, state that the Enemy is scientifically far inferior to ourselves. There is no evidence that the Enemy even has a working stardrive now, though unquestionably at some past time they colonized the scores of star systems which they still inhabit.

Enemy beam weapons are admittedly very efficient. The Enemy achieves outputs from hand-held devices which our forces can duplicate only with large vehicle-mounted units. Our scientific staff still has questions regarding the power sources which feed these Enemy beam weapons.

Thus far the briefing files. I have examined the schematics of captured Enemy lasers. The schematics show no power source whatever. This is interesting, but it does not affect the certainty of our victory.

Initially, the Enemy outpost to which I have been

tasked was not using weapons more powerful than the small arms which our own infantry carry.

I watch:

The infantry is well trained. Three-man teams shoot and advance in a choreographed sequence, directing a steady volume of fire at the outpost. At the present range it is unlikely that their rifles and lasers will do serious damage. The purpose of this fire is to disrupt the Enemy's aim and morale while more effective weapons can be brought to bear. The heavy-weapons section is deploying back-pack rockets and the company's light ion cannon.

An infantryman ripple-fires his four-round rocket pack. The small missiles are self-guiding and programmed to vary their courses to the laser-cued target.

Three of the rockets curve wildly across the bleak terrain and detonate when they exhaust their fuel. They have been unable to fix on the reflected laser beam which should have provided the precise range of the target. The anomaly has absorbed the burst of coherent light so perfectly that none bounces back to be received by the missiles' homing devices. Only the first round of the sequence, directed on a line-straight track, seems to reach the target.

The missile vanishes. There is no explosion. At .03 seconds after the computed moment of impact—there is no direct evidence that the rocket actually hit its target—the Enemy outpost launches a dozen small missiles of its own. One of them destroys the ion cannon before the crew can open fire.

Puffs of dirt mark the battlefield. The infantry is using powered augers to dig in for greater protection. The Enemy outpost continues to rake the troops with rockets and small arms, oblivious of the infantry's counterfire.

Seven hours before planetfall, a human entered the bay where we Bolos waited in our thoughts and memories. He wore the trousers of an officer's dress uniform, but he had taken off the blouse with the insignia of his rank.

The human's face and name were in my data banks. He was Major Peter Bowen, a member of the integral science staff of our invasion force. My analysis of the air Bowen exhaled indicated a blood alcohol level of .1763 parts per hundred. He moved with drunken care.

"Good evening, Third Battalion," Bowen said. He attempted a bow. He caught himself with difficulty on a bulkhead when he started to fall over. I realized that the bay was not lighted in the human-visible spectrum. Bowen had no business here with us, but he was a human and an officer. I switched on the yellow navigation lights along my fender skirts.

Bowen walked toward me. "Hello, Bolo," he said. "Do you have a name?"

I did not answer. My name was none of his concern; and anyway, it did not appear that he was really speaking to me. Humans often say meaningless things. Perhaps that is why they rule and we serve.

"None of my business, hey, buddy?" said Bowen. "There's been a lot of that goin' around lately." He was not a fool, and it appeared that he was less incapacitated by drink than I had assumed.

He reached out to my treads. I thought he was steadying his drunken sway, but instead the scientist's fingers examined the spun crystal pads of a track block. "Colonel McDougal says I'm not to brief the battalion tasking officers because that's been taken care of by real experts. Colonel McDougal's a regular officer, so he oughta know, right?"

The situation shocked me. "Colonel McDougal is your direct superior, Major Bowen," I said.

"Oh, you bet McDougal's superior to me," Bowen said in what should have been agreement but clearly was not. "He'll be the first to tell you so, the Colonel will. I'm just a civilian with a commission. Only—I figured that since I was here, maybe I ought to do my job."

"Your job is to carry out your superior's orders to the best of your ability," I replied.

Bowen chuckled. "You too," he said. His hands caressed my bow slope. My battle honors are welded to my turret, but the flint-steel of my frontal armor bears scars which tell the same story to those who can read them.

"What's your name, friend?" Bowen asked.

My name is my password, which Bowen is not authorized to know. I do not reply.

He looked at me critically. "You're Maldon," he said, "Grammercy's your tasking officer."

I am shocked. Bowen could have learned that only from Captain Grammercy himself. Why would Grammercy have spoken what was his duty to conceal? It is not my duty to understand colloid minds; but I sometimes think that if I could, I would be better able carry out the tasks they set me.

"You know the poem, at least?" Bowen added.

It was several microseconds before I realized that this, though inane, was really meant as a question. "Of course," I said. All the human arts are recorded in my data banks.

"And you know that the Earl of Essex was a fool?" said Bowen. "That he threw his army away and left his lands open to pillage because of his stupidity?"

"His bodyguards were heroes!" I retorted. "They were steadfast!"

The bay echoed with my words, but Bowen did not flinch back from me. "All honor to their courage!" he snapped. I remembered that I had thought he was drunk and a disgrace to the uniform he—partly—wore. "They took the orders of a fool. And died, which was no dishonor. *And* left their lands to be raped by Vikings, which was no honor to them or their memory, Maldon!"

The retainers of the Earl of Essex were tasked to prevent Vikings under Olaf Tryggvason from pillaging the county. The Earl withdrew his forces from a blocking position in order to bring the enemy to open battle at Maldon. His bodyguards fought heroically but were defeated.

The Earl's bodyguards failed to accomplish their mission. There is no honor in failure.

"What did you wish to tell us, Major Bowen?" I asked.

The human coughed. He looked around the bay before he replied. His eyes had adapted to the glow of my running lights.

My comrades of the 3d Battalion listened silently to the conversation. To a creature of Bowen's size, fifty-one motionless Bolos must have loomed like features of a landscape rather than objects constructed by tools in human hands.

"The accepted wisdom," Bowen said, "is that the Anceti are scientifically backward. That the race has degenerated from an advanced level of scientific ability, and that the remnants of that science are no threat to human arms."

He patted the flint-steel skirt protecting my track and roadwheels. "No serious threat to you and your friends, Maldon."

"Yes," I said, because I thought a human would have spoken . . . though there was no need to tell Bowen what he already knew was in the official briefing files.

"I don't believe the Anceti are degenerate," Bowen said. "And I *sure* don't think they're ignorant. Nobody who's turning out lasers like theirs is ignorant. They've got a flux density of ten times our best—and there's not even a hint of a power source."

"The Enemy no longer has stardrive," I said, as if I were stating a fact instead of retailing information from the briefing files. This is a technique humans use when they wish to elicit information from other humans.

"Balls!" Bowen said. He did not speak as a human and my superior. Instead, his voice had the sharpness of a cloud as it spills lightning to the ground, careless and certain of its path. "Do you believe that, Maldon? Is that the best the mind of a Bolo Mark XXX can do synthesizing data?"

I was stung. "So the briefing files stated," I replied, "and I have no information to contradict—"

"Balls!" Bowen repeated.

I said nothing.

After a moment, the scientist continued, "There's a better than 99% probability that the Anceti are reinforcing their outpost worlds under threat of our attack. How are they doing that if they don't have stardrive, Maldon?"

I reviewed my data banks. "Reconnaissance shows the strengthened facilities," I said. I already knew how Bowen was going to respond. "Reconnaissance does not show that the equipment and personnel were imported from outside the worlds on which they are now based."

"We're talking about barren rocks, some of these planets," Bowen said. His tone dripped with disgust. I choose to believe that was a human rhetorical device rather than his real opinion of my intellect. "The Anceti and their hardware didn't spring from rocks, Maldon; they were brought there. A better than 99% probability. We just don't know how."

"The briefing files are wrong," I said. I spoke aloud to show the human that I understood.

They rule and we serve. We know one truth at a time, but colloid minds believe contradictory truths or no truth at all. So be it.

There was a question that I could not resolve, no matter how I attempted to view the information at my disposal. I needed more data. So—

"Why are you telling us this, Major Bowen?" I asked.

"Because I want you to understand," the human said fiercely, "that the Anceti's science *isn't* inferior to ours, it's just different. Like the stardrive. Did you know that every one of the star systems the Anceti have colonized at some point in galactic history crossed a track some other Anceti star system occupied? Or *will* occupy!"

I reviewed my data banks. The information was of course there, but I had not analyzed it for this purpose.

"There is no indication that the Enemy has time travel, Major Bowen," I said. "Except the data you cite, which could be explained by an assumption of time travel."

"I know that, I know that," Bowen replied. His voice rose toward hysteria, but he caught himself in mid-syllable. "I don't say they have time travel, I don't *believe* they have time travel. But they've got something, Maldon. I know they've got something."

"We will accomplish our mission, Major Bowen," I said to soothe him.

Some humans hate us for our strength and our difference from them, even though they know we are the starkest bulwark against their Enemies. Most humans treat us as the tools of their wills, as is their right. But a very few humans are capable of concern for minds and personalities, though they are encased in flint-steel and ceramic rather than protoplasm.

All humans are to be protected. Some are to be cherished.

"Oh, I don't doubt you'll accomplish *your* mission, Maldon," Bowen said, letting his fingers pause at the gouge in my bow slope where an arc knife struck me a glancing blow. "But I've failed in mine."

He made the sound of laughter, but there was no humor in it. "That's why I'm drunk, you see." He cleared his throat. "Well, I was drunk. And I'll be drunk again, real soon."

"You have not failed, Major Bowen," I said. "You have corrected the faulty analysis of others."

"I haven't corrected anything, Maldon," the human said. "I can't give them a mechanism for whatever the Anceti are doing, so nobody in the task force believes me. Nobody even listens. They're too happy saying that the Anceti are a bunch of barbarians we're going to mop up without difficulties."

"We believe you, Major Bowen," I said. I spoke for all my comrades in the 3d Battalion, though they remained silent on the audio frequencies. "We will be ready to react to new tricks and weapons of the Enemy."

"That's good, Maldon," said the human. He squeezed my armor with more force than I had thought his pudgy fingers could achieve. "Because you're the guys who're going to pay the price if Colonel McDougal's wisdom is wrong."

He turned and walked back to the hatchway. "Now," he added, "I'm going to get drunk."

I wonder where Major Bowen is now. Somewhere in Command, some place as safe as any on a planet at war. Behind me, the main battle rages in a fury of shock waves and actinic radiation. It is hard fought, but the exchanges of fire are within expected parameters.

The mission to which I have been assigned, on the other hand . . .

The infantry company called in artillery support as soon as the Enemy outpost began strafing them with back-pack missiles.

I watch:

The first pair of artillery rockets streaks over the horizon.

The missiles' sustainer motors have burned out, but the bands of maneuvering jets around each armor-piercing warhead flash as they course-correct. They are targeted by triangulation from fixed points, since the outpost itself remains perfectly absorbant throughout the electro-optical band. These are probing rounds, intended to test the Enemy's anti-artillery defenses so that the main barrage can be protected by appropriate countermeasures.

The Enemy has no defenses. The shells plunge into the center of the anomaly and disappear, just as all earlier projectiles and energy beams have done. Neither these shells nor the barrage which follows has any discernible effect on the Enemy.

.03 seconds from the first warhead's calculated moment of impact, the research facility begins to bombard our attacking infantry with artillery rockets.

The Enemy is firing armor-piercing rounds. They are already at terminal velocity when they appear from the anomaly. When the warheads explode deep underground, the soil spews up and flings dug-in infantrymen flailing into air. Sometimes the hard suits protect the infantry well enough that the victims are able to crawl away under their own power.

Back-pack missiles and small arms fire from the outpost continue to rake the infantry positions. The company commander orders his troops to withdraw. 5.4 seconds later, the acting company commander calls for a Bolo to be assigned in support.

The air over the battlefield is a pall of black dust, lighted fitfully by orange flashes at its heart.

I am now within the extreme range even of small arms fired from the research facility. The Enemy does not engage me. Shells launched from the anomaly continue to pound the infantry's initial deployment area, smashing the remains of fighting suits into smaller fragments. The surviving infantry have withdrawn from the killing ground.

Friendly missiles continue to vanish into the anomaly without effect.

Thus far I have observed the outpost only through passive receptors. I take a turret-down position on the reverse slope of a hill and raise an active ranging device on a sacrificial mounting above my protective armor. Using this mast-mounted unit, I probe the anomaly with monopulse emissions on three spectra.

There is no echo from the anomaly. .03 seconds after the pulses should have ranged the target, the outpost directs small arms fire and a pair of artillery rockets at me.

The bullets and low-power laser beams are beneath my contempt. The sacrificial sensor pod is the only target I have exposed to direct fire. It is not expected to survive contact with an enemy, but the occasional hit the pod receives at this range barely scratches its surface.

As for the artillery fire—the Enemy is not dealing with defenseless infantry now. I open a micro-second window and EMP the shells, destroying their control circuitry. The ring thrusters shut off and the warheads go ballistic. Neither shell will impact within fifty meters of my present location.

.03 seconds from the moment I fried the Enemy warheads, a high-amplitude electromagnetic pulse from the anomaly meets the next of the shells raining in from friendly artillery batteries. The warhead has already made its final course corrections, so it plunges into the calculated center of the target. The electronic fuzing will probably have failed under the EMP attack, but the back-up mechanical detonators should still function.

It is impossible to tell whether the mechanical fuzes

work: there is, as I have come to expect, no sign even of kinetic impact with the anomaly.

The outpost launches two more missiles and a storm of small arms fire at me. The missiles course-correct early. They will strike me even if their control circuits are destroyed.

To the east, the air continues to flash and thunder over the Enemy's main line of resistance. Casualties there are heavy but within expected parameters. My comrades will make their initial breakthrough within five hours and thirty-seven minutes, unless there is a radical change in Enemy strength.

This research facility is far from the population centers of this planet. Did the Enemy place it in so isolated a location because they realized the risk of disaster at the cutting edge of the forces they were studying desperately to meet our assault?

I know they've got something, Major Bowen told me. He was right. The real battle will not be decided along the main line but rather here.

I open antenna apertures to send peremptory signals to Command, terminating the artillery fire mission. I use spread-transmission radio—which may be blocked by war-roiled static across the electromagnetic spectrum; laser—which will be received only if all the repeaters along the transmission path have survived combat; and ground conduction, which is slow but effectively beyond jamming.

Friendly artillery has no observable effect on the outpost, and it interjects a variable into the situation. All variables thus far appear to have benefited the Enemy.

While I deliver instructions and a report to Command, and while my mind gropes for a template which will cover my observations thus far of the Enemy's capabilities, I deal with the incoming missiles. I spin a pair of fluctuating apertures in my turret shielding. The gaps are aligned with the lifting muzzles of my infinite repeaters and in synchronous with their cyclic rate.

I fire. Pulses along the superconducting magnets in the bores of the infinite repeaters accelerate short tubes of depleted uranium—ring penetrators—to astronomical velocity. Miniature suns blaze from kinetic impact where my penetrators intersect the warheads. The missiles lose aerodynamic stability. They tumble in glowing cartwheels across the sky.

.03 seconds after I engage the warheads, a burst of hyper-velocity ring penetrators from the anomaly shreds my sacrificial sensor pod.

My capacity to store and access information is orders of magnitude beyond that of the colloid minds I serve, but even so only part of the knowledge in my data banks is available to me at any one moment. Now, while I replace the sensors and six more missiles streak toward me out of the anomaly, I hear the baritone voice of the technician replacing my port-side roadwheels during depot service seventy-four years ago.

He sings: *Get in, get out, quit muckin' about—*
Drive on!

My data processing system has mimicked a colloid mind to short-circuit my decision tree. I have been passive under attack for long enough.

I advance, blowing the hillcrest in front of me so that I do not expose my belly plates by lifting over it.

Both direct and indirect fire have battlefield virtues. Direct fire is limited by terrain and, if the weapon is powerful enough, by the curvature of the planet itself. But, though the curving path of indirect fire can reach any target, the warheads have necessarily longer flight times and lower terminal velocities because of their trajectory. When they hit, they are less effective than direct-fire projectile weapons; and the most devastating artillery of all, directed energy weapons, can operate only in the direct-fire mode.

The worst disadvantage of direct fire weapons is that the shooter must by definition be in sight of his target. Bolos are designed to be seen by our targets and survive.

My tracks accelerate me through the cloud of pulverized rock where the hillcrest used to be. The infinite repeaters in my turret hammer the anomaly with continuous fire. I am mixing ring penetrators and high explosive in a random pattern based on cosmic ray impacts.

I hope this will confuse the Enemy defenses. The only evident effect of my tactic is that, .03 seconds from the time the first HE round should have hit the anomaly, the Enemy begins to include high-explosive rounds in the bursts which flash harmlessly against my electromagnetic shielding.

I am clear of the rock dust. I align myself with the anomaly and fire my Hellbore from its centerline hull installation.

Even *my* mass is jolted by the Hellbore's recoil. A laser-compressed thermonuclear explosion at the breech end voids a slug of ions down the axis of the bore, the only path left open. The bolt can devour mountains or split rock on planets in distant orbits.

My Hellbore has no discernible effect on the anomaly; but .03 seconds after I fire, an ion bolt smashes into me.

I am alive. For nearly a second, I am sure of nothing else. Circuits, shut down to avoid burning out under overload, come back on line.

I have received serious injuries. My hull and running gear are essentially undamaged. Most of the anti-personnel charges along my skirts have gone off in a single white flash. This is of no importance, since it now appears vanishingly improbable that I will ever see Enemy personnel.

87% of my external communications equipment has

been destroyed. Most of the antennas have vaporized, despite the shutters of flint-steel which were to protect them. I reroute circuits and rotate back-up antennas from my hull core.

My infinite repeaters were cycling when the ion bolt struck. Ions ravening through the aperture in my electromagnetic shielding destroyed both infinite repeaters, bathed the hull and wiped it clean of most external fittings, and penetrated the turret itself through one of the weapons ports. All armament and sensory installations within my turret have been fused into a metal-ceramic magma.

The turret ring is not blocked, and the drive mechanism still works. I rotate the turret so that the back instead of the hopelessly compromised frontal armor faces the anomaly.

Data clicks into a gestalt which explains the capabilities which the Enemy has demonstrated.

I brake my starboard track while continuing to accelerate with the port drive motors. My hull slews. The change in direction throws a comber of earth and rock toward the outpost. Though my size and inertia are so great that I cannot completely dodge the Enemy's second ion bolt, the suspension of soil in air dissipates much of the charge in a fireball and thunderclap. My hull shakes, but the only additional damage I receive is to some of the recently replaced communications gear.

I am transmitting my conclusions to Command via all the channels available to me. I load a message torpedo intended for communication under the most adverse conditions. This is a suitable occasion for its use.

The Hellbore discharge has disrupted the guidance systems of the artillery rockets the Enemy launched at me seconds earlier. In the momentary silence following the bolt's near miss, I release my torpedo. It streaks away to warn Command. The Enemy ignore the torpedo in the chaos of their own tumbling shells.

The Enemy is not mirroring matter. Rather, the Enemy mirrors facets of temporal reality. Our forces have seen no evidence of Enemy stardrive because for the Enemy, a planet can fill a point in space where it once existed or will one day exist. The Enemy need not transit the eternal present so long as there is a congruity between Now and When.

Personnel of the research facility I have been tasked to eliminate have developed the technique still further. They are creating a special space-time in which whatever can exist, *does* exist for them so long as there is an example of the occurrence in their reality matrix.

Their tool is the anomaly that appears from outside to be a non-reflecting void. It is a tunable discontinuity in the local space-time. The staff of the research facility use this window to capture templates, copies of which are in .03 seconds shuttled into present reality and redirected at their opponents.

The research facility can already mimic the firepower of an infantry company, a battery of rocket artillery, and—because of my actions—a Mark XXX Bolo. I have only one option.

There is no cover for an object my size between me and the research facility. Though my drive motors are spinning at full power, nothing material can outrun the bolt of a Hellbore. The third discharge catches me squarely.

The shockwave blasts a doughnut from the soil around me. My turret becomes a white-hot fireball. The electromagnetic generators in the turret were damaged by the initial bolt and could not provide more than 60% of their designed screening capacity against the second direct hit. My port skirts are blasted off; several track links bind momentarily. My drive motors have enough torque to break the welds, but again I slow and skid in a jolting S-turn.

My target is a research facility. It is possible that the Enemy will not be able to develop similar capabilities anywhere else before our forces have smashed them into defeat. That is beyond my control—and outside my mission. *This* is the target I have been tasked to eliminate.

I open the necessary circuits and bypass the interlocks. A disabled Bolo is too valuable to be abandoned, so there have to be ways.

I have no offensive armament. My Hellbore is operable, but the third ion bolt welded the gunport shutters closed. A salvo of armor-piercing shells hammers my hull, lifting me and slamming me back to the ground in a red-orange cataclysm. The multiple impacts strip my starboard track.

I think of Major Bowen, and of the Saxon bodyguards striding forward to die at Maldon:

Heart grow stronger, will firmer,
Mind more composed, as our strength lessens.

The citizens do not need to know what the cost is. They need only to know that the mission has been accomplished.

My sole regret, as I initiate the scuttling sequence that will send my fusion pile critical, is that I will not be present in .03 seconds. I would like to watch as the Enemy try to vent an omnidirectional thermonuclear explosion into their research facility.

FALLEN ANGELS

Two refugees from one of the last remaining orbital space stations are trapped on the North American icecap, and only science fiction fans can rescue them! Here's an excerpt from *Fallen Angels*, the bestselling new novel by Larry Niven, Jerry Pournelle, and Michael Flynn.

*   *   *

She opened the door on the first knock and stood out of the way. The wind was whipping the ground snow in swirling circles. Some of it blew in the door as Bob entered. She slammed the door behind him. The snow on the floor decided to wait a while before melting. "Okay. You're here," she snapped. "There's no fire and no place to sit. The bed's the only warm place and you know it. I didn't know you were this hard up. And, by the way, I don't have any company, thanks for asking." If Bob couldn't figure out from that speech that she was pissed, he'd never win the prize as Mr. Perception.

"I am that hard up," he said, moving closer. "Let's get it on."

"Say what?" Bob had never been one for subtle technique, but this was pushing it. She tried to step back but his hands gripped her arms. They were cold as ice, even through the housecoat. "Bob!" He pulled her to him and buried his face in her hair.

"It's not what you think," he whispered. "We don't have time for this, worse luck."

"Bob!"

"No, just bear with me. Let's go to your bedroom. I don't want you to freeze."

He led her to the back of the house and she slid under the covers without inviting him in. He lay on top, still wearing his thick leather coat. Whatever he had in mind, she realized, it wasn't sex. Not with her housecoat, the comforter and his greatcoat playing chaperone.

He kissed her hard and was whispering hoarsely in her ear before she had a chance to react. "Angels down. A scoopship. It crashed."

"Angels?" Was he crazy?

He kissed her neck. "Not so loud. I don't think the 'danes are listening, but why take chances? Angels. Spacemen. *Peace* and *Freedom*."

She'd been away too long. She'd never heard spacemen called *Angels*. And— "Crashed?" She kept it to a whisper. "Where?"

"Just over the border in North Dakota. Near Mapleton."

"Great Ghu, Bob. That's on the Ice!"

He whispered, "Yeah. But they're not too far in."

"How do you know about it?"

He snuggled closer and kissed her on the neck again. Maybe sex made a great cover for his visit, but she didn't think he had to lay it on so thick. "We know."

"We?"

"The Worldcon's in Minneapolis-St. Paul this year—"

The World Science Fiction Convention. "I got the invitation, but I didn't dare go. If anyone saw me—"

"—And it was just getting started when the call came down from *Freedom*. Sherrine, they couldn't have picked a better time or place to crash their scoopship. That's why I came to you. Your grandparents live near the crash site."

She wondered if there was a good time for crashing scoopships. "So?"

"We're going to rescue them."

"We? Who's we?"

"The Con Committee, some of the fans—"

"But why tell me, Bob? I'm fafiated. It's been years since I've dared associate with fen."

Too many years, she thought. She had discovered science fiction in childhood, at her neighborhood branch library. She still remembered that first book: *Star Man's Son*, by Andre Norton. Fors had been persecuted because he was different; but he nurtured a secret, a mutant power. Just the sort of hero to appeal to an ugly-duckling little girl who would not act like other little girls.

SF had opened a whole new world to her. A galaxy, a

universe of new worlds. While the other little girls had played with Barbie dolls, Sherrine played with Lummox and Poddy and Arkady and Susan Calvin. While they went to the malls, she went to Trantor and the Witch World. While they wondered what Look was In, she wondered about resource depletion and nuclear war and genetic engineering. Escape literature, they called it. She missed it terribly.

"There is always one moment in childhood," Graham Greene had written in *The Power and the Glory*, "when the door opens and lets the future in." For some people, that door never closed. She thought that Peter Pan had had the right idea all along.

"Why tell *you*? Sherrine, we want you with us. Your grandparents live near the crash site. They've got all sorts of gear we can borrow for the rescue."

"Me?" A tiny trickle of electric current ran up her spine. But . . . *Nah.* "Bob, I don't dare. If my bosses thought I was associating with fen, I'd lose my job."

He grinned. "Yeah. Me, too." And she saw that he had never considered that she might not go.

'Tis a Proud and Lonely Thing to Be a Fan, they used to say, laughing. It had become a *very* lonely thing. The Establishment had always been hard on science fiction. The government-funded Arts Councils would pass out tax money to write obscure poetry for "little" magazines, but not to write speculative fiction. "Sci-fi isn't literature." *That* wasn't censorship.

Perversely, people went on buying science fiction without grants. Writers even got rich without government funding. *They couldn't kill us that way!*

Then the Luddites and the Greens had come to power. She had watched science fiction books slowly disappear from the library shelves, beginning with the children's departments. (That wasn't censorship either. Libraries couldn't buy *every* book, now could they? So they bought "realistic" children's books funded by the National Endowment for the Arts, books about death and divorce, and really important things like being overweight or fitting in with the right school crowd.)

Then came paper shortages, and paper allocations. The science fiction sections in the chain stores grew smaller. ("You can't expect us to stock books that aren't selling." And they can't sell if you don't stock them.)

Fantasy wasn't hurt so bad. Fantasy was about wizards

and elves, and being kind to the Earth, and harmony with nature, all things the Greens loved. But science fiction was about science.

Science fiction wasn't exactly outlawed. There was still Freedom of Speech; still a Bill of Rights, even if it wasn't taught much in the schools—even if most kids graduated unable to read well enough to understand it. But a person could get into a lot of unofficial trouble for reading SF or for associating with known fen. She could lose her job, say. Not through government persecution—of course not—but because of "reduction in work force" or "poor job performance" or "uncooperative attitude" or "politically incorrect" or a hundred other phrases. And if the neighbors shunned her, and tradesmen wouldn't deal with her, and stores wouldn't give her credit, who could blame them? Science fiction involved science; and science was a conspiracy to pollute the environment, "to bring back technology."

Damn right! she thought savagely. We do conspire to bring back technology. Some of us are crazy enough to think that there are alternatives to freezing in the dark. *And some of us are even crazy enough to try to rescue marooned spacemen before they freeze, or disappear into protective custody.*

Which could be dangerous. The government might declare you mentally ill, and help you.

She shuddered at that thought. She pushed and rolled Bob aside. She sat up and pulled the comforter up tight around herself. "Do you know what it was that attracted me to science fiction?"

He raised himself on one elbow, blinked at her change of subject, and looked quickly around the room, as if suspecting bugs. "No, what?"

"Not Fandom. I was reading the true quill long before I knew about Fandom and cons and such. No, it was the feeling of hope."

"Hope?"

"Even in the most depressing dystopia, there's still the notion that the future is something we build. It doesn't just happen. You can't predict the future, but you can invent it. Build it. That is a hopeful idea, even when the building collapses."

Bob was silent for a moment. Then he nodded. "Yeah. Nobody's building the future anymore. 'We live in an Age of Limited Choices.'" He quoted the government line without cracking a smile. "Hell, you don't *take* choices off a list. You *make* choices and *add* them to the list. Speaking of which, have you made your choice?"

That electric tickle . . . "Are they even alive?"

"So far. I understand it was some kind of miracle that they landed at all. They're unconscious, but not hurt bad. They're hooked up to some sort of magical medical widgets and the Angels overhead are monitoring. But if we don't get them out soon, they'll freeze to death."

She bit her lip. "And you think we can reach them in time?"

Bob shrugged.

"You want me to risk my life on the Ice, defy the government and probably lose my job in a crazy, amateur effort to rescue two spacemen who might easily be dead by the time we reach them."

He scratched his beard. "Is that quixotic, or what?"

"Quixotic. Give me four minutes."

FOR COMPLETISTS: COMPLETE IN ONE VOLUME

Some concepts are too grand, too special to be confined to one book. The volumes listed below are examples of such, stories initially published in two or more volumes, collected together by Baen Books to form one unitary work.

The Fall of Atlantis
by Marion Zimmer Bradley

65615-5 • 512 pages • $5.99

The saga of an Atlantean prince. Combines *Web of Darkness* and *Web of Light*.

The Complete Compleat Enchanter
by L. Sprague de Camp & Fletcher Pratt

69809-5 • 544 pages • $5.99

Includes *all* the de Camp & Pratt Harold Shea *Unknown*-style stories of the Incompleat Enchanter and his intrepid adventures in lands of fable and story.

The Starchild Trilogy
by Frederik Pohl & Jack Williamson

65558-2 • 448 pages • $4.99

Epic, galaxy-spanning adventure, beginning with an Earth enslaved by the rigorously logical Plan of Man, and ending with the creation of a newborn intelligent star....

The Compleat Bolo
by Keith Laumer   *69879-6 • 320 pages • $4.99*

Combines all the Laumer stories dealing with Bolos,

the ultimate weapon and the ultimate warrior in one. Includes the Retief Bolo story.

The Devil's Day
by James Blish   69860-5 • 320 pages • $3.95
A bored multi-billionaire hires a master of black magic to summon up *all* the demons in Hell and release them upon the world for a night—but once released the infernal legions have no intention of returning to Hell ... Combines *Black Easter* and *The Day After Judgment* in one of the scariest apocalypse stories ever written.

Wizard World
by Roger Zelazny   72057-0 • 416 pages • $4.95
Banished as a child from his universe of sorcery, Pol Detson must return from Earth to defeat a master of technology who is conquering his lost homeworld—but will he return as a liberator or a new conqueror ...? Combines *Changeling* and *Madwand*.

Falkenberg's Legion
by Jerry Pournelle   72018-X • 448 pages • $4.99
The governments of East and West have created a tyrannical world order that will not rule the stars— because of John Christian Falkenberg, a military genius who will not permit mankind to be cast into eternal bondage. . . . Combines *The Mercenary* and *West of Honor*, two of the cornerstones of Pournelle's future history.

The Deed of Paksenarrion
by Elizabeth Moon   72104-6 • 1,040 pages • $15.00
The brilliant saga of grittily realistic fantasy. Combines *Sheepfarmer's Daughter*, *Divided Allegiance*, and *Oath of Gold* into one BIG trade paperback.

POUL ANDERSON

Poul Anderson is one of the most honored authors of our time. He has won seven Hugo Awards, three Nebula Awards, and the Gandalf Award for Achievement in Fantasy, among others. His most popular series include the Polesotechnic League/Terran Empire tales and the Time Patrol series. Here are fine books by Poul Anderson available through Baen Books:

THE GAME OF EMPIRE

A *new* novel in Anderson's Polesotechnic League/Terran Empire series! Diana Crowfeather, daughter of Dominic Flandry, proves well capable of following in his adventurous footsteps.

FIRE TIME

Once every thousand years the Deathstar orbits close enough to burn the surface of the planet Ishtar. This is known as the Fire Time, and it is then that the barbarians flee the scorched lands, bringing havoc to the civilized South.

AFTER DOOMSDAY

Earth has been destroyed, and the handful of surviving humans must discover which of three alien races is guilty before it's too late.

THE BROKEN SWORD

It is a time when Christos is new to the land, and the Elder Gods and the Elven Folk still hold sway. In 11th-century Scandinavia Christianity is beginning to replace the old religion, but the Old Gods still have power, and men are still oppressed by the folk of the Faerie. "Pure gold!"—Anthony Boucher.

THE DEVIL'S GAME

Seven people gather on a remote island, each competing for a share in a tax-free fortune. The "contest" is ostensibly sponsored by an eccentric billionaire—but the rich man is in league with an alien masquerading as a demon . . . or is it the other way around?

THE ENEMY STARS

Includes for the first time the sequel to "The Enemy Stars"; "The Ways of Love." Fast-paced adventure science fiction from a master.

SEVEN CONQUESTS

Seven brilliant tales examine the many ways human beings—most dangerous and violent of all species—react under the stress of conflict and high technology.

STRANGERS FROM EARTH

Classic Anderson: A stranded alien spends his life masquerading as a human, hoping to contact his own world. He succeeds, but the result is a bigger problem than before . . . What if our reality is a fiction? Nothing more than a book written by a very powerful Author? Two philosophers stumble on the truth and try to puzzle out the Ending . . .

MERCEDES LACKEY

The Hottest Fantasy Writer Today!

URBAN FANTASY

Knight of Ghosts and Shadows with Ellen Guon

Elves in L.A.? It would explain a lot, wouldn't it? Eric Banyon is a musician with a lot of talent but very little ambition—and his lady just left him lovelorn in a deserted corner of the Renaissance Fairegrounds, singing the blues and playing his flute. He couldn't have known the desperate sadness of his music would free Korendil, a young elven noble, from the magical prison he has been languishing in for centuries. Eric really needed a good cause to get his life in gear—now he's got one. With Korendil he must raise an army to fight against the evil lord who seeks to conquer all of California. And Eric's music will show the way....

Summoned to Tourney with Ellen Guon

Elves in San Francisco? Where else would an elf go when L.A. got too hot? All is well there with our elf-lord, his human companion and the mage who brought them all together—until it turns out that San Francisco is doomed to fall off the face of the continent. Doomed that is, unless our mage can summon the Nightflyers, the soul-devouring shadow creatures from the dreaming world—creatures no one on Earth could possibly control....

Born to Run with Larry Dixon

There are elves out there. And more are coming. But even elves need money to survive in the "real" world. The good elves in South Carolina, intrigued by the thrills of stock car racing, are manufacturing new, light-weight engines (with, incidentally, very little "cold" iron); the bad elves run a kiddie-porn and snuff-film ring, with occasional forays into drugs. *Children in Peril—Elves to the Rescue.* (Part of the SERRAted Edge series.)

HIGH FANTASY

Bardic Voices: The Lark & The Wren

Rune could be one of the greatest bards of her world, but the daughter of a tavern wench can't get much in the way of formal training. So one night she goes up to play for the Ghost of Skull Hill. She'll either fiddle till dawn to prove her skill as a bard—or die trying....

Also by Mercedes Lackey:

Reap the Whirlwind with C.J. Cherryh
Part of the Sword of Knowledge series.

Castle of Deception with Josepha Sherman
Based on the bestselling computer game, *The Bard's Tale.*™

The Ship Who Searched with Anne McCaffrey
The Ship Who Sang is not alone!

Wheels of Fire with Mark Shepherd
Book II of the SERRAted Edge series.

When the Bough Breaks with Holly Lisle
Book III of the SERRAted Edge series.

Wing Commander: Freedom Flight with Ellen Guon
Based on the bestselling computer game, *Wing Commander.*™